MY MAN, MICHAEL

LORI FOSTER

BERKLEY BOOKS, NEW YORK

THE BERKLEY PUBLISHING GROUP
Published by the Penguin Group
Penguin Group (USA) Inc.
375 Hudson Street, New York, New York 10014, USA
Penguin Group (Canada), 90 Eglinton Avenue East, Suite 700, Toronto, Ontario M4P 2Y3, Canada
(a division of Pearson Penguin Canada Inc.)
Penguin Books Ltd., 80 Strand, London WC2R 0RL, England
Penguin Group Ireland, 25 St. Stephen's Green, Dublin 2, Ireland (a division of Penguin Books Ltd.)
Penguin Group (Australia), 250 Camberwell Road, Camberwell, Victoria 3124, Australia
(a division of Pearson Australia Group Pty. Ltd.)
Penguin Books India Pvt. Ltd., 11 Community Centre, Panchsheel Park, New Delhi—110 017, India
Penguin Group (NZ), 67 Apollo Drive, Rosedale, North Shore 0632, New Zealand
(a division of Pearson New Zealand Ltd.)
Penguin Books (South Africa) (Pty.) Ltd., 24 Sturdee Avenue, Rosebank, Johannesburg 2196,
South Africa

Penguin Books Ltd., Registered Offices: 80 Strand, London WC2R 0RL, England

This is a work of fiction. Names, characters, places, and incidents either are the product of the author's imagination or are used fictitiously, and any resemblance to actual persons, living or dead, business establishments, events, or locales is entirely coincidental. The publisher does not have any control over and does not assume any responsibility for author or third-party websites or their content.

MY MAN, MICHAEL

A Berkley Book / published by arrangement with the author

PRINTING HISTORY
Berkley edition / February 2009

Copyright © 2009 by Lori Foster.
Excerpt from *Servant: The Kindred* by L. L. Foster copyright © 2008 by Lori Foster.
Front cover photo: *Young Boxer Resting on Ropes in Boxing Ring with Ropes in Foreground* by
Christopher Thomas/Photographer's Choice/Getty. Stepback photo: *Young Man and Woman
Embracing and Kissing in Pool, Dusk, Side View* by Digital Vision/Getty.
Cover design by Rita Frangie.

All rights reserved.
No part of this book may be reproduced, scanned, or distributed in any printed or electronic form
without permission. Please do not participate in or encourage piracy of copyrighted materials in
violation of the author's rights. Purchase only authorized editions.
For information, address: The Berkley Publishing Group,
a division of Penguin Group (USA) Inc.,
375 Hudson Street, New York, New York 10014.

ISBN: 978-0-425-22629-2

BERKLEY®
Berkley Books are published by The Berkley Publishing Group,
a division of Penguin Group (USA) Inc.,
375 Hudson Street, New York, New York 10014.
BERKLEY® is a registered trademark of Penguin Group (USA) Inc.
The "B" design is a trademark of Penguin Group (USA) Inc.

PRINTED IN THE UNITED STATES OF AMERICA

10 9 8 7 6 5 4 3 2 1

If you purchased this book without a cover, you should be aware that this book is stolen property. It was
reported as "unsold and destroyed" to the publisher, and neither the author nor the publisher has
received any payment for this "stripped book."

To my sister, Monica Flowers, aka Moni, aka Mo.

Let me tell you, you are one tough cookie! You also happen to be a lot of fun, even when bruised and broken. The wreck, the hospital stay, and the very long recuperation were awful, but even under those circumstances, we really enjoyed having you around.

We look forward to taking the "Little Angel" RVing with us again!

Love ya bunches,

LoLo

CHAPTER 1

MORNING brought the sounds of muted footsteps, soft chatter, and the rattling of trays and machines. Life disturbed the quiet that had settled over the hospital during the long night. Unshaven, sullen, bordering on depressed—though he'd never admit it—Mallet shifted, and winced in pain.

All that had happened still seemed surreal—except for the awful pain. That was real. Very real.

Dawning sunlight flickered through the frozen layer of lacy frost that climbed the bottom of the window, blocking a dull view of the parking lot. Mallet stared at it, brooding, wishing for a change.

For uplifting news.

It was futile, and he knew it, but he wouldn't accept it. He couldn't.

Tomorrow they would release him from the hospital, and a few days later he'd be expected to start therapy to learn to walk with only one good leg.

Closing his bloodshot eyes and swallowing around the pain left in his throat from the resuscitation tube, he considered his destroyed future. How could everything change so drastically in such a short time?

In the last four years, he'd made a strong name for himself in the SBC. At twenty-six, he was considered a major contender in two weight classes and one of the most feared competitors in the sport. In another month, he would have fought for—and won—the title belt.

His hands fisted. His jaw flexed and tightened.

Thinking of the wreck brought an invisible weight to his chest, crushing his lungs.

Crushing his legs.

Through closed eyelids, he saw it all, felt it and smelled it and relived it again and again. Flashing lights, metal grinding against metal, the acrid stench of burnt rubber as tires squealed and brakes ground without success; the lash of the seat belt cutting across his body, trying in vain to pin him in place.

The impact of the wreck sent his brand-spanking-new, shiny black sports car tumbling like a snowball going downhill. Each flip had compressed it more, disfigured it, destroyed it.

Only when it slammed into a concrete wall did it finally stop.

With Mallet trapped inside.

"Good morning, Michael. Are you ready for your breakfast?"

Disinterested, sick at heart, Mallet looked at the nurse with dead eyes and a trampled heart. "I'm not hungry."

"Oh, come on now." Light fingers touched his biceps. "A big fellow like you has to eat."

Knowing she brought the meal herself as an avenue to flirting, he looked away. What use was he to a woman with one leg shot to hell and the other a long way from healed?

What use was he to anyone, or anything?

Her sigh, subtle and filled with frustration, sounded loud in the silent room. "How about I just leave this here in case you change your mind?" Sidled up beside his narrow bed, she began the morning routine of checking his vitals.

"You're due for your pain medicine, but I'd prefer you eat first—"

"I don't need it." He relished the pain. It was his hair shirt, a reminder that no matter how hard he worked, everything could be stripped away in the blink of an eye.

"Do you at least want some coffee or—"

"No."

Giving up, she started out of the room. "The doctor will be in to see you shortly."

To do what? Mallet wondered. He'd seen the hospital staff, had every test done, talked to specialists, all without a change in his prognosis.

How many ways did they want to tell him that his mangled right leg would never again function? Should he be thrilled that with a lot of therapy and several surgeries, he might be able to keep it—useless as it'd be?

Was he just supposed to accept that no matter how hard he worked at recovery, he would never again fight?

What else did he know but fighting? All his life, he'd been a competitor. First and foremost with himself. In so many ways, he was his own worst enemy.

But he'd found a family with the SBC, the only real family he'd ever known. They'd knocked him off his high horse, then built him back up, better, stronger. Accepted and befriended, even respected.

If he no longer fit in with them, what would he do?

What would he be?

"I've never seen anyone sulk so much."

Startled, because he'd thought himself alone, Mallet looked toward that deep, melodic voice and found a slight woman sitting in front of the frost-covered window. Or more like . . . she perched, butt and feet both on the window shelf, arms crossed over her knees. A sleeveless gray tunic covered her upper body.

At either side of her, colorful flower arrangements, sent by fighters' wives, made a bizarre frame.

How had she gotten in without him noticing?

Palest blond hair in a deep side part hung straight and

baby-fine to her shoulders. Large, heavily lashed hazel eyes studied him.

Bemused, Mallet looked her over, from her odd positioning against the window to her lithe limbs to a mouth that defied description.

Only in a fantasy, *his* fantasies, had he seen a mouth like that.

"How'd you get in here?"

"Ah, so you can speak in complete sentences. I was wondering if I had the wrong man." She slipped off the ledge with grace and agility, her hard-soled ankle boots tapping the floor as she stood. Long, trim legs encased in black leggings ate up the distance until she stood close by. Her arms, as gangly as her legs, were bare, lightly muscled, and very smooth. She was tall for a woman, but slightly built.

At his bedside, she tilted her head, sending that platinum hair swinging in a silky, distracting dance, as smooth and fluid as a fall of water.

Entranced, Mallet stared up at her.

Voice soft and rich, she said, "You mope for no reason, sir. A warrior, no matter the condition of his limbs, remains a warrior for all of his life."

Warrior? *Mope?* Her assurances—if that's what they were—annoyed Mallet enough that he stopped wondering how and why she'd come in, and instead turned defensive. "What do you know of it? Of any of it?"

Perching a trim, tight derriere on the edge of his mattress, she surveyed him in unadorned sympathy. In a ballsy move that shocked him stupid, she put both hands on his right leg, the one with the most damage.

Using an impersonal butterfly touch that somehow aroused as much as it offended, she stroked the length of his thigh and along his knee and shin. Through the thin layer of the sheet and the bulky padding of bandages, her touch stirred him.

"Stop that!" Though appalled, both by her daring and his reaction to it, Mallet didn't move to catch and restrain her hands. He couldn't. It was as if invisible steel bands held him in place.

Her gaze lifted, warm as honey, as intoxicating as whiskey, and that killer mouth spared the smallest of intriguing smiles. "Sir, what I know is that you can be whole in body again."

"Whole in body?"

"Yes, sir. I can take you to a place that will again make you a complete warrior, a man with two legs that serve him." She tipped her head. "But you'd have to accept my proposition."

Her strange appearance was made more so by her strange speech. "Your pro—".

The door swung open and the doctor, so damned jovial, stepped in. "Michael. How we are we faring today? Anxious to get out of here, I bet."

Mallet blinked at the doc, then looked back to see . . . the woman gone. Just like that.

She wasn't anywhere.

What the hell?

Now he was losing his mind, too? Had he imagined her, their conversation and the effect of her touch?

If so, why didn't he drum up a sexy and willing woman instead of an impish vision of long legs, soul-sucking eyes, and a mouth made of sin, captured in a confusing package that addressed him as "sir"?

"Give me the fucking pain pill."

The doctor hesitated at his foul mood. "Your pain has worsened?"

Yeah, in a way it had. On top of a useless leg and a shit attitude, he now had a boner.

If that didn't call for drugs, nothing did.

Now that he slept again, Kayli Raine circled his bed, studying him from many angles. It wasn't fear that nearly stole her breath away.

Knowing the differences of their worlds, she'd done her studies and tried to prepare herself—but she'd failed.

He was so big.

So dark and powerful.

The sheer size of him fascinated her. Even forewarned with reports of a larger people, he was more than she'd ever imagined, at least six feet five inches tall and two hundred pounds or more. In her world, men were only slightly larger than the women, who averaged a few inches over five feet.

She knew the reasoning; she'd studied her history books well. Once additives, especially steroids, were stripped from the food source, giants no longer grew.

Yet there he was, not only huge, but layered in muscles . . . everywhere. Her natural curiosity made her long to explore those muscles, to test their resilience, their durability.

His potency.

She didn't dare. Not again.

She'd assessed his leg and found it not irreparable, but the strength in that damaged limb, the brawn . . . Kylie shivered.

He'd make a valiant warrior. He would make things right again.

Once she convinced him.

While she stared at his face, making note of the high cheekbones and chiseled jaw, the kink in his nose no doubt caused by a past contretemps, his eyes opened.

Bright, vivid blue.

As they had the first time, they took her aback, and she had to check her reaction so that he didn't see her as vulnerable. He needed to know that they were on equal footing, both warriors, both with a higher purpose.

"Hello, sir."

He blinked hard, and as Kayli watched, his brows pinched down into a ferocious frown.

Belying the severity of his injuries, he sat up and looked around the room. "You," he said, pointing at her, "are not real."

Kayli didn't know what to think of that. "I assure you that I am." Desperate to convince him, she moved closer, took his large, warm hand, and put it to the side of her face. "Touch me."

"No!" He snatched back his hand as if she'd burned him, when he was the one with the fevered skin. "Stop that."

"Why?" Kayli tipped her head, somewhat perplexed. "You wanted verification that I'm—"

"I want to know what the hell you're doing in my room!"

Ah. Right to the point. It was a good quality for a warrior, for a savior. She liked that. She liked *him*—despite his current sour mood and lack of initiative.

"I'm here to negotiate with you." She glanced at his big body, started to look away, but her gaze returned. At the top of his thighs, the sheet lifted in a curious way. "What—"

"Get out." He pulled the pillow from behind him and slapped it down over his lap. "Now."

This wasn't going well at all. All her life, Kayli had known her flaws as well as her assets. Diplomacy was not her strong suit. Candor was counted a flaw.

"Please, sir, I would ask that you calm yourself." His raised voice might bring rubber-soled nurses running, and that would only delay their talk.

His jaw locked and the blue of his eyes burned like the hot center of a flame. "Do not call me sir."

"As you wish." Wondering how she should address him, Kayli sat on the side of his bed. She couldn't afford to exacerbate his temper, so she made every attempt at affability. "What shall I call you then?"

"Don't call me anything." Already his burst of strength waned, leaving him pale as he slumped back on one arm, half sitting up, half reclining. "Just get out of my head."

In his time period, anything unexplainable was explained as imagined. But she couldn't afford for him to think her a figment of fantasy. "I assure you I'm not in your head. I'm real skin and bones, just as you are." But then, not like him at all. "You felt me, did you not?"

"Not as I'd like, no." Groaning, he dropped to his back and stared at the ceiling. Kayli looked, but saw nothing of interest there to hold his attention.

Though he looked pained, she knew it wasn't a physical ailment. "How may I prove my existence to you?"

Outside his door, voices sounded. Michael locked his gaze on hers. "You want to prove you're here? That you're real?"

"It's necessary, yes." If he didn't recognize her existence, how could she convince him to accept her proposition?

"Then don't move."

The voices grew nearer. The urge to disappear coursed through her. "You have guests coming."

His lip curled. "A real woman wouldn't care, now would she?"

"You doubt I'm a woman?"

His eyes flared. His gaze moved over, and he croaked, "No." He cleared his throat, brought his attention back to her face, and spoke again. "No, I see that you're female, all right. I just don't know if I'm delusional or not."

"Oh." Kayli considered the situation, and decided her presence now would cause no negative impact. "To prove that you are not delusional, I'll stay." She moved away from the bed. "And afterward, we must talk."

The door pushed open and an impressively sized man with a clean-shaven head led a parade of visitors. Behind him, a blond woman and a dark-haired woman conversed, and behind both of them, strode another large, silent man.

They all pulled up short when they saw her.

Knowing her garb to be out of fashion for them, and sensing their protectiveness toward their wounded friend, she held out a hand in the universal sign of peaceful intent.

"Hello. I'm Kayli Raine."

They all stared. The bald man moved first, stepping forward while the others remained in mute fascination. His massive hand engulfed her own, so warm but gentle. "Simon Evans. How are you?"

"Tired from my journey, but not as tired as our friend here. He's just awakened from a short nap."

Simon lifted one brow, stared some more, and without sparing a glance for his warrior-friend in the bed, motioned the blonde forward.

"Kayli, this is my wife, Dakota. And that's Dean Connor, and his wife, Eve."

Husbands and wives.

Life mates.

Something kicked inside Kayli's heart; possibly yearning. But her life was not meant for such sharing with another. She knew her duty, had long ago accepted—even relished— her fate.

While Michael lay in the bed, disbelieving, Kayli spoke with each person, talking her way through a mild interrogation and a lot of suspicion.

"Michael." Kayli watched, and when the daze faded from his eyes, she smiled.

That just made him dazed again.

"Would you care for refreshments? Since you skipped your morning meal, I could locate a drink for you."

"No." He looked at each of his friends in turn, all of whom were looking at her, then brought his gaze back to Kayli. "I'm good."

Simon shook himself and finally gave his attention to Michael. "Good, huh? Well that's one hell of an improvement. Should I give credit to your lady friend?"

"No."

Dakota put her hands on her hips. "She's here, and you're sitting up, so I'm giving her credit."

Dean lounged against the wall. "Where'd you two meet?"

"Here, in this very room," Kayli said. "Just this morn."

"Ah." Dean nodded. "Now I get it. You weren't already acquainted."

"No, we were not. I knew of him, of course. But he knew nothing of me."

The one named Eve pasted on a smile. "Are you a fight fan, Kayli?"

Their attempts to mask curiosity with social conversation made her head swim. "Warriors are impressive, and Michael in particular is very honorable."

"Honorable?" Dean glanced between Michael and her. "What do you mean?"

"You should ask the truck driver who caused the accident." With that said, Kayli walked over to stand beside him. "Satisfied?"

"No."

So surly. "What more can I do?"

"Nothing." He glanced up at his friends, his complexion turned ruddy, and he beckoned her down closer.

When Kayli complied, he whispered, "Go away now, okay?"

"If that's your wish. But I will be back for us to have much discussion."

Without reply, he stared at her mouth, kept on staring until Kayli straightened.

Confused by his attention to her lips, she headed for the door. "It was pleasant to meet you."

A round of farewells and more curious stares followed Kayli as she left the room. Once in the hall, she looked left and right, saw no one, and disappeared to her shuttle where she could observe him unnoticed. She'd give his friends one hour to visit him, no more, and then she'd be back to finalize her plans with Michael.

The timing was important. He wouldn't have the luxury of getting used to her or the new circumstances.

She needed him—now.

SIMON folded his arms over his chest. "Okay, give. Who was that?"

"Is she far enough away from the door that she won't hear us?"

Dean poked his head out, then stepped all the way into the hall. When he stepped back in, he was shaking his head. "She's gone."

Frowning, Dakota, too, walked out to the hall, but she held the door open. Looking back into the room, she said, "Where did she go?"

Simon shrugged. "Elevator? Another room?"

"There's nothing. Just hallway. She must've run off in a hurry," Dakota said, "and she must be fast."

Because he'd already seen her vanish once, Mallet wasn't surprised. He was, however, glad to know she was real. But what the fuck? No really . . . *What the fuck?*

"I think they're giving me some really heavy-duty dope."

Eve sat by his side. "They're taking good care of you, Michael."

"Yeah, such good care that I'm hallucinating."

Simon and Dean came to the other side of the bed. "What do you mean?" Simon asked.

"Until you met that crazy chick that was just in here, I thought she was an illusion or something."

At the foot of his bed, Dakota laughed. "That's your go-nads talking, big boy. She's a hottie."

Dean and Simon both cleared their throats.

"Oh, come on," Eve said to the men. "You're married, but we don't expect you to be blind."

Dean frowned a little. "She has a certain . . . waif-like appeal."

Eve snorted. "You were tongue-tied."

"She looked athletic," Simon noted, "but also frail."

Dakota rolled her eyes. "She looked like walking sex, and you both know it." She nodded at Mallet. "He sure knows it."

Putting an arm behind his head, Mallet ignored the banter of his married friends and stared at the ceiling. Would she be back? What in God's name did she want to discuss with him?

And . . . "Where did she come from?"

"Good question." Simon raised a brow. "She has a faint accent, but I don't recognize it."

Dean stepped closer. "Maybe she's visiting someone here in the hospital."

"And your charm drew her in," Eve added with a grin.

Charm? He had no charm. Not anymore. He had . . . nothing. Well, good friends, he thought as he looked around at the encouraging faces. But hell, when they accepted that he couldn't fight, what would they have in common?

Jack shit.

"Michael?" Dakota seated herself at his other side on the mattress, but it didn't have the same effect that Kayli's nearness did. "She said you were honorable."

"She's weird."

Dakota took his hand. "She said we should talk to the guy who ran into you. Have you seen him?"

God, he didn't want to talk about this.

Simon crossed his arms. "Might as well tell her. You know she worries about you. If that bozo said something to you, or is giving you a hard time—"

"He's actually a nice guy."

Everyone went silent. And no wonder. The driver of that truck had stolen Mallet's life. But . . . it hadn't been his fault. Fate. Just unlucky fate.

"Look, I'll tell this once, then I don't want to talk about it again, okay?" Mallet waited for the nods of agreement before continuing. "The guy—his name is Travis Stockham— came to see me. No, before you all start getting up in arms, he was apologetic, and worried about me, and losing sleep because of what happened."

"And no wonder," Dakota said. "If he hadn't run into you—"

"He's fired from his job, but he has two kids and a wife and a mortgage—the whole shebang." Sometimes, Mallet thought, life just sucked.

He drew a deep breath. "The accident wasn't really his fault. There were kids playing in the street. One of them kicked a ball, and Travis saw it out of the corner of his eye. He thought it was a kid, or thought maybe a kid was following, and he swerved."

"Shit," Dean said.

"Yeah. He lost control and . . . he ran into me." Mallet shrugged. "In his situation, to avoid a child, I might've done the same thing."

Eve put a hand to her throat. "You forgave him, didn't you?"

Well hell. If the women got weepy, he wouldn't be able to take it.

Going gruff, Mallet frowned. "Nothing to forgive. I saw the police reports. He told the truth." There hadn't been many times in his life where he could make a difference. In the face of all he'd lost, Mallet knew he wanted to do something right, something noble.

He wanted to make a difference. He needed at least that.

"Lawyers came to see me. They wanted to settle out of court so I wouldn't sue the trucking company."

"Bloodsuckers," Simon complained.

"What happened?" Eve asked.

"We settled. I told them that as long as they gave Travis back his job, all I needed are my medical bills paid."

"That's pretty damned generous of you, Mallet, considering."

He shrugged at Dean. "Shit happens. It's not like he was drunk or high. He wasn't speeding. My career is over, and nothing will change that. I couldn't see fucking up Travis's life, too."

Simon moved closer. "Don't talk stupid. One bum leg won't keep you out of the SBC."

Saying it hurt, but he had to find a way to face the truth. "I can't fight."

"But you can announce, train, coach. . . . You have a huge following." Simon indicated the basket filled with notes and letters from Mallet's fans. "There's a lot you *can* do to stay active and contribute to the sport."

None of that would be enough. As a fighter, Mallet didn't want to take part from the sidelines. Kayli understood that. She knew he was a . . . warrior?

No. Not that. He had ultimate respect for soldiers, and he knew the difference between what they gave and what he did. But fighting was in his blood.

Mallet shook his head. "I appreciate the pep talk, I really

do." To appease his friends, he added, "I'll think about it, okay?"

"Kayli's right." Dakota squeezed his hand. "You are honorable."

Damn it, he wanted to think so. But how had Kayli known about the deal? Until now, no one other than Travis and the lawyers had been privy to that information.

"I'm getting tired," Mallet lied, because he didn't want to chat about little things while monumental problems weighed on his mind. He didn't want to be in a position of deflecting good intentions and false encouragement, when the true outcome was so grim. "I'm sorry you came all the way down here—"

"It's a ten-minute drive, goofy." Dakota ruffled his hair. "Of course we came. And we'll be back tomorrow to drive you home."

Once, what seemed a lifetime ago, he'd been half in love with Dakota. Now, he was happy that she and Simon had such a good life together. "You don't need to do that."

"We'll be here," Simon said. "No arguments. You're like family, and family doesn't check out of the hospital alone."

CHAPTER 2

MALLET sat up in the bed, waiting for her. After an
hour, he decided she probably wouldn't return. But
damn it, he had a lot of questions for her.

Uncomfortable, he shifted, and pain screamed through
his body. The worst of it radiated through his leg. One surgery had left him stitched and swollen, but he'd need more.
A lot more.

Two fractured ribs made a deep breath difficult. Bruising
everywhere, combined with strained muscles and damaged
ligaments, kept him sick to his stomach.

Locking his teeth, Mallet closed his eyes a moment to
regain control.

A gentle touch startled him.

He opened his eyes, and there she was, sitting on the edge
of his bed, her hands again drifting over his right leg.

"Is the pain extreme?"

Some things never changed, Mallet decided, and he lied,
saying, "No. It's fine."

In a way that now seemed familiar, she tipped her head.

"You're being stoic. I understand. It's not good for a warrior to show weakness."

Of all the . . . "Okay, first, not another word from you unless it's to answer one of my questions, understood?"

"I understand." She studied him. "Your friends found me attractive. I thought that odd."

Forgetting the order he'd just issued, Mallet stiffened. "Did one of them say something to you? Did you see them again before they left?"

"No, but they told you I was a hottie." She straightened and folded her hands in her lap. "I studied your colloquialisms for this journey, and I know that referring to me as a hottie indicates that they find me attractive."

"How . . ." Mallet stopped, regained control, and took her hand. He didn't want her poofing away—good God, she did sort of poof—before he finished with his questions.

Holding her hand had an outrageous effect on him. Okay, so he'd been a couple of weeks without getting laid. He'd had other things on his mind, and then the wreck . . .

But damn it, *a hand*? Just her hand? He felt sultry inside, tense outside.

Insane.

Squeezing her slender fingers a little, Mallet asked, "How did you know they said that?"

"May I show you something?"

"Will it answer my question?"

"I think it will answer your question more easily than will my explanations."

He nodded, and she eased her hand away from his and stood. Lifting up her tunic, she revealed a wide, supple black belt circling low on her trim hips.

Mallet stared. He saw her navel and her smooth skin, and his heart punched hard. She wasn't wide in the hips, but she had curves. The way the leggings clung like a second skin, he saw the protrusion of hip bones, the soft mound between her thighs.

"Sir?" From the belt, she withdrew a small, flat device

not much bigger than a calculator. The tunic fell back into place, and she said again, "Sir?"

"What?" He still stared at her body, distracted, hot.

"I would show you this, to explain how I know of you and what you do and say."

Right. She wanted to show him something *other* than her body. Collecting himself—barely—Mallet looked at her face. "Shoot."

She tipped her head, then acknowledgment shone in her eyes. "More jargon, yes? You don't want me to fire upon you, you want me to proceed."

"Yeah," Mallet said, deadpan. "Proceed."

Kayli turned the device toward him, touched a circle on the front; it came on, projecting a small but crystal-clear image into the air. Not like a television or computer or projector, but like . . . life.

It looked real.

It looked like him in miniature, in bed, talking with his friends.

"What the hell?"

She handed him the device.

No matter how he turned it, the image remained there in the air in front of him. "Fucking incredible."

She cleared her throat. "Everything you do is captured within space. With my viewer, I can tune in to observe you."

"Anytime?" Oh God, horrible possibilities crept in, like earlier, when he'd limped, cursed, and dragged his way into the john. He could feel his face getting hot. But damn it, he would not use a bedpan like an invalid.

Kayli shook her head. "It's not that simple. I speak into the machine and request specific data within a certain time frame, and it depicts episodes to exemplify the data. As an example, when I requested recent shows of compassion, I saw your conversation with Travis Stockham."

She'd seen him with Travis? No way.

Kayli went silent, looking down at her feet for a moment.

"Perhaps you'd be rewarded to know that later, he cried at your generosity and compassion."

Mallet stiffened.

Kayli's gaze lifted, locked on his. "On his knees beside his bed. He thanked God, and he thanked you, sir. He prayed for you."

A new weight, not the weight of despair, squeezed Mallet's lungs. "You can't know that."

"I could show you if you're inclined."

"That's an intrusion on that man's privacy!"

She tucked her hair behind her ear. "Yes, I know, and I felt uncomfortable with it. I didn't view him long. I only wanted to ensure that he hadn't taken advantage of your intentions."

Mallet found himself again struggling for composure. For once, he didn't feel for himself and his situation. He felt glad—glad that he was able to relieve some of Travis's burden, both financial and emotional. If he'd been in Travis's situation, he knew he would have been miserable.

"You are truly an honorable man, sir. You are the man we want. The man we need."

"We?" Now what was she suggesting? That there were more of her? Not that he wasn't interested—hell, he was male, so he was interested. But still—

"My colony."

Mallet blinked at her. "Your . . . ?"

"Colony." She turned serious and again sat beside him, her hip brushing his and setting off sparks inside him.

With a single touch, she turned off the viewer. "In the twenty-third century, there are no states, no nations. We are a people divided into colonies, ruling ourselves without interference from big government. We rely on bigger government only for the strictest rules, which means—"

Mallet smashed a finger over her mouth. His head swam, and it wasn't the pain meds. "You said the twenty-third century?"

She nodded, caught his wrist, and lowered his hand—to her lap.

Oh good God.

He felt the heat of her. He knew what lay just beneath his hand and that knowledge coursed through him like a hot, wet lick.

"Specifically," she said, oblivious to his turmoil, "I'm referencing the year 2220. That is my current year, the year where your presence is needed. You see, sir, my colony—"

He didn't want to, but he took his hand from that warm, soft lap and smashed his fingers over her mouth again.

She started to pull away.

"No," he said. "Just be quiet. Let me think."

Through large hazel eyes, she watched him. And she waited.

Finally Mallet asked, "You're saying that you're from the future?"

Not looking the least bit insane, she nodded.

"From 2220?"

She nodded.

So if she wasn't nuts, she had to be pulling his leg. Did she expect him to believe that? Did she think the accident had also muddled his brain? The more he considered it, the more annoyed Mallet got. "How stupid do you think I look?"

And just like that, she was gone. Without her mouth behind his fingers, his hand fell. He was a large man, a fighter, more capable than most—and her disappearance scared him.

"Damn." It seemed lame and unbelievable, but he carefully stretched over the side of his bed and looked under it.

Nope. She wasn't tucked under there, hiding. She was just plain gone.

When he straightened again, she stood right before him. Mallet jumped so hard in surprise, it hurt like hell.

"God damn it, don't do that!" His heart thumped and his skin crawled. He didn't like being startled. It made him feel like a frail little girl.

Kayli apologized with a shrug. "I wanted to show you something, but I required permission."

"Permission from who?"

"My mother."

Mallet stalled. Her *mother*? Of all the idiotic . . . Hopefully that woman wasn't lurking around, popping in and out, too. "What does your mother have to do with anything?"

"Everything. You see, our ancestors started our colony, so my mother, as the oldest remaining relative, is now the Arbiter."

"Arbiter?"

"She is the person empowered to make weighty decisions concerning the colony—our people, our futures, our . . . everything. Most often she confers with the Council Mavens, to ensure all colony members' opinions are appropriately represented within her decisions."

"The council is elected?"

"No. They're appointed by my mother, but with feedback from the members of the colony."

"Are you one of these Council Mavens?"

She shook her head. "I lead our defense team, and as such, was appointed Claviger."

"Claviger, huh? And that means . . . ?"

"Technically, I am the one who carries the keys. For our colony, it means I have the computer which locks or unlocks any given area of our colony. In many ways, my position is the most important to the colony members."

"Sounds like you and your momma have things all wrapped up."

His sarcasm stung her, given her expression. "My family would be similar to what your time period considers royalty."

In other words, he had a princess visiting him from the future? Mallet's eyes narrowed. "Now you're just fucking with me, aren't you?"

She went quiet, fidgeted, and then looked at him with clear disapproval. "I'm sorry, sir, but your language unsettles me. It's not appropriate for where we will go."

"Your colony?"

"Yes. If you'll agree." This time she pressed her fingers

to his mouth. "And if you agree, I, as Claviger, can make your leg whole again. It will be as if the damage never occurred. You will be the same man you were before the accident, but in a different time and place. You will stand with the members of my family to take responsibility for my people."

Despite the craziness of her assertions, her audacity turned Mallet on. He nipped the tip of her middle finger with his teeth. Not hard, just enough to get her attention before he licked, tasted—

She jerked back fast, disappeared, and reappeared again almost immediately.

"I'm sorry," she said in a rush, for the first time with an inflection of emotion wavering in her tone. "You must not do such things with your . . . your teeth and your . . . tongue? Yes, I'm sure it was your tongue."

Wow. Such a reaction. He raised a brow and smiled. "It was."

She took a step back, then caught herself and stiffened her shoulders.

"How'd you do that flickering in and out?"

Her face tightened. "I tried to leave, my computer insisted I stay." Her chest expanded on a breath. "Because it is important that I stay to finish our discussions, I'm asking you, please do not do anything so . . . perturbing again."

Grinning, Mallet shifted to face her more fully. "I perturbed you?"

She nodded. "Such things leave me unsure how to react."

"I could show you how to react." Okay, so pain kept him more immobile than not, and he couldn't do squat without breaking a sweat. On top of his pathetic condition, she was probably looney tunes, but her sweetness made the lunacy irrelevant. Even under such absurd circumstances, Mallet couldn't help but turn on the charm and give it a shot.

She intrigued him more than any other woman he'd met.

After drawing another deep breath, she flipped back her hair and lifted a stubborn chin.

Though Mallet hoped for agreement, he waited for her anger. He waited for a typical female rejection, maybe even a slap in the face.

"I'm sorry, sir," she stated, "but I may not breed. It is forbidden for a warrior."

That statement wiped all thought from Mallet's brain. She couldn't *breed*? Okay, so maybe her lunacy mattered a little after all.

Mallet took in the seriousness of her expression and decided to play along. "Sorry, sugar, but I ain't going anywhere I can't *breed*."

She blinked hard and fast. "Oh, no, you misunderstand. It is forbidden for *me*—for most warriors. But you are an exception. You would be accepted as a prominent placeholder in the hierarchy, equal to the Arbiter. You would be expected, even encouraged to procreate."

"No shit?"

"It would be wonderful if you filled our ranks with your offspring."

Damn, but he couldn't help it. Not since the accident had he found anything remotely funny, but several times now she'd made him smile. Now, with this craziness, he guffawed aloud, and once he got started he couldn't stop.

She was a warrior?

From the twenty-third century?

She wanted to take him back there with her, and once there, he'd be encouraged to "get it on"?

The more that Mallet laughed, the more her expression soured until she pinched up and said, "Sir, your humor is misplaced."

His leg hurt like hell, his ribs screamed in protest, and the rawness in his throat caused real agony, but it just didn't matter.

"You think?" Wiping tears of mirth from his eyes, he settled from robust laughter to a warm smile. "Tell me this, honey, who am I supposed to procreate with?"

Her hazel eyes burned. Her lips went stiff. "You will be offered a selection of available women."

Mallet howled with laughter. Forgetting the pain of his injuries, he fell back on the bed and shook with the hilarity of it.

Yeah, he had to be dreaming.

Someone would make his leg as good as new, *and* give him his choice of fine-looking women? A desperate fantasy for sure.

Or wait—maybe the women weren't so fine. Maybe he'd be a sacrifice.

Choking down his amusement, Mallet turned toward her as far as his ruined leg would allow. He couldn't stifle the wide grin. "Got a bunch of dogs in your colony, is that it?"

Her arms folded. "Animals are rare and cherished, but a few do reside within our boundaries."

So cute, even for a nut job. "I meant the women, sugar. Are they homely, desperate hags?"

She went so rigid, a brisk wind would have broke her. "They are not unattractive, I promise you."

"Do the others look like you?" If so, what the hell, he might just go with the delirium and have himself a good time while it lasted.

Color splotched her cheeks. "They do not. Unlike me, they're more feminine."

That rid him of his smile. "More feminine, huh? How so?"

"Women who are not warriors are . . . softer. Most in our colony have darker hair and bluer eyes, as your own, though some do have brown hair and green eyes. My fairness and height, along with my coloring, have made me an aberration of my colony—an irregularity within my family."

Did all that mean that she found herself unattractive? She had acted surprised that his friends called her a hottie.

Mallet snorted. She was a looker, no two ways about it. But judging by her expression, he'd embarrassed her when that hadn't been his intent.

"All that, huh?" Taking his time, Mallet looked over her long legs, trim torso, and proud shoulders. With the tunic she wore, it was tough to judge her breast size, but it didn't matter. He liked them all—large or small, soft or firm. Whatever she hid, he'd be satisfied.

All in all, there was nothing irregular about her sex appeal that he could see. "How are the other broads more feminine than you?"

"The women are delicate, whereas I am sturdy."

"Sturdy?" He snorted again. "I don't think so."

"That would be your singular perception as an oversize man. In my colony, the men do not grow as . . . *large* as you."

Though he figured none of it was real, he couldn't help asking, "So the men are shrimps, too?"

Her exasperation showed. "The men are not as powerful as you, but they are good at what they do."

"Just not so good that you couldn't use some outside help—from me?"

"This is true. Our men are not fighters. They are builders and breeders, and they—"

"Okay, hold up." Mallet started snickering again. "Breeders?"

Her hands landed on her hips, giving away her vexation over his frequent interruptions and overall chauvinism.

"There is a shortage of males. With the future of our colony dependant on offspring, it is too dangerous to risk a man in confrontations with other colonies."

Outraged on behalf of all mankind, Mallet sat up again. "Wait one damn minute. You're telling me the guys cower at home while the women go out to fight?"

"They do not *cower*. The men of my colony are brave and understanding of their circumstances. They build our walls, which require heavy lifting. They supervise our perimeter and alert us—"

"The women?" he sneered.

"The *warriors*."

"All the warriors are women?" Time to switch drugs. That was too screwy even for him.

"Yes, the warriors are all women. We're selected early in life based on our growth plates and aptitude toward physicality."

"Looking for the big hardy ones, huh?"

She ignored that. "The men alert us when a hostile group approaches. But they also tend to the children, and when appropriate they endeavor to reproduce with the nonwarrior women."

Despite himself, Mallet got caught up in her outrageous tale. It sounded to him like she had a bunch of wusses in her colony. What kind of men would sit home while the women went out to fight?

To distract her from her pique, he lifted the viewer. "Why don't you just use this to keep up with your enemies?"

"The viewer only goes back in time, not across time, and not forward."

Mallet studied the little box again. "How's it work?" When she didn't answer, he glanced up to see her blushing again. One brow lifted in question.

"I don't know the specifics of it."

"You don't know?" Assuming her story ran short on those details, he snorted. "Figures."

Rather than scramble to make her tale more believable, she snatched the viewer out of his hand and returned it to the strap in her belt. "How do your microwave ovens work?"

Hell, he didn't know. "You push a button and it cooks food."

"But how is that accomplished? What does the pushed button do?"

He shrugged. "Um . . . microwaves? They cook the food somehow. Hell, I'm not a chemist or anything. I'm a fighter."

She slanted him a smirk of her own. "How do your video cameras capture an image, save it onto a selected format, and allow you to play it back again?"

Giving up, Mallet held up his hands. "No idea."

"And your ancient cell phones that you all seem to carry without fail? How do they permit you to communicate through space?"

"You've got me. I'm clueless."

Satisfied, she gave a nod of her head. "And so it is. Each

generation has made use of tools and toys available to them
with no concept of how they actually function."

She had a point. "All right, let's let that go for now." He
eyed her, and went with a different source of curiosity. "You
don't consider yourself a hottie?"

Her chin went up. "Compliments are not necessary, I assure you. I take great pride in being honest with myself. I am
strong and fast and brave. But no, I am not blessed with the
appearance that draws men."

"Really?" Sure as hell drew him. In a big way. His injuries had all but incapacitated him, yet she got a rise out of
him anyway.

"I have endeavored not to let that flaw affect me as I meet
my fate for my colony. My mother has two other daughters
to fill the ranks with offspring who will carry on our family's destiny. I am needed only to keep the peace, not the
standing of our name."

Mallet took extreme pleasure in saying, "I think you're
gorgeous. And that's not the same as being hot. A chick can
be hot, but not beautiful. Vice versa, too."

Kayli frowned a little. "You're saying that she can be
beautiful but not . . . hot?"

"Yeah. And for the record, hot means doable, as in easily
fucked." He watched her waver, saw the color that first
leeched from her skin, then flooded back, red hot and ripe.
"You, Kayli Raine, are both."

She shook her head in frantic denial. "No, I'm not—"

"Yeah, you are," he interrupted. "Very." He watched her
blanch. "You aren't going to disappear on me again, are
you?"

She again shook her head, but remained mute.

"Cat got your tongue?"

That confused her. She put a hand to her chest. "My heart
is racing. You disconcert me."

Sounded fair, considering what she did to him. "And
maybe I turn you on a little?"

More confusion swam in her mellow eyes. "Turn me on?
I am not a machine. We already established that."

Mallet chuckled at her misunderstanding. "No, turn you on, as in make you hot?"

She put a hand to her cheek. "Yes, you do bring a fever to my skin with your brazen way of speaking."

Enough teasing already. With his blood stirring over his sexual intent, Mallet lowered his voice. "Come here, Kayli."

Gaze flaring, she backed up a step. "Oh, no," she said, and then added with great wariness, "Why?"

Mallet watched her. "I want to see if I turn you on."

"No." She denied him with a raised hand. "My instincts tell me that I should keep a fair distance from you while you're in this odd confrontational mood. It would be best if we got back to business."

"First things first." He didn't feel a single ache in that moment. "Come here."

She breathed harder, and said in desperation, "I can not. What you do, whatever you plan, it is not proper, not for me."

"How so?"

"I told you," she said on a high, nearly hysterical note. "I am forbidden involvement with a male. I must focus on my duty alone. I am here to gain your agreement for assistance, nothing else. If I fail at that, I fail at everything that is important to me. I fail my colony. Please, can we not come to terms?"

Mallet saw her urgency, her near-pleading, and changed his direction. "All right, just calm down."

"I can't!"

He did his best to look neutral. "Come sit by me and we'll talk about everything."

Caution kept her entrancing hazel eyes glowing gold. "*Only* talk?"

He didn't want to scare her. He knew she believed everything she said. Hell, a tiny part of his mind was beginning to believe, too. "I promise."

She inched closer, then drew a breath, summoned up her nerve, and walked bold and brave to sit beside him. "Thank you, sir."

"So what exactly would you need me to do if I accepted your proposition?"

Before she could answer, the door started to open, and right before Mallet's eyes, she disappeared.

Again.

Damn it.

CHAPTER 3

"TIME for your bath, Michael."

Damn, damn, damn. Alesia, a cute little nurse's aide who took her time with a sponge, wheeled a cart into the room. Red lips curved in a smile and bright eyes shone with anticipation.

It didn't move Mallet at all. "I don't want a bath."

"Now don't be grumpy. You know it'll make you feel better." She glanced at him in sultry invitation. "I promise to be very gentle."

Frustration mounted until Mallet thought he might shout. "Leave that shit and get out."

She blanched. "But, Michael, I can . . ."

"Look, Alesia, I haven't fucking moved, right? I haven't sweated or gotten dirty. You spent an hour washing me last night and I'm still clean, I swear. I know my leg is shot, but my arms are fine so I can damn well clean my own face and brush my own teeth, and I don't need any fucking help to do it."

By the time he finished, frustration turned his face an angry red and sent his voice into a shout. With a sad, wounded nod, poor Alesia turned tail and ran out.

The door hadn't quite shut behind her before it was shoved open again.

"You're fucking kidding me, right?"

Drew Black! Mallet hadn't expected to see him.

Everywhere the SBC president went, he brought loads of presence with him. Muscular and fit, he stood several inches shorter than Mallet, and still the room felt smaller with him in it.

Brown eyes mocked Mallet, and that perpetual smile flickered over Drew's face. "You turned down *that* chick for a fuckin' sponge bath?"

Flustered, Mallet said, "Yeah."

"What? You went blind in the accident?" He walked into the room. "Did you see the ass and legs on that girl?" Drew clutched his heart. "Are you out of your fuckin' mind?"

"No, it's just—"

"Did that truck smash your balls as well your leg? Hell man, she was steaming." Drew laughed. "Call her back. I'll let her wash my fuckin' back."

Mallet couldn't help it; he grinned. "I'm sure you could charm her into doing it, too." Known as the guy with the foulest language in the biz, Drew used one adjective more than any other. Somehow "fuck" found its way into his every sentence.

Holding out a hand to Mallet, Drew said, "You crazy motherfucker. How the hell are you?"

"I'm okay."

"No fucking way. The Mallet I know would have had that chick in the bed naked already. You made her cry, you heartless bastard." Being a little heartless himself, Drew grinned as he said it.

"It's not easy to get it going when my leg is shot, my ribs are cracked, and they keep filling me with drugs."

"Wouldn't slow me down."

No, but then nothing ever slowed down Drew. "I believe that."

He turned a chair closer to the bed and sat down. "So

seriously, man, how the hell are you doing? When can I expect you back?"

Mallet felt sick. "Maybe no one told you, but I'm done."

Drew made a rude sound. "Fighting, maybe. But hell, man, we need you, and fighting is only one facet of this game. You know that."

"I'm a fighter."

"Fuck yeah, you are. One of the best. So teach it, talk it, explain it, but don't fucking give up on me." Drew grabbed his forearm. "That's not like you, man. It's not like the SBC. We're here for you. You do what the fucking doctors say, no arguments, and whatever you need to get going again, you tell me. You got that?"

"Yeah." He didn't, not really, but Mallet nodded his appreciation. "Thanks, Drew."

"Fuck that. I don't need any thanks. I need you back with us, doing what most people can't." At Mach speed, the only speed Drew knew, he started wheeling and dealing with Mallet. "The sooner, the better. So let's work this shit out. Tell me what I have to do and what you need from me so I can get you under contract again."

Mallet was struggling for a reply when Kayli reappeared behind Drew. "Hello."

Drew jerked around. It wasn't often that anyone or anything got by him. That Kayli would take him by surprise amused Mallet.

Drew looked at her, then looked at Mallet.

Mallet groaned.

With his gaze hot on Kayli, Drew said, "Knock off the dying cow sounds, you crazy fuck, and introduce me."

KAYLI wasn't about to let this crude, pushy man convince Michael to commit to anything when she'd approached him first, and needed him more. Somehow she had to thwart the man's plans.

Killing him was out.

Though Michael seemed less than thrilled to see him, she felt his appreciation and loyalty.

She held out a hand. "I'm Kayli Raine, a friend to Michael."

"Just a friend?"

Kayli started to say yes, but Michael said, "Off limits, Drew."

"The hell you say." Enjoying the situation, he held on to Kayli's hand. "Drew Black. Now tell me, sweetheart, is he yanking my chain? Has he spoken for you?"

Drew Black had the oddest way of speaking. "Michael and I are working out an agreement."

Drew's brows shot up. "An agreement, huh?" He turned to Michael. "You want to explain that?"

"No. And let go of her hand."

Grinning, Drew released her. "So that's why you sent the little nurse running, huh? Had a sure thing already lined up?"

Kayli bristled at his assumptions. "Michael would never take advantage of a woman in the manner that you're suggesting."

Both men went mute in surprise, Drew to cough down a laugh, Michael to roll his eyes.

While she had the opportunity, she explained further. "Michael is not interested in your offer, kind as it is. He is a warrior, nothing less."

"A warrior? What the fuck's up with that shit, Mallet? Is she from some upstart organization? You know no one else will treat you as good as the SBC."

"I will," Kayli promised.

Drew sat back in his chair, deceptively bored, feigning a lack of concern, but Kayli felt the keen tension emanating from him. "So she speaks for you, Mallet, is that it?"

"I do," Kayli said.

"No one speaks for me," Michael said at the same time. He glared at Kayli, then addressed Drew. "I'll think about it, okay? That's all I can promise right now."

"I can take a promise. So promise me, too, that whatever

her offer is, you fucking will give me a chance to counter it."

"Will do."

Kayli stood aside while the men tried to ignore her. Though they discussed logistics of various opportunities and the overall tone of the SBC organization, she felt each of them taking turns watching her.

Her piercing sagacity paired with primal instincts had saved her many times in the past. With Michael, she felt she lost some of her advantage, but not so much that she'd fail her colony.

She couldn't.

Too many people, men and women alike, depended on her.

Finally, after she'd waited in silence for an extended period, Drew Black decided to take his leave. He stood, clasped Mallet's hand. "She's a strange broad, isn't she?"

Mallet flicked a glance her way. "That's putting it mildly."

Withholding her acrimony wasn't an easy task, especially when Drew continued with a grin, "Never knew one to be so quiet so long, especially when she's already made it clear she disagrees with my motives for dropping in."

"Don't worry about it." Mallet's expression sent a clear warning. "She's not going to cause any problems."

Kayli kept silent, but she knew that she would cause a problem—several problems—if Drew Black got in the way of her mission.

"She's a looker," Drew said. "Go easy on her." And with that, he took his leave.

Standing several feet from the bed, her gaze locked with Michael's, Kayli waited.

As they stared at each other, a strange tension pulsed in the air, leaving her chest tight, her limbs quivering in a most unfamiliar way. Only during battle did she ever feel so alive.

"Shall we talk now?"

"I wish the damn door would lock."

"There have been numerous interruptions."

He held out a hand. "Come here."

Why did such a simple gesture send heat spiraling through her? "Can we not talk as we are?"

"No, we can't. I want to hold on to you and I want you to stay put, no matter what."

"The more who see me, the more I risk."

"Then come here and let's get things settled."

That was as close to an agreement as she'd gotten, so Kayli moved forward, sat beside him, and accepted his hand.

Again, the dissimilarities astounded her. His hand was easily twice the size of hers. Even in a sickbed, partially drugged, and in pain, she felt the strength in his gentle hold.

Jerking herself back to her purpose, Kayli brought her gaze to the burning blue of his eyes.

Looking at him made it more difficult to explain, but she needed every connection to him in order to convince him.

"I need you to return with me, the sooner the better."

His thumb rubbed a slow circle on her palm. "As in— now?"

She shook her head. "It would be best if you depart with a believable tale. I can assist you with that. It's possible to make arrangements that will satisfy your people in the next twenty-four hours."

"Then we both . . . poof?" His thumb moved to her wrist and stole a measure of her breath.

Warmth filled her face, her whole body. It was the oddest sensation, one she'd never quite experienced before.

She cleared her throat. "I will transport you to my vessel, and from there we will travel forward to my time. This will be done seamlessly. That is, once we leave here, you will next find yourself in my time."

He skipped much of what she said to ask, "Your vessel?"

"It hovers above, unseen and yet there."

"Huh."

"Transporting has become a much simpler means of travel."

"You don't say."

Was he humoring her? "At first there were some mishaps,

of course. But over time it has been perfected. You mustn't worry about lost body parts or rearranged molecules—"

"Yeah, like in *The Fly*. That dude's whole body got tangled with an insect."

"Such doesn't happen, I promise you." Not anymore.

"Good to know." The corners of his mouth tilted up the smallest bit.

He didn't believe her, Kayli could tell, but she wouldn't give up. "You will be apprised of the situation as soon as we're home, and in very short order you will undergo a ceremony to take your place in the hierarchy."

"I hate ceremonies."

"Yet it is necessary." She didn't want to go into that aspect of the deal with him just yet. She had a feeling that the idea of a union, more than time travel, would put him off. "Afterward, all will defer to you, the same as they do our Arbiter and the Council Mavens."

"Your mother and her cronies?"

Growing used to it, she skipped right past his cynicism. "It is our hope that you will be able to teach us to fight in the manner you deploy so that we are better able to defend ourselves, and so that we can retrieve those of the colony already taken prisoner."

Using both hands, Michael explored her fingers, opening each one, smoothing with his thumb. It was as if the size of her hands fascinated him in the same manner that his fascinated her. He lifted her hand to his mouth. "I need to know I can trust you."

That was not what she expected to hear. Questions, disbelief, yes, she had anticipated both.

"How do I—"

He drew the tip of one finger into his mouth and curled his tongue around it.

Her heart stopped, then skipped several beats. Her breath caught, straining her lungs. The touch of his tongue felt . . . indescribable.

Without conscious thought, her eyes closed, but quickly opened again. "You . . . you must stop that."

"Hmm-mm."

"Is that a no? Oh!" He drew another finger in, treating it to the same damp exploration.

Deep inside her, something curled in the sweetest way, giving both pleasure and an ache.

"You are so small-boned, Kayli. So delicate." His thick lashes lifted and he caught her in his gaze. "And you taste good."

"No." That raspy voice didn't sound like her own at all. "That is, I am large for a female."

"Not the females I know." He sucked her middle finger into the heat of his mouth.

The curl of pleasure expanded; the ache deepened. Kayli gulped in air so fast, she almost choked; frowning at herself, she tried to pull away.

He didn't let her. His grasp was firm but gentle.

"Sir, I have seen your females." It wasn't easy to speak with him doing that to her fingers. Inside her boots, her toes curled. "The blond one called Dakota was taller than the other, but yet not so tall as me."

"Dakota is a big girl." He kissed his way down to her palm, then the inside of her wrist. "Sexy as hell, but no one would call her frail."

Sexy? Did that mean she appealed to him? For some reason, that irritated Kayli. "Perhaps not."

"You," he said while nibbling on her, "are very delicate."

Compared to him and his friends, she had to agree. "I'm still fast and strong, and I'm well practiced."

"Interesting. If I wasn't stuck in this bed, I'd let you show me how practiced you are."

Kayli scooted closer to him on the bed. "Accept my proposition and I will get you out of this bed. I will make you whole and then we can start sparring immediately. I'm most anxious to learn your moves."

Michael smiled lazily. "My best moves are done in a bed."

"Really?" That left her bemused. "I observed you in action and it seemed to me that you needed adequate room to maneuver. You were especially good at using your legs to devastating effect."

Michael gave a crooked grin. He held her hand to his chest. "I wasn't talking about moves in fighting."

Kayli stared at him. "I was."

"I know."

Even with all the studies she'd done, he could be *so* confusing. "Sir, I'm not convinced that you're taking this seriously." Annoyed, she pulled her hand away and stood.

It was time to give him a nudge. "If you are unwilling, or unable, to meet the duties I require, I must not waste any more time with you. I will go to my next choice of savior. He is not as promising as you, but perhaps—"

"You've been checking out another guy?"

Ah, now she had his attention. Finally. "Yes, sir, I have. Several in fact." She hadn't found anyone else as suitable, but a small exaggeration wouldn't cause any real harm. "My situation is most dire. I need a commitment from you."

He studied her for a long minute. "Okay, lady, let's get down to it. First, you said you had an idea on how I'd disappear without anyone getting too nosy about it. What's the plan?"

"You would tell your friends that you cannot accept being disabled."

"I can't."

She softened. "You, sir, would adjust if there were no other alternatives. I have not a single doubt that you'd not only adjust, you would excel in a new venture that would allow you to grow as a man and would assist others in the process."

He tucked in his chin. "Got a little hero worship thing going on there, don't you?"

"You *are* a hero. You will be our hero." Kayli pressed a fist to her heart. "I sense it."

"You're getting nuttier by the second."

Knowing it was his discomfort at compliments that caused the insult, Kayli dismissed it. "They will believe you when you say that you've heard of a treatment in a faraway place, a procedure that is reputed to bring about miracles. You want to go there to explore the possibilities."

"I suppose I heard about this treatment from you?"

"Yes."

"It might work. They'd buy that I wouldn't give up easily."

"No, you wouldn't." Already she recognized him as a dedicated, and stubborn, man.

"Okay, one more thing." His eyes glinted at her, giving fair warning. "Before I commit, I want something from you."

"You can have anything that is within my power to give to you."

That vow brought about a toothy grin. "Glad to hear it. So Kayli, come here and give me a kiss."

She was certifiable, what with all her talk of vessels and transporting through time. But what would one kiss hurt?

He had to taste her.

If his legs and ribs weren't fucked, he'd want more than that. But he knew his own limitations, and he wasn't about to embarrass himself by starting something he couldn't finish.

Biting hard enough to bruise, Kayli caught her lush bottom lip in her teeth.

Poor little girl. She looked like a deer caught in the headlights. "Is the idea of kissing me really so bad?"

She didn't move, barely breathed. "That is what you want before you'll agree? Truly?"

"Oh, trust me, sugar, I want more than that. But while the mind is willing, the body isn't able." Later, if she stuck around and didn't seem a threat . . . no, that'd be taking advantage of the worst kind.

And as she'd said, he was too honorable for that.

As if weighing the problems of the universe, she paced away in deep thought.

Mallet laughed. It hurt his ribs, his throat, but damn, he couldn't remember the last time a woman had so thoroughly rejected him. It was sort of . . . refreshing. "You're demolishing my ego, you know."

Mind made up, her shoulders back with grim, almost suffering resolve, she turned around to face him. "I'll do it."

Such a lack of enthusiasm. The stoic way she presented herself, you'd think he'd asked her to throw herself off the side of a high cliff. Determined to figure her out, Mallet kept his grin at bay as he watched her. "You're very brave."

"But first," she said, ignoring his jibe, "you must alert your friends. I want to know that you're serious, and that you will follow through with our agreement. I'll have your word that you won't renege once you've taken your toll."

"My *toll*?" Would kissing him really be so awful that she considered it a debt to be paid?

As if a thought occurred to her, Kayli lifted a hand. "In fact, to ensure your cooperation I will transport us during the kiss. Agreed?"

What the hell? In for a penny, in for a pound. "Why not?" Mallet picked up the phone and dialed Simon. He got his answering machine. "Sorry, he's not home."

"It would make things simpler if you left a note anyway." Rushing around to the bedside table, she opened the top drawer and located a pad of paper and pen.

She handed them to him.

"You want me to write it all out?"

"Yes. One of the nurses will find the note and alert your friends, and they'll have no option but to accept that you've made your own decision."

"My decision to jump ship without talking to them first?"

"You're distraught," she explained. "You're in a difficult stage of your life. It would not be uncommon for you to flee."

"Flee?" Now that just plain pissed him off. "I don't *flee* from anyone or anything."

Witnessing the level of his insult had her fighting a smile. "Very good to know, truly, but it would be understandable if you did—as I'm sure your friends would agree. Also, there won't be the uncomfortable issue of them trying to talk you out of your decision."

Which, she likely figured, would force her to talk him into it again.

She waited, and when he did nothing, she finally said, "Go ahead, sir. Write your note."

Disgruntled, Mallet put pen to paper. He didn't take it too seriously because, really, who would get a chance to read it? But just in case Kayli wanted to see it for herself, he made the explanation believable enough.

He told his friends not to worry about him because he planned to travel a bit. With Kayli at his side, he would explore surgical options for his leg in various countries, and have some fun along the way. As he added, "She's hot, and I'm ready," he anticipated her reaction. He signed it with a flourish.

There. It all sounded plausible, didn't it?

Hovering anxiously at his beside, Kayli asked, "All done?"

Pushy broad, when she had a goal in sight. "Yeah, sure."

She rolled in her lips, fretted, and then asked, "Did you make a special notation to your friend who was just here?"

"Drew?" At her nod, he said, "No, why would I?"

"He wanted to hire you for specific employment. I think it would be nice if you gave him the courtesy of turning him down."

"Turning him down is a courtesy?"

"Wouldn't that be preferable to giving him false hope, to leave him waiting for you without knowing if you planned to accept his offer?"

"Maybe." Not that Drew really waited for anyone. He was a mover and a shaker, always on the go with new plans, better plans. He was never content to be idle, either in body or mind, for too long.

Mallet jotted a P.S. to Drew, thanking him for his offer but refusing. He handed Kayli the paper. "I know you're dying to take a look, so go ahead."

She read it in a mere glance. Toward the end, she frowned at him, but said nothing.

"It appears convincing." She fidgeted a moment, and

then, somewhat unwillingly, said, "You could tell them that you'll be in touch. It's not impossible. If you found it necessary for your peace of mind, you could make contact with them, even from my time period."

"That's done, huh?" In a way, her spacey imagination was adorable. She should be a writer. Maybe she *was* a writer.

"I'm here, aren't I?" Her mouth softened into a smile. "Time travel is not encouraged because it's costly to execute. Only the most advanced systems—known as supercomputers—have the capability."

"I take it that you have yourself a supercomputer?"

"One of the very best, yes. Even so, we don't utilize it often because to do so leaves open the possibility of causing a rift in the future. But as I explained, you will be an important part of the hierarchy, and as such you will be given more freedom."

Yeah, almost like he'd be a king. Mallet shook his head at that absurd image. He was better suited to grunt work than leadership.

Although, when it came to sex, he enjoyed being in charge—a lot. With just that thought, his voice deepened and his flesh warmed.

Patting the side of his mattress, he said to Kayli, "Now that we have the note all right and proper, how about you come a little closer? We have some unfinished business, remember."

Her smile disappeared and a new wariness turned her hazel eyes glittering gold. "Yes, of course."

She placed the note on his nightstand and then . . . stood there.

She looked almost ill, causing Mallet to sigh. "Kayli, I'm not going to hurt you."

"I trust not." A deep, fortifying breath gave her courage to move nearer to his bed. But a few feet away, she stalled once more.

Trying an encouraging smile, Mallet again patted the mattress. "Sorry, honey. I'd get up and woo you proper, but with my injured leg, I'd only fall on my face."

That got to her, and with blatant sympathy she seated herself beside him. "Very soon, it will be as if nothing happened to your body at all. All your bruises will be gone. All your aches and pains—"

"Yeah. Can't wait." Mallet caught her upper arm and tugged her resisting body slowly down to him. He stared at that oh-so-sexy mouth of hers, watched her lips part, saw her tongue slip out to wet dry lips.

Damn, he was hard again, and he hadn't even kissed her yet.

"Closer," he whispered, his voice deep and rough. "A little more."

He felt her hot breath touch on his face, felt her palpating fear, strange as that seemed. And then his mouth brushed hers, and though he wasn't a man given to poetic inclinations, he knew her mouth intoxicated him—that was the only way to describe the rush of sensation that jumbled his emotions and fired a deep physical response.

Using his free hand, Mallet clasped her warm nape to keep her close. He deepened the kiss, turned his head for a better fit, and slicked his tongue past her teeth to explore her sweet mouth.

At first, she gasped and stiffened. Mallet kept it up, tasting her, teasing himself, and reveling in how a simple kiss had turned so carnal.

As he burned, she gradually slumped into him, and by small degrees flattened over him.

To fully relish the feel of the soft female body covering him and her cautious, surprised response, Mallet kept his eyes closed.

It wasn't until his hand moved down her back to her behind that she stiffened and jerked back on straightened arms.

Panting a little, her eyes cloudy with confusion and uncertainty, she asked, "Satisfied?"

Keeping Kayli's gaze locked in his, Mallet shook his head. A warm breeze moved over them, dancing over his heated skin and causing her fine, silky hair to move. "I won't be satisfied until I'm well enough to put you under me."

To his right, a man said, "You are well enough."

Shock sliced through Mallet.

Keeping a hold on Kayli, he jerked around—and discovered he wasn't in his familiar hospital bed any longer.

Oh shit, oh shit, *oh shit.*

Purest sunlight shone through a tall wall of windows built along one side of a white room with a very high ceiling. There were tables and chairs, but unlike any he'd ever seen. Through an open corridor, warm, fresh air circulated.

He gulped. "Toto, I've a feeling we're not in Kansas anymore."

Kayli blinked. "Sir?"

Several robed people stood around him, all of them strangers to him, all of them with impersonal expressions on their faces.

Scowling at Kayli with accusation, incredulity, and a healthy dose of caution, Mallet accepted the truth. "You transported me!"

CHAPTER 4

RATTLED from the unexpected intimacy of Michael's kiss, Kayli tried to free herself without success. Michael's hands were so tight on her, she winced. Knowing it was a reaction to the circumstances, and not a bent toward brutality, she leaned closer to him. "It's okay, Michael. They're only android assistants."

"Android assistants?" His vigilant gaze never wavered from their audience. "As in . . ." He shook his head with disbelief. "Not real?"

"They're real, sir. Very real. They're just not human. These are my friends and companions."

"Robots? Are you yanking my chain?"

The things he said . . . "They're anthropomorphic systems." At his blank look, she clarified, "Designed to be human in appearance, but freethinking only to a limited degree."

"Who designs them?"

"These were of my preferences."

Shock faded under censure and his brows pinched down over burning blue eyes. "They're all *male*, Kayli."

He appeared to want an explanation for that. "Well . . . yes, I know." Kayli shrugged. "I prefer male company."

The scowl darkened. "Is that so?"

With his intent gaze zeroed back in on her, she again tried to wiggle free. "Sir? Could you please loosen your grip?"

He glanced down at his taut hold, and released her with a rush. "Shit, I'm sorry, honey. Are you okay?"

At his curse, the scandalized assistants all murmured to one another. It was unheard of for anyone, human or humanoid, to speak so crudely.

"I'm unharmed." Kayli sent the assistants a look to quiet them before bestowing an encouraging smile on Michael. "Would you like to stand?"

"I can't—" The words dropped off. Going pale with shock, he gazed down at his body—and blinked. "Christ almighty, woman, I'm naked."

So she had noticed.

So she had *felt*.

Flustered, hot-faced, and shaky, Kayli nodded at an assistant, who hurried to retrieve a covering. "Your clothing was not designed to withstand the rearrangement of molecules during transportation, as mine is. Likely it was destroyed in transit."

Mallet didn't hear her. He was too busy staring fixedly at his legs, or more to the point, the lack of scars on his legs.

With heavy precaution, he pushed up on one straightened arm. Over his entire body, muscles flexed and bunched in an impressive display.

Kayli did her best not to gawk, but she'd never seen, never even imagined . . .

Again the assistants murmured.

With a large hand flattened on the floor, Mallet bent one leg, paused with his breath held, flexed it, bent, straightened it again. At the lack of agony, he sucked in his breath and turned to Kayli with so much hope, her heart melted.

"Yes," she whispered, so happy to be the one to tell him. "It's as I said—your body is healed and whole again."

Michael's Adam's apple bobbed as he audibly swallowed. Slowly, he rose to his feet. "They're gone."

The assistants, all very capable, scurried back from the breadth and height of Michael as he gained his feet. Awe and alarm widened their eyes, making Kayli wish that, for this instance alone, she hadn't given them so many emotions.

Gently, she asked, "The scars?"

"The pains."

Yes, of course. Just because he hadn't complained didn't mean he hadn't suffered. Michael was a warrior, a man conditioned to take great agony without ever giving voice to the pain.

She touched his arm and encountered tensile strength and incredible power. "I'm happy for you."

He took two steps and turned, watching the movement of his legs, the flexibility and strength, and a slow grin brightened his expression. "I feel . . . fine."

He looked fine, too. Very fine. Never had she imagined a man such as him. Yes, he was bigger, but that only covered half of it. His muscles were so delineated that each small movement sent them into an impressive display. The simplest gestures showed inspiring power. Even the way in which he held himself, with so much confidence and attitude, was in stark contrast to what she was used to.

She'd dropped him into a totally unfamiliar time and situation, and still he looked ready to take charge of them all.

"Hell," he said with an ear-lifting grin, "I feel *great!*"

His infectious good mood had her smothering her own grin. The time was inappropriate to excesses of glee, for her at least.

After accepting the robe from an assistant, Kayli glued her attention north of his broad shoulders and held it out to him. "I'm glad that our exchange pleases you." Repaired health was the least she could give him for his upcoming aid.

"Well, yeah." He paid no mind to the proffered covering. "I mean, I must be nuts to be buying into this, but who gives a damn?"

His comfort at being naked before an audience of strangers astounded her. The members of her colony considered modesty a most-important virtue—and Michael obviously had none.

"Sir?" Unwilling to get close enough to touch him again—or have him touch her as he'd already done—she thrust the robe toward him insistently. With any luck, he'd take the not-so-subtle encouragement to cover his nakedness.

Instead, he used her extended arm as a leash to snag her, and then haul her in close. Her mouth dropped open as he scooped her up against his body, against all that hot male flesh. Against her protests, he swung her in an exuberant circle. Her flying legs made the assistants duck out of the way.

Laughing aloud, he shouted, "Kayli, love, I can stand on my own!"

"Michael, please!" Blushing to the roots of her fair hair, Kayli braced against his inflexible shoulders and glanced at her assistants. They all stared back at her with indulgent if astounded humor.

This display amused them?

Lower, near his ear, Kayli insisted, "You *must* show some decorum."

Michael brought his face close to hers and, in a low rumbling growl, he said, "I'd rather take you to bed."

A flash of heat left her mute and unseeing. She shook her head to clear it. "What? No!"

He nuzzled her jawline. "Why not?"

He had to stop saying such outrageous, impossible things to her. "I've already told you," she whispered in a rush. "It is forbidden for me."

Leaning back to see her, he smiled and said, "Yeah, well, as the almighty chosen one, I'll have to change that now, won't I?"

Chosen one? Doing her utmost to gather her composure, she pushed him away. Instilling much gravity into her voice, she said, "*First*, you must cover yourself. I insist."

His smile spread with insidious good humor. "I think it's adorable when you take charge."

She had to ignore that. She was a warrior, a respected member of her colony; there was nothing adorable about her. "And," she continued, unwilling to reply to his comment, "I need to orient you to our colony and the time period. I must show you your new surroundings, help you become acclimated to your new environment—"

"That'll wait." He hugged her tight again, and there was nothing she could do about it without engaging in actual combat. "Right now, I just want to celebrate with some good lovin'."

Good lovin'?

Nonplussed, Kayli shoved back yet again, this time as far as she could, and stared at him. How was it that she continually found herself flattened against him?

She tried to ease the press of her lower body against his, but with one arm around her waist and the other scooped just below her bottom, he kept her snug to him, forcing her to feel every extraordinary inch of his maleness—and there were . . . several inches.

"Now don't faint," he teased. But he did ease his hold just a bit.

It didn't help, not when her wiggling attempts to escape him only added new heat to his vibrant blue eyes and an intensity to his entire mien that bespoke male interest in the extreme.

Kayli sucked in needed oxygen. "You are very quick to be accustomed to time travel."

"Nah." He put his forehead to hers and stared into her eyes. His breath was warm, his look warmer. "I just figure I'm dreaming or hallucinating or something. Whatever it is, I want to make the most of it before I wake up."

He still didn't believe her?

Dismay all but flattened her. She'd already transported him. He was in her vessel. What more could she do to convince him? "Sir . . ."

Another voice intruded, this one so strident it had the

power to snap the mood and gain everyone's attention. "Kayli!"

Wincing in dread, Kayli stiff-armed Michael. "You must release me. *Now.*"

Before she could free herself, the voice continued with icy censure. "How dare you behave this way? Kayli Raine, this is not how you were raised to represent me. This is *not* how you serve your colony!"

From bad to worse. "Of course. I was just—"

"I won't hear your excuses, young lady, because there are none. This is a most inappropriate time for such displays of impropriety. As you well know, the day of our next sacrifice approaches."

His eyes narrowing at the censure, Michael loosened his hold and turned to her mother. Gloriously naked, he asked, "And just who the hell are you?"

So cheerful that he wanted to whoop, to do cartwheels and kicks and then carry Kayli off for some very private one-on-one celebration, Mallet barely held himself in check.

That is, until the pinch-faced broad showed up, and all the joy sucked out of the room as if her cold presence freeze-dried all happy emotions.

Given how Kayli squirmed beside him, any dope could figure out that she was horrified. Mallet disliked that most of all.

"Mother," Kayli said, "I can explain."

"Mother?" Mallet looked at the woman more closely. She looked to be a well-preserved forty-something, old enough, he supposed, to have mothered Kayli, if she'd gotten an early start at that sort of thing.

The coloring differed, with Kayli blond and hazel-eyed, and her mother dark-haired with striking blue eyes. Still, he saw a resemblance in the stubborn chin and high cheek-bones, the shape of the nose and arch of the eyebrows.

But where Kayli was lean and lithe, her mother was

voluptuous. The older woman spilled curves, attitude, and indignation.

For many reasons, not the least of which was how she'd spoken to Kayli, Mallet disliked her on sight. "So that's her, huh? The head honcho?"

Kayli groaned.

The mother puckered up like she'd just bitten into a very ripe lemon. "Kayli, what does he say?"

Kayli cleared her throat. "It's his native colloquialisms, Mother. He's only confirming—in his own way—that you're the Arbiter, our matriarchal leader."

"I see." She gave a graceful but hoity nod. "This is my colony, yes."

"Own it lock, stock, and barrel, do you?" He didn't wait for her to reply. "Well, I hope you're not looking for me to bow or kneel or anything subservient like that. Ain't in my nature."

She pinched even more. Unlike her daughter, her gaze never once wavered from his face. "Not at all. It is our hope that you shall take a place in the hierarchy, and bow to no one. To the contrary, our people will hail you."

"Yeah, I'm not much into that, either." He didn't mind a horde of screaming fans while he fought, or some sexy female groupies outside of a bout. But other than that, he preferred to be treated like everyone else.

Ignoring his dissention, the mother tried to forge on with her purpose. "Shall I call you Michael?"

"Whatever floats your boat." Her uptight, aloof attitude continued to nettle him. He'd never been a big fan of social classes, and he wasn't about to start liking the separation now.

Again, Kayli rushed to explain his meaning. "If it pleases you to address him by his first name, he's agreeable."

The mother said, "Thank you, Michael. And you may address me by my given name, Raemay."

"Sure thing." Now that his playtime with Kayli had been demolished, he supposed he should find out about the business at hand. Crossing his arms over his chest, he faced Kayli's mother and quirked a brow. "Now what, Rae-may?"

Put off by his casual speech, she nonetheless mustered up her diplomacy. "I wish you to meet my daughters, Idola and Mesha."

He glanced back at Kayli with surprise. "You have sisters?"

"Yes. I informed you previously, remember?" Her gaze took another quick trip down and then back up his body again.

Pleased that his body kept drawing her attention, he smiled.

When her flustered gaze clashed with his, more color warmed her face.

Amused, Mallet accepted the robe that two squirrely fellows kept trying to get on him without actually getting close enough to touch him. He held it up, then shook his head.

"You realize there's no way this'll fit my shoulders?"

When Kayli looked grieved, he shrugged and wrapped it around his waist, tucking in the edges.

Hoping to tease Kayli out of her tense mood, he asked, "Better?"

Her attention went to his still naked chest. "Marginally, thank you." She rushed into speech. "My sisters will be presented to you first, before the rest of the available females. It would be ideal if you chose one of them."

"Chose one of them for what?"

Kayli blinked hard and fast, and her mouth moved, but no sound emerged.

Raemay filled in. "We would be honored for you to take union with our family."

"Take union?" Mallet didn't like the sound of that at all. "What's that mean, take union?"

But no one seemed inclined to explain. Instead, Raemay cast her daughter a chiding look. "You haven't told him of the ceremony?"

"I . . . ah . . . I did, just not in detail."

Raemay dismissed her with a frown. "I can start them preparing now," she said. "There is no time to waste."

Balking at that idea, Kayli gave immediate protest. "But, Mother, Michael must have time to look around."

"Yeah," Mallet said, without knowing why he felt compelled to complain. "I need time to look around."

"And to get to know our ways." Kayli didn't look at him, but instead beseeched her mother, "He needs to be fed and rested and, as you can see, properly attired."

Raemay took in his size in a single scathing glance. "He appears more than capable of feeding and bathing himself."

Heat scalded Kayli's cheeks. "Yes, of course. But he's yet to know how to acquire nourishment here, and we need to find something suitable that'll fit his unusual proportions."

Listening to the two women, Mallet decided he needed to know what the hell this union business was about. He had his suspicions, but he hated to jump the gun with a wrong assumption.

Kayli had mentioned a ceremony for him to take his place in the hierarchy. But if the ceremony was a union—with a woman—well, they'd just have to appoint him some other way.

Raemay tapped a finger to her chin as she assessed him. "I doubt there's anything prepared to suit him. He is rather large."

"We'll need to improvise, I fear."

"Had you forewarned us of this issue to give us time to properly prepare, I wouldn't have suffered him so improperly attired in my presence."

"As I recall," Mallet told her, "I wasn't attired at all, improper or otherwise."

"*Sir,*" Kayli warned, as if speaking back to her mother was a cardinal offense.

Because of Kayli's unusual jitters, he disliked the mother even more. She spoke down to her daughter, and sounded like a nag.

To redirect the conversation, he asked, "I don't suppose you have any jeans?"

"Genes?" Bewilderment had her brows pinched down. "But of course. We're advanced, but every human still has their genetic makeup—"

"No." Mallet shook his head at the misunderstanding. "I mean blue jeans. Denim."

"Ah." Kayli nodded. "It's a material," she explained to her mother. Then she said to Mallet, "I saw it on your friends, yes? I believe we could replicate it."

"Great, because I'm sure as hell not wearing what they wear." His gaze went over the android assistants with disgust. They looked like a bunch of sissies in their flowing robes and draping pants.

Her mother's features tightened. "Fine. Any other . . . demands?"

"I could use a big juicy steak and a baked potato."

Raemay eyed him as if he'd turned into a Neanderthal. "We do not consume beef here."

"No kidding?" A colony of vegetarians? Hoping he wouldn't have to follow suit, Mallet asked, "Is that a religious or dietary restriction?"

"Neither," Kayli interjected. "I can have the meal prepared for you immediately. Would you like to dine here or elsewhere?"

"I don't know what elsewhere you have, sugar. So far, I don't know much of anything except that your assistants wear PJs and your mom curls her lip over the mention of a steak." So saying, he faced the older woman. "So, yeah, Mom, how about giving us a little time to check out the joint, get familiar and all that?"

"But you must meet Idola and Mesha."

Mallet held up a hand. "Afterward, I'd be happy to meet Kayli's sisters, just don't pin any hopes on me leaping headlong into any fancy unions of any kind. Ain't gonna happen."

Raemay went rigid with displeasure.

And so what? If he didn't miss his guess, the whole union thing was a way to leg-shackle him and, no matter the level of his gratitude, he wasn't falling for that.

And if he was wrong, at least Mom would know up front how he felt.

"My daughters are very beautiful young ladies."

With his look aimed at Kayli, Mallet said, "No argument there." Now that he'd met Kayli, kissed her and held her, he wasn't about to start any hanky-panky with her siblings, regardless of how hot they might be. Most could call him a down-home yahoo, but he wasn't a complete fool. Sisters were definitely taboo.

Raemay wasn't amused by his lack of deference. "You, sir, are misguided in making light of such a serious situation."

"Mother," Kayli implored. "He needs some time."

Outrage simmered off Raemay, but she finally relented. "Very well." She addressed Mallet. "You have until the morning, and then you must choose."

The hell you say! "Why the rush?" he asked, hoping to buy himself some time from whatever odd customs they had in mind.

"Whomever you choose will be removed from availability. The decision must be made before noontime, when the next sacrifice will be selected."

Sacrifice? Now just what the hell did *that* mean?

Mallet started to ask, but Raemay poofed into thin air, just as he'd seen her daughter do on too many occasions.

He rounded on Kayli. "It's damned annoying the way you women disappear without warning."

Distraught, Kayli pressed her fingertips to her temples. "Yes, well, you'll become accustomed." Then under her breath, she added, "I hope."

A little paler and a whole lot more strained, she got down to business. "Tyehim, Darian, please order up suitable clothing and shoes. I believe you heard his preferences. Hadar, prepare a room. He'll need a bigger bed, obviously. You'll find us shortly in the dining area."

The one she'd addressed as Tyehim inched nearer. "I would scan you, sir."

"Scan me?"

"It's painless," Kayli said. "Just hold still a moment."

"Arms out, please," Tyehim directed. When Mallet, wearing a pained expression of annoyance, lifted both arms straight out, he nodded. "Excellent."

In the next instant, a bluish beam came from Tyehim's eyes, fanning out to encompass Mallet's size as it slid over him, head to toes.

Freakin' amazing.

Tyehim nodded. "Thank you, sir."

"Look . . . Tyehim is it?" At the man's nod, Mallet said, "You don't need to call me sir. Mallet will do."

"Mallet?"

"My fight name. You know, hardheaded? Like a big sledgehammer?"

Tyehim glanced at Kayli with confusion, then back to Mallet. "Thank you, Mallet. I will have the clothing anon."

Mallet watched some of the men scurry off, leaving several others behind. Kayli sure had a crew of them, and they were all fair-haired, lean lightweights. He supposed, to a woman, they'd be considered handsome.

He didn't like it.

Temper pricked, he asked, "Will your lackeys know my size?"

Kayli seemed too distracted to react as he wanted. "They are not lackeys, sir, but highly developed AMAs."

"AMAs?"

"Android male assistants. There are but a few AFAs, or—"

"Android female assistants. Got it." Taking their measure, Mallet strode a wide circle around the AMAs remaining in close proximity. He enjoyed the sheer pleasure of walking under his own steam.

The AMAs looked as human as he did, not at all like machines. "So they're sexually oriented android robots, like in *Terminator* and *Alien*?"

"Sexually oriented only in part." Kayli held out a hand. "Our time is limited, so I'd prefer to brief you on the way."

Though skeptical, Mallet looked forward to her explanations. He took her hand and she started him down the long, narrow corridor.

That, too, he enjoyed. Hell, he wanted to run. He wanted to jump and kick and train.

He wanted to fight again. Right now. Not in anger, but in competition, just to assure himself that he was back, as good as ever.

But Kayli's gentleness, her undeniable femininity as she walked beside him, tempered his desire to test his strength and speed. Instead, his thoughts went to her, what made her tick, what motivated her.

What excited her.

Her hand felt small and cool in his. And damn it, he felt protective. Not because of whatever malevolence she claimed against the colony, but because of her own misconceptions about her appeal, and her mother's emotionless interaction with her.

Little by little, he was starting to believe.

Everywhere he looked, he saw things unfamiliar to him. It was all too vivid, too substantial to be a dream. His friends had seen Kayli. Drew Black had held her hand, the same as he himself did now.

She existed—which meant he really *had* transported to the future.

Kayli needed him, and he wanted to help her—not only with the problems she described, but with the inner turmoil he detected, too.

She glanced up at him, then away. "I understand that your media entertainment often focused on the future. That's what you meant by *Alien* and *Terminator*?"

"Kick-ass movies, yeah. I enjoyed all the sequels, too."

"Our AMAs are unlike those ill-tempered creatures of your films."

Windows lined the corridor and through them, Mallet saw grasslands, towering trees, and flowers everywhere. The colors were brighter than any he'd ever seen; the sky so blue it hurt his eyes, the grass lushly green, the flowers a rainbow of hues.

Mallet moved to a window. "If we're in a spaceship, we aren't that high in the sky."

She came up beside him. "We're in my vessel, but while moored, we have restrictions on visibility. We must be close enough for all to see, but not so low that other vehicles might have to avoid us."

"So if I jumped out—"

"You can't!" She latched onto his arm with alarm. "The fall would extirpate you."

"Extirpate?"

"Kill you. You would be beyond repair." She shook his arm, anxious to make him understand. "I would not be able to make you whole again."

Mallet covered her hand. "Sorry. Bad joke." He lifted her hand and kissed her fingertips. "I'm not planning to damage myself again anytime soon."

Her scowl showed just what she thought of his humor. With a tug, she steered him into a sterile room in direct contrast to what he'd seen out the windows.

There was no color here at all.

The warm, white stone floor held soft white chairs, odd in their design. Only the single door they'd entered broke the windowless white walls.

After one last stern look of reprimand, Kayli returned to their previous discussion. "Our AMAs are freethinking, but never provided with more strength than the person who acquires them. However, they are often more intelligent, and they can be designed with a varying assortment of human emotions."

Mallet turned a circle in awe. The temperature of the room wasn't cold, but the atmosphere felt stark and frosty. Distracted, he pointed out, "Yours have emotions."

"Yes, they do. I paid extra to have them fully equipped with all known sentiments. It makes it easier to enjoy their company."

Because her mother kept herself so aloof? What about her sisters? Did they treat Kayli the same way? Like a stranger, an employee, rather than family?

That thought bothered Mallet a lot. He knew what it was to be without family. To have family but be distanced from them would surely be worse. "They're like friends to you, even though they're not real?"

"They are real," she insisted again. "They're just not human."

Her tone showed her defensiveness of her AMAs. The same defensiveness one would have for a friend.

Mallet softened his tone. "All right."

That just made her pricklier. "Please remember that things are very different here. I know that for you, your world consisted of one planet and one known being. Here, with me, you will discover many planets with many forms of beings."

Enjoying her gumption, Mallet tweaked her chin and smiled. "Am I going to be freaked out?"

Proving she had an adequate grasp on his lingo, she fell into a smile, too. "Quite possibly." Turning back to the room, she lifted her arm. "This, sir, is a media room. Here you can relax and take in an assortment of depictions of our colony and the worlds that surround ours."

Mallet surveyed all that blank white space and cocked a brow. "All I see are walls."

"That's because nothing is activated yet."

"Yeah, well . . ." Still skeptical, he pointed out the obvious. "I don't see anything to activate."

She sighed. "Everything is voice-activated. Everything is also prerecorded, so you don't have to worry about intruding on anything or anyone in a personal manner, as I did with you and with your new friend, Travis Stockman."

Travis wasn't really a friend, but Mallet let that go. "Good to know."

"I'll enter your voice into the database, and then you can command the system to show you our wildlife, our food sources, our housing, and education. Anything you like."

"How about your firearms?"

"Oh, no." She looked appalled at such a question. "Weapons of that sort are forbidden."

She had to be kidding. "I thought you were at war."

"We are, but it is hand-to-hand combat. That's why we need a man of your ability, power, and . . . size."

"So there're no guns, no bombs?"

Her hazel eyes flared, and she hushed him in a rush. "No," she whispered. "Even the mention of such a thing can cause alarm."

"So . . ." He tried to think through the idea of a weapons-free existence. "Are knives, sticks, things like that allowed?"

"Yes, though they're frowned on as being the tools of cowards."

Ingenious. The world would rid itself of a lot of problems without fear of one group annihilating another. "So we're to go it *mano a mano*?" When Kayli just looked at him, Mallet said, "Men, or in your case, women, going at it hand to hand."

"That is the preferred way, yes." She paced a little while formulating more explanations. "I told you how the colonies are self-sufficient, each tending to its own problems. The Cosmos Confederation, which is our form of government that spans the galaxies, issues very few rules. One of them is a strict forbiddance of weaponry, lest it be used to unfair advantage against another."

Nodding as much to himself as to her, Mallet said, "I like it." He gestured at the room, which looked like a barren, hygienic rubber enclosure meant for nut jobs. "So how's this work?"

Kayli put her hands together. "Hauk, wildlife please."

Mallet grinned. "Is that a pun?"

"Not at all. Hauk is—"

"Spelled with a *u*," said a thick masculine voice that resonated throughout the room, giving Mallet a start. "Not a *w*, like the extinct fowl."

Eyes heavenward, Kayli continued, "Hauk is the name of the system in charge of this room."

"In charge of everything," clarified the voice. "I have ultimate control of the vessel in every conceivable way. I just set your voice to the system so that you are now able to issue commands of your own."

Crossing her arms under her breasts, Kayli said, sotto voce, "Hauk can be a little . . ."

"Cocky?" Mallet asked. But he understood, and added, "He's male. I get it."

"He has a male voice," Kayli clarified, "but he's a computer."

"A male computer," emphasized Hauk. "Unlike some gender-free units." Then he added, "And Kayli, I'm quite pleased you didn't say *just* a computer."

"Now Hauk, would I insult you that way?" Kayli taunted.

"On a daily basis," Hauk confirmed. "But I tolerate it because I love you."

She snorted. "More likely because I own the ship."

Hauk sniffed in return—but didn't refute that.

Chuckling at their sibling-like banter, Mallet asked, "You name all your robots and computers?"

"But of course, otherwise, what would I call them?"

Hauk asked, "Shall I proceed, Kayli?"

"Yes, please."

And suddenly Mallet found himself in a heavily wooded setting. He could smell rich earth and moss and the scent of running water carried on a balmy breeze. All around him, leaves rustled, large unfamiliar birds screeched, and animals snarled.

Shocked, he took Kayli's hand and pulled her behind him as he searched the area, looking for the source of those angry animal roars.

"That's enough, Hauk. Thank you."

The woods disappeared, placing Mallet back in the stark white room.

He stared at Kayli. "Holy shit."

Disapproval warred with amusement. "I see that I've surprised you."

"Again." He ran a hand over his head. "I take it we weren't transported?"

Amusement won out. "We were not. The room provides a three-dimensional vision of all commands. To get the full benefit, you need to sit in one of the chairs. They can provide simulated motion and air disturbance, along with temperature changes."

"No, thank you."

She laughed—and the sound was so rusty, but rich and pure, that Mallet found himself heating with temptation.

"It's all an illusion, Michael. The chair will simulate other affects of your command, but no harm can come to you." She lifted their laced hands. "Or me. That is why you put yourself in front of me, isn't it? To protect me?"

Feeling self-conscious in the face of her amusement, he shrugged. "I guess." And as his irritation grew, he added, "It's instinctive."

"And perfect for our purposes. We need a warrior like you, a man capable and caring."

That reminded Mallet of something her mother had said, and he jumped on it, anxious to ease the awkwardness of the moment. "What did Raemay mean about a sacrifice?"

Kayli avoided his gaze. "I would prefer to explain that later. For now, we should take you to eat, and then you may either return here to familiarize yourself with our community, or retire to your room to get some rest."

Mallet caught her chin and brought her gaze around to his. "I'm not tired, Kayli. Food can wait. And I'm not ready to explore this room further just yet. So how about you just answer my question?"

"It is complicated."

"Un-complicate it."

She sighed. "Very well. As you know, we are under siege from a neighboring colony. The men are bigger than our norm, though nowhere as massive as you. More along the lines of my height."

"And you're a runt," he teased. But he recalled that her

mother stood no more than a few inches over five feet—much shorter than her daughter.

Kayli's expression contorted with anger. "They are savages. Marauders taking what they want without consideration. At first, we tried to fight them, but that only caused damage to our homes and lands without success in defending our people. When we engage, they go after our men, knowing that we have a shortage and that our men are most valued."

More valued than the women? Mallet was too astonished to comment. He couldn't imagine a bunch of women trying to protect men. It wasn't natural.

"Have they killed many of your men?"

"None."

"None?" He grunted. "Then . . . ?"

"Sheltering the males leaves our untrained women vulnerable for abduction." Her hands fisted. "We've lost several to them already."

A knot of dread twisted in his guts. "They murdered *women*?"

"We don't know!" She paced away, but came right back. "I hope not, but the first was taken almost a year ago, several more since then, and we never again hear from any of them."

So while warring, they grabbed up available women. Bastards. "What do they want?"

Kayli's hazel eyes filled with sadness, anger, and impotence. Her ripe mouth turned down in distress.

Eyes closed, she whispered, "Women." She swallowed, lifted her shoulders with helplessness. "From what we can tell, that's all they want—our women."

A very bad feeling came over Mallet. "And the sacrifice?"

She started to turn away, but Mallet caught her shoulder. "Kayli?"

She didn't look at him; her voice was small, filled with shame. "To avoid attack against the entire colony, we . . . that is, the hierarchy . . ."

"Spit it out."

She met his gaze with stoic determination. "It was decided to give them one woman on the first day of every second month."

Outraged, Mallet dropped his hand and took a step back. "Meaning you hand over six women a year to your enemy?"

Again, she closed her eyes as if unable to face the truths of her colony's decision. "So far," she whispered, "the intruders are satisfied with that quota, and our colony is safe from further retribution. Whoever you choose tomorrow will be protected from the practice. That's why Mother is anxious for you to decide."

"And whoever I don't pick?"

"Will be among those determined suitable as a peace offering. A name is randomly drawn from all available women."

He didn't believe it, any of it—how could he? But still Mallet went rigid with rage. He was a natural-born fighter; it was the only thing he'd ever found in life that made him feel complete.

But damn it, he fought as a sport, not as a way of bullying others. He detested brutality, especially against anyone smaller or weaker than himself. The thought of cruelty toward children or women left him raging. He hadn't lied about his instinctive inclination to protect.

Now those instincts slammed into him. "No fucking way."

Kayli drew a deep, shuddering breath, and nodded. "Yes. And the time for choosing the peace offering—"

"Sacrifice, you mean."

"Yes. The time grows near. Unless you get familiar with our situation and offer a better solution, another woman will be left in the glen for them to take."

"Oh, I've got a better solution, all right." Mallet turned and headed for the door. "You fight. Each and every fucking time."

Kayli ran after him, her voice raised with excitement. "Sir, wait. It was not my decision to cower and give in. Perhaps with your aid, we can convince the others . . ."

"Stop calling me sir!"

She faltered, then launched after him again. "Michael, wait. Where are you going?"

"To find your mother the Arbiter," he ground out. "And the chicken-shit council who lets her pull this stunt again and again." He was to choose a woman? Ha! He'd choose them all, and then they could start to figure out another way.

Kayli wrapped both hands around his upper arm. "Wait!"

"For what?" He dragged her along a few steps.

"You have no idea where you're going."

That brought him up short. Knowing she had a point, he turned to face her. "Take me to them."

Kayli grinned, and it made her look so beautiful, Mallet felt like he'd been punched in the solar plexus. "You're happy?"

Tears filled her eyes as she nodded. "That you're here, *yes*. That you feel the same as I do, *yes*. That you're willing to do whatever you can to assist in ending this horrid—"

Mallet couldn't help but snatch her up and kiss her silly. Her mouth was soft and damp—and quickly pulled back from his. "Come here."

She fought her way out of his arms. "Michael, you must stop that!"

"Sorry, babe, no can do." He crossed his arms, and stared her in the eyes. "Now take me to your leader."

CHAPTER 5

I T was such a corny line that Mallet almost lost some of his steam.

Almost.

But Kayli's reaction to his kiss, not at all encouraging, kept his temper on a high note. How was it she'd uprooted him, zipped him through time, turned him inside out—and managed to stay mostly unaffected by the sexual chemistry snapping and crackling between them?

As he watched her rub her mouth with her fingertips, he was far from unaffected.

He wanted to see her smile again, hear her laugh. He wanted to taste her.

All over.

Kayli drew in several calming breaths, and took another step away from him.

Hoping he hid his annoyance, Mallet raised a brow and waited.

"There is a certain way of doing things here," she said with tentative care. "Because she is the Arbiter, you can not just storm in on my mother and make demands. She will need to hear an alternate plan, and that will require you to have at least a rudimentary understanding of our surroundings and manners. I beg of you—"

"No, never beg."

Exasperation took her back another step. "Very well, Michael. I *ask* of you, please, will you eat, don more appropriate attire, and then make use of our media room? In the morning we will speak again and you may tell me of any alternate plan you might conceive. But understand up front, whatever your intentions, I'm for defending our people, *all* of our people. I will back you in any effort to end the sacrifices."

He supposed her suggestions made sense, but patience now didn't sit quite right. Rubbing the back of his neck, he nodded. "When do they choose the next poor female to throw to the wolves?"

Her breath shuddered in and out. "Not until tomorrow midday."

That'd give him a little time to think things through. Already, a plan formed. Harebrained, but hell, it was better than forfeiting someone to an unknown fate.

"All right. I'll try to slow it down." He pointed a finger at her. "But no one is getting sacrificed."

Her smile quivered. "Thank you, sir."

He threw up his arms in frustration. "I told you, no more 'sirring' me, damn it!"

"All right, Michael."

Her humble response irked, and blunted the edge of his temper. What had she thought—that he'd go along with such a barbaric thing? No way.

Less heated but still grumbling, he said, "For a supposedly civilized colony, I'm not real impressed."

"Understandable, under the circumstances."

"Yeah, well . . ." He hated seeing her like this, on pins and needles. "I'm hungry and I guess I could use some clothes that fit a little better." He flipped one end of the robe over his knee. "At least if I'm covered a bit more, it'll keep you from ogling me so much."

And with that, he gestured for Kayli to show him to the kitchen, or the eating place, or whatever she called it.

A little tongue-tied, her cheeks again pink, Kayli darted around him to take the lead down the hall. Mallet didn't mind. He enjoyed the rear view of her as much as the front. Heck, maybe even more.

So she wanted to defend her people.

He liked that. He liked her. A lot.

The future, and all it held, looked a whole lot brighter than it had yesterday.

KAYLI'S heels echoed on the floor as she approached the pristine food preparation room. As one interconnected unit, it selected, cooked, and served each menu requested.

She stopped inside the door. "How do you like your steak?"

Arms folded over his chest, he propped one boulder-shoulder against the framing of the unit. "Medium well would be great."

Despite his casual stance, he looked impatient, and Kayli could guess why. He knew only the cooking methods familiar to his time, and was disappointed not to see the meat already seared. She shuddered at the repulsive thought.

"Your potato?"

He eyed her, then shrugged. "What the hell. I'm not in training, so load it up."

"Load it?"

"Butter, sour cream, bacon bits, cheese—throw it all on there."

"Of course." She faced the mainframe—which consisted of one tiny circular microchip—and repeated Michael's order.

A quiet hum sounded, and seconds later a seamless space stretched opened in the counter. A tray arose filled with the steaming food, a glass of iced juice, condiments, napkins, and utensils.

Seeing Michael go wide-eyed in amazement gave Kayli

some satisfaction; he'd certainly taken her by surprise more than once. "Like much of my vessel, the galley is voice-activated."

Dumbfounded, Michael looked at her, then at the fragrant food with much doubt. "You named the food, and it . . . appeared."

"Prepared just as you requested," Hauk said.

"In the future, while on board, you may order up your own food." Kayli watched as Michael sniffed the food with suspicion. "If you don't want to come here to do so, you can instruct Hauk and he can have it delivered to you by one of the AMAs."

"Taste it," Hauk said. "Go ahead."

"He's anxious," Kayli explained with an indulgent pat to the counter. Hauk was great, very cocky as Michael had claimed, but also determined to please. "He probably sees you as more of an equal, so your opinion matters greatly to him."

Hauk took exception to what she said. "I can speak for myself, Kayli."

Still a little shell-shocked, Michael picked up a fork and knife, and cut into his steak. He took one bite, and his eyes closed on a groan. "Oh God, that's good."

"I'm not a god," said Hauk, "but thank you. I would serve you nothing less than perfect food."

Kayli wished for a way to rein in her domineering computer. "That was just another colloquialism, Hauk. Remember I gave you that history on our guest and his speech mannerisms? If you would only take the time—"

"It took me only minutes to absorb it all, of course." Hauk sniffed with all the disdain usually reserved for humans. "It was an understandable mistake."

"It was," Michael said around a mouthful. "You are a god—of fine cooking."

"There, you see, Kayli? The big man sees my worth."

If possible, Hauk would have probably stuck out a tongue. It was fortunate he didn't have one.

"His name is Michael."

"I know his name."

"Call me Mallet," Michael said. "I'm more used to it."

"Indeed," Hauk said. "It suits you, Mallet."

Annoyed at how they'd excluded her, Kayli picked up the tray and handed it to Michael, put her hand on his forearm, and said, "We're going to the dining room now, Hauk."

Hauk sighed, but agreed. "Very well."

Before she could say another word, they were in the formal dining area.

Michael stiffened in shock to find himself transported yet again. "Did we just—?"

"Yes. Hauk moved us here."

Annoyance darkened his features. "I don't like it. I have legs, you know."

And no doubt he wanted to use them, now that he could again. "I understand. Once we leave the vessel, we'll rarely transport, so you don't need to get accustomed to it."

"Why do we transport here, and not elsewhere?"

His interest pleased her. The more he learned about them and their ways, the more effective he'd be in correcting the wrongs. "Hauk has the ability to do the transports easily, but it uses a lot of his power to access that function when we're not on board. Most in our colony do not have a computer like Hauk."

"No one else has a computer like me, thank you very much."

Kayli considered shutting Hauk down, but knew she wouldn't. "True. My mother has a powerful unit, but not as powerful as Hauk. A few of the more established families have comparable units. But again, nowhere as powerful as Hauk. As head of our warriors, I have use of him." She smiled because really, despite his quirks, she was quite fond of Hauk and considered him one of her closest friends. "He and I have been together for a long time."

"Since she was seventeen," Hauk said, and he didn't sound as pleased with that memory as she was. "The point is that Kayli makes more use of my far-reaching ability when she's on board. Away from me, she conforms to what the average colonist can and cannot do, so that she can better fit in with them."

"Got it. No reason for them to see her as superior, right?"

"Exactly."

"Admirable. But no more transporting me unless I request it. Understood?"

Kayli didn't like it, but she nodded.

Hauk, filled with deference, said, "Of course, Mallet. It will be as you wish."

Still scowling, Mallet ignored the seats to study the room Hauk had prepared. Great panels were open to reveal the glass dome ceiling. It made him feel like he was surrounded by the blue sky and fluffy clouds. Soft music played from a hidden console, and at the center of the oval stone table, several thick candles flickered.

It hit Kayli that the room was set for romance.

"Hauk," she warned.

But the cantankerous computer didn't reply. Later, she'd have to remind him of her duty as a warrior. She had serious responsibilities that prohibited any attempts at pairing her with their guest.

He was not meant for her.

No man was meant for her. She would spend her life alone, first defending her colony, and later, teaching others to defend it.

Michael looked at her. "This is some room."

Did he realize Hauk's intent? Hopefully not. "It's been determined that proper digestion is necessary to a healthy body, so mealtimes are of utmost importance. A soothing ambiance is as crucial as the food consumed."

"Yeah?" Michael took a step closer. "Seems more seductive than soothing to me."

"Hauk's idea," she blurted, and moved to the head of the table. "I'll speak to him about it."

"Don't bother." His smile came slow and sexy. "I don't mind."

Kayli could have sworn she heard Hauk snicker.

But truly, what did it matter? Tomorrow, Michael would be presented with the available women, all of them very pretty, more than appropriate, and anxious to be chosen by him. Why bother explaining things to him again now, when he'd soon make a choice all on his own that would end his playful flirting?

"Please." She pulled out a chair. "Sit down and enjoy your meal."

"Good idea. I don't want it to get cold."

"It wouldn't. The plate is fashioned to keep it at the proper temperature."

"Great. Now that's an invention that makes sense." He gestured for her to be seated. "Ladies first."

"All right." As Kayli sat, the chair cuddled her, again giving Michael a start. "Each chair has a microchip to inform it of your size, muscle mass, and body temperature. When you sit down, it will conform to your highest level of comfort—or as closely as it can, given your unusual size."

With caution, Michael sank into the seat, remaining stiff while it moved around him. Gradually, he relaxed. "Wow. Heavenly." He patted the arms, shifted a little, and picked up his fork to continue eating. "I could really get used to all this added comfort."

Kayli's heart stuttered. "I hope you do." Now that he was here, she didn't want him to leave. Ever. She wanted him to be content in her colony, to stay with her . . . or rather, her people.

Other colonies offered great allures, each more unique and appealing than the other, so she'd have to see what she could do about keeping him gratified.

"I can't wait to try out the beds." He consumed several more bites, all the while watching her. "Are they the same?"

"Fashioned for your comfort? Yes." The intensity in his direct blue gaze kept her edgy, and she cleared her throat. "Your pillow will remain cool, and your coverings will determine the proper body temperature to best suit you."

"Huh." He finished off his last bite of steak and sat back. "I've got a question."

Never had Kayli seen anyone devour a meal so efficiently. He wasn't crude in his habits, but the food had disappeared in very short order.

"Dessert?"

His gaze warmed with humor—and something more. "Not unless you're on the menu."

Her heart slammed into her chest. Good heavens, the way he spoke, and how he looked at her as he said those outrageous things. . . . No one had ever looked at her like that. Certainly no one had ever dared to speak to her that way. It was rude and invigorating and a little bit thrilling.

She needed to get herself in check. "I am not." She tried to relax. "You had a question?"

"I do." One side of his mouth kicked up. "If the bed conforms to a person's comfort, what happens when two bodies are in the bed?"

Kayli blinked. "Two bodies?"

Losing the relaxed posture, he leaned forward and folded his muscled arms on the tabletop. "You people don't make love in a bed? Huh." His eyes glinted. "Kinky. I'm game, but for kicks, why don't you tell me what the norm is here now? I'm burning with curiosity."

Her mouth opened. She felt it. But . . . nothing came out.

Hauk came to her rescue. "Mallet, you really must behave before you send her into vapors." A cool breeze brushed over Kayli, aiding in her recovery.

"Yes." She found her voice, though it sounded oddly thick and raspy. "Thank you, Hauk."

Hauk continued without acknowledging her gratitude. "You should understand, Mallet. Kayli is a virgin and destined to remain that way."

"Hauk!" She jerked so hard and fast, the chair went into spasms beneath her, unsure if it should firm or soften to accommodate her posture.

Michael sat back again, this time both shocked and fascinated. "Seriously? You've never . . . not even once?"

Kayli shot out of the traumatized chair. "Shut up, Hauk!"

"Now Kayli, compose yourself. When the man is presented with the horde of anxious virgins tomorrow, he'll know something is up."

Michael swiveled his chair around, looking for Hauk. "What the hell are you talking about? What virgins? A horde of them, you said?"

"Shut. Up. Hauk!"

Instead, Hauk tsked at her tone. "Kayli is a warrior, Mallet, and thus forbidden to take union, the reasoning being that a warrior's life is too fraught with risks and family is far too valued to put to chance. Instead, she is in union with her duty to the colony. A lonely existence, yes, but she convinces herself that she is at peace with her decision."

Red-faced and teeming with fury, Kayli slapped a hand down on the table. "Shut down, Hauk."

"And let your vessel drop from the sky?"

A growl rumbled in her throat. "You mistake me on purpose and it is not appreciated. Shut down your intrusion into this room. Immediately."

"Very well."

In an instant, his voice left, the candles went out, the music died, and the ceiling closed.

Somehow, being sealed into the room with the reduced light and silence only made Kayli's proximity to Michael more intimate.

With her heart pumping hard and fast, she couldn't look at him, yet she felt his gaze, burning hot, piercing with ripened male curiosity.

Arms wrapping tight around herself, she walked to the opposite side of the room, giving Michael her back. "I apologize for Hauk," she said, and the mortification she felt sounded in her terse, strained tone. "The emotions supplied to him have commingled to where he considers himself something of a best friend, brother, and father figure, all in one. It drives him to overstep himself on occasion."

Silence droned on, adding to her tension until she thought she'd snap in two.

And then she heard Michael's chair as he pushed it back.

The urge to flee the situation was so great, her breath strangled in her lungs. She stood her ground only by force of will.

Right behind her, close enough for her to breathe in his compelling scent, Michael said, "Did he lie?"

He was right there, right behind her.

As a warrior, she could fell him in any number of ways—but of course she wouldn't.

As a warrior, she had no inspiration how to deal with a man who stole into her personal space without harmful intent.

"No." She hugged herself tighter. "Hauk is incapable of lying."

"But he's sure got sarcasm nailed, huh?"

Despite her thrumming tension, she managed a credible half laugh. "Oh yes. He excels at sarcasm."

Warm hands settled on her shoulders, almost prompting her to leap away.

"Kayli?" he whispered.

She swallowed twice before saying, "Yes?"

"You're a virgin?"

Oh, how the times had changed, for a man to ask a woman that. In his day, such a question might seem as proper as the uncertainty in his tone.

Now, here, it simply wasn't done. Wasn't discussed. Wasn't mentioned.

"Michael . . ." Best to explain this as a history lesson. She'd remove all personal influences. Yes, that's what she'd do. "You must understand that society goes in cycles. During your time period, promiscuity was accepted, for men and women alike. It was more uncommon for a person to reach adulthood as a virgin than otherwise."

"Depends on your definition of adulthood."

She didn't bother clarifying that, because it hadn't much changed. Some were adults earlier than others, legally or otherwise. "Now, after many diseases and a collapse of moral institutions, we have come full circle. It is rare and highly frowned upon, for most—male or female—to engage in intimate activity outside of a legal union sanctioned by the Council Mavens."

His hands drew her back into him until her shoulders rested against his broad, hard chest.

It felt . . . remarkable.

And far too tempting.

"So." He bent closer until his nose touched her hair. "You've never had sex?"

He did seem caught on that fact. "No." And she never would.

"How old are you?"

He sounded both incredulous and challenged. "I am twenty-five."

She heard him breathing in, as if smelling her, her hair and her skin, and it did funny, disturbing, but pleasant things to her stomach. Things she'd never before felt.

"Let me get this straight. If you remain a warrior, you'll never be allowed to have sex?"

"I'll never be permitted to form a union. Sex outside of a union would be scandalous and reason for discharge from my position as Claviger."

The silence hung heavy around them as he considered what she'd said. "All the warriors are women in the same boat as you?"

It took her a second to decipher his meaning. She had a good grasp of his lingo, but when flustered—as she was now—she had to concentrate more. "Some are widows who out of loyalty to their deceased partner chose a life of defense. Some are, as you said, like me. I'm sure that each of the women has reasons of her own."

His hands weren't idle. They caressed her shoulders, warm and firm but with so much gentleness. "And your reasons are?"

Inside, she trembled, but when she spoke her voice sounded strong enough. "I can't abide injustice, so I want to do what I can to keep our colony safe for all." She didn't add that her mother had made the decision for her at a very early age. She'd schooled her in her duties, encouraged her in her beliefs until now, Kayli wasn't sure what she thought on her own and what she thought out of a sense of fostered responsibility.

She would never admit that to anyone though, certainly not to Michael Manchester.

Silence stretched out as Michael held her. His hands left her shoulders so that he could lace his arms around her, keeping her in a gentle but iron embrace.

"So no sex, but what about anything else? Any smooching? Any foreplay?"

So much heat came off him, she felt enveloped in it, and it left her faint. "I . . . I don't understand."

He gave her a tender squeeze, and his voice lowered. "How many times have you been kissed?"

No, no, no. She did not want to discuss this. "I don't know."

"Can't keep count, huh?"

His teasing did nothing to relax her, not with him still so close, smelling so hot, and feeling so powerful.

"Okay, let's come at this from another angle. How many men, other than me, have kissed you?"

Her brain refused to function. Nothing clever, or even believably deceptive, came to mind. "A few."

"Do you remember names? Places? Or are they all so forgettable?"

He mocked her, but in a nice way, probably meant to help her relax. "What does this matter to you? We have important matters to discuss, and—"

"Real important, I know." His mouth brushed her temple and it felt like the sweetest of kisses. "The thing is, Kayli love, I'm not sure you realize what all the issues are."

Kayli *love*? She tried to turn to face him. He held her firm. "Meaning?"

"My questions first, then maybe we'll talk about it. So quit dodging it, Kayli. How many men have had their mouths on you?"

The way he phrased things! She gave up. "Two."

For a heartbeat he said nothing. Then: "When?"

Her sigh was loud enough to activate the fans in the

room. It was fortunate, because a stirring of the air helped to cool her burning flesh. "When I was fifteen, one of my fellow students kissed me. I didn't like it and I reported him."

Michael's laugh sounded with humor and pleasure. "Did he get in trouble?"

"He was reprimanded, yes. Not for kissing, so much, but for kissing a girl already declared for the service of her colony."

"Huh. So even at that young age, you knew you wanted to be a warrior?"

From the time she could talk, she'd been told she was perfect for service to her colony—and imperfect for anything else, especially a union. "Yes."

He thought about that before asking, "And who else kissed you?"

To get the interrogation over with, Kayli rushed through the rest of the telling. "When I was seventeen I started my training and a man my age tried to . . . discourage me."

"With a kiss?"

"Yes." And more. And truthfully, she *had* been discouraged. She'd been led to think about things she'd never before considered. Possibilities she'd thought forever out of reach.

Then her mother discovered them and . . . heart aching, Kayli shook her head. "He moved away after I refused him. I haven't seen him since."

"Did you care about him?"

The words stuck in her throat. The truth hurt, but the reason for the truth hurt the most. "No."

She hadn't loved him. But she had loved the idea of having a family of her own, a person dedicated to her, to their children.

"He was a nice young man, and I hated seeing him disappointed."

Michael's hand opened over her waist, stroking the tiniest bit, just enough to make her tingle, to make her every nerve ending spark with awareness of him. "When I kissed you, you didn't like it."

Untrue—but should she tell him that? He already understood that much of her reaction was from inexperience.
Leaving it at that would be best for all concerned.

"I'm not used to . . . the *way* that you kissed me was . . .
the dampness and heat and . . ." She swallowed down the
rest of her stammers and just spoke her thoughts aloud.
"Never before had I felt a man's tongue."

Against her temple, she felt his smile. "The kisses you'd
had were just pecks."

"Extended pecks, but yes, nothing more than that." With
Michael, it had been more. More emotion, more effect, more
reaction, and more *need*. "You should not kiss me again."

"Right," he said, and he made it sound like anything but
an agreement. "At least not until we have a few things
cleared up." After a brief hug, he released her and walked
back to the table. With one gulp, he finished off his juice.
"What is this stuff? I like it."

Freed so abruptly from his touch and unnerving conversation, Kayli wallowed in confusion. "It's a mixture of our
fruits." She braced one hand on the wall to steady herself.
"I'm glad it pleases you."

"It was all great. Do you have some kind of special cattle
here, to produce a steak like that?"

Kayli stiffened. "The barbaric ritual of slaughtering animals ended after most nearly became extinct, or toxic to
humans. Many diseases resulted before nature was righted.
Now animals, *all* animals, are treated as kind pets."

He looked from her to his empty plate and back again.
"So the steak I ate was . . . ?"

"We have only ersatz meats, manufactured based on your
preferences."

"*Ersatz*, huh? I'll look that up later. What about fruits,
vegetables, breads, all that?"

"Grown in our fields, but also scientifically reproduced
as needed." She tried to encourage him without sounding
impatient. "You can acquaint yourself with all our advance-
ments by spending some time in the media room."

"Unbelievable." Michael looked again at his empty plate

and shrugged. "Well, however you got the steak, it was perfect. I can't wait to try a burger or fried chicken."

"I'm sure there are many things you will be curious about, and of course you should try them all."

"Yeah?" He looked at her, and that same heavy sensuality was back, hot enough to knock her over. "I think I'll hold you to that."

WHILE Mallet watched Kayli flounder with her feelings, he thought of all he wanted to do to her, how novel it'd be to have a virgin.

And how sweet.

A deep voice harrumphed. "I know I was ordered to disappear, but Mallet's clothing is available."

She welcomed Hauk as a grand distraction. "Thank you, Hauk. You may present them."

"How gracious of you, Kayli." They appeared, folded, on the tabletop.

"Hauk," she warned. "I am in no mood for your dictatorial attitude—"

"Now, children." Mallet laughed as he scooped up the clothing to examine it. He found a dark T-shirt, jeans—minus some of the rivets—odd underclothing, and brand-new low boots. They'd do. "Let's try to get along, why don't we?"

Hauk ignored that to ask, "Shall I put them on you, or would you prefer to bathe first?"

"No one is dressing me but me. And yeah, I'd like to shower first, thanks. With my wreck, it's been a while since I got to stand under hot water and scrub up real good."

No one replied to that, so he looked at Kayli. "I assume I have a room for that sort of thing?"

"Your own suite has been prepared, but—"

"With my preferences, right? Great. I'll go there now, and give you a break from my company."

"But how can you leave now? We have a lot more to discuss, most especially that cryptic comment about issues not yet revealed to me."

"We'll get to all that tomorrow morning." Deliberately dismissing her, he said, "Now Hauk, if you'll just guide me, I'll walk. No poofing me around, okay?"

"Suit yourself, but it's a long jaunt."

"Perfect. It'll give me time to think." With the clothing tucked under his arm, he headed for the door.

Appearing dumbfounded, Kayli rushed after him. "Think about what?"

Looking over his shoulder, Mallet winked at her. "Kisses, virgins, and sacrifices. What else?"

CHAPTER 6

BEYOND agitated, Raemay rushed through her chambers. Her hair, long and dark, fell loose from the feminine clips that had kept it atop her head.

So like her other daughters.

So different from Kayli. *His* daughter.

No, she wouldn't think it. She wouldn't consider it.

They needed the stranger here, she understood that, but he threatened everything.

Everything.

In the common room, she spoke into her digital telecom, summoning both her daughters. "Make haste," she ordered.

Given her state of near panic, Raemay would have liked to telecommute to them, but her computer didn't have the same far-reaching capabilities of Hauk, a fact that nettled like a gnarled weed. She could request, at any time, that Hauk take her to Kayli, but not to anyone else, because ultimately, Kayli had control.

She was Arbiter, the leader of the council.

She was the one all others looked to.

Yet her daughter had the most powerful system of control

in their entire colony. When the rest of the council had named it so, how was she to dispute the necessity of the defense system?

She could not.

Only she saw the ludicrousness of it. They'd had little enough use for defenses—until now.

Her pulse raced until she felt light-headed. "Oh heavens, where are those girls?"

Within minutes, twenty-year-old Idola and eighteen-year-old Mesha rushed through the door.

Dressed in a froth of gossamer fabrics and ribbons, her hair curled and her lips rouged, Idola led the way. "Mother, what is it?"

Right behind her, hair tied up with bows and misted with a light, sweet fragrance, Mesha asked, "Are you all right?"

Raemay waved off their concerns. "Tomorrow you will meet the stranger." Too frantic to remain still, she paced as she spoke. "He is a giant of a man, but you won't be timid, do you understand? Don't let his size and overbearing manners deter you. You are both beautiful. Very beautiful."

With their long dark hair and pale blue eyes, skin like porcelain and lush figures, they should be all a man would want—especially given their connection to the council and the power that came with being in the hierarchy.

But . . . Raemay closed her eyes and put a fist to her heart. She knew, oh how she knew, the appeal of fair hair and golden eyes.

"Mother?"

Collecting herself, Raemay said, "I'm arranging a private audience with each of you before the other females present themselves. It is imperative that one of you win him over."

Slightly rebellious, yet at the same time more than a little tentative, Mesha asked, "Which of us?"

"Either of you!" Regretting the outburst, which caused each of her frail daughters to quail, Raemay rubbed her forehead. "Either of you would suit. But one of you must. *Must*. Do you understand?"

Idola touched her mother's shoulder. "Shh, now Mother.

It will be all right. I will see to it. He'll find no fault with me, I promise you."

Poor, misguided Idola. She discounted Kayli without a thought. But then, Raemay had discounted her as well until she saw the way the stranger looked at her oldest daughter, a look she recognized only too well.

The thought sent a shudder down her spine. Raemay didn't know if it was disgust . . . or yearning.

"It must be more than that." She grabbed Idola's hands, squeezing for emphasis. "He must want you more than any other." He had to want her more than he'd want her fair-haired, golden eyed daughter.

"Mother!" Scandalized, Mesha went pink in the cheeks and lowered her tone to a breathy whisper. "Do you suggest we tempt him?"

"Yes! Yes, you must tempt him. In every manner that you can." Drawing in a calming breath, Raemay forced a smile for her offspring. "And after you win him over, he will take you in union and your life, our lives, will be set—as should be."

Raemay watched as the two sisters looked at each other and smiled. Neither of them gave Kayli a thought, not in terms of tempting, not in terms of a union.

Kayli wasn't competition for them; most times, they barely accounted her as a woman. Unfortunately, Michael Manchester saw Kayli as exactly that—a woman—and not much else.

Raemay had raised foolish children. She herself had been foolish. And selfish.

Now she'd have to do her utmost to manipulate things to her advantage. If the stranger had to stay—and she supposed he must—then she needed an alliance with him.

And *not* through Kayli.

Never that.

She couldn't chance it.

"THE mother plots."

Striding along, examining the massive spaceship as he

went, Mallet gradually got used to the idea that he'd been teleported into the future, and into a very unpredictable situation.

Maybe it was his lack of roots, or maybe it was his gut reaction to Kayli, but all in all, none of it shook him up as much as it probably should have. He had his body back. He had a purpose here. And he had Kayli.

As package deals went, it wasn't bad.

"The mother, huh?" The floor grid felt strange beneath his feet—not iron, but not cushioned, either. Hauk hadn't exaggerated about the length of their journey to get to his room. Kayli had one hell of a vessel. "I take it you mean Raemay?"

"Yes."

That didn't surprise him. One look at the woman and he'd recognized her as a schemer, a manipulator. Some women just screamed trouble, and not the "fun to overcome" type, either, like Kayli. No, Raemay was mean-spirited, not multilayered or defensively independent like her adorable daughter. She wasn't staunch in her determination to assist others. She wanted only to help herself.

"So who's she plotting against? Me?"

"In part, yes. But mostly she conspires against Kayli."

An instinctive surge of anger stopped Mallet dead in his tracks. To his left was a series of rooms, all doors closed. To his right, the windows showed a sun setting over strange, beautiful lands. "You better explain that."

"I would give you some history, if you're open to it."

Fuck history. He had a more pertinent concern. "Is Kayli in any danger?"

"Right now, no. At this moment, she frets, concerned only with you."

"Frets? How so?"

"She doesn't understand you or her reaction to you."

"Ah." Nice. He wondered what conclusions the little virgin would come to. Just thinking of her innocence turned him on. Mega turned him on. He knew he'd have her. Eventually. But he didn't want to rush things too much. "I've put her in a tailspin, huh?"

"Yes. More than you realize, most likely."

"Then by all means, Hauk. Educate me." Anything and everything about Kayli fascinated him, most especially her indescribable scent. Every time he got close to her, his insides clenched with desire. The smell of her hair and skin made him nuts.

And that was novel to him. He'd wanted women before, but not on such a gut-grinding level.

He also enjoyed her inner strength that seemed so at odds with her gentleness and caring. She was a complex woman, and he'd enjoy learning all the facets to her personality.

One of the doors opened and a man walked out. He looked startled to see Mallet, but he didn't linger. After a nod of welcome, he went on his way.

"An AMA?"

"Yes. Currently you are the only human male on the vessel. That one, Denay, has the duty of supervising maintenance of the interior whenever we're moored." Hauk sniffed in disdain. "He'll report to Kayli that all is well, of course, otherwise I would have notified her of any malfunction myself."

"You're a real hands-on kind of supercomputer, huh?"

"I live here so yes, I like to keep account of all functions."

Mallet liked the idea of Kayli having a power like Hauk to look after her. "Do you *only* live here? On the ship I mean."

"I have the ability to go where Kayli goes—unless she blocks me, something she does on occasion when she wants her privacy."

"Privacy for what?" Mallet hoped it wasn't time to spend with another man.

"Thinking. Brooding." With a verbal shrug in his tone, Hauk said, "Like all humans, she sometimes likes to be alone. But it's rare because she needs an open channel with me to be alerted of any difficulties, either with the ship or the people of her colony."

"What about the warring colony? Can you go there?"

"No. Their coordinates have never been configured into my system. Someone needs to go there first, to set the location, and then return the data to me. Thus far, anyone who has gone has not returned."

"Hmmm." Another thought occurred to Mallet. "Are the humanoid robots capable of transmitting data?"

"If programmed to do so, yes."

Little by little, the pieces of a plan came together. Mallet started walking again. "Would you be able to follow a person there? You know, like lock a beacon onto her or something?"

"If Kayli deemed it." Hauk missed Mallet's meaning to boast, "Kayli needs only me for most every task, but she does like the interaction with her many AMAs."

"Great." A twinge of jealousy added an edge to Mallet's tone. After all, Kayli's AMAs all shared a storybook handsomeness. No cauliflower ears, scars, or broken noses for them. That was enough on that. "Now what were you saying about Mommy Dearest?"

As if he guessed at Mallet's mood, Hauk snickered before continuing. "The mother has always adjudged Kayli a warrior. From the time of her birth, Raemay insisted on burdening Kayli with a deep sense of responsibility toward the colony. Kayli matured thinking it was her own inclination, when in fact, the mother fostered it bone deep."

So it wasn't Kayli's destiny or personality as much as her mother's wishes being fulfilled? "Why would she do that?"

"It is not for me to say. Yet." Mallet started to protest but Hauk continued, "I will tell you more after you've seen the defense techniques. I believe you'll take issue with Kayli fighting."

"No shit." Mallet didn't need the visual to know how he'd feel, because he already felt it in spades. "It's nuts for her, for any woman, to stand in the front lines of danger."

"No, it is simply our way." Hauk continued to guide him along the corridors. "And moreover, it is important that you not interfere with who she has become."

Not who she is, but who she has become—through her mother's machinations. "A warrior?"

"Misguided as it may be, it is how she now defines herself, what she knows and respects most about herself." Hauk all but teemed with glee. "It's what makes *you* so appealing to her."

Because he felt foolish for talking to air, Mallet understood Kayli's need for a human form—her AMAs. It would be much easier to have this conversation with Hauk if he had a body. "Do you know for a fact that she finds me appealing?"

"There are no doubts."

Mallet paused to briefly study a narrow passageway. "Where does this lead?"

"To the dock for small vessels meant for short-term travel."

"Like jets or something?"

"Similar, but our various modes of transportation are all solar-powered."

Not surprising. Solar power was gaining popularity even in his time. "What if there's no sun?"

"There is always sun or the planets would cease to exist."

"No, I meant, what if it's a cloudy day and the vehicles don't get enough solar power?"

"The answer to that is complicated. In the media room, you will see that solar power is not the unwieldy method of your generation. It has been streamlined and defined, concentrated to get much power out of little light. But it should also be noted that we have learned to control the weather."

"The hell you say!"

"Our lands are so perfect because they are nurtured with the right formula of sunshine, rain, temperature changes, and night rest."

"All specifically programmed, I guess?" He'd heard a few doozies since coming here, but that took the cake.

"Indeed. The weather is most predictable now."

Sports fans would love that. But with that topic exhausted,

Mallet sighed. "Okay, I'll bite. How do you know that Kayli likes me?"

Ready to brag, Hauk gleefully explained. "I am Kayli's closest confidant in all things. She can hide nothing from me."

"You can't be sure." But Mallet wished for assurances. He'd like to know where he stood with Kayli, if he set her to trembling because of her inexperience or because he frightened her. If she didn't share his overwhelming need, he'd have to find a way to pull back, to move more slowly with her.

And given how much he wanted her, going slowly would be damned difficult.

"I am positive. Along with monitoring the ship, I also monitor every aspect of Kayli's health. Her pulse rate and body temperature spike whenever you get near. She grows breathless and nervous. She has no allergy to you, so that makes a human attraction accountable for the physical discrepancies."

Relieved, and ready to believe, Mallet grinned. "She hides it well."

"Not from me."

He laughed. "You sure annoyed her plenty with the romance routine during dinner." She'd looked like a rabbit facing a wolf, even though Mallet hadn't instigated the ambiance.

"Not at all. Kayli might suffer temporary annoyance toward me, but she loves me too much to stay angry for long."

"Yeah?" Mallet considered Hauk's role in Kayli's life. "What does a supercomputer know of love?"

"I understand love for the emotion it is, and what it engenders in people. But in this instance, it's more about what I know of Kayli. She petitioned for me when she first took over her duties as head of defense."

"At seventeen?" Mallet had a hard time swallowing that. Kayli hadn't been much more than a kid. At that age, she should've been pushing boundaries—not protecting them.

"She was always mentally and emotionally advanced for

her age. Very responsible, very mature. But also, we'd never before been threatened from outside the colony. Most of Kayli's early years in defense centered on easily controlled internal disputes between citizens and the occasional petty crime."

"So you don't have much crime here?"

"Very little. Upon purchase, homes and establishments are wired into my database for safekeeping. Any attempts at breaking and entering are instantaneously routed through my alarm system."

Mallet pictured that scenario. "Your systems go on alert, and Kayli goes running?"

"Yes. I can tell her who is being burgled, and by whom. She never has to go in blind for a conflict."

"And she takes backup?"

"When necessary. She used to thrive on the occasional alarm. She would handle domestic arguments, conflicts over merchandise exchanges, bad tempers flaring and causing a physical fight. Everyone respects her so much that her presence has an immediate calming effect. But that was all before the intruders came."

Hauk paused, and it made him seem very human. "We'd become close before she was appointed Claviger. Since then, we are inseparable. Kayli will never give up being a warrior, because to do so would mean giving up me."

Well, hell. That could complicate things. "Why are the two tied together?"

"Kayli obtained me from her mother by convincing the Council Mavens that the head of defense should have control over the most powerful computer system. Raemay fought the edict, but in the end, she knew she chanced alienating council members, and through them, the citizens of the colony, if she didn't agree."

It wasn't uncommon, Mallet thought, for more than one person to want ultimate control of a group. Given Hauk's power, he could see two strong-minded women fighting over possession of him. "So mother and daughter have had strife since then?"

"Raemay has caused strife since the day Kayli was born. It's as if she feels she must keep an emotional distance between herself and her oldest offspring."

Lights blinked on the floor in front of Mallet, and Hauk said abruptly, "This is the entrance to your quarters."

He paid no mind to Hauk's not-so-subtle attempt to change the subject. "Why would Raemay—"

"We will talk more of that later. One thing at a time, sir."

"Don't call me sir."

"Don't press me for more information."

Grinning, Mallet gave up. "Fair enough." He pushed the door open, looked inside, and found an empty room. He didn't see a bed or a chair. He didn't see anything.

Was he expected to crash on the floor? God knew that he'd done worse in his lifetime, but somehow he'd gotten the impression they were going to pamper him a little.

With a mental shrug, he asked Hauk, "I guess this means our chat is over?"

"Where it concerns Kayli, yes. But I must accompany you inside. You'll need instructions for your new quarters." Lights preceded Mallet, as if to show him the way.

"I'm not a dunce. I can find my own way into an empty room."

"Ah, but the room is not empty, Mallet. It only appears so."

So they'd given him . . . what? Invisible furnishings?

"Whatever you require can be added," Hauk said after Mallet's extended silence.

"Yeah . . . a bed?"

"Far right wall." As Mallet looked at the wall, guiding lights blinked across the floor and up to a small square notch.

The wall opened and a bed folded down, spacious, and luxurious with fluffy pillows and a generous down-like coverlet.

"I opened the bed remotely," Hauk explained, "but whenever you want to rest, touch the circuit—it resembles a small etched square in the wall."

"Huh." Neat trick. "What else?"

"The bed tidies itself when you touch the square again to fold it away."

"That cuts back on housework."

"On the side of the bed is a pen-like container. Do you see it?"

Again, tiny lights in the floor blinked on. Mallet followed the lights to the pen and picked it up. "Yeah. Am I supposed to start a diary?"

"At the base of the pen you'll find a small circle."

"Another circuit?"

"Microchip, yes. You touch it to stabilize the pen. A magnetic field will keep it from tipping over. Set it wherever is comfortable for you."

Mallet chose to hold it.

"Two buttons on the pen will give you distinct projections. Touch the button at the top of the pen for your control panel."

Mallet lightly grazed the button, and a blue light beam ejected from the pen, displaying a panel across his midsection. He had no idea what to do with it. "It's just light, that's all."

"The buttons all work. Try one."

Right above his navel was a button labeled "On/Off." He touched it and a much larger projection of a man and woman filled the air in the opposite direction. Though the couple didn't move, they looked as real as if the two people had poofed into his room.

Very cool. "A hologram?"

"Not quite. This would be the equivalent of your television. What you see there is a local program that welcomes you to our colony, but you have hundreds of entertainment choices. The pen has a protective coating, so you can watch in the shower if you like."

"Don't see a shower." He touched the button and the projection disappeared.

"We're getting there. Let's take it one thing at a time, please."

Fascinated, Mallet put the pen back at the side of his bed. It would take some time to get used to all the gadgets in this new world.

For the next twenty minutes or so, Hauk walked Mallet through the functions in the beige, square room.

With Hauk's help and the light path to guide him, he learned of the touch control window blinds and the self-heating blankets on the bed. He found more clothing in his size hanging in a large hidden closet. Again, with just a touch, the wall closed to conceal the space.

"Okay, so now how about that shower?"

Lights outlined a slim opening. "Step inside, give the command, and you will be showered."

Mallet stuck his head in and saw nothing. "Where does the water come from?"

"It mists from tiny pores in the tiles."

"Mists? I don't want to be misted. I want to soak. I want to scrub. I've had nothing but sponge baths for too damn long."

"You are so barbaric." Hauk tsked. "I can arrange more water flow for you, but if you really enjoy water play, you should do as Kayli does."

"And that is?"

"Go swimming. She does so every night."

Mallet's attention sparked. He pictured her in a bikini, under the setting sun, her skin and hair wet . . . "Tonight?"

"She has completed her water play and is returning to her sleeping quarters." Hauk paused, then said, "And she's still thinking of you."

Mallet grinned. Somehow he had to get a leash on his libido. He had a hell of a lot to learn, and it'd be easier to do it without an obsession for Kayli. He figured the quickest way to gain her favor would be to rescue her colony from the asses causing her trouble.

One thing at a time. "So how does the shower work if there isn't much water?"

"Stand on the white square. Your body will first be misted with an enzyme that breaks down all undesirable pollutants.

After that, water will be misted over you to remove the enzymes. Lastly, a brush of warm air will dry your hair and skin."

Freaking amazing. Misty showers. That was one invention he didn't really care for. Soon as he could arrange it, he'd go swimming with Kayli. "Hauk?"

"Yes?"

"Not to be a bother, but I could use a toothbrush, too."

"It's no bother. Unlike you, I can be everywhere, doing everything, all at once."

Mallet rolled his eyes. "Within your network . . . is that right?"

"Yes." Lights blinked near a small plastic tube protruding from the shower. "This room has been sanitized for your use. You close your mouth over the cylinder, and it will clean your teeth."

"No toothbrush?"

"No."

"So how long does it take—"

"Mere seconds, if you'd only stop talking and do it. I assure you, it's painless."

"I'm not worried about pain. I just don't like it." Mallet stripped off the robe and stepped naked into the shower. "The command is?"

"Shower on."

Seconds later, as Hauk had promised, Mallet felt as clean as if he'd soaked in a hot tub for an hour. He followed instructions for cleaning his teeth and, forgoing the clothing, sprawled out in the cozy bed. It plumped, firmed, and softened in all the right places.

With a sigh, he stacked his arms behind his head and settled in. "Hey, Hauk? I don't suppose you can be my alarm clock?"

"What time would you like to arise?"

"Early enough to spend some time in the media room and then meet with Kayli before I have to pay a visit to her mother."

"I will awaken you."

The room dimmed, the air adjusted, the bed morphed yet again to accommodate his relaxed posture—and Mallet fell off into a deep slumber . . . only to dream of Kayli.

LOST in deep thought, Kayli pulled her tunic on over her head and flipped her hair loose from the collar. She was just reaching for her pants when Michael appeared in her room.

No one other than her mother had ever dared to transport in on her unannounced, and it so surprised her that she screeched and automatically kicked out at him.

The blow, aimed at his sternum, was hard enough to do serious damage.

That is, if it had connected.

Michael caught her foot and held on. He grinned at her. "Whoa. Deadly kick, babe. Good girl."

Praise? He offered her praise for trying to maim him? "Are you insane?" She hopped on one leg to keep her balance. "You can't just—"

"Hauk did it, not me." Using the press of his elbow, Michael tucked against his body as he looked her over from her freshly brushed hair to her state of undress.

Standing there on one leg, Kayli struggled to keep from falling. "Hauk sent you here?"

"Yeah, I told him I was ready to see you and—poof. Here I am."

Spellbound by the warmth of Michael's smile, not to mention his touch, Kayli remained mute for several seconds. Then indignation kicked into overdrive. "Hauk!"

"You rang?"

"I did not *ring*," she snapped. "I bellowed."

With a shrug in his tone, Hauk said, "The result is the same. You have my attention."

"Make a note, Hauk. You are *not* to transport anyone into my private quarters ever again."

"Now hold up a minute." Michael stroked behind her knee. "What if it's an emergency? What if I'm dying and need your help? What if it's your mother, the all-mighty Arbiter?" Driving the point home, he added, "Should you really make a blanket statement like that when you know Hauk will enforce it?"

Hauk said, "He has a valid point. Shall I use my own discretion, then?"

With the way they ganged up on her, Kayli couldn't think of an appropriate rejoinder.

"Hey Hauk, I've got a question," Michael said. "Do futuristic chicks wear panties?"

"Some do, and some do not."

"No kidding?" His look heated, Michael bent a little to see for himself, causing Kayli to screech in very real alarm.

He was far too outrageous, and she had to get a handle on the situation.

While slapping at him she shoved her tunic down low between her thighs. "Michael," she said as reasonably as she could. "Let go of my foot. Right now!"

He straightened again with a teasing grin. "No more kicking?"

"Not right now, no." She'd make no promises if he continued to behave so scandalously.

Stepping forward, he brought his hand up her leg until he cupped behind her knee. Taking one more step and guiding her leg alongside his hip, he stepped up flush to her body, sort of . . . between her legs.

She was practically wrapped around him, and oddly enough, it felt scintillating.

"Good morning," he whispered low. And then he pressed his mouth to hers in a firm but gentle kiss of greeting.

She would have fallen if he wasn't so quick to wrap his free arm around her waist.

She didn't pull away. She couldn't. And then both his arms were around her, holding her tight but allowing her to put both feet on the floor, where they belonged.

When he lifted his head and smiled at her, Kayli stared dazedly for several moments before she mustered her decorum.

"I'm sorry, Michael, but you must understand a few rules, the first being that you are not to kiss me."

"Hmmm." He touched his mouth to her chin, the corner of her lips, the tip of her nose. "I hate to start off by breaking rules, but . . . I'm going to kiss you, Kayli. Lots. All over." He stroked her cheek. "You may as well get used to it."

His open disobedience made her mouth fall open.

Before she could get too outraged, he asked, "Have you eaten?"

"Yes!"

"Good. Me, too."

Oh, she hadn't expected that.

He took her hand and led her toward her bed. As her heart punched into overtime, he sat down and patted the spot beside him, urging her to sit down, too. "That means we can get right into solving some problems."

Solving problems? So he didn't intend to . . . He hadn't come to . . . A little deflated, though she wouldn't admit it to anyone, Kayli accepted that she'd jumped to a wrong conclusion.

Michael studied her face, then asked, "What is it?" with convincing innocence.

No, obviously his purpose was not to seduce her. She felt foolish, but covered it with a question of her own. "Do you have a plan for us to discuss?"

"I do." He eyed her. "Will you sit down?"

She didn't want to. Not *there*.

On a bed.

But . . . "As you wish." Kayli seated herself beside him. Their hips touched. The mattress adapted, conforming to their individual weights and levels of comfort.

What he said first surprised her: "Your room is smaller than mine."

Her room was cozy—something not easily accomplished on a vessel of such size. She enjoyed the soft yellow walls and cream-colored floors. Rather than go into her simple preferences, she said, "You're an esteemed guest soon to be part of the hierarchy."

"So? You're the Claviger, right?"

Hauk said, "She can have any room she wants, Mallet. She enjoys this one for the simplicity."

He looked around again, then nodded. "Thank you, Hauk."

For some reason, Kayli felt insulted that he'd so readily accept Hauk's explanation. Her eyes narrowed. "Hauk says it and you believe it?"

"You said he can't lie."

Oh. She *had* divulged that quirk of his program, hadn't she. Blast.

His eyebrow lifted in question. "So you're not happy with your room?"

She felt more foolish than ever. "Of course I am, but . . ."

"Even if I could," Hauk said, "I would not lie about something such as this."

Kayli let out an exasperated sigh. "Go away, Hauk."

"Stop picking on Hauk." Michael touched her chin and brought her face around to his. "He's been very helpful to me."

With Michael so close, his touch so warm and his gaze warmer still, her breath hitched. "How so?"

"I wanted to spar this morning, and Hauk suggested some of your AMAs."

Alarm shot through her. "You didn't break any of them, did you?"

"I know you care for them, Kayli. I wouldn't hurt any of them. That is, even if I could have, which isn't certain. They're strong and fast. And they don't get frustrated the way people do."

Pride eased a modicum of the tension wrought by his close proximity and the intimate way he looked into her eyes. "They're perfect for sparring because they counter whatever you do. I use them all the time."

That statement sent a new light into his eyes—one of

disgruntlement. "Let's not talk about you *using* them, okay? I get weird connotations and I don't like it."

Grasping his meaning, her face went hot. "I didn't mean—"

He dismissed her explanations with a shake of his head. "They match what I do, but Hauk tells me they won't fight."

"They're not programmed for violence of any kind. Not even in sport."

His grin came, spreading out slowly. "I think we should use them as defense."

"But . . ." Kayli had always considered her AMAs above such human conflicts. "I don't want them damaged."

"They're like machines, right? If something breaks, they can be repaired?"

"To a point."

"So we amp up their strength a bit. It'd be perfect for what I have planned."

"And that is?"

Hauk spoke just then. "Raemay is waiting for you, Mallet." And with doom in his tone, he added dramatically, "It is time."

Michael scowled. "Time for what?"

Kayli groaned. "Time for you to view the virgins." Distraught by the idea—though she shouldn't have been—she started to stand. She wanted to be far away when Michael was presented with his many choices.

He caught her hand before she could put any distance between them. "Don't run off, woman. You're coming with me."

She pulled back. "Oh, but I can't. It's not proper."

"Screw proper." His hand was firm on hers. "I have a few choice things to tell your mother, and it'll be best if you're there."

More alarm. "Michael, you must understand. You can not insult her."

He stood and pulled her into his embrace. "I'm going to explain to her why we don't need to sacrifice anyone."

Well . . . she did want to hear his plans. The curiosity of it had gnawed on her peace of mind all night.

Kayli caught her bottom lip in her teeth, considered for only a moment the indecency of accompanying him to a choosing, and then nodded. "I suppose I can tell Mother it was your wish for me to be there."

"Won't be necessary." Michael slung an arm around her shoulders. "Old Raemay will figure it out real quick. Trust me." And then he said, "Hauk, I'm ready. Do your thing."

Kayli didn't have much choice in the matter when in the next instant Hauk transported them out of the vessel and into the reception hall of the council building.

Her mother waited there.

So did Idola and Mesha.

CHAPTER 7

R AEMAY watched as Michael took in the scene before
him. He stood obscenely tall and broad-shouldered,
large enough to set the council members gaping. One by
one, they began to murmur to each other, no doubt scandalized as much by Kayli's presence at a choosing as by Michael's bold and arrogant stance.

He stood with his long legs braced apart, his eyes narrowed, and one thickly muscled arm draped possessively
around her daughter.

Raemay struggled to unglue her tongue from the roof of
her mouth. She had to take control. "Kayli, what is the
meaning of this?"

The second she spoke, Michael squeezed Kayli closer
before she could offer up an explanation. His piercing gaze
bored into Raemay, giving her pause. "You want me to
choose a woman, right? That why you summoned us here?"

"We want you to form a union, yes. It will cement your
position in our colony and ease concerns about your priorities."

"Because if I'm tied to a female member of the colony,

everyone will figure I have a vested interest in the colony's well-being."

"Yes." Sensing she couldn't dictate to this . . . this Neanderthal as she could with ordinary colony males, Raemay said no more about Kayli. Instead, she gestured toward her two younger offspring. "These are my daughters, Michael. Idola and Mesha Raine."

He nodded at them without much interest. "I'm pleased to meet Kayli's sisters."

For her part, Kayli looked ill.

Idola, unused to the lack of attention, moved toward him, one delicate hand extended. Her long dark hair curled all the way to the small of her back and her big blue eyes, though clouded with a touch of fear, held direct to his.

"It is very nice to meet you, sir. Mother has told me that you'll save us."

He took her small hand into his mammoth mitt, gave it a clumsy, ungallant shake, and released her. "I'll be helping Kayli with that, yeah."

Nonplussed, Idola flipped back her hair to show her breasts to advantage.

And Michael looked.

It might have been a reluctant, even grudging glance, but he was male and therefore not immune to a woman's ripe charms.

Putting her hands on her hips, Idola showed off her small waist at the same time. The draped fabric of her short dress was sheer enough to tease while still protecting her modesty.

"I promise that I would please you well in a union."

His brows shot up, and then he . . . laughed.

Not a subtle snicker, or a quick chortle. No, he laughed out loud, robust and hearty, as if he'd just heard a fabulous joke.

Raemay couldn't believe it. The boneheaded Philistine had no sense of propriety.

Wiping his eyes, he said, "Sorry, sugar," without any sincere remorse. "Luscious as you might be, it just ain't gonna happen."

Though she fought it, tunnel vision closed in on Raemay. She saw everything slipping away. Everything important. Everything she'd worked so hard to conceal, to protect.

"Mesha!" Because she'd sounded far too shrill, Raemay took a breath to moderate her tone. She even worked up a smile. "Come forward, my dear, and meet our guest, Michael Manchester."

With a sigh, Michael shook his head at her. "You can bring her on, Raemay, but I'm telling you right now, it won't matter."

Beside him, Kayli closed her eyes. At least she recognized his behavior as reprehensible.

Mesha, already swaying toward Michael, faltered for only a second. A blush climbed her neck to her cheeks and on up to her hairline. It didn't help that she had her hair up to show her slender neck and pale shoulders in the low-cut gown. Unlike Idola's, the dress wasn't short, but it parted in the middle so that with each step her shapely legs showed.

With a nudge, Raemay got her moving forward again.

"Save it, honey," Michael told her. "It's a great show, but you're wasting it on me."

Kayli gripped his upper arm, yanked him down toward her, and groused something into his ear. But he only smiled and shrugged, and when she tried to separate from him, he hauled her right back.

Putting a hand to her stomach, Raemay fought to quell the queasiness churning there.

Michael's direct blue gaze zeroed in on her. She saw it there, in the depths of his soul, what he intended.

"All right, Raemay." His smile didn't reach his eyes. "Are there more girls lined up somewhere?"

Too sick to speak, Raemay just nodded.

One brave, and possibly nosy, council member stepped forward. "The rest of the women are through the doors in the antechamber, sir. Just there." He pointed at the ornate double doors.

Michael started in that direction. "Let me have a look then, so we can get this over with." He dragged Kayli along beside him, his steps so long that she had to rush to keep up with him.

He pushed the heavy doors open with laudable ease, and was enveloped in the collective gasp issued from the many eligible ladies in their colony.

Raemay knew it was his phenomenal size that caused the women to react so. Of course, he was handsome, as well. She'd even find him attractive if he wasn't so mammoth in height and muscle.

His brows lifted at the vast gathering. "Damn, got a lot of them, don't you?" He looked over his shoulder at Raemay. "And they're all virgins? Seriously?"

He made a jest of them. He ridiculed them and all they held dear. Her throat burned with anger, but she said evenly enough, "Yes, they are pure, as is proper for one out of union."

Glancing down at Kayli, he murmured, "No offense, babe, but damn. A hundred or more virgins? That's like a wet dream, except that I'm awake."

Raemay's mouth fell open at such a crude disclosure.

Her daughter, lacking her reserve, offered up immediate retaliation. Kayli scowled, and landed a solid punch to his shoulder.

Raemay held her breath, fearful of his reaction to a physical assault. What should she do? Should she try to intercede on Kayli's behalf?

She was still pondering protective measures when, to her surprise, he caught Kayli's fist, kissed it, and smiled.

He wasn't in the least injured, or even a little offended or angry.

Still holding Kayli's hand, he said, "And hell, I'd go along with it, except it doesn't suit my purpose in the long run."

Still riled, Kayli asked, "What purpose?"

Pretending not to hear her question, Michael donned a charismatic smile and waved to the women. "Sorry, ladies. You're all knockouts, no doubt about it. I'm sure whoever nabs you in a union is going to be thrilled. Thing is, I'm off the market."

Hearing her worst fears confirmed, Raemay groaned. He was a buffoon. An imbecile with brawn. But she was the Arbiter, a woman of power. She would not tolerate this farce any further.

"Sir," she got out through gritted teeth, "I'd have a word with you."

"Sure thing, Arbiter." He gave her an insolent bow. "You can even have more than one, but it won't change anything."

Rage and insult burned through Raemay, helping to mask her fear. She knew it was inevitable, but still, the second he got close enough, she tried her best to reason with him. "I must point out that despite the differences in our worlds, your behavior is inexcusable."

"I find offering up virgins to be inexcusable, so I guess we're at an impasse, huh?"

She wouldn't relent. "You have made a mockery of a most serious ceremony for my colony. You have rejected my daughters in a callous manner—"

"Now there's where you're wrong."

Raemay took a step back. "What are you saying?" Was there hope after all?

Both Idola and Mesha, expressions buoyant, took an anxious step forward.

The brute squeezed Kayli. "I didn't mean to mock anyone. I probably lack the finer social skills you're used to, but then, you had to have had some sort of background check on me before bringing me here, right?"

What could she say? She'd known he was an uncouth caveman, but Kayli had insisted, and as Claviger her opinion counted a lot with the council.

"I knew you lacked sophistication, yes." Raemay put up her chin. "But that offers no excuse for deliberate cruelty."

"I meant to be decisive, not cruel, so acquit me of that, okay?" He squeezed Kayli again. "I made my choice, but I figured you had your own ideas about that, and I didn't want you saying I hadn't taken the time to at least look at all the . . . options."

Crushed by what she knew was to come, Raemay folded

onto a settee. She sent Idola and Mesha an apologetic glance. "I see."

Finally finding her voice, Kayli shoved away from him. "Well, I don't see, not at all. What are you doing? What is this purpose of yours?"

"I've chosen."

Kayli's eyes widened, then a mask came over her features, hiding any emotion at all. "Who is it?"

As if he hadn't just destroyed years of careful planning, Michael grinned, looked around at them all, and announced loudly enough to deafen ordinary men, "Kayli Raine, I choose you."

All the oxygen escaped her body in one giant shock wave. No! Surely Michael hadn't . . . of course he hadn't . . . *or had he*?

Colorful dots in rainbow hues swam before Kayli's eyes, gradually closing in to pinpoint black as her mind and body went limp with the thought of losing it all, everything, even her reason for existing.

From far away, she heard Hauk's voice saying, "Er, Mallet, I do believe she's about to faint."

"What the—!" In the next instant, her world dipped and swayed as Kayli felt herself scooped up by solid arms, cradled to Michael's big hard chest. "Hey, easy now, sweetheart."

Sweetheart? No, she was not his sweetheart. She wasn't any man's sweetheart.

She couldn't be.

Her pulse raced so fast it made her tremble; she continued to feel woozy with disbelief. Her palms got sweaty and her skin itched with incredulity.

"Probably overcome with joy," Michael murmured, and even to Kayli's dazed senses, he sounded amused and mocking.

"Perhaps," Hauk agreed uncertainly. "But I somehow doubt it."

Joy? Kayli thought with near hysteria. How could she feel joy when he wanted to make a union with her?

Oh God, oh God. What was she to do?

"I do like how in tune you are to her," Michael praised Hauk. He didn't walk anywhere with her, didn't seem to strain with her held in his arms. He just stood there, at his ease.

Conversing with Hauk.

With a large part of her colony looking on.

"All polymorphous computers can decipher a wide variety of signals," Hauk explained, "be they networked, verbal, coded, or physical."

"And are there a lot of polymorphous computers around here?"

"No." Hauk's voice thrummed with pride. "I am the only one in this colony or, for that matter, any of the surrounding colonies."

Kayli could not believe how cavalier they both behaved, while her entire universe crumbled out from under her.

"Here," her mother demanded in shrill, almost concerned tones. "Put her down over here."

"I don't mind holding her," Michael said.

"*You're* the reason she's in a dead faint!"

"No," Kayli protested, her voice sounding thin and high. "I didn't faint." She wouldn't do something so weak. She'd *never* fainted before, and she wasn't about to start now.

Michael grumbled, but he carried her to the settee and lowered her gently to the padded cushions. The seat immediately shifted around her.

Needing a moment to compose her thoughts, to grasp her disappointment and hide her dismay, Kayli rested her head back and kept her eyes closed. She felt limp, but her thoughts churned in a fevered rush.

With malicious accusation her mother said, "Look at what you've done to her," and took Kayli's hand to pat at it.

"I shocked her a little, that's all." Michael's hand, much larger and warmer than her mother's, cupped her face. "Come on now, Kayli. Open your eyes and talk to me. No more playing possum."

He knew! Somehow Michael realized that she'd already

regained her wits. But she just wasn't ready to face him yet.

"She doesn't want you!" Raemay shrieked. "Surely, even a man as dense as you are can determine that much."

Oh no, Kayli thought, from bad to worse. Michael was not a man to accept such insults, but as offensive as her mother could be, she was still the Arbiter.

Kayli lifted her lashes and found Michael looming over her, his face a study of deep concern.

Ha!

A concerned man would not have done such a thing to her. Brows coming down, she said, "I'm fine."

His palm flattened to her abdomen, keeping her still when she would have sat up, and sending a jolt through her already traumatized system.

"Take it easy, baby. Warriors aren't supposed to lose consciousness over a little thing like a union. I don't want you rushing yourself now."

Her eyes closed again. *A little thing?* How could he say that? A union with him would strip her of everything important to her, all she held dear. Didn't he understand that she'd long ago resigned herself to her life, accepted it, and embraced it?

If he stole that from her, she'd have nothing. She wouldn't be herself anymore. Worse, she didn't know who she'd be.

As if her mother divined her thoughts, she clapped her hands to call attention from the council and colony members.

"Everyone, please. Quiet now." When everyone went silent, Raemay looked at them all. "If our guest claims Kayli, then we have some very serious ramifications to consider."

Like an impending storm, Michael crackled with energy. "More serious than your daughter's health?"

"She said she's fine."

"I *am* fine," Kayli assured them both, and again she started to sit up.

Again, Michael held her still.

Her mother rallied. "If you take Kayli in union, she will

no longer be eligible for the position of Claviger. She will no longer claim control of Hauk. He will belong to me again, as is right and proper."

Putting her hands over her face, Kayli struggled to accept the loss—and then Michael said, "Not so fast, Raemay. I haven't finished yet."

Kayli dropped her hands to stare up at him. "There's *more*?"

Dear God, what next? Would he claim her vessel, too? Not that it mattered. It went with the position of Claviger.

Unconcerned with destroying her life, Michael winked at her, and his hand on her abdomen caressed. "It's your fault I didn't get it all said right up front."

Her temper simmered. "My fault?"

"Yeah. If you hadn't keeled over, I wouldn't have gotten distracted."

Raemay rushed into speech. "What else is there to say? You claimed her, she can't possibly refuse you, knowing what it'd mean to our colony, and so—"

"I want Kayli," Michael repeated, as if those words didn't nearly put her into another faint, "but I have stipulations."

Stipulations?

Kayli felt new hope.

Shoving Michael's hand away, she sat up to pay attention. "Go on."

"Stipulations?" Her mother gasped in outrage. "You're not allowed stipulations!"

Undaunted by Raemay's statement, Michael touched Kayli's chin. "You're okay now, honey?"

"Yes, of course I am." She'd settled small riots, handled virulent disputes, and faced off with the warring colony.

Never had she "keeled over," as Michael put it.

Embarrassed over such a weak display, Kayli straightened her shoulders and lifted her chin. "I'm quite all right, I promise you. I didn't get enough sleep last night, that's all."

His expression softened. His touch softened. In front of God and everyone, he bent and kissed her lips. "Good."

In the next instant, he reverted back to a demanding warrior. "I'm taking Kayli—and Hauk."

"But—" Raemay said.

"I'm taking over as the head of defense," Michael said. "That means Hauk is mine."

Kayli's heart sank. "You're taking my position?"

He didn't look at her, but instead addressed Raemay and the Council Mavens. "I'll do this, but only with Kayli at my side. Because of her experience, expertise, and term of service so far, she'll retain the official position of Claviger."

The words felt like a punch to Kayli's solar plexus. Pride kept her from staggering, but inside, she shriveled. What use would her position as Claviger be without any real authority behind it?

She'd be utterly useless.

A tense hush fell over them all, and why not? Never had anyone dared to make such outrageous demands. For as long as Kayli could remember, the rules had been followed to the letter.

Damn him, she'd *earned* the right to be Claviger, to control Hauk, to head up the defense.

Except . . . Her shoulders slumped as she forced herself to face the awful truth. She had sought out his help, because she couldn't handle the current situation on her own. And luckily for them all, he was willing.

In fact, his quick adjustment amazed her.

He took charge with ease, accepting the challenge, mixing things up without any hesitation or apprehension. He stood there before them all, defiant, confident in his decisions—rather amazing.

Kayli's lips felt stiff and cold, but she managed to speak. "A position for me, even in name only, can not be assigned just because you deem it so. Such a thing is not done here." Such a thing would leave her feeling like an utter fool.

Michael folded his arms over his chest. "It's done if they want my help."

Raemay laughed. "Given your behavior, I'm no longer so certain of the worth of your contribution."

The members of the council inhaled—and waited.

Though he spoke to everyone, Michael stepped away from Kayli and approached Raemay. "My contribution will be to end the sacrifices."

The crowd stirred, encouraged by his confidence.

Raemay drew back. "That's impossible! We'll be destroyed if we try such a thing."

He shook his head, refuting that. "My contribution will be to bring back those women already taken—if they want to return."

Raemay backed up two steps, then caught herself and stood her ground, shoulders back, expression stony. "You dare to doubt their dedication to this colony?"

Michael let that go. "My contribution will be to train the defense team to defend the colony against further attacks and kidnappings. I spent a few hours in the media room and I have a grasp on what needs to be done. When I've finished training the warriors, no one will have to be afraid, because we'll be strong and capable."

"We?" Raemay taunted with a sneer. "You make outrageous demands, and you think that makes you one of us?"

His conviction didn't waver. If anything, Raemay's derision only made him more determined. He gave her a chilling look, and stated, "I'm going to call on the men of the colony, too."

Raemay floundered at that outlandish claim. "The men? But . . . why?"

Michael rolled his eyes. "Why? Because they're a part of the colony, too."

"They're not warriors!"

"Yeah, well maybe that'll change."

Lips parted and eyes wide, Kayli stared at Michael in stupefaction. He not only flaunted his disregard for their longestablished rules, and harassed her mother, but he planned to enroll the men in defense?

The wives would never stand for it.

The council would send him back to his own time.

She had to do something—but what?

"Hauk," she said, near panic.

"We examined every angle," Hauk assured her, "and it's a solid plan with a high probability of success."

Oh, perfect. He'd won over *her* computer.

"I know what I'm doing." Michael held his own against both her and her mother's skepticism. He turned to look at Kayli. "But I need you by my side. You've been one hell of a defense leader. From what I saw, the warriors appear well trained—by you. You know everyone, their strengths and weaknesses. To succeed, it'll take both of us, babe. I can't do it alone."

Was that supposed to be a balm to her lacerated ego after he declared his intent to strip her of everything she held dear?

"What about children?" Raemay challenged. "Do you plan to contribute to the growth of our colony through offspring?"

Everyone saw the surprise on Michael's face before he pulled in his chin, crossed his arms. "I've got nothing against kids."

He said that calmly enough, but one and all saw that the very idea of children left him thunderstruck.

Raemay sensed the weakness, too, and verbally pounced on him. "And when Kayli is carrying your baby, what then? Would you have her endanger the child just to be at your side?"

Going red with some indiscernible emotion that was at least in part anger, Michael pointed a finger that almost touched Raemay's nose. "Arbiter or not," he said, "that is none of your business. It's up to Kayli and me, and we'll make those decisions when we need to."

Which meant . . . what? Kayli sucked in a shuddering breath and waited. She could do nothing else, not after the mention of children—Michael's children—had almost flattened her.

He turned to face the rest of the assembly. "But while

we're on the subject, you all should know—there's no way in hell I'd want to bring a kid into a situation as unstable as this."

A shocked, insulted gasp issued from the crowd.

Kayli covered her mouth with stunned disbelief. They needed children to survive. Without them, the colony would die out.

But Michael wasn't finished.

"I'll tell you what else, I'd want my son or daughter to know that I fought against bullies, that I didn't cower or give in to threats. I'm willing to do whatever's necessary to ensure that *all* children, mine or yours, will never have to worry about growing up only to become a damned sacrifice!"

Because she'd always felt the same, his assurances bolstered Kayli, taking some of the sting from her sense of loss and betrayal.

Suddenly Michael turned and stormed back to her. If the inferno of heat in his blue eyes wasn't enough to cause alarm, his stomping stride and clenched fists were.

Not that she feared him. But she definitely respected his strength, and at the moment, she wasn't at her best.

He snatched up her hand before she could even think of retreating.

Facing the crowd, he raised their clasped hands so high that Kayli went on tiptoe to keep from stretching too far.

"Together," he shouted to the crowd, "to the best of our combined ability, we'll protect the colony."

Michael's promise, given with so much assurance, won the plaudits of everyone in attendance. The cheers sounded, subtle at first, but quickly growing loud enough to rattle the thick structure in which they stood.

Never had Kayli heard such a roar of approval.

The council lauded him. The available women idolized him. Someone had opened a window and out in the streets, the colony hailed him.

It made her head swim to think how easily he'd won them over.

Though still uncertain how to regain what was rightfully hers, or if, given what was best for the colony, she should even try, she looked out at her people and considered their reaction.

Their contagious elation seeped into her heart. Despite the demolishment of her identity, she almost felt like smiling over the miracle she'd just witnessed, the hope that Michael had given them all.

But then she saw her mother, her two sisters.

They were furious.

They were hurt.

And, she could tell, they blamed her.

CHAPTER 8

BENDING down to be heard over the roar of her people, Mallet touched his mouth to Kayli's ear. She smelled soft and warm, and like a woman.

His woman.

He'd just claimed her, right?

The thought didn't alarm him as it should have. Sure, he'd started this farce thinking that if he had to accept a woman to keep the higher-ups happy, he wanted it to be Kayli. She was familiar, and he had a bad case of lust for her.

But now that it was out in the open . . . a deep contentment had settled into his bones, and he couldn't deny that he was happy to change her life. Hopefully, for the better.

"I'm sorry I shocked you, babe." He leaned back to see her face. "Are you okay now?"

"I won't faint again," Kayli promised him. Then her beautiful golden eyes narrowed. "I appreciate your assurances to the colony, but I hope you don't expect me to accept the theft of my position, and my computer, without a protest."

He grinned, so pleased with her that he almost forgot the enmity of her family. They were all staring daggers at her, more Raemay and Idola than Mesha, though the youngest sister looked none too happy either.

He felt it, so surely Kayli did, too.

He'd have to talk to Hauk to find out why so much animosity existed. Looking at Kayli, at her beauty and pride and confidence, he'd think their dislike was based in pure jealousy. Except that her sisters weren't exactly dogs themselves. And as Kayli had said, she was so different not only from her family, but from much of the colony, that he didn't think envy of any kind factored in.

She might suit his idea of drop-dead sexy, but compared to the other females, she stood out as the odd duck.

When he'd looked at all those virgins, despite his teasing words for Kayli, he hadn't felt lust. They'd gaped at him, some with curiosity, some with anxiety, and some with desire. But all he'd felt was . . . itchy. Uncomfortable. Like a man facing the noose.

At that exact moment, he'd lost the last of his doubts on his plan to claim Kayli.

Before the "transported into the future" thing, he hadn't really planned to settle down anytime soon. He'd been much more interested in furthering his fighting career by winning a title belt.

But life had kicked him in the butt big-time, thrown him through some twists and turns, ripped his career away without giving him time to even think about it. And now here he was, in the freakin' future, in Kayli's colony.

Since it looked like he'd be staying, no way did he want to be saddled with some simpering, too soft, deferential marshmallow.

He looked at Kayli, taller than the others, more toned, sleeker.

Just as he liked a woman to be.

She had the stance and manner of a person in charge, but when he touched her, she trembled. He liked that. A lot.

In many ways, it seemed as if she'd been designed specifically for him. He looked at her mouth and wanted it bad, under his mouth, on him, everywhere.

He looked at her body, and couldn't wait to see her exposed, to touch her, to explore every inch of her in detail.

But most of all, he spoke with her and heard her dedication and loyalty and determination, and it won him over in a way no one and nothing ever could. He respected her. He liked her.

He kept a raging jones for her.

Plenty of good reasons to make a union and keep her colony happy.

If in the bargain he could remove her from the dangers of being a warrior . . . all the better.

Hauk made an abrupt sound. "Everyone is waiting while you two make eyes at each other."

Kayli jerked to attention.

Mallet took his time, letting her know—letting them all know—that she was the one and nothing would change that.

"I have a plan to keep everyone safe," he said to the crowd at large. "If you'll all excuse us now, Kayli and I will talk things over and finalize details."

Raemay protested. "What of the union?"

He raised a brow. "Is that something we do right now? Or are there arrangements for that?"

Kayli went red-faced.

Hauk said, "The Council Mavens must approve the union. Then the colony will witness your kiss as a pledge."

"I'm with you so far." Hell yeah, he had no problem kissing Kayli, even if he had to do it with an audience of slathering virgins and uptight Council Mavens watching on.

"And then—"

Kayli said, "Hauk. I'll explain it from there, if you don't mind."

"I just bet you will," Hauk teased.

Raemay, flanked by her fussy daughters, made a snarling sound of disapproval. "Hauk! You will *not* join our guest in making a mockery of our rituals."

"Wouldn't dream of it."

After rolling her eyes, Kayli said, "He's picking up your bad habits."

"Yeah, I like him." Mallet waited for the explanations she claimed she would give.

Kayli rubbed her forehead, hesitated; then, with a glare aimed at one and all, she grabbed his hand and tugged him as far from the center of the room as she could.

Once they reached a corner, she freed her temper. "I can't believe you did this to me."

Mallet had expected the worst. Hauk had told him how important her duties were to her. She'd built her life around the position of Claviger, and without that responsibility, she'd feel at loose ends.

So he'd left her the position. And still she was pissed? He propped a shoulder against the wall and gave her a questioning look. "This?"

"Putting me in this awkward position."

Oh, he could think of a lot of positions to put her in, only a few of them awkward, but he probably shouldn't mention them now.

Smiling at her, Mallet put his arms around her waist and rocked her in a teasing way, hoping to lighten her mood. "Look at it from my perspective, sugar. I'm expected to do this whole union thing, but you're the only woman I want."

"How can you say that? You don't even know the rest of the women."

"Didn't appear to me that I was going to be offered a chance to get to know them." He touched his nose to hers, and wanted to kiss her silly. But this was important, so he stayed on track. "Your momma was breathing down my neck, all but shoving your sisters on me, and babe, they are not you."

Kayli tried to look angry, but instead, a heart-wrenching vulnerability filled her golden gaze. "Meaning?"

"They wouldn't do." He did kiss her. Damn it, he couldn't help himself. But he kept it brief. "Not even close."

"I don't understand you."

Mallet didn't mind that. He didn't completely understand her, either. The women he'd known were . . . fluff. Nice, warm, fragrant, sexy fluff, but they didn't have Kayli's mettle, her confidence.

And damn, but it turned him on.

He kissed the end of her pert nose. "It's simple. I think you're hot."

"I know," she said, somewhat deflated. "You've told me that before. But I'm unsuitable to a union."

"Only because you thought that, as Claviger, you were off-limits. But I worked around that. You heard me tell everyone that you're staying on."

Her laugh sounded brittle. "As a . . . a useless appendage? An unnecessary advisor?" She shoved against him, putting space between their bodies. "I want my life, Michael, the life I've built for myself, not crumbs of it just to keep me quiet."

Well, hell, was that what she thought? That he didn't really need her?

But really, what did he know of warrior women and wars without weapons? He was feeling his way here, acting out of honor and an instinctive hate of injustice. Now that he'd watched the media files, boned up on the colony and how it functioned, he'd sort of gotten into the mood of the thing. He damn well intended to see it through.

He tried to reason with her. "It's not like that, Kayli."

"Then what is it like?" She stood up to him, against him. "Will you be my advisor, an assistant of sorts, and leave the major decisions to me?"

Not likely. One reason he'd chosen fighting as a career instead of a regular nine-to-five job was that he didn't like taking orders from anyone. Just because he was in a new world didn't mean he planned to start now.

Somehow he had to sway Kayli to his way of thinking.

"Hear me out, okay?" She looked resistant, but she stayed quiet. "After Hauk explained how things work, that you could lose him and your position in defense if I got my way, I figured this was a good compromise."

"It's not allowed. Even now, my mother is cautioning the

council about changing rules arbitrarily and what the repercussions might be to such a drastic shift in tradition."

Mallet peered over his shoulder and saw that Kayli was right. Raemay railed at the council members, browbeating them to her way of thinking.

He turned back to Kayli. "Just because it hasn't been done already doesn't mean it won't fly now. You came all the way back to the past for me, so the council must want me enough to give me a little leeway on rules and rituals, right?"

She fisted her hands in his shirt. "You can't dismiss a lifetime of customs."

He covered her hands with his, gentling her, soothing her, hoping to convince her. "When they're dumb customs, I damn well can."

She stiff-armed him. "You're calling us *dumb*?"

"Not you." Damn it, this was frustrating. "Just the opposite, in fact. I think you're smart enough to make your own decisions, including decisions on your career. I trust you, Kayli."

That stilled her. "You do?"

He nodded—and knew it was true. "I understand why your colony wouldn't want to put marriages . . . that is, a union, at risk, but that should be a decision for the two people involved. If you think you can fulfill your part of the union and help run the defense—"

"*Help* run it?" She snorted with contempt at that option.

Mallet sighed. He might as well clue her in now on how things would be. "All right, you want the straight of it? I'm here, and I'm not leaving anytime soon. If you think I'm a hands-off kind of guy, think again. I will be in charge, babe, but I'm happy to share the responsibility with you."

She crossed her arms. "And by share, you mean that you'll always get your way?"

"In some things." She looked so cute when she got pissed off. And he sensed, he *hoped*, he was wearing her down a little. "But I'm willing to hear you on all major decisions. So what's the real problem here?"

"I don't know what you mean."

He saw the color that again stained her fair complexion. Ah. Maybe he knew the way to convince her after all. "You don't want me? Is that it?"

Her mouth pinched shut.

"Mute again, huh? Well, let me tell you, I think you do."

"That's because you're horribly conceited."

"Maybe." Why deny it? He had a lifetime of success with women to shore up his beliefs. "I get it that you're lacking experience and all. But you do warm right up for me." He wouldn't mention Hauk's assurances.

"I don't know what you're talking about."

He trailed one finger down her bare arm and watched her shiver. Smiling, he said, "You see?"

Silence ticked by, and then she met his gaze and nodded. "I will be truthful, too, Michael. If I could keep Hauk and maintain my position as Claviger without interference, I would be happy to have a union with you."

Here we go again. Mallet stared up at the ceiling, and for the first time noticed all the pinpoint lights embedded there. Before Kayli could storm away from him, he brought his attention back to her. "You'll still be Claviger, babe, just with me at the helm. And as to Hauk . . ." Feeling magnanimous, he offered, "Maybe we could share him?"

"No, that's not possible."

He didn't even try to contain his aggrieved and impatient sigh. "Why?"

"All polymorphous computers ultimately need one person in charge, one person who can make the final decision in case of disputes. Believe me, you do not want Hauk caught between two controllers, forced to make his own decision as to who is right and who is wrong."

Damn, damn, damn. She had a valid point. Hauk was great, but Mallet didn't want him controlling things any more than he already did.

If he wasn't worried about Kayli, if he didn't really care for her . . . But he did. As Hauk had predicted, when he sat in the media room and watched the scenes of Kayli fighting, his blood had gone ice cold.

The men attacking her colony were big. Not as big as him, but certainly more substantial than the men of her colony, the men she was used to. They were far more layered in muscle than a woman as fine-boned as Kayli. She'd fought well, but she was no match for the intruders.

If one of them had struck her in the face . . . Never mind that she wore a clear polymer-type helmet that Hauk said turned dark while she fought, concealing her features but allowing her to see clearly. Hit hard enough, the helmet wouldn't have mattered at all.

It crushed Mallet to think of her with bruises or maybe even breaks to her beautiful nose, jaw, and cheekbones. He'd had his share of each, still carried the scars, and knew the pain involved.

But he was a man, not a delicate woman, so the difference was as clear as night and day to him.

With a visual of her hurt cramping his brain, he started shaking his head, as much to deny her as to rid himself of the awful images. For whatever reason, the attackers hadn't seemed bent on causing any real damage to the female warriors.

They'd deflected blows, tripped, taunted—all in all played with them, without ever really striking out as Mallet knew they could have.

They'd controlled the women enough to take what they wanted, and then they'd left.

"No."

She frowned at that one abrupt word. "No what?"

"No, you can't have Hauk." She started to turn around and he jerked her back. "Damn it, woman, give me a break here, will you?"

At the loss of his temper, she didn't quail. No, she planted her small feet, straightened her shoulders, and jutted her chin toward him.

"A break?"

Hell. Now her attitude was more heated than his own. "That's right." Mallet tried to moderate his tone. "Cut me some slack. Ease up. Stop pushing me."

"You're the one pushing!"

Being reasonable now wasn't easy. "No, I'm doing the best I can, in the situation *you* put me in. And I'm telling you right now, if only one of us can be in charge, well then, sorry, sugar, but it's going to be me."

That way, he'd know for certain she couldn't order Hauk to transport her away from him. She couldn't leave him.

She couldn't endanger herself.

Though she said nothing, her golden eyes burned with hurt and offense.

"He'll still be with you, Kayli. You'll still talk to him and order him and do . . . whatever it is you do with him. I'll just have the final say."

"That's not good enough."

Thanks to years of training, and because he knew this was so important to her, Mallet was able rein in his temper. "Look, I promise that whenever possible, you'll have the last word. If I feel I need to countermand your decision, I'll talk to you about it first."

When that didn't convince her, Mallet tried yet another tack. "I really do need your help with the warriors. In that, you'd be the one in charge."

Curiosity edged in around her vibrating anger. "How so?"

At least she sounded interested, giving Mallet hope for a peaceful resolution.

"What I'd like is to train with you, and then the two of us can work with the rest of your army. We need to do this at Mach speed, and I have a feeling you're a fast learner. Since everyone learns in a different way, I'll trust you to know the best method for instructing the others."

Now he had her. Her eyes gleamed with the challenge. "I suppose that might work."

"I also want the men involved, if they want to be involved. We'll let some of the AMAs help us train, too. In record time, I need to bring you all up to speed on unarmed tactics."

"When would we start?" Excitement over the challenge helped to drown out some of her upset.

Relieved, Mallet shrugged. "That's up to you. I watched some fighting in the media room, but it doesn't give me the whole picture. I'm unfamiliar with what you and the others already know. I'm unfamiliar with your routines. I don't know anyone, and they don't know me." He took her hands in his. "I *need* you in charge, Kayli, so that I can make an impact."

She looked hopeful, and he hated that he'd brought her to that.

"Think about it, sugar. To your colony, you'll still be the Claviger, and in reality you will be in charge of the troops." He scooted her resistant body closer to his, relishing the feel of womanly curves and softness. "You'll also have me. Now isn't that enough?"

In a move that he chose to see as surrender, she dropped her forehead to his sternum. Mallet wasn't sure, but she might have been snickering at him.

"Please tell me that's a yes."

She swallowed, and when she looked at him, she appeared resigned. "I admit that you make it all sound good. But I didn't approach you blind. Before choosing you, I watched many of your fights."

"Yeah?" He liked the idea of her studying him at what he did best.

She gave a slow nod. "You're going to take over. Everything. Why not just admit it now?"

Damn, she had him pegged. "Maybe just a little." Mallet kissed the top of her head. "But I promise to try to defer to you, and I swear to never, ever take your opinions lightly."

She remained unconvinced, but said, "I suppose that for now it will have to be enough."

For now? Mallet let that go. He'd pushed her enough for one day. "So what do you say, woman? Can we get this union business under way?"

She shook her head at him, and this time there was no

mistaking her humor. "Did Hauk, by chance, explain to you any part of what happens with a union?"

"He didn't go into detail, no. We had a lot of other stuff to discuss."

"I see." She cleared her throat. "Well, do you understand that once we're joined in union, we're expected to share our lives?"

"Yeah."

"In *all* ways."

"Yeah." Sounded good to him. He'd enjoy keeping her close at hand.

That flush of color tinted her skin again, and she looked away. "Physically, too, I mean."

Oh yeah. He put his forehead to hers and spoke low. "Trust me, babe, making love to you won't be a hardship." Then something occurred to him, and he straightened. "Unless . . . I'm not expected to do that with your busybody mother and the council looking on, am I?"

Horrified by just the thought, she gasped. "No!"

"Thank God." In some things, he was an exhibitionist. But definitely not in the sack.

She shoved him in the shoulder. "The problem is that we're expected to *celebrate* our union right after the council approves."

"Celebrate? Like a party?" Or maybe a reception, the way they do at weddings.

She glared at him so hotly, her meaning sank in.

"Ohhhh, *celebrate.* I get ya." Hell yeah. He'd called love-making many things, but never a celebration. Come to think of it, though, the word suited, especially if he was celebrating with Kayli. "Right after, you say?"

"Yes. We exchange a pledge, the council approves, and we are dismissed to . . . to . . ."

"Consummate?" Mallet provided, trying to help her out.

"Yes."

The old John Henry sat up and took note of that. "No kidding? So it'd happen like . . . now? I mean, as soon as we do the whole kiss thing?"

She nodded.

Damn. He'd have to face the council with a boner if he didn't get himself under control. Being more noble than he ever thought possible, Mallet said, "Then how about we ask for a short reprieve? Much as I'm hankering to get you under me, I don't want to rush through it, so I think we need to deal with the whole sacrifice issue first."

He expected Kayli to welcome the reprieve, but instead, she appeared equal parts disheartened, relieved, and insulted.

She shrugged. "I agree. It's best if we prioritize. I'll explain to the council that we'd like to settle the most immediate threat first. The fact that you don't want to procreate until the matter is settled makes it a moot point anyway."

"How so?"

"Every available male is encouraged to join in union and procreate to help strengthen the ranks of our colony. Since you announced to everyone that you wanted the matter of the sacrifices settled first, waiting shouldn't be an issue."

In other words, they'd planned to use him as a brood mare. "Gee, thanks."

She looked beyond him to her mother and the Council Mavens, distracted by duty. "You have yet to tell me what your plan might be."

Mallet gathered her to his side. "How about we head back over to the council and your mother, and I'll explain it all at once to save some time. What do you think?"

"And the union?"

He started her on her way, smiling at the thought. "It's on the agenda, babe, trust me. First opportunity, consider it done."

THEY wanted to postpone the union?

Raemay had a difficult time disguising her joy, but after Michael's dominant display, this was better than she could have imagined. She agreed with Michael and Kayli, of course, and praised them for their sense of responsibility and duty to the colony.

Priorities, she told them. They all had them.

Now her priority would be finding a way to sabotage the union so that it never happened. Michael had unwittingly given her the tools, and Kayli would benefit from her scheme.

She'd make the most of the opportunity. She had to. Her future depended on it.

CHAPTER 9

A T the edge of a high ridge, the wind in his hair, Valder
Wildoon sat atop his sleek orbiter, the obsolete engine
purring like a pleased cat as he surveyed the neighboring
colony below.

Just yesterday, he'd spoken with Kaimani, the twenty-
year-old woman they'd last taken *prisoner*. He grinned.
Labeling Kaimani a prisoner was a running jest among his
people, because no woman was treated poorly under his do-
main.

Certainly no woman would ever be sacrificed to an enemy.

Like the rest of his people, Kaimani had smiled before
him, unafraid of him, happy and carefree despite his reputation as a scofflaw. He kept order through strict discipline,
but he was not harsh to his people.

Just the opposite. Under his studious care, they flour-
ished.

Not that Raemay would ever accept that. Evil bitch. His
skull burned just thinking of her and the spell she'd woven
around him. She'd drawn him in, pretending to be thrilled

by his wild rejection to conformity, his daring reputation—
only to leave him, reducing him to a heartsick fool.

For years he'd worried for her, searched for her. When,
from a reliable source, he'd finally found her location, he'd
wanted to go to her, to win her love all over again.

But he was older, wiser. He'd asked around, at the Cosmos Confederation, at other colonies. Raemay had a reputation as an iron-willed ruler. Within the borders of her own
colony, she was safe.

He learned that she was happy, that she had married and
had children.

He'd harbored his love for decades, but now that love had
turned to hostility.

He knew where she was, though he'd yet to see her. But he
wouldn't give up. Never. He'd find her. He'd have her again.

On his terms this time.

She could continue to hide while offering virgins for his
men. It was a bounty he wouldn't refuse, not when they ran
short on women but high on lust. He'd take and take, and
then, when he'd reduced the ranks of her colony, he would
storm the lands until he uncovered the rock that shielded her.

He'd have his revenge.

Thinking about it set his heart thundering, his loins burning. He could almost feel her velvety skin, the silken texture
of her hair, the warmth of her catchy little breaths while
she . . . *No.*

He wouldn't indulge those fantasies.

She had changed, aged, grown into a woman he didn't
know, a woman he no longer loved.

For now, he'd only bide his time while planning, advanc-
ing, gaining ground.

Kaimani was happy with the man who'd claimed her. She
had bragged to Valder that she was already with child. It
pleased him, especially since she'd wanted him first.

He'd had to disappoint her with his rejection, of course.
The wants and needs of his men always took priority over
his own.

And besides, for what he ultimately wanted, Kaimani

wouldn't do. So she'd gone with another, and now she claimed to be happier than she'd ever imagined being.

It seemed that Raemay's rule hadn't served her any more than it had served him.

Soon, Raemay's rule would end.

EVEN though he knew that Kayli would miss him if he didn't return soon, Mallet lingered. Hours ago, he'd snuck out with Hauk's help, pretending that he wanted to explore the lands. And they were beautiful lands, no doubt about it. Fields and valleys, hills and lakes. Forests of thick trees and wildflowers everywhere.

Never had he seen anything so . . . surreal. It was like a painting, or a vision from a song.

At exactly two P.M., just as Hauk had claimed, it rained. Not a vicious thunderstorm, but a heavy, drenching rain that kept streams full and watered all the lush foliage.

Mallet didn't mind getting wet.

He turned his face up to the sky and let the water run over him. It felt good, being free like this to think, to just be a man.

Life felt good. Having his strength back, standing on his own, felt better than good.

But being with Kayli felt . . . incredible.

He didn't want to hurt her, but he also didn't want to sit idly by and allow her to be hurt by others. Interfering with her mother . . . well, that'd surely lead to trouble. Relatives were always a pain in the ass. But he had to do something. When he looked at Raemay, he saw that she was consumed by the strangest animosity toward Kayli.

She was a darling girl, a woman to be proud of, so why would her mother feel that way?

Denying her company on this little excursion wouldn't sit well with Kayli, either. But having her pissed was preferable to risking her safety.

He walked a long time in the direction Hauk had indicated. On the media viewer he'd seen the path, so he felt pretty sure of his route. Along the way he saw creatures un-familiar to him, but Hauk had assured him he wouldn't run into anything too dangerous as long as he didn't venture into the woods.

And if he did go into those thick, dark woods, according to Hauk the most treacherous things he'd find there were . . . birds.

Really fat, ugly birds, given what he'd seen on the media viewer. Not the type to fly overhead, but some strange breed that sat in trees and swooped down on prey, big or small, tearing with razor-sharp beaks and long claws.

Sounded pretty gross to Mallet, but he'd hidden his re-vulsion; he wasn't a wuss to start worrying about feathered fiends, even the futuristic kind.

After a time, the rain let up and the sun came back out, and that, too, felt pretty damn good. At the top of a rise, Mallet stopped and, going low over rock outcroppings, crept to the edge until he could see to the valley below.

A sacrifice had been left there, all alone and vulnerable to danger.

She was a necessary tool to his overall plan.

Serene and poised, she looked lovely waiting there on a smooth boulder, her long, dark brown hair blowing in the breeze, her hands folded in her lap. She wore a diaphanous gown that reminded him of the expensive lingerie of his own time.

A transport—sort of like a floating car minus the rubber wheels—had taken her out to the valley and left her there to await her fate. Mallet thought of the women who had come before her, the fear they might have experienced, what they'd thought about while waiting.

Fury tightened his muscles.

He'd waited so long that his clothes had nearly dried when he heard the rumble of an engine, a foreign sound in the smooth-gliding solar vehicles of the colony. A big blond dude, dressed in an open-necked shirt and black pants, rode in fast and hard. He spun his purring vehicle in a tight circle around the sacrifice.

She barely moved.

The intruder grinned. He looked to be in his midforties, but still solid in the way of a man used to being physical.

A man in his prime.

Behind him, several other large men rode in on different forms of transport, just as fast but without the throaty growl of the leader's vehicle. They all circled their prey; they all looked pleased.

Mallet's eyes narrowed. Fucking perfect.

When the leader again circled, Mallet surveyed the guy's transportation. It was unlike anything he'd ever seen, in his own time or since arriving here. It didn't touch the ground, but it had more muscle to it than the other vehicles he'd seen.

It was louder, faster, showier.

He'd have to ask Kayli about it . . . His attention went back to the sacrifice when the leader asked, "What is your name?"

She said without inflection, "I am Lydina."

"You will come with me now, Lydina," he ordered, indicating that she should climb onto his transport.

Without a word, she climbed onto the back of the machine, put her arms around the man, and rested her head on his back.

The engine revved, but before leaving, he leaned down and dropped a package on the boulder where the sacrifice had waited. Then, in a blink, he and the others flew away, darting into the woods, shielding them from Mallet's sight.

Not being an idiot, Mallet waited several more minutes before standing and dusting himself off. He could hear nothing, and trusted that they were completely out of range.

He looked over the edge of the rise and decided that, despite the recent rain, it was navigable.

"Going somewhere?"

Oh hell. He recognized that annoyed female voice. Playing it casual, amused at her stealth, he shrugged and smiled as he pivoted to face Kayli. She stood there, feet braced apart, frown fierce, arms folded under her breasts.

"Yeah. I was." He put his hands on his hips. "I didn't hear you ride up."

She relaxed her stance enough to wave a hand toward a floating vehicle. "I rode my aircycle." At his questioning look, she said, "It's silent, but fast enough to suit a trip out here."

Even as Mallet noticed, and regretted, the fine tension in her lithe little bod, he said, "Our intruder rode something noisier." He hadn't wanted to upset her again, but she'd have to learn that he needed his space—especially when doing something he considered too dangerous for her.

"An orbiter." She didn't look at him as she neared the edge of the hill and peered over. "I've seen them, but never ridden one. Few people still have them since most colonies, including ours, have forbidden them." Her brows pinched down as she moved farther away from him. "Not only are they against eco-friendly codes, they assault the ears and disrupt everyday life."

Mallet said, "Huh." Truthfully, he thought it was pretty damned cool. Sort of like a spaced-out Harley. But given her contempt when she described the orbiter, he decided it was better not to admit that to her. "He also left behind a package."

Kayli, still stiff with irritation, looked toward the boulder where the sacrifice had waited. In a low murmur, she said, "He's never done that before."

"Maybe he sensed something this time. Want to go see what it is?"

"I intend to, yes." Her arms crossed again. The sunshine was bright here, glistening on her pale hair and making her golden eyes glow. "You know the rules, Michael. My mother has declared that no one is to witness the exchange."

"I'm not much for rules." Especially when he didn't understand why they were made in the first place. How the hell could they fight an enemy if they refused to ever confront him, or even lay eyes on him?

"Your being here could have disrupted things if you were spotted."

Mallet shrugged. "But I wasn't."

His cavalier attitude almost caused her exasperation to boil over. "Is this how we work a partnership? You sneak off without me?"

"I didn't sneak," Mallet lied. "I wanted to look around, familiarize myself with your colony, and I just ended up this way."

Unconvinced, she glared daggers at him.

Time for an offense, Mallet decided. "Why were you sneaking up on me anyway?" He moved closer as he spoke. "What if you'd startled me and I went over the side of this damn hill?"

"You'd likely have broken something." She said that as if it didn't matter to her. "And then I would have had to repair you again."

"Yeah, we never really discussed that, did we?" Glad for a new topic, he kept walking until she was near enough for him to touch. "How'd you, ah, repair me the first time?"

Her gaze turned wary. "Hauk did it during transportation."

"No shit?" He put an arm around her and led her with him as he searched for the easiest route down to the valley. "Hauk is a damned medic, too?"

"No." She slipped away from his hold. "This is one of those things that, while I understand the end result, I don't entirely comprehend the specifics of how it actually works."

"Give it a shot anyway."

Shrugging, she bent and plucked a beautiful blue wildflower growing from between two rocks. "During transport you are entirely under Hauk's control. Across airwaves or something, he sends nano-pulses throughout your system. They detect all damage, feed the information back to Hauk, and with those same pulses, he directs an electrical charge at healthy cells to activate at a highly accelerated pace, healing bone, tissue, ligaments . . . whatever."

"So the health rate here must be something, huh?"

"We get our fair share of illnesses, which are treated by physicians and lesser, yet still competent, computer systems.

But they're all plugged into Hauk, so he monitors all activity to ensure correct diagnoses. Whenever damage is severe, Hauk intercedes and does what he can. But some injuries can't be corrected."

"Like?"

She stared out at the horizon. "A failed heart. Limbs that have been too long severed. Decapitation."

"Good God, you have beheadings here?"

Her gaze came back to meet his. "Such hasn't happened in a long time."

"Well, that's a relief." Mallet took the flower and tucked it behind her ear. He smiled, liking how pretty that looked, how pretty she looked. "Let's get that package now."

After holding her hand, he started to take a cautious step over the edge, and Kayli snatched him back. "Are you insane? We can't climb down."

"Sure we can. We just need to be careful." He expected her to appreciate his consideration in including her. Given the treachery of the climb, he'd have preferred for her to wait around until he returned.

Or better still, not had her there at all.

But she was here, and already piqued, so he hoped to coax her out of her sour mood.

"We'll take the aircycle." She pulled away from him and went to the floating vehicle. She swung one leg over the narrow seat and then, as if by magic, glided over toward him. "Get on."

Mallet eyed the slight framework, the delicate handles. "Yeah, uh, I kind of doubt that thing will hold me." It looked to be made of some very thin type of aluminum. "If I put my weight on there, we'll both end up mired in the mud."

Kayli looked him in the eyes, and said by way of a challenge, "Trust me."

"A dare!" He grinned at her, liking how she'd chosen to test him. "You're saying it'll hold us both, and still get us where we want to go?"

"Without any difficulty."

"All right, lady." He stepped over and straddled the seat,

hesitated, and then eased down. The cycle didn't move. "So far so good, but if I get dumped on the hillside, I'm blaming you."

"Lift your feet onto the running boards and hold on to me."

"No problem with that." He settled his feet alongside hers until his long legs caged her in. The position put her firm butt snug against his crotch. Choking down a groan, he slipped one arm around her waist, far enough to open his hand on her trim midriff. Beneath his palm, her muscles tensed. "Let's see what you've got."

She smiled, and vaulted them forward—and over the hillside.

To his credit, Mallet didn't shout at the unexpected sensation of falling headfirst off a cliff. He did hug Kayli a little tighter, hoping to protect her with his body when they dumped.

But they didn't.

Staying close to the ground, darting and tilting to avoid rocks and small bushes, she wove her way down the hill—all without once jarring him from his seat.

It was . . . exhilarating. The wind in his face, the scent of nature, the scent of Kayli wrapped in his arms.

Leaning forward, Mallet put his nose to her nape. God Almighty, she was delicious, smelling just as fresh and pure as the outdoors, but stirring him on a much deeper level.

He closed his eyes, thinking what it'd be like once he claimed her as his own, once he had all the rights of a man in union with his woman.

Waiting wasn't easy. But he had his reasons, beyond the priorities of the colony.

Kayli didn't yet understand lust; she didn't understand her own need, so how could she understand his? Until she did, he knew their first time together would be awkward for her at best, uncomfortable at worst.

He wanted so much for her than that.

He wanted . . . everything.

"Michael?"

He opened his eyes, and realized they'd stopped. "Hmmm?"

"What do you think? Did you enjoy the ride?"

He'd enjoy riding her more, but bit back that carnal sentiment. "Enough that next time, I want to drive."

"As soon as you watch the media instruction."

"I'd rather you teach me."

"Oh." She glanced over her shoulder at him, then away. "I could do that."

"Thanks." He hugged her, kissed her ear.

"I think you'd enjoy riding above the clouds, too."

"You can do that with this . . . what'd you call it?"

"Aircycle, and no. I have a Sky Slider for that. It's enclosed so that our oxygen is regulated properly. But I love flying up high, especially at night when it almost feels like I'm darting in and around the stars—" She broke off abruptly. "Anyway, if you'd like to take a ride with me sometime, we could fit that in."

"Definitely." For whatever reason, he was very turned on by the idea of her sharing new things with him. "I'll look forward to it."

To show she was done cuddling, Kayli asked, "Shall I open the package, or will you?"

Stepping off the aircycle, Mallet surveyed the small package, really not much more than a padded envelope. "I'll do it, just in case it's booby-trapped somehow."

"That's not necessary." She withdrew a small, blunt pen and clicked a button. "Hauk?"

"So *now* you want to talk to me?"

She sighed. "What's in the package?"

"Nothing more dangerous than a note. You don't need to fear for Mallet. He'll be fine opening it. But I should point out that it wouldn't be necessary—"

"Thank you." She clicked the pen again and put it away, caught Mallet's curiosity, and said, "A remote connection to Hauk. Through the remote, he can only speak when I allow him to." She patted the pocket holding the pen. "It's an indulgence I'm seldom afforded."

Oh, Hauk just had to love that, Mallet thought with a laugh. Given his lecturing tone before Kayli had shut him down, Hauk didn't appreciate being silenced in any way. "You're mad at him?"

"Not at all. I preferred to confront you on your jaunt today without his assistance, that's all."

Teasing her, Mallet said, "You figured he'd take my side again, huh?"

Her expression darkened and she gestured at the package. "If you aren't going to open that, I will."

Mallet laughed again. "Patience, lady." He retrieved the envelope, which was more like folded papers with a colorful seal around them. The seal was something he hadn't seen before, very different from the lick and stick envelopes of his time. Carefully, he pried it open. There were two thick papers, one blank but waxy, used to protect the contents.

And the other . . . a brief, handwritten note in a big bold scrawl.

Damn.

Kayli tried to see the note. "What's the matter? What does it say?"

Mallet handed it to her, but didn't wait for her to read it. "Next time, he wants two women instead of just one."

"That fiend!" Kayli scanned the note. Her anger got the best of her and she slapped it back down on the rock. "Two. He'd soon rob us of all available women."

"Until you had nothing left to offer but warriors. I'm wondering if that's not his plan." He sat down on the rock and studied Kayli as she fumed. "He took the sacrifice without a single suspicion."

"Good." She edged closer, distracted in some odd way. "It probably won't take him long to discover that we substituted an AFA for a human, though."

"We don't know that. If he doesn't try to force her, then how would he tell? I sure as hell can't. We did equip her with the right parts, more or less. She has enough of a . . ." Mallet coughed, searching for appropriate words. "Um . . . *female façade,* that unless he gets into the nitty-gritty—"

Kayli shot him a hot look.

"—we should be able to buy some time."

She propped a hip beside him on the big rock. "It's a good plan, Michael."

He looked up at the bright sun, still high in the sky. "Unless he rapes her." An uneasiness crept over him. How pissed would the guy be when he realized he'd been duped? Would the other women, already kept captive, be in danger? "But hell, even then he might not notice."

"You're jesting."

Mallet shrugged. "Rape isn't about paying attention. It's about dominating and abusing." Thinking what the other sacrifices might have suffered, his hands fisted. "Any bastard twisted enough to rape isn't someone I'd count on being real astute."

Her hand slid over his. "Then let's hope he doesn't force any of them. In the meantime, we'll begin preparing for his return."

Her touch had a gentling effect that almost scared him. No one had ever gotten to him that way before. He turned his hand and opened it to lace his fingers with her. "Thanks."

"For what?"

"Making me feel a little better about this." Jesus, he was so new to all of it, he felt like a blind man trying to find his way through broken glass. It was so hard for him to understand, much less follow their ways.

In his time, he'd have called the cops and let them handle it all. But here, everyone relied on him.

And if he screwed up, it could hurt Kayli, and that was something he didn't dare contemplate.

He felt her smiling at him.

"What?"

She lifted one shoulder. "You'll be pleased to know that your announcement about recruiting males has reached the general masses."

"Yeah?" Another rebel cause on his part. But damn it, surely other men, even futuristic dudes, felt as he did—they'd want to protect their women . . . wouldn't they? "How'd they take it?"

"They've been volunteering ever since you snuck off."

Relief, and something more, filled him. It was Kayli's smile doing the trick.

"Woman." Mallet pulled her onto his lap. "I did not sneak."

"Of course you did." Losing her humor, she touched his face with cool fingertips and deep gravity. "But please, Michael, it's not necessary. If you want to be without me, I'd prefer that you tell me so, not leave me to find out from others."

Who had told her? Had it embarrassed her, to be left in the dark? "Okay, so you want it up front, point-blank, huh?"

"I want us to be honest with each other, yes."

His grin came, further lightening his mood while also setting a spark to his constantly burning lust. "All right." He smoothed a thumb over her cheek. *So damn soft.* "I do need time away from you every now and then. But not for the reason you think."

"What reason then?"

"I want you pretty fucking bad." There was plain speaking for her. "Always. More every minute because being around you only sharpens the edge of lust."

Her lashes flickered; her lips trembled.

She tempted him without even trying.

Mallet inhaled for control, and reminded himself of his reasons for waiting. "But we're not in a union yet, are we? And I respect you too much to do anything that might make you ashamed."

She didn't say a word, just watched him.

She wanted more? Fine. He'd be happy to give her more. "I'm going to kiss you again."

Eyes flaring, she started to ease away.

Mallet didn't let her. "Now, don't get spooked."

"No, no, I'm not." But she continued to strain away from him. "It's just that I don't think—"

"Thinking at a time like this is never a good idea." He

slipped his hand under her hair and around her nape, affording him a hold that made controlling her easy. "You need to get used to me, Kayli, to kissing and more, before we go through any union business. I'm already on the ragged edge here. Once I know you're mine, I'm going to be on a very short fuse."

Incomprehension filled her gaze.

Mallet laughed at himself. Of course she didn't understand. How could she? He barely understood.

Throughout his lifetime, he'd had plenty of women, and not once, not even when he'd been a green virgin fumbling around in the dark at a drive-in theater, had he been so lost to control.

Kayli was special. He knew it, and she needed to know it, too. "Come here," he said as he encouraged her closer.

"Michael . . ."

"Shhh." He gazed at her mouth. God, she had a pretty mouth. "Just relax and don't fight me." As she stilled, he said, "It's only a kiss, that's all. No big deal for a warrior, I promise."

Her lips parted—either to protest or for a deeper breath—and he took advantage. He didn't push her, keeping the kiss light and easy, but he tasted her, slipping just the tip of his tongue over her lush bottom lip.

"Damn." The taste of her, the heat of her mouth . . .

She clutched one hand to his shirt.

That was encouragement enough for him. Putting his mouth more firmly over hers, Mallet deepened the kiss. She leaned into him, flattening her breasts to his chest, her breath coming fast and hot.

His hand opened over her back, spanning the breadth of her shoulder blades, then coasted down, tracing her spine, moving toward that fetching little bottom that he'd already dreamed about.

But just before his fingers encountered that firm flesh, another voice said, "Well, hello you two."

Mallet lifted his head and found Idola standing there, her

blue eyes narrowed, her mouth tipped up in a secret smile of devious satisfaction.

Kayli panted, her gaze first vague with need, then stark with embarrassment. She stiffened in shame.

Well, hell.

CHAPTER 10

H ER heart in her throat, her face hot, Kayli addressed her sister. "Idola." She hated the guilty sound of her voice and strove to subdue it. "What are you doing out here?"

Her sister gave her a snide "caught you" smile. "Mother sent me, but not because she suspected such an intimate tête-à-tête." The smile disappeared. "There is trouble at the market and you're needed."

Kayli tried, and failed, to put space between Michael and her. His hold was so secure that Idola couldn't miss it. It was a hold of possession, and protection.

But Michael couldn't shield her from her sister's perception of things. "Trouble? Where we set up for men to volunteer?"

"Yes." Idola shrugged one bare, rounded shoulder. "Some of the women protest because they don't want their men involved with the ugliness of defense." She tilted her head, studying Michael's embrace with critical disdain. "You should go, and quickly, before things turn more violent."

Michael nodded. "We'll leave together."

"That won't do, sir." Idola swayed closer still. "Mother wants to see you."

Michael's temper sizzled in the air like the lightning from an imminent storm. "Mother," he said with insult, "isn't running the show anymore."

As Kayli freed herself, she said, "Yes, she is, Michael." She still understood her duty, even if he didn't. "She remains our Arbiter, and nothing has changed that."

He caught her before she could mount the aircycle. "I don't want you going off by yourself." Looking pained, he leaned closer to her, his voice barely a whisper. "Not now."

Kayli put up her chin. She had to make him understand the importance of abiding by their code of conduct. "I see. So despite all the assurances you just made to me, you are already refusing to let me do my job as Claviger?"

He held his position, staring down at her as his features slowly tightened with angry frustration. "Well, God forbid I interfere with your job. Go on then, see to your *duty*. I'll catch you later." His gaze slanted to Idola, and she smiled at him. He shrugged. "Or maybe not."

From that heated visual exchange, the bottom dropped out of Kayli's stomach. It took an effort to keep her shoulders straight, her expression haughty.

Would Michael succumb to Idola's charms? The men of their colony, and even from colonies far away, all wanted her. Idola represented not only extreme beauty and grace, but a legacy of power, a hierarchy, and substantial inheritance.

Idola wouldn't be confused by Michael's attentions.

She wouldn't be intimidated by his masculinity.

She also wouldn't belittle herself with unseemly physical exchanges outside of a union.

Whatever he did or didn't do, she had her own obligations to worry about. Kayli looked straight ahead. "That's fine, then. I have things to attend to anyway." And with that not-so-great parting shot, she zipped away.

She heard Michael call after her, but she didn't slow down.

She wouldn't.

Either he'd be taken with Idola, or he wouldn't. But as she drove, she pulled out the pen. "Hauk?"

"He's trustworthy."

Why did Hauk always have to anticipate her concerns so adequately? "All the same," Kayli gritted from between her teeth, "you are still loyal to me and I . . ." The words choked her, because they represented insecurity, something she hadn't ever felt so deeply before. "I ask that you supervise."

"Done."

To her relief, Hauk said nothing else, so Kayli stored the pen—but left the link open. If Hauk wanted to confide in her at any point, he could.

Tonight, she'd get a full report. It was unfortunate, but she dreaded it already.

As she looked at their visitor, at his impressive height and incredible hard build, Idola felt tingly inside. Never had she seen a man such as him. He was a visual delight. Even his bold and disrespectful manners somehow titillated her.

She took a swaying step toward him, smiling in a complimentary way that he couldn't possibly misinterpret. "You really are a big one, aren't you?"

"It's all relative." He had his large hands on his hips, his head down as he paced. Every line of his muscular body vibrated with agitation. When he looked at her again, it was as if he didn't even really see her. "Can you take me to your sister?"

She was not used to men ignoring her this way. "You, sir, have a one-track mind." She tried another sly smile. "I already explained that my mother has a need to meet with you."

"That'll have to wait," he grumbled. He appeared eaten up with guilt over something.

Her sister?

Idola couldn't understand that. Kayli had never before

garnered so much male attention. As a warrior, she was exempt from such attentions. "No, I'm afraid it will not wait."

His head snapped up and he took two annoyed steps toward her. "Look—"

Refusing to be cowed, Idola met his gaze and smiled. "I saw you kissing Kayli."

He drew up short, assessing her as he would an insect. "So?"

"Not just kissing," she purred, determined to break through this wall of indifference. "But . . . somehow more." He'd held Kayli with so much possession, kissed her with such heated passion.

She shivered.

Seeing Michael that way—despite the fact that her sister had been the focus of his attentions—had stirred something deep inside Idola, something forbidden and exciting.

He stood before her now, so tall that he blocked the sun, making her feel very small and vulnerable. Very womanly.

"You're into voyeurism, huh?" His tone mocked her. "Not nice, Idola."

The insult didn't faze her. Unable to help herself, she put one hand to his chest and wanted to melt at the incredible heat and inflexible strength. He was like a human time capsule, a dangerous caveman, a brute—but oh so sexy.

His blue eyes flashed amusement. "I'm starting to feel like a Thanksgiving dinner here."

Her tongue came out to moisten her lips. "My apologies, sir, it's just that . . . you are *so* big."

"Yeah, you mentioned that already." He caught her wrist and moved her hand away, down to her side, then released her. "So are we going to see the Great Oz or what?"

Not understanding him, still unsettled by the dominating potency of him, Idola tilted her head. "The Great Oz?"

Solid arms crossed over that substantial chest. "Your mother."

Her rapt gaze went to his bulging biceps, and she shivered deep inside herself. He could easily break them all, and instead of frightening her, it sent delicious heat swirling throughout her.

"Yes, of course." Trembling inside, filled with anticipation, she gestured to her aircycle. "This way, please. I'll take you to her."

He held back with a look of distaste. "I'd prefer to walk." He sounded very inflexible.

"Oh, but . . . That would take far too long." She wanted him wrapped around her. She wanted to feel his body against hers. So forbidden, and yet so delectable.

He remained indecisive for a heartbeat before giving in with ill grace. "Fine. But let's make it fast." And then under his breath, "I'm definitely going to learn to drive one of these contraptions."

Idola seated herself first and then waited, her breath bated, her skin tingling with eagerness.

She'd spied on him since he'd wandered from the center of the colony. She'd seen his expression of pleasure when Kayli joined him, and she'd watched as he'd wrapped his strong arms around her on the aircycle, holding her as a lover might.

He'd pawed Kayli with his big hands, hugged her within the circle of his arms, even smelled her hair.

Yet now, he managed to sit without touching her, and Idola's disappointment was extreme. She was unused to seeking out attention; it usually came her way as the normal course of things. She could be bold when pushed, but it wasn't natural for her.

"Michael, sir?"

"What?" He leaned back, his hands braced behind him on the seat, his legs kept wide so that his thighs wouldn't close on hers.

And he didn't request a lack of formality, the way he had with Kayli. He let her address him as "sir" without protest.

Irritation edged in, diluting her desire.

"You need to hold on." Her heart fluttered. "To me—or else you might fall. You're far too valuable to our colony for me to risk any injury against you."

"I'm fine. Get it going."

Obstinate man. "I don't understand you." Perhaps he needed more direction. Perhaps he didn't understand her esteemed position within the colony. "You do realize that everyone wants me?"

His laugh was coarse and mean. "Not everyone, dollface, because I don't."

Even the endearment reeked of contempt. "But I get sent to the council, and to the Cosmos Confederation meetings, and one day I'll be the one to carry on the family name in a very prized union."

"All that, huh? Well, aren't you special?"

"Yes." Thinking she at last had his attention, Idola added, "I have my pick of suitors."

"I see." With insulting amusement, he asked, "Then why are you hitting on me?"

"Hitting on you?"

"Flirting. Flinging around the inviting looks. Coming on to me."

Curse the man, she got his meaning. Why *did* her mother want her to engage him? He was beyond impossible, and not in the least bit suitable to her rank. Being honest, Idola said, "I'm not really sure."

"Twit," he muttered, only half under his breath.

She gasped and twisted around to see him. "Is that an insult?"

He rolled his eyes. "Just drive, okay? I want to check on Kayli."

Seeing no hope for it, Idola straightened and pulled the cycle forward. She tried speeding, but maneuvering on the aircycle wasn't her forte and she was as likely to dump herself as him, so she slowed again, resigned to losing this round.

But it burned her pride, so much so that she had to point out the obvious. "Kayli does not require your assistance."

"She gets it anyway."

Idola narrowed her eyes in frustration. "She's as capable as most men, you realize. Strong and fast. She has the physique of a—"

"Hottie."

The way he said that, with a growling purr, left no misunderstanding on his meaning. Aghast at his lack of decorum, she breathed, "Excuse me?"

"She's a real babe." *Now* he leaned forward to speak in her ear. "Sexy, sensual, and all woman. She's so damn gorgeous that I can barely keep my hands off her. It's only my respect for her that keeps me in line." She felt his smile. "No other woman compares. Not even close."

Idola felt mortified heat flood over her skin. No one had ever dared to insult her so throughly, to speak to her in such an improper way. "You are not yet in union," she reminded him.

With a shrug in his tone, he said, "Yeah, it's a tough time. Lots of shit going on." Then he leaned forward again, his breath hot, his body hotter. "But it will happen, Idola, take my word on that. You'd be wise to stop shooting barbs against her. They only piss me off, and lady, that's something you don't want to do."

The threat didn't alarm her. Kayli would never bring such a beast into their midst, someone who would physically injure the women. Besides, Idola's position in the colony made any insult to her very foolhardy. The reprimands for such an offense were swift and severe.

But she didn't want to continue to suffer his insults, either. She'd have to be more subtle in her efforts. Because she doubted they'd work, despite her mother's encouragement, she decided once she delivered him to her mother, she would try her best never to see him again.

MALLET was still irked when Idola ended their snail's-pace journey at the grand entrance to the reception hall. At the top of the steps, beneath an ornate portico, Raemay waited.

The slow ride back to the center of the colony had been excruciating. Again and again, Idola had come on to him, reaching back to touch him—and once almost crashing because of it. She'd smiled at him, scooted back against him, and attempted to insult Kayli in the subtle but catty way of jealous women everywhere.

Apparently, she hadn't taken his warnings to heart, and he wasn't a man who hurt women, which left him with only a cold shoulder to dissuade her. That had been about as effective as a frown.

Idola had a sweet, lush body and a pretty enough face, but even if she weren't Kayli's sister, it wouldn't matter, not to him.

He'd made up his mind.

Stepping off the cycle the second it stopped, Mallet let his temper carry him up the steps to Raemay. Fuming, he said loud enough for her and her daughter to hear, "Don't sic any more women on me, family or otherwise, you got that, Raemay? I don't like it."

Raemay slowly withdrew the hand she'd offered in greeting. Slim brows came down, creasing her forehead. "I have no idea of what you're speaking."

He tossed a look toward Idola, who appeared shamed in defeat. He almost felt sorry for her. *Almost.*

"I have no idea what you have against Kayli, but lady, I've had my fill of that shit, so knock it off."

"Have against her?" Her back went straight as a flagpole. "Kayli is my daughter."

"Yeah, I know it," he said, more than aware of the family ties, and lack of emotion that should have been there because of them. "Do you?"

Raemay leaned into his anger. "I appointed her Claviger of our colony. As such she is held in high esteem. She—"

"Is forever doomed to be without love?"

Emotions flashed over her face in wild panic until contempt finally settled there. Giving him an insulting perusal, Raemay curled her lip. "What, sir, do *you* know of love? You barely know my daughter. She is content in her duty."

"After she's mine, she'll be more than content." That boast took Raemay back a step. Were they all prudes here? Dumb question. The look on Raemay's face said it all.

Done debating the point, Mallet said, "Don't send Idola after me again, not unless she can learn to keep her hands to herself." With an evil smile of promise, he added, "If you do, I'll put her off the cycle and return alone. Don't doubt me."

Raemay glanced at Idola, then waved her away. Mallet was relieved; there was no reason to insult the twit further.

After she'd sped away in a sulky temper tantrum, leaving Mallet alone with Raemay on the steps of the reception hall, Raemay folded her hands together. "Are you finished?"

He hadn't expected her direct approach, but only shrugged. "As long as we understand each other, then yeah, I'm done."

She nodded. "Walk with me, please."

Unsure about this mood of hers, Mallet weighed his options. Curiosity got the best of him, and he agreed. "For a few minutes. And then I want to find Kayli." He fell into step beside her as she descended to the street. Because he couldn't quite keep himself from looking around in awe, he said, "You have beautiful architecture here."

"Thank you. I'm very proud of it."

"Designed by locals?"

"Designed and built by members of our colony, yes."

Mallet made note of the pleasure in her face. "You've got some major talents here then."

"I'm aware of that." She pressed her lips together in thought, glanced at him, and Mallet saw her decision to share. "Our colony is set up so that everyone who can work, does. Anyone able-bodied who won't work is sent away from the colony."

As he was of the mind that everyone should contribute in some way, he didn't find fault with that. "Have you lost many from that rule?"

"Very few, in fact. Most take great pride in exhibiting their talents, as you can see from the work of our craftsmen. But there are other contributions not so readily visible. Teaching, cleaning, cooking, or serving . . . everyone has a special flair if people are patient enough to find it."

"Cleaning, as in maids?"

"The job includes both men and women, and is a valuable talent to have. Not all are organized and tidy. Not all see the necessity of cleanliness. In my colony, all contributions are valued."

He found no fault in that reasoning, either, so he walked on with her in silence.

The heartbeat of the colony boasted elaborate buildings, beside more functional structures, beside more humble abodes. It was an eclectic mix that probably worked against exclusivity and social classes. "What about those who can't work?"

"We only have a few. Even those injured beyond repair are capable of contributing in some way, be it supervision or advising. Those who can not are cared for by their family, neighbors, and the community as a whole."

She glanced up at him, and again, despite the difference in coloring, Mallet saw the same beauty in her that he saw in Kayli. She was older, but she still had a youthful appearance and grace.

If she wasn't such a witch, she'd probably have more than her fair share of men chasing her.

"We all work together," she said, unaware of his scrutiny, "to ensure the health, well-being, and safety of our people."

Sounded good to him—to the point of being idealistic. "One of your rules?"

She gave an arrogant lift of her chin. "One of my policies, yes."

So maybe she wasn't all bad. Not that he was ready to forgive and forget yet, not after she'd sent Idola after him with the purpose of blowing his union with Kayli. And he knew it was Raemay behind that brazen stunt. For whatever reason, she didn't like the idea of Kayli settling down with him.

But because Kayli's life would be easier if they could get along, he would give her mother a chance to redeem herself in his eyes. *If* she could convince him that she truly cared for Kayli and had her well-being as a priority.

He looked up at the bright sun, the vivid blue sky, and the occasional fluffy white cloud. "The day is getting away from us." He wanted to see Kayli, to know she was okay, to assist her and . . . just be with her.

He didn't like that they'd separated as they had. That last kiss . . . she'd singed his eyeballs with her enthusiasm. But then he'd seen the shame she felt when Idola busted them, and knew the moment was forever spoiled for her.

He needed to be with her, to talk, to explain.

Okay, so he wanted to more than talk with her. A lot more. He'd force himself to be patient, until Kayli wanted the same.

Raemay led him to the shelter of a tall tree. The broad, waxy leaves provided plenty of shade. "She won't appreciate your hovering, or your interference with her duties."

Mallet leaned back on the tree. On a neatly groomed acre of land, he saw a three-story house more elaborate than the others. Rather than the stark white of so many of the buildings, it boasted a warm toast color with dark red trim. When Raemay noticed the direction he looked, she looked, too.

"That is my home."

"No kidding?" Figured she'd have the grandest place around. Mallet made note of the long, paved walkway, the ornate door and steps, the flowery landscape. No driveway, but then, what they drove here didn't require driveways. "Pretty fancy."

"Yes." Her jaw tightened. "I've worked hard for what I have, Michael."

Ignoring that, Mallet appeased his curiosity with a question. "Kayli got a house? Or does she just live on her spaceship?"

"Spaceship? You mean her vessel?"

"Yeah." Thinking of her forever in that pile of cold metal—as amazing as the spaceship might be—didn't sit right with him. "Is that where she lives?"

"Kayli has a home. A very lovely home." Turning her head, Raemay studied him with interest. "She hasn't yet shown it to you?"

"No." And that made him wonder why she hadn't. Did Kayli want to keep him on the spaceship to ensure a forced distance in their personal life?

God knew, with him at one end and her at the other, unless he got Hauk to transport him, it'd take nearly an hour just to reach her.

"I would have thought . . ." Raemay barely bit back a smile of satisfaction. "That is, if you're to form a union, it'd only be right for her to share with you. I know she's proud of her property."

"We've been busy." Mallet kept all inflection out of his tone. "Where is it?"

Pointing to a quaint cottage on a much smaller plot of land, Raemay said, "Over yon."

Mallet looked, and . . . "Huh." It was a cute little house, about a fourth the size of Raemay's. Nicely landscaped, with plenty of trees, very tidy but otherwise . . . plain. It was white, like most of the houses, but with a red tile roof and arched wooden door. He recalled the simplicity of her room, and pondered his perceptions. "She's not into fancy, I take it."

"If you knew Kayli as well as you think, you'd know that she's highly opposed to ostentatious displays."

Because that sounded too much like a slur, Mallet said, "Unlike her mother?" When Raemay only tightened her mouth and frowned, he let that go. For now. "I like it. It's quaint."

"Yes, it is." Raemay continued to look at the house. "You should understand, Kayli is not limited in her means. But she fell in love with the place."

"Why?"

A surprised laugh escaped her. "I asked her the very same thing. She told me that she would not get lost inside."

Mallet knew Kayli hadn't meant figuratively. Her spaceship was so big, with so many corridors and rooms and subrooms, that a person *could* feel lost wandering around the interior.

Harking back to Raemay's earlier comment, Mallet asked,

"What makes you think I plan to interfere with Kayli's duties?"

That had her laughing again. "You've created quite the reputation in the short time that you've been here."

Couldn't deny that. But then, he was from the past, and that was enough to shake up anyone. "Sometimes an outsider sees things you can't. You get caught in the circle and can't see your way out of it."

"You think I'm caught in this circle?"

"Maybe." Again he looked at the beautiful sky. "I didn't set out to interfere, Raemay. Mostly I just want to give a new perspective to things." The same way Kayli had given him a new perspective on just about everything. His body, his health, his life.

Love.

Before Kayli, he'd never really pondered the future because fighters lived fight to fight. If you won, you went forward with more training, more diet, more prestige, and money. If you lost, it was back to the gym, studying tapes, honing moves, refiguring angles and strategies.

Long-term plans were foolish.

Now, without a single sanctioned competition in sight, his future looked more promising than he'd ever imagined. It was a future with Kayli, and it was brighter and more optimistic than that near-perfect sky.

Raemay laced her hands behind her back and paced in front of him. Her slipper-covered feet crushed dewy blades of grass and filled the air with a freshness Mallet had always associated with spring. He had a feeling that here, in this place, spring happened year-round.

"We seem to be conversing in a more general tone now."

He acknowledged that with a grin. "Beats scrapping, doesn't it?"

"Yes." She firmed her mouth again. "For that reason, I hesitate to press you."

But she wasn't hesitant enough to let it go, he noticed. "Let's get it over with then."

She inclined her head in a show of assent. "The problem, sir, is that many of the ladies here are discouraged. You appeared to make your choice so precipitously, and in such an unorthodox manner."

God, he was tired of that tune. "But my choice *is* made, so what is it you want, Raemay?"

"I want us to work together." She stopped pacing in front of him and put her head back to look into his eyes. "I spent the night thinking on what you've said, the decisions you've made."

A fancy butterfly, larger than any he'd ever seen, flitted by. It almost landed on Mallet's shoulder, then took flight again. "About Kayli, you mean?"

She frowned at his distraction. "Contrary to what you might think, Michael, I adore my daughter. I'm proud of her and her contributions to our colony. Almost as proud as I am of my own contributions."

She admitted that her own feelings came above her daughter's? He shouldn't be surprised. "At least you're honest about it."

She flushed. "I've worked hard for my colony and for my family. I won't be ashamed of taking satisfaction in success."

"Guess not."

"Yesterday, you won over many of my people." Puzzled by that, she again paced. "Before your speech, the men had seemed so content to remain secure within our boundaries, protected so that we could ensure the continuation of our people."

"I've thought about that, too." At a loud chirping, he looked up to see a fat orange bird perched on a limb above his head. It seemed prudent to move. He had no idea what type of droppings futuristic birds might produce. "The way I figure it, men are men, no matter the time period they live in."

They began walking again, heading down the center of town. Some people waved. Others watched with curiosity.

Raemay seemed to know them all and greeted them with kindness.

"I might not be up on the twenty-third century, but I did my history lessons like everyone else in my time. Historically, men are aggressive and protective. Unless you're putting some sort of passivity chip in their noggins, it goes against basic male instinct to sit back, excluded from risk, while women put their necks on the line. It's just not natural."

"Given your . . . colorful colloquialisms, I sometimes have difficulty following your reasoning. This time, however, I believe I get the gist of it."

She wanted plain speaking? Fine. "You had your guys brainwashed."

"Brainwashed?"

Mallet saw some children playing with a floating ball. Out of the ten children, only one was a boy. It was clear that they had some issues with getting more males into the colony. Mallet felt sorry for that kid. The girls were squealing, teasing, sometimes clustered together to whisper. And the boy obviously just wanted to play.

Venus and Mars, he thought with a smile.

At first, he thought the noise came from the cluster of kids, but the farther they walked, the louder it got. It came from somewhere at the outskirts of the colony hub.

Curious, he continued on in that direction. "Yeah, brainwashed. You convinced them to your way of thinking without them even realizing that they'd been swayed. Tell a person something often enough, and they start to think it's their own idea."

Which, he figured, was what she did to Kayli. She'd convinced her daughter that she was a warrior, and now Kayli believed it.

Frustration, maybe a hint of irritation, chased away some of Raemay's congeniality. "I see. Brainwashing." Her brows lifted with disdain. "You don't harbor a favorable opinion of us, do you?"

He didn't, not so far, but Mallet kept that thought to

himself. "When you get the women on board, and they start laying down the rules—and withholding from anyone who doesn't follow their rules—well hell. Those poor male schmucks didn't stand a chance."

"Withholding . . ." His meaning sank in and Raemay scowled darkly. "I assure you, it was never our intent to manipulate—"

"Yeah, maybe not a universal plan. But that's been a historically proven method, too. Since the beginning of time, women have used sex to get their way." He grinned, shrugged with an admission of his own. "And let's face it, men have let them."

They turned a bend in the town walkway and Mallet found himself facing a field of battling men and women. Because of Kayli's bright blond hair, he spotted her right away.

Standing on a platform, back rigid and shoulders straight, she shouted at them all.

And was ignored.

Raemay held out a hand. "You see what your new decree has caused? Families in turmoil. Men and women in dispute. Chaos within a normally peaceful colony."

"Like hell." One guy stepped up to the platform to shout at Kayli—and Mallet saw red.

All his training came to the fore. He didn't get enraged, no, not that. Whenever he fought, he did so with a clear head and the intent to counter any and all moves.

He went cold with deliberation; no one would rage at his woman.

Without even thinking about it, he broke into an agile sprint, heading straight for Kayli.

He didn't have to plow his way through the crowd; they parted for him as if sensing a tornado ripping through. With every step he took, his instincts gained ground until he was reacting purely on basic male protection mode.

Reaching the offensive guy in less than fifteen seconds, Mallet grabbed the arm he had outstretched toward Kayli—and tossed him.

The bellowing man landed on his back with a loud thump, causing men and women alike to scatter. Mallet wasn't breathing hard. He hadn't strained himself in the least. He stood there, waiting to see what the guy would do, if he'd have the sense to stay down.

All turned to see what had happened; little by little, silence settled over the field.

Standing there, hands on his hips and determination still ripe, Mallet waited until he had their undivided attention. When all stared at him, he joined Kayli on the platform.

One glance at her and he saw her narrowed eyes, the tension in her shoulders.

Uh-oh.

Too late, he remembered Raemay's warning: Kayli would not appreciate his interference.

Damn. Hoping to remedy things, he looked out at the crowd, raised a hand, and said, "Your Claviger has something to say to you. How about you all shut the hell up and listen?"

CHAPTER 11

KAYLI felt the shock in the crowd as vividly as she felt their awed stares. Some had met Michael already, but many had not. Judging by their expressions, his powerful, take-charge manner had diverted their arguments.

Off to the side of the confusion, she noted her mother's look of smug displeasure.

Her once-simple world was now so complicated, she could barely keep her thoughts straight. And it was all because of Michael.

When he'd first come charging through the crowd, she'd assumed he would embarrass her by robbing her of credibility, by taking over.

Instead, he calmly tossed the irrational man blasting her with his displeasure, then turned and deferred to her.

She was still flummoxed by his display. In her colony, men did not throw other men.

And yet, Michael had made it look so effortless that she knew she'd made the right choice in him.

"You have their attention, babe, but I don't know how long it'll last. If you've got something profound to lay on them, I suggest you get to it." He put his hand to the small of her back, caressed lightly. "Or would you rather I knock a few heads together first?"

Was he . . . serious? It appeared so.

Forcing a smile for the crowd, Kayli said, "A moment, please."

She pivoted, giving the assembly her back, and dragged Michael a few feet to the rear of the platform. This was the second time she'd found it necessary to seek privacy with him, in front of an audience.

Ready to set him straight, she looked up at him, and he gifted her with the cheekiest, most endearing smile she'd ever seen.

It made her knees weak and obliterated her resolve.

In a flash, she remembered that heated kiss, the touch of his tongue, his taste. If Idola hadn't interrupted them, what might she have done?

After Idola had interrupted, what had he done?

When she just stood there, Michael said, "Seeing you in take-charge mode is a turn-on. Confident women are so sexy."

Sexy? Is that what he truly thought? With his experience, he had to have known many attractive women—not that she wanted to ponder that too much. So far she'd managed to keep most thoughts of him with other women from her mind—but it got more difficult by the day. "I'm sorry, Michael, but you can not just bully your way into our assembly."

"Assembly?" Raising a brow, he glanced down at the hand she still had clasping his arm, then covered her hand with his own.

Warm, gentle, soothing.

In direct contrast to her inner turmoil, a turmoil he engendered.

"Is that what it was, honey? An assembly? Because it looked more like a riot to me."

It had looked like a riot to her, too. Too quickly for her to keep up, tempers of the colony members had escalated out of control. And no wonder. Their world was now as confused as her own.

Trying to block his charm so that it wouldn't scatter her thoughts, she asked, "Why did you throw that man like that?"

"He shouted at you." Face darkening with grave sincerity, he lifted his head and spoke loud enough for all to hear. "If he shouts at you again, I'll throw him again. Or worse. You might want to let them all know that."

Dryly, she rolled her eyes. "I imagine they all just heard you."

Unapologetic, he nodded. "Good."

Her teeth clenched. "Fine. No shouting. Anything else?"

"No shouting at you. I don't give a damn if they want to chew each other to bits. Unless you're trying to get their attention. Then they damn well better show some respect."

She pulled her hand free from his and crossed her arms. "Respect. Check. Anything more?"

Michael grinned. "Yeah." He leaned closer until she felt the warmth off his body and saw the striations in his intense blue eyes. "You're even more adorable now that you're all hot under the collar. A man can only take so much, Kayli."

Her eyes widened.

"Do you think they'd start rioting again if I kissed you?"

Alarm took her fast away from him and back to face the crowd. She held up her hands—and noticed they shook.

"Henceforth," she announced to one and all, "if you're here at the arena, it is to join our ranks. That means that when I speak, you will show appropriate respect by listening. I do not expect to have to raise my voice again. Is that understood by all?"

Heads bobbed, but then one woman stepped forward. "I have a question."

Kayli gave her leave to speak.

"What if we don't want our men joining? Do we have any say in—"

Michael spoke before the woman had finished her questions. "You do not, not here."

They all turned to him, and Kayli wanted to throw up her hands in exasperation. Instead, trying to maintain a façade of control, she gestured Michael forward.

The women went mute with lusty greed.

The men slumped from comparisons.

It was quite the odd reaction for both.

Shaking off that observation, Kayli looked over her people. "As many of you already know, Michael Manchester has come here to share his expertise in hand-to-hand combat methods, and to assist in defeating the invaders. You will show him the same respect that you show me."

No one said a word.

Kayli cleared her throat. "Michael, do you have anything to add?"

"Yeah. Those of you in unions, if you disagree about who's to join and who isn't, stay at home until you get things settled. For now, the only people here should be people willing to fight for their colony. And the sooner we get started, the better. So I want men over there, and women over here."

He *was* taking control. But before she could show him her frustration, he said, "Your Claviger has done a remarkable job training the women, and I'd like her to continue with that while I go through the ranks of men to see what potential we have."

A murmur of excitement rose from the crowd, then died when Mallet raised his hand.

"Plan to sweat, people, because from here on, it's all hard work. We're not going to stop until we're able to defend this colony, men, women, and children, from all invaders. You have my word."

The silence stretched out, stretched, and then—the enthusiastic cheers erupted.

Again.

Kayli was still staring at her people when Michael tipped up her chin. "Okay?"

Once again, her heart softened. He was simply the most amazing man she'd ever encountered. "Listen to them." She smiled at him in gratitude for what he'd brought to her people—hope. "What do you think?"

"I think you've done a great job of heading the defense, that's what I think." He bent and kissed her hard and fast, shattering the cheers into silence once again. "Go ahead and take them through your routine training. I'll keep an eye out while I sort through the men." He cupped her cheek. "And then tonight, you and I have some unfinished business."

Unfinished business.

Did he mean of the sensual sort? Because God knew, she hadn't a clue in that department.

And again, thoughts of Michael with other women, women who basked in their femininity, women comfortable and even practiced in sexual activity, nearly drowned her in her own misery.

How could she ever compare?

How could he *ever* be happy with her?

"Kayli? I'm not sending you to the gallows, babe, so don't look so glum. You'll damage my ego."

Given the size of his ego, he grinned as he made that outrageous comment.

Kayli shook off her worries. "I'm fine."

Regardless of her jumbled personal feelings, they had to prepare for the return of the invaders. The sooner they got the defense organized, the better their odds of success.

She'd have to worry about her lack of sexual knowledge and hands-on practice at a more convenient time. For now, she'd do well to impress Michael with the skills of the defense women. When he saw their abilities and knew that she had taught them, he'd know that she was capable.

And then, if he wanted her, it would be maybe because he cared, not because he felt some associated sense of obligation to protect her.

Keeping that plan in the forefront of her mind, Kayli strode into the ranks, issuing instructions and directing her people to get the most out of them.

But even as her troops put on a remarkable exhibit of

strength, speed, and agility, her mother stood there, watching with what appeared to be a mix of worry and resignation.

Once Kayli had everyone busy with differing facets of routine training—some exercising, some sparring, some studying new formations of defense—she approached her mother.

"Kayli," she said, and her strained smile put Kayli on edge.

"Mother." Even though Michael often took her off-guard with his ways so different from hers, she realized that nothing made her tense like facing her own parent did. "You seldom visit the training yard. Is everything all right?"

Raemay shook her head, but said, "Yes, of course." She turned to walk and Kayli naturally followed, not far, just to . . . move. "Michael and I had a talk."

A fresh wave of unease crept up Kayli's spine. Just as she knew it'd be disastrous for Michael to alienate her mother, she could not afford to have her mother chase Michael away. The colony couldn't lose him. Watching him, seeing how everyone reacted to him, brought home that they needed a change even more than they needed Michael's instruction on hand-to-hand combat.

Hoping to hide her concern, she asked, "How did that go?"

Raemay shrugged. "He saw your home, and mine. He seems to think you've been treated unfairly."

Relaxing a little, Kayli rolled her eyes. "I'll explain to him."

"Will you?"

"Of course." Seeing that her mother watched her with keen interest, Kayli touched her arm in assurance. "I love my home. It's perfect for me."

Her mother nodded, hesitated, walked a little more. "Daughter, you know that when it comes to defense, I trust you implicitly. But in this, in a union of the heart, I have to wonder if you know what you're doing."

Kayli wasn't sure how to reply to that, so she said nothing.

"Do you?" Her mother paused to give her a keen look. "Do you know what you're doing?"

No, she didn't. Not even close. "About defense?" Kayli hedged. "Yes. You know I never liked the idea of submitting to the invaders. I'd much prefer to fight them, even if we lose."

"Sometimes . . ." Raemay hesitated, drew a breath to start again. "You're a very wise young lady, and I'm so proud of you. But you *are* young, and that makes it difficult to always see the big picture."

"Meaning?"

"It's possible that losing isn't the worst that can happen."

"No?" Kayli had never seen her mother like this, teetering on uncertainty, at a loss for words, unable to make her position clear. Suspicions surfaced, but Kayli kept her tone and expression neutral. "What would be worse than losing?"

Donning a false smile, Raemay stopped and turned to face her. "I trust your instincts as Claviger, you know that. But with Michael? He's unlike our people. He's not what any of us is used to."

"I know." She shrugged. "Everyone knows." Within a minute of meeting Michael, it was clear that he had his own way of seeing and doing things.

"He is bold and demanding, controlling and inflexible."

Kayli could not deny any of that. "Yes."

Brows pinching down, Raemay asked, "Has he . . . pressured you in any way?"

She smiled. "No, Mother." In truth, he had, but somehow she enjoyed his form of pressure. It was . . . stimulating.

Raemay took her hands. "Do you agree to a union with him for the sake of our colony, or because he's the man you want for the rest of your life?"

Everything about her mother was different now. Never before had she been so passionate about something. Not with Kayli. Not over a man.

With her sisters, yes. Many times, Kayli had sat in on long discussions about choosing the right man for the right reasons. But it was assumed that Kayli would never have that bond, so why talk of it?

Trying a dose of honesty, Kayli said, "He hasn't pressured me, not in the way that you mean. He influences me just by being himself. I'm . . . intrigued by him."

Raemay gave her close scrutiny. "And you're a little afraid?"

"Mostly of what he makes me feel."

Her mother paled; her voice dropped in alarm. "Would he ever harm you?"

"No!" Kayli knew that with a bone-deep certainty that she couldn't understand. She held her mother's shoulders. "He's not that way, Mother. Michael is a protector. He would never hurt any woman."

"How can you be so certain? How do you know he isn't misleading you in some way?"

Memories lightened Kayli's mood. "There are so many ways. I studied him before I chose to bring him here. I witnessed him with his closest friends, and with the female medical staff in the hospital who tried to gain his attention. But most of all, when I told him of our problems, of the women being taken, his reaction was honest and pure. It was a true indication of him as a man."

"And?"

"It enraged him. He would give his life to protect a woman, any woman." As her confidence with the subject grew, her smile grew, and Kayli hoped it would bolster her mother. "Given how he'd care for a stranger, can you imagine what he'd do to protect a woman he considered his own?"

By small degrees, Raemay relaxed, and finally nodded. "Impressions can be deceiving, so I hope you're right."

"I'm sure of it." Other things, like Michael's overwhelming sexuality, she wasn't so sure about. What she knew of sexual matters was laughable. Other than a kiss or two, she had zero experience—whereas he was well practiced and would likely prefer a partner who was, too.

"There's something else."

Drawn from her own worries, Kayli lifted her brows. "Yes?"

"I . . . tested him."

A confession? From her mother? That, too, was unusual. The stunt she'd pulled was expected, but not an admission of remorse. "If you mean with Idola, I already know about it."

Guilt darkened Raemay's eyes. "You do?"

"Hauk kept a close watch for me. He reported back that Michael was as blunt as you just claimed he could be in rejecting Idola."

"I did it for you, Kayli. I wanted to make sure—"

"Mother, please." It was a special moment for Kayli, a rare instance of pure honesty between them. "As Arbiter, you don't need to make excuses to me. You wanted to test him and you did."

Using one daughter to do your dirty work, and willing to hurt the other to make a point. Kayli shook her head. "I understand."

"Do you?"

No. But then she seldom understood her mother's motives. "Let's forget about it. Michael turned down Idola— she's not too hurt about it, is she?"

"I haven't spoken to her yet."

"Well, I hope she isn't." Kayli rushed through the rest of her sentiment. "He turned her down, and made it clear that he's determined on his course. I hope that puts your . . . concerns to rest."

Raemay remained unconvinced. "Are you positive you want him, Kayli? That you want to risk everything in your life for him, all that you've built, all that you've accomplished?"

To hear Raemay, it sounded as if marrying Michael would be the greatest of sacrifices. Kayli didn't think it would be. In some ways, she believed sharing her life with him might be wonderful.

But it was a moot point.

Like Michael, she'd sacrifice anything to protect the members of her colony. "I'm positive."

After Raemay let out a defeated breath, Kayli hooked their arms and led her back to the fields where the women now practiced and the men worked out.

It was an odd sight to see. In an uncommon display, no doubt following Michael's lead, the men had all removed their shirts. With the vigorous exercise, sweat-sleek muscles flexed.

The women, usually so dedicated to their workouts, were now only halfheartedly going at it, distracted with ogling the men.

When they noticed Kayli, they launched back into their practice.

Kayli couldn't blame them for the preoccupation. For an extended moment in time, Michael held her attention. He was magnificent.

"It's indecent," Raemay grumbled, pulling Kayli out of her reverent stare.

"It's just his way, Mother." She nodded to the women in approval, and continued on. As they got nearer the group of men, one of them stopped sparring and put his hands on his knees.

Michael said, "I didn't call a stop yet. Let's go."

"But my legs hurt," the man complained, bent double and huffing air. Kayli recognized him as a successful merchant, and a man unused to heavy physical activity.

Not that Michael cared for his excuses.

He stood over the man with an expression of disgust. "Does your vagina hurt, too, you big wuss?"

Shocked, the man sputtered in response.

Raemay gasped.

Kayli, God help her, had to stifle a laugh, as did a few of the other women who bit their lips or hid their mouths behind their hands.

Michael pointed to the female warriors, all of them practicing with a vigorous show of energy. "They're still at it, and even with an idle job, you've got bigger muscles and should have more stamina. If you want to be part of the defense, you have to learn to push through the pain. You have to be at least as good as the women."

Though it took a visible effort, the man straightened and

went back to work. Michael nodded in satisfaction, noticed Kayli and Raemay watching, and gave them a brief nod as well.

Not long after that, though, he called a halt and gave everyone a moment to grab a drink or stretch.

Raemay touched Kayli's arm. Her eyes were disapproving, her mouth tight in a sign of annoyance. But she didn't voice a complaint. Instead, she whispered to Kayli, "What is a wuss?"

CHAPTER 12

FOR several days, Kayli managed to dodge any heartfelt discussions with Michael. It was easier than she had imagined, given how he threw himself into the training. The man proved tireless.

He set up three sessions a day, allowing the women to join them, even appointing some of the better female fighters the task of instruction.

On the third day, the men and women mixed, all working at various skill levels. There wasn't a single unutilized space on the fields. Michael effectively divided groups, giving each a specific task, then rotating them at intervals.

On the forth day, he took it further than field training. He wanted everyone to pay attention to diet, too, which meant he ate many of his meals with the trainees. After a long consultation with the cooks, he came up with a specific menu for everyone. He praised as often as he corrected, harassed as often as he commiserated.

And he sought Kayli's input.

He truly made her feel an important part of the equation. If she noticed a lapse in technique, he stood back while she offered the correction, then smiled at her with pride. So often, the way he looked at her made her blush.

Even now, with everyone working hard, he found time to seek her out with his gaze, to look her over and smile in that appreciative way.

"Your heart is racing," Hauk pointed out.

"We've been working for hours." Kayli used a forearm to wipe the sweat from her brow, turning away from Michael.

"You're in incredible shape, so exercise has nothing to do with it, and you know it."

"Do you want something, Hauk?"

"Yes, as a matter of fact I do. Mallet wants to speak with you."

"Now?" He often conferred with her during practices, and in the middle of explaining a technique, he'd tell her that she smelled good, or that she looked good sweaty; sometimes he'd just say that he wanted to hear her voice.

Little by little, he was softening her. She didn't know if that was a good thing or not.

"At the end of the practice," Hauk explained. And then, in a chastising tone, he added, "You've been avoiding him, Kayli, and he's been patient. But it's not like you to cower."

"I am not cowering!" She was giving herself time to get her thoughts together, to . . . prepare herself. She glanced over and saw that Michael had gathered everyone together. He did that each day, going over what they'd learned, offering encouragement, and answering questions. She sighed.

"Fibber," Hauk accused. "You're uncertain of how he might affect your neatly organized life, but Mallet deserves your attention."

She rolled her eyes. "What are you, his defender? He can handle himself, you know."

"Indeed. He is most capable of handling many things, including your insecurities."

Gnashing her teeth, Kayli said, "I'll talk to him later." Because she wasn't ready to face Michael and his expectations, she slipped away before he could wrap up his pep talk to the assembly.

She'd denied it to Hauk, but she knew it was cowardly to flee this way. But blast it, she needed time to herself, time to sort through her feelings.

Time to prepare herself.

In a very short time, she'd gone from acceptance of a solitary life of duty to dealing with the flirtatious courtship of a very large, very sexual man who claimed to want her, and who made her want . . . things, too.

Hoping Michael wouldn't notice her retreat, she hopped on her aircycle and drove away. The air had cooled a little as the hours slipped away, and the breeze on her face dried the sweat on her heated skin. She felt itchy, as much from her unresolved feelings toward Michael as from her strenuous activity.

When she reached the lake where she liked to swim, she turned off her aircycle and dismounted. The sun hung low in the sky, sending a splash of crimson color over the horizon.

Sitting on a large, flat boulder, Kayli pulled off her boots, loosened her belt, and sprawled out on her back. The surrounding trees allowed a dapple of sunlight to dance over her face. The whistle of a bird and the water lapping on the shore lent musical whispers to the air. "Hauk?"

"Hmmm?"

The computer's easy tone matched her melancholy mood. At least with Hauk, there was no reason for pretense. "You're right, you know."

"About you being insecure? Of course I am. But you shouldn't be."

Easy for him to say. No one expected the same things of him. "I don't know anything about sex."

"You took the basics, Kayli. You know the mechanics."

"Just barely."

"So?"

"Michael knows much more."

"I'm sure he does. He lived in a different culture than you."

"It's not just that." Though God knew, that was more than enough. "He's more innately sexual. I feel it when I'm around him."

"I'm positive that he'll be happy to teach you anything you need to learn."

She had the feeling that Hauk deliberately missed her point. "I feel like an idiot."

A voice, not Hauk's, said, "Perhaps I can help. I have a modicum of experience."

Kayli shot upright and twisted at the same time to face the intruder. "Dormius!" She hadn't heard him approach, and Hauk, blast him, hadn't warned her. "What are you doing here?"

"I followed you." Cautiously, he strode toward her and sat close on the rock. "Do you mind?"

Eyeing him, Kayli tried to figure a reply. Dormius was a little younger than her, attractive with boyish charm and an easy smile. Though both of her sisters had whispered about him, their hands over their hearts, he didn't interest her one whit.

Because her sisters liked him, Kayli had always made a point of looking over him, beyond him, or through him.

"What is it you want?"

He pushed breeze-ruffled brown hair from his forehead. "The rules have changed of late."

"The rules?"

Gaze direct, compelling, and enveloping, he stared at her. "Until the outsider came and named you as available, no one dared pay you too much attention. But I have always noticed you. I've always . . . admired you."

Drawing back, Kayli frowned. Oh no. No, no, no. "Don't be ridiculous."

He reached for her hand, shocking Kayli and making her realize how different Michael's touch felt to her. Less unwanted and intrusive. Less . . . repugnant.

"You are very different from other women here."

"Is that a compliment?"

"Oh yes. I admire the differences." His gaze moved over her face and he took a deep breath. "I've seen the way the outsider—"

"His name is Michael." For some reason, she did not want Michael forever labeled an outsider.

Dormius nodded. "I see how he kisses you. Often. Everyone sees." His gaze met hers, pinning her in place. "You like it."

She leaned farther away. "Michael is impulsive and isn't yet accustomed to our ways."

"But you are—and still you allow the kisses."

How was she to stop Michael? He often did things even before she knew . . . No, that wasn't true. If she told him, in no uncertain terms, not to kiss her, he wouldn't.

But she'd never told him not to.

She was to blame.

Dormius smiled. "I heard you speaking to Hauk, but what can an asexual computer really tell you?"

She started to stand, and Dormius caught her arms. Not hard, not really restraining her, but making his preference for her to stay well-known.

Without another word between them, Kayli's training kicked in, shored up by her natural resistance to things unfamiliar.

And this, with a certainty, was unfamiliar.

Her eyes narrowed. "Coming here was a big mistake, Dormius."

"Let me be the judge of that." And he stood with her.

MALLET took a long drink of the crispest, purest water he'd ever tasted. Like most things here, the water was better. The sky, the scents, the laughter. He liked it all.

Since he'd started training, everything else seemed to have fallen into place for him. He belonged, more so than he ever had. He enjoyed the people, different as they might be. Except for his lack of communication with Kayli, he was having the time of his life.

Two of the women from the defense team gave him the once-over. It wasn't the first time that had happened, but for the most part, he pretended not to notice. After a cordial nod of greeting, he picked up his shirt and swiped the sweat from his face, then drew it over his head. He found that they sent him fewer covetous looks when he was covered more. Given that he didn't want to encourage them, it'd be best to stay fully dressed when possible.

"Sir?"

He looked up to greet a young man still red with exertion. "Call me Mallet."

Hesitant, the man said, "I am Kamir. Could I beg a moment of your time, please?"

"You can't beg, no, but my time is yours." He smiled at him. "What's up?"

For a moment, Kamir looked confused before cautiously returning the smile. "It's true that you speak very differently."

"So I've been told."

"I enjoy your informality."

"Good to know. So Kamir, what can I do for you?"

Kamir stepped closer, struggling with what he wanted to say. "I enjoyed our activities today."

Knowing he'd worked them hard, ramping things up to get them all ready in record time, Mallet grinned. "No complaints, huh?"

"No si . . . Mallet. I like the way it feels to use my body this way." He stretched out a leanly muscled arm, flexed it back. "I'm tired, but in a good way."

"I know exactly what you mean." Mallet slapped him on the shoulder. He'd often felt the same, enjoying each new muscle he discovered, each new measure of strength. "Keep at it, and you'll be totally ripped in no time, I promise you."

"Ripped?"

"Shredded. In shape." He shook his head. "As good as a body can get."

"Ah, I see." Very serious now, Kamir said, "That brings

me to my point. I was wondering if there were more activities I could practice at home."

Mallet loved the enthusiasm. At first, he'd been concerned that the men would be total wimps, since they'd been
so willing to hide behind the women.

Now he knew that it had never been by choice, it was a
concession made to the women they loved. He couldn't do it,
but then, he hadn't been born and raised in this atmosphere.

So far, every guy who'd joined him—and just about every able-bodied man had—gave it his all. They got into the
fun of it, ribbing each other, competing, and at the same
time showing off for the women who trained beside them.

Of course, the women showed off a little, too. He hadn't
lied when he told Kayli she'd done a phenomenal job. The
women were not to be dismissed. They'd be a valuable asset
in fighting off foes—if Mallet could get beyond the fact they
were women putting themselves at risk.

Even now, he wasn't sure if he could take it once the real
conflict began.

"There are things you can do in your spare time, and we
can go over them later, after you've become accustomed to
the ones I'll cover here, at the arena." The last thing he
needed was some overenthusiastic kid hurting himself. "In
the meantime, just stick with the menu and make sure you
show up every day."

"But—"

"I don't want you to overdo." As he spoke, Mallet scanned
the area for Kayli—and didn't see her. Damn it. Had she already slipped away on him again? "Understand me, Kamir,
if you overdo it and pull a muscle now, you could put us behind. Let's keep to our pace, and once you're in general
bulked-up shape—"

"Like you?" he asked with optimism.

"Uh, yeah. Sure." *Not.* The kid didn't have the frame to
pull it off, but he could definitely add some muscles. "Then
you can start expanding the routine on your own."

A little defeated by that, he still accepted Mallet's instruction. "I'm sure you know best."

"That's why they pay me the big bucks." Where the hell had Kayli gone?

"Big bucks?"

"A joke."

"Oh." Kamir laughed, even though Mallet knew he hadn't understood. "Very funny, sir."

"Yeah, I'm a regular comedian." Blind adoration made him uneasy. "So Kamir, where do you work?"

"I'm an entertainer."

"No shit?" Surprised, Mallet stopped looking for Kayli and instead focused on Kamir. "What's your talent?"

Nonplussed by Mallet's sudden attention, Kamir stammered, and finally managed to say, "I sing."

"Live singing, or recording in a studio, or what?"

"We, ah, don't record things anymore. Not in the way you probably mean. We create audio files that can be picked up anywhere within the designated radius. You see—"

Hauk's voice came out of nowhere. "I beg pardon for interrupting so rudely, but Mallet, you are needed elsewhere."

At the intrusion of the computer's voice, Kamir paused. Mallet, going on alert, said to Kamir, "Excuse me. I think that's my cue to cut out."

Again confused, Kamir said, "Yes, of course," to Mallet's back as he strode away.

After a few feet, Mallet stopped. "Hauk?"

"Yes?"

"Just where exactly am I needed?"

"The lake." Hauk hummed a little, then added, "Kayli is there."

Needing no more prompt than that, Mallet took off in an easy jog. To any onlookers, they'd think he was only continuing his stamina training: He jogged almost every night. Of course, he did that to burn off sexual energy. Being celibate sucked.

Once he was a safe enough distance away from the group to ensure privacy, he asked Hauk, "What's wrong with Kayli? Is she in trouble? Is she all right?"

"My, my, my. Aren't you the worried one?"

"Hauk," he warned, in no mood for games. For too long now, Kayli had kept a deliberate distance from him. What really rankled was that he could barely keep his focus on anything *but* her. Again and again during each training session, his gaze found her in the crowd, lingered, devoured.

Right after training, she found one reason after another to stay well out of his reach.

God, he wanted her. Bad. This business of showing consideration and patience was for the birds. Thanks to being an SBC major contender for the title belt, he'd been chased by more women than he could count. Now the woman he wanted most, more than any other, avoided him like he had the plague.

"Kayli is fine," Hauk assured him, and in the next second, announced, "but it does appear that she might have an eager suitor—"

"A *suitor*?" Mallet snarled. He gave up jogging to outright run. Damn it all. He'd made a point of giving her some space, and now some other knucklehead wanted to move in?

Like hell.

He dashed across the landscape, not in the least tired now that anger had given a boost to his adrenaline supply.

"Yes, a young man who appears anxious to answer some of her more—" Hauk simulated a perfect cough. "Intimate questions."

Mallet almost fell over his own feet. He growled, "Explain that, Hauk, and make it quick without any jokes, or so help me, I'll yank a wire or two."

"I don't have wires, so it's an idle threat. Not that I consider this a teasing matter. Kayli, as you know, has been raised in a very puritan lifestyle. You and your steamy sexuality have her all atwitter."

"Atwitter?" A stupid word that didn't really sound horrible, but not really good either. "Seems to me that she's put me entirely from her mind."

"Seems to you." Hauk laughed. "But she's been plenty preoccupied thinking about you, and what you want to do with her. That, Mallet, is why she's been avoiding you."

"She's afraid?"

"More like insecure. You have experience and she does not. She doesn't want to disappoint you or embarrass herself."

Damn. She'd been thinking of him, worrying? He never should have let her have so much time alone.

"She was asking me about some specifics so she could measure up to your expectations, when Dormius showed up. I believe *he* might be willing to educate her."

Mallet saw red. "Dormius is a dead man."

"It's quite possible. My Kayli is not a woman to trifle with."

"*Your* Kayli?" Mallet paused to scan the area. "Which way is the lake, damn it?"

"Just over the rise yon. Beyond the tree line. It's a very private area, in fact."

Private! "Great. Just freaking great."

"Mallet, please understand. When I left, it was more to keep Kayli from mangling the young man than to have you rush to her rescue." Hauk waited the perfect beat of time to draw emphasis, then added, "And of course, it'd be best if she learned from you, rather than me."

"Learned?"

"Yes. As Dormius pointed out, I'm asexual. I could tell her what she needs to know, but it would be rather cold and clinical, not at all what she needs to encourage her in this union."

"So now I have to encourage her?"

"Well, you haven't been all that charming, have you?"

Hauk's idea of diplomacy didn't sit well. "If you don't have wires," Mallet asked, "do you have a plug? A chip or circuit I could yank?"

Hauk sniffed. "There's no reason to threaten me. I want Kayli to be happy. I think, with proper guidance, you can make her happy."

"Gee, thanks." Mallet spied the lake and started toward it.

"But please note, I would not allow you to 'pull my plugs' as you say. I have defaults in place to stop any such sabotage."

Damned annoying think box. "Yeah, well, what about water? If I tossed a bucket—"

"She's just over there," Hauk quickly assured him, then went silent.

As Mallet jogged over the rise, he saw Kayli below, her knee on the throat of a young man who lay still—the only form of defense left to him. "Well, what do you know." Dormius wasn't a big guy, not by any measure, but he was still a man, and from what Mallet remembered, he was in decent shape.

Yet Kayli had him pinned down and as helpless as a child. Mallet smiled with pride. "Damn, she's something, isn't she?"

"Told you so," Hauk said. "Now please do not allow her to hurt him. It would start rumors that she doesn't need."

Now that he saw Kayli had it under control, Mallet welcomed Hauk's advice. "Such as?"

"Such as the impression that being raised a warrior, she's incapable of being as womanly as a woman needs be for a union. Can you imagine how she'd be injured to know such denigrating rumors circulated, affecting not only her, but you as well?"

Damn. He knew exactly how she'd react, and it bothered him. "Yeah." Mallet gave himself a single moment to catch his breath, then shouted, "Kayli! What the hell are you doing?"

Hauk groaned.

Kayli looked up with a dark scowl.

Jogging forward the rest of the way, Mallet stopped beside her. "I know that being free to explore is new to you, but you'll be doing all your exploring with me, babe, not any other bozo."

She released the young man to stand toe to toe with Mallet. *"Explore?"*

Mallet cupped her cheek. "You are one beautiful, vibrant, sexy woman. But you agreed to be mine, and even though we've both been busy with training and other responsibilities, I'm not about to share you." As he spoke, he *acciden-*

tally stepped on the fellow still sprawled on the ground, earning a groan from him that both he and Kayli ignored.

Stupid putz.

"He," Kayli said, pointing a finger to the ground without drawing her gaze from Mallet's, "insinuated that I'm easy."

Son of a bitch. Hauk hadn't told him that.

"I didn't!" the young man protested. "I would never! I only wanted . . ."

Though it wasn't easy, Mallet kept his tone mellow, without a hint of the real threat involved. "Want me to kill him?"

"No!"

The boy yelled, "No! Really. I wasn't—"

"I wouldn't mind," Mallet assured her. "Any asshole who insults you that way deserves nothing less than a sound thumping."

Her eyes widened at his language. In a choked whisper, she said, "Asshole?"

Mallet shrugged. "It seems appropriate for a jerk that'd make such an assumption about your character." He smiled at her. "You're the most honorable, moral, *good* person I know. If he's too stupid to know it, he's useless to the colony."

"She's great," the guy whined. "Perfect. A real paragon."

Mallet looked down at him. He had a bloody nose and a fat lip, prompting Mallet to cock a brow. "Given your bludgeoned face, buddy, 'paragon' is a little overkill, don't you think?"

Finally Kayli realized that Mallet's foot was on Dormius's shoulder.

"Michael!" She pushed him to the side, freeing the knucklehead on the ground, who immediately rolled to his knees and tried to scoot out of range.

"What?" As usual, her defense of everyone amused Mallet. She'd obviously popped the little weasel, but she didn't want anyone else to abuse him.

Through her teeth, Kayli said, "I can handle this myself."

" 'Course you can. Never had a doubt. But you're mine, so allow me the right to defend you just for the fun of it, okay?" He reached out a hand to Dormius.

When the fellow warily accepted the offer, Mallet hauled him to his feet—and held on to him. "She *is* mine, and you should understand up front that I don't share. Kayli can kick your ass from here to Sunday, and I imagine she probably will if you offer another insult."

"No insult was intended, I swear!"

Mallet paid no mind to his protests. "But know this— when she's done, you're mine. And I'm not nearly as nice as she is."

"Understood," Dormius said in a rush, and the second Mallet released him, he apologized to Kayli. "I swear, Kayli, insulting you was never my intent. I had only hoped to inquire about the differences in the colony now."

Her eyes narrowed. "Fine. Be gone, then."

"And to compliment your daring in forging new ground for *all* of us—"

Kayli sighed. "Go, Dormius."

But he appeared to be on a roll, determined to get his piece voiced. "—and to tell you how much most of us appreciate the new freedom now afforded, because we, too, have romantic interests—"

"Go!"

At her raised voice, Dormius jumped. "Right. Sorry." He dashed away, limping a little, wiping at his bloody nose. At the last, he called back, "Say hello to your sister for me."

Watching him, Mallet said, "That's just plain pathetic."

Kayli simmered for a moment, then socked him in the shoulder. "How *dare* you charge in here and play the defender?"

With a scowl, Mallet rubbed his shoulder. For a dainty thing, she packed a wallop. "Actually, I wasn't playing." Then he pulled off his shirt.

Aghast for new reasons, Kayli rasped, "Michael!"

"Hmmm?" Seating himself on a large rock, Mallet tugged off his shoes and socks. He felt Kayli's rapt attention on him, heightening with every piece of clothing he removed.

Hands clasped in worry, brows pinching down, she rushed over to him. "Just *what* do you think you're doing?"

"I'm still sweaty from the practice, and I haven't had a chance to shower." He glanced at her, caught her wide eyes filled with both indignation and something akin to anticipation. Smiling to himself, he said, "So I'm going to do the next best thing—I'm going to take a swim."

Mallet heard her gulp, saw her eyes widen even more. But he didn't hear a protest.

Damn, but she pleased him.

CHAPTER 13

M ALLET knew that Kayli was reserved, modest—and still she couldn't entirely tamp down on her own sensual inclinations. He glanced at her bare feet, knew she'd had the same intention to swim before Dormius had interrupted her, and asked, "Any chance you want to join me?"

Her head snapped back. "Oh no, we can't."

"Why not?" In the face of her agitated denial, his calm felt comical. He had a feeling he'd always enjoy the contrasts in their personalities.

"If someone found out—"

"Hauk can tell us if anyone approaches. Can't you, Hauk?"

"Certainly. I will be most vigilant. I can guarantee your privacy by alerting you well in advance to any visitors."

"Hauk," Kayli complained, and then, while visually devouring Mallet's naked chest, she said, "It is unseemly for us to be alone together at night, especially when only partially clothed—"

"Partially? Honey, I don't swim in my clothes—partial or

otherwise." So saying, Mallet stood and shucked off his pants.

Kayli went dead silent, even her breathing suspended. When he turned to her, buck naked and a little too wired to look truly calm in any way, she sucked in a quick breath that almost strangled her.

He was hard—something that seemed to happen every time he got in her vicinity. Not much he could do about it, even if he'd wanted to. But he didn't. He needed her to understand the effect she had on him.

As Kayli's gaze slid over him like a heated touch, she remained silent. Mallet locked his knees and let her look her fill.

Watching her watch him was a unique turn-on.

He wanted her to be familiar with his body. He wanted her to become comfortable with him so that when he took her, she wouldn't be too nervous or tense.

But hell, *he* was so tense that he didn't know how he'd last through her intense curiosity.

The last crimson rays of the setting sun reflected off the surface of the blue lake. That, combined with the land and dark velvet sky, created a gorgeous setting.

But nothing compared to Kayli's bright hazel eyes or the way her fair hair lifted from a faint breeze. Yes, she was different from other women here, but to Mallet, she was by far the most beautiful—anywhere in time.

Her concentrated stare tested his resolve in a very big way. He took a step toward her. "You've seen me before, Kayli."

Without blinking, she pointed at him. "Not like that."

Mallet glanced down at a boner that couldn't be missed. "Oh yeah." With her innocence, he doubted Kayli realized he was above average. "Don't worry about that right now."

He was about to coax the oh-so-lovely Kayli Raine into the lake, hopefully with few if any clothes on. They were alone, she was sexy in her innocence, and he was so fired up, he thought he might self-combust.

"Not worry?" She looked dubious. "But, um . . ."

With another shrug, Mallet turned matter-of-fact about things. "I want you, honey. You know that. When a guy wants a woman, he gets hard."

"And . . . bigger?"

Mallet took a deep breath through his nose. "Yeah. Bigger, too."

Kayli's tongue slicked over her bottom lip and she sought his gaze with a measure of disbelief. "Perhaps . . . too big?"

"No, never that." Hell, he'd had women go nuts over his size. Never had he thought his endowment would be a hindrance to lovemaking.

Without deliberate provocation, she licked her small pink tongue over her bottom lip again, twisting Mallet inside out.

Her expression turned quizzical. "I felt that before." She nodded at him. "Hard like that I mean, when you were still in the hospital."

"Yeah, I remember. You turned me on then, too." Hell, from the get-go, he'd reacted to her in extreme ways, wanted her like crazy. She'd dragged him out of his near depression just by showing up. "I won't apologize because I can't help it. It's a very natural thing whenever you're around me, looking so good."

That brought her attention to his face. "But I'm sweaty."

"So am I." He shrugged. "We both worked hard. The difference is that you smell good sweaty. Sort of earthy and warm and—"

Quickly interrupting, she asked, "What will you do. With"—she nodded at his lap again—"that."

He wished she'd quit talking about his dick like she expected it to perform some amazing trick. Right now, about all he could manage was strained conversation. "I won't take you tonight, if that's what you're wondering." God, it hurt to make that promise.

"Take me? Where?"

"I meant . . ." Mallet ran a hand over his face. This was more difficult than he'd ever imagined. "I won't make love to you."

"You mean have sex?"

He took another step toward her. "I mean make love, there's a difference. You'll have to trust me on that one."

Her frown reappeared. "Why not?"

"Why not what?"

"Why won't you make love to me?"

Did she have to sound so put out? It weakened his resolve to do the noble thing and wait. "First off, you've been avoiding me. If you're not comfortable in my company, how the hell can I expect you to be intimate?"

She flushed with guilt. "I've been busy."

He gave her a look to let her know he wasn't buying that, but he didn't outright challenge her on it. "Second, we're not yet joined in this whole union business. I don't want to do anything that you might later regret."

Having thought about it a lot, the rehearsed words came easily. "And lastly, I respect you and care for you too much to take advantage."

"But you're . . ." She gestured at his pride and glory. "You know."

Did he ever. "We could do some other things," Mallet suggested. Just thinking it made his muscles constrict and sent liquid heat through his veins. His voice dropped as he added, "Things we'd both enjoy that would help you get accustomed to me, but wouldn't require you to lose your virginity."

"Really?" The curiosity returned to her bright hazel eyes. "Like what?"

She couldn't expect him to spell it out. Hell, just saying "virginity" nearly toppled him over the edge. To his knowledge, he'd never had a virgin. Anticipating the moment when he'd get her under him kept him on the ragged edge.

Keeping things vague, he said, "I promise you'll enjoy it."

He waited while she pondered it all, seeing one emotion after another cross her beautiful face.

"You know I would never hurt you, don't you, Kayli?"

"Yes." Narrowing her eyes, she studied his body. "I know all about sex."

"Is that right?"

"The basic mechanics I mean. I know that men get erect before they can enter a woman." Her gaze flashed up. "Right?"

"Yeah." He sounded like a dying man.

"I also know there's some preparation that's necessary to make it enjoyable for a woman, but I'm fuzzy on what that preparation might be."

"It's called foreplay, and it's something men like a lot, too, babe."

"They do?" When he nodded, she made a face. "So the 'other stuff' you mentioned is like the foreplay? I assume that's kissing and . . . something more?"

This was worse than the inquisition. "I swear to you, I'll explain it all once we're in the water." Where he could touch her, and show her, and enjoy her.

But she didn't seem convinced, and continued to over-think things until Mallet said, "Kayli? You're killing me here, babe. Make a decision, okay?"

If she said no, he'd find a way to accept it. It'd take a nice long soak in the lake, but he wouldn't pressure her.

She drew a deep breath, bit her bottom lip—and nodded. "All right."

Damn, but her acquiescence nearly took out his knees. "Yeah?"

Further torturing him, she paused with her slender fingers on the top hook of her shirt and gave him a severe look. "But I want you to go in the water first. And don't peek."

Heart pounding, Mallet felt like a kid who had just had his candy taken away. "The thing is, honey, I *really* want to look at you." He was dying to see her. All of her. Head to toes and everything in between.

"I don't think so." She lowered her head so that her hair half concealed her expression. "I'm sorry, Michael, but no one has seen me without clothes since I was a very young girl."

"No one male you mean, right?" Surely her mother or her sisters had done the whole shopping-till-you-drop thing with her. Massive shopping sprees weren't his thing, but he knew Eve, Dean's wife, could spend an entire day at the mall. Dakota, Simon's wife, wasn't all that into fashion, but on occasion she'd gone along just for fun and company.

"No one," Kayli reiterated. With Mallet still watching her, she folded her arms around herself. "Not even my family."

"Why not? They don't have shopping in the future? Do you just zap clothes out of thin air?"

"Of course not. We have shops to obtain the styles we like. But I've always been very . . . private."

"You have a kickin' bod, babe. You should be flaunting it, not hiding."

Her brows beetled down. "I prefer to find my clothes on my own, usually cyber-ordered, without voyeurs." Her arms tightened and her voice grew impatient. "So are you going to get in the water or not?"

Damn. "It's a deal breaker?"

Her mouth pinched and she glared at him. "I am not taking off anything as long as you're standing there looking at me."

Definitely a deal breaker then. "Okay, okay, I'm going in." Mallet turned and waded into the dark water until he was knee deep. It lapped gently against his body, cold and crisp—which was a good thing. Maybe it'd help him hang on to his self-control a little longer so he wouldn't embarrass himself.

A thought occurred to him, and he asked, "There's nothing deadly in here, is there?"

"No. It's safe for swimming."

Trusting her on that, he went a little deeper until the water hid his boner. It felt good—but not as good as Kayli would feel once he finally got her in there with him.

Night came quickly as the sun finished its descent behind the hills, leaving everything in shadows. One by one, stars blinked on across the inky sky, creating ribbons of light on the surface of the lake.

Impatient, burning up, Mallet splashed his face and his

sweaty chest. When he couldn't take it anymore, he called out, "Kayli?"

She popped up in the water in front of him. "I'm here."

Damn. His heart punched hard at the sight of her.

Her pale hair looked darker slicked back on her head. Water spiked her lush lashes and glistened on her sleek shoulders.

That killer mouth of hers smiled shyly, almost melting his good intentions.

Thanks to bright moonlight, Mallet could just see the upper swells of her small breasts in the water. Her nipples would be hard now, and knowing that was pure torture. He wanted her in his hands, in his mouth.

Since he didn't want to spook her, he tried not to stare. But it wasn't easy. He pasted on a strained smile and wrestled his gaze to her face.

She waited, her expression serious and nervous and brave. Damn, he adored her. "Come here."

She shook her head—and dipped a little lower in the water until it touched her chin. "It's shallower where you're at. I'd be . . . exposed."

"Yeah. But just a little." Just enough.

She considered that for too long, then said, "You come to me."

"A control freak huh? I can dig it."

She took him seriously. "As head of the defense, I am used to being in control. But then, so are you." She chewed her bottom lip. "It worries me some, giving up my control to someone. But since I'm unfamiliar with all things sexual, I suppose I have to a little."

"I'd never hurt you."

As she continued to consider the logistics of sexual involvement with a take-charge man, she shrugged off his reassurance. "I'd never let you."

Mallet smiled at that. She had a lot of spunk, and that added to his admiration . . . which added to his lust. "How do I know you won't hurt me?"

"I won't." She was far too serious, almost making him

laugh. Then she added, "Do you think you can compromise and meet me halfway?"

"You're a diplomat." Finding no fault with her suggestion, Mallet moved out the few feet to reach her. When he stood right in front of her, the water reached his upper abdomen. He couldn't get too close, or she'd feel his erection, and that might send her out of the water before he'd gotten a chance to learn her a bit.

She gazed up at him. "Now what?"

Such a loaded question . . . "What I'd like to do," he told her, "is kiss you. Just a kiss, nothing more. Not tonight anyway."

She rolled in her lips, considered things, and nodded. "Okay."

He lifted his arms from the water and, voice gruff, whispered, "Give me your hands." When she did, he laced his fingers through her own as insurance that he wouldn't forget himself and start groping.

Because he'd never dealt with anyone like Kayli before, he didn't trust himself to use finesse. He was used to women who knew the score, who practically ran the show in bed. More often than not, he'd had women all over him, and he'd reveled in wresting control from them—a playful game they'd both enjoyed.

But Kayli was different. Having a woman shy away from him was a novelty.

"There are all kinds of kisses, Kayli. If I'd realized sooner how innocent you are, I wouldn't have gone so far, so fast with you." Hoping she'd understand his sincerity, he said, "I apologize for that."

Her gaze drifted over his chest. "It's all right. I didn't dislike being kissed. I just . . ."

"Wasn't used to it, I know." He was so hot, Mallet wondered that steam didn't rise off the water. She had a strong grip, but her hands were so small and trusting in his.

He would *not* blow this.

"Here's the deal." He lifted one of her hands to his mouth and kissed her wrist. "This time, you call the shots."

"How? I don't know enough—"

"You'll catch on, trust me. And when you want more, take more."

Her eyes were huge and dark and so serious. "I don't understand."

"You will." Leaning down by small degrees, he lightly touched his mouth to hers, exploring with a gentleness that was almost as foreign to him as it was to her. Even the girl who'd taken his virginity hadn't been as unschooled as Kayli—and he loved it.

Knowing that he'd be her first in so many ways, that she would learn everything from him, with him, was more of a turn-on than the most practiced expertise could ever be.

As Mallet teased with small, light touches, her soft lips followed his, parting just a little so that her sighing breaths escaped, tempting him and adding to his tension.

From the moment he'd met her, her mouth had drawn him. She had a mouth that'd drive any man nuts, and now it was his.

When she licked her bottom lip, her tongue touched his lips, too. Just to let her know how much he liked that, he gave a low, measured groan. It encouraged her, and she did it again, more deliberately this time, slowly stroking his bottom lip.

Yeah, he'd figured her for a quick learner—and he wasn't wrong.

Mallet opened his mouth to match her, greeted her tongue with his own. Her hands gripped his, a telling reaction that thrilled him. She leaned closer and he felt her tight little nipples graze his chest.

Everything masculine in him clenched hard.

She tasted so good and felt so right, it took concentrated effort not to rape her mouth. He breathed deeper, turning his head a little to let her seek a more intimate kiss.

"Michael?"

The whispered, husky way she said his name was as effective as a hot stroke along his dick. Shaking a little from the restraint, he kissed the corner of her mouth, her chin, her bottom lip. "Whatever you want, baby."

She leaned back the tiniest bit, looked at him, then melted into him again, her mouth full on his, wet and hot, her movements unschooled but hungry.

Damn.

Anxious to advance things a bit, Mallet teased the seam of her mouth with his tongue, and when she opened, he sank in, slow, deep, and hot. Moaning, she squirreled closer to him, letting him feel her naked breasts on his chest, her belly on his abdomen.

No way did she miss his hard-on, considering it was caught between their bodies, getting stroked by her squirming movements.

She tried to free her hands, but he held on, knowing that if she started playing touchy-feely, he'd never get through this as planned.

Against her lips, he said, "I love your mouth, Kayli. I swear, girl, I've dreamed about it."

Before she could try to respond, he kissed her again, letting her feel some of his urgency.

"But there are other places to kiss, too." As he said that, he trailed small, damp kisses to the corner of her mouth, along her jawline to her neck, then down to her shoulder. "Do you like that?"

Her eyes closed; her head tipped back. "Yes."

"You'll like this, too." He opened his mouth on the sensitive hollow where her neck met her shoulder. Very gently, he let her feel his teeth, then the stroke of his tongue.

She gave a shuddering inhalation, then a throaty purr of building excitement.

"Yes."

After another gentle love bite that made him want to eat all of her and caused her to shiver, he licked his way back up her throat to her ear. "God Almighty, woman, you taste so damn good." He touched his tongue to her ear, traced the delicate whorls, and then nipped her earlobe.

A willing participant, Kayli tipped her head to accommodate him, and parted her kiss-swollen lips on increasingly hungry breaths.

Perfect, Mallet thought. Better than perfect. At this rate, she'd be ready for him in no time.

Forcing himself to keep to a slow pace, Mallet moved their locked hands to the small of her back, arching her body into his, hugging her close.

It was a perfect pose for a woman as strong as her, a supplicating pose in direct contrast to all she was used to. Seeing her like that made his lust rage.

Her breasts were fully exposed now, small, but firm, rising and falling with deep breaths. He moved her against him, and the feel of her breasts on his chest was sweet and exciting.

Feeling pretty damned powerful in this role of instructor, he licked her throat again, kissed her temple, and then took her mouth as he wanted, with all the heat and need he felt.

Her response was electric, without an ounce of reserve.

Trying to get closer, Kayli pressed her breasts to his heated skin, rolled her slim hips against his straining cock.

Mallet couldn't take it. He wasn't a saint, or a monk, or a eunuch. He felt himself on the verge of snapping.

Before he totally lost sight of his plan, he released her and dipped backward into the chilled water. The dousing did little to cool his lust, but at least it gave him a moment to collect himself.

God knew that with Kayli, he'd need all the help he could get.

CHAPTER 14

WHEN Mallet emerged, he found Kayli still standing where he'd left, waist deep now, her arms wrapped tight around herself. The sight of her body drew him, but even more than that was her expression. With only the moon for illumination, he saw her confusion, her hurt—and her desire.

Hoping for inspiration, he shoved his hair back and kept his distance. "I'm sorry." Man, was he sorry. "We have to stop now."

She barely moved except for a fine trembling and uneven breaths. After a prolonged stretch of time that felt like the ticking of a bomb, she nodded, but asked, *"Why?"* And then, even more agonized, she added, "Did I do something wrong?"

She looked so sexy standing there, so small and female and so much *his* that he barely got the words out. "Oh no, babe, don't ever think that. You're . . . perfect. More than perfect. Truth is, you've singed me—and that's a good thing. It's just that things aren't going quite the way I expected."

"Oh." She looked away from him, her head lowered, her

arms squeezing even tighter around herself. "I didn't behave as you thought I would. I was . . . too immodest."

A jolt went through him.

"What?" The little goof actually thought she'd disappointed him? Not possible.

Mallet came toward her so fast, with so much purpose, Kayli gasped and tried to get out of his way.

She wasn't quick enough.

He lunged, caused a big splash, and then he had her back in his arms, where she damn well belonged.

Water dripped down her face, off the lashes of her wide eyes. Her mouth opened with a startled gasp.

Opening one hand on the back of her head, the other on the small of her silky back, he pressed her close. "You're incredible. Don't ever think otherwise. But I'm only a man, Kayli. Before meeting you, I'd gone through a long stretch of celibacy because of the damn injuries. After meeting you—well, hell, not only have we traveled time, but I don't want anyone else now, and the fact is, I'm not good at denying myself."

She stared at him with stark incomprehension. Mallet felt like smacking himself. How could Kayli understand uncontrollable lust when she was a virgin? A woman who'd barely been kissed, much less indulged red-hot need?

"Here's the thing. We need to go slow, but I'm not a guy known for my patience or my finesse." He had to kiss her, and he did, quick and hard. "Being a fighter . . . women throw themselves at me. I've never had to go without, and I've never had to go slow."

That wasn't quite right, and he shook his head. "That is, I've gone slow, but only to tease, because that's what we both wanted. Not because the lady needed time to adjust . . ." He sounded like an ass, telling her about other women. Damn. "Look, Kayli, this is new for me, too. I'm trying to be really considerate—"

"Maybe you shouldn't." Warm and a little dazed with unfamiliar need, she slipped her fingers over his collarbone, then down into his chest hair. Her gaze flickered up to his. "Deny yourself, I mean."

God, she looked so ready.

His heart started thumping double-time. His dick twitched with encouragement. Mallet had to remind himself that Kayli didn't know what she was saying, that sexual desire was new to her.

He had to be the strong one, and damn it, when it came to sex, he usually just gave in.

He stopped her hand from the sensual exploration and kissed her palm. "Not right now, honey. Not tonight. Not like this."

"But . . ." Her lashes fluttered; heat poured off her. "I don't want to stop."

Futuristic chicks were into torture, he understood that now. His smile hurt, but he managed it anyway. "I know how it is, Kayli. I know what you're feeling, believe me. The problem is that lust distorts things, and makes us forget our priorities."

Offended, she drew back a little.

He pulled her close again, determined to make her understand. He would be considerate damn it, even if it killed him.

"But before this, before *now*, you've made it clear how you feel. Your colony has some pretty strict moral codes about showing . . . affection." What a crock. Affection? He was dying for her. "If I did to you what I want to do to you, it'd definitely cross a line. And later, when you had time to think about it, you'd regret it, and then you'd be pissed at me."

Maybe. He looked at her, at her warmed eyes and trembling shoulders and thought, *But maybe not?*

Then he shook himself.

No. Damn it, he would be noble. Kayli deserved that much.

She deserved everything he could give her.

Her hands flattened on his chest. In a small but daring

voice, she tested her newfound feminine wiles. "What is it that you want to do to me?"

Mallet couldn't believe it. Despite his hesitation, she felt comfortable enough to tease him? He'd call that definite progress.

Fighting a triumphant smile, he said, "You little temptress."

"Am I?"

Now she sounded pleased with herself. "Oh yeah. You're sure as hell tempting me." He searched her face in the moon shadows. "We're both naked, Kayli. We're alone. And we haven't done the whole union thing yet. But you're not worried or afraid?"

"I was," she admitted, her eyes dark and her voice breathless. "Now I'm just . . . warm and shaky and my stomach feels . . . tingly."

Oh God. He needed to drown himself. "Good." He sounded like a dying man. "Those are all signs that you want me."

Somehow, she snuggled closer without seeming to move. "I want something. I'm just not sure what."

It hurt, but he said, "You're a smart girl. Try guessing."

Challenged, she said, "Okay." She looked at his mouth with scorching intensity. "I want more kisses."

"Not a problem. On that score, I'm happy to oblige." He started to do just that, but she put her fingers to his mouth.

Her sigh, ripe with frustration, warmed his skin. "Somehow, I know that kissing won't be nearly enough."

It was a dangerous game, heightening his own need as much as hers, but Mallet couldn't call it quits. Not while she was being so daring, and not when it might work to his advantage in the long run, getting him closer to her.

"No? Then what else do you want?"

"I want you closer." As she spoke, she moved, almost without thought, driven by basic desire to brush her body into his.

To still those tantalizing movements, Mallet hugged her close, as near as two people could get without making love.

Her fingertips pressed into the muscles of his chest and her forehead rested against his sternum. Voice broken with need, she whispered, "Closer than that, even."

Tilting his head back, Mallet stared up at the glowing moon. He could feel Kayli's heartbeat, the tremors that shivered through her. Knowing this was probably the first time she'd felt the overwhelming swell of sexual desire, he couldn't bear the thought of leaving her unfulfilled.

His plan to ease her into things had backfired in a big way, mostly because he'd underestimated how innately sensual she was.

Not that long ago, it had felt like his entire world had crashed in on him. Now, here with Kayli, Mallet knew he wouldn't change a single thing, because all that had happened had brought him here, to this moment.

Knowing how badly she needed him tempered his burning lust with an even hotter tenderness. The feeling was new to him, but then, everything with Kayli was new. And wonderful. And fun.

Using fresh insight and an altered plan, Mallet tangled his fingers in her fair hair and tipped back her head.

A pulse beat wildly in her throat. She looked hot and ripe. "I can help you if you'll let me."

Her fingers continued a deep caress on his pectorals, but she seemed unaware of it. "Help me how?"

Anticipation swelled inside him. "I can make you feel better, honey. Much better. More relaxed." He brushed his mouth over that telltale pulse in her throat, touched with his tongue, teased with his teeth.

"I am . . . tense." Her eyelids drooped, her lips parted. "It's the strangest thing, Michael. The way I feel, I mean."

"Tell me." As he said it, he began easing them toward the shoreline where large rocks offered stability for what he intended to do next. To her. For her.

His heart swelled with his purpose. He'd have his fingers on her, in her, stroking her until she came, and it didn't matter if it was selfish or altruistic.

The end result was a lot of eagerness on his part.

Her tongue slicked out slowly over that killer mouth of hers. "I feel . . . jittery inside, but also warm and thick and . . ."

"And?" he prompted, wanting her to continue.

A little embarrassed, she whispered, "Wet."

Hell yeah. Not kissing her wasn't an option. He ravaged her mouth, and she loved it, pressing hard against him until he started moving again. "You should be wet, you know. That's what makes it all easier for a woman."

"How so?"

"I'll show you." Not the way he wanted, but it'd have to do for now.

He found a large, flat rock half out of the water, hidden in deepest shadows. After sitting on the very edge, which kept his lower half submerged, he coaxed Kayli closer. She didn't resist, and in fact seemed eager to his sex-starved libido, so he brought her up onto his lap and guided her legs around him.

As he cupped her waist, keeping her away from his erection, her breathing came faster, harder.

Mallet heard an odd sound, like the rustle of weeds, and lifted his head to listen.

Hauk said, "Just the wind."

Mallet jumped at the sudden intrusion. Cursing, he scowled at the air around him.

"No reason to worry," Hauk assured him. "Carry on."

Some things in the future were more difficult to adapt to than others. He liked Hauk well enough. For a high-tech, state-of-the-art, futuristic computer, he wasn't too arrogant.

But right now, he wished Hauk was more than a mere voice so he could punch him. "Do you have to hover over us, Hauk? It's like having a damned voyeur around."

"I do not hover," Hauk told him. "But Kayli is my responsibility, so I'm not going anywhere."

Kayli chuckled in a teasing, flirting way as she leaned into Mallet and kissed his chin. "Usually he makes me nuts, too, but Michael, he's just a computer."

"Just?" Hauk harrumphed. "You don't think that when I'm—"

"Hauk!" Mallet glared some more. "Could you please just ensure our privacy without the running commentary?"

"Fine."

When it stayed silent, Mallet took a deep breath, forced himself to relax, and smiled at Kayli. "Now, where was I?"

With incredible timing, a breeze moved the tree limbs overhead, allowing through a shaft of moonlight that highlighted all of Kayli's best features.

Her mouth, her eyes.

Her proud shoulders.

Her breasts and belly.

"Ah, damn." He held her shoulders and looked his fill, and it almost did him in. "Trust me," he said in a raspy, unrecognizable voice. "You *really* have no reason for modesty."

She turned her head shyly. "I'm not as rounded as most women."

True enough, but not a reason for inhibition. "Forget other women. None of them matter." He swallowed, and said, "Let me tell you, woman, there are a lot of places that I'd like to kiss you."

She didn't say anything, so Mallet lifted her hand. "You enjoyed my mouth on yours."

"Yes." She stopped hiding and turned back to watch him.

"And on your throat?" As he spoke, he pressed a warm, damp kiss to the center of her palm.

She nodded. "It was . . . wonderful."

He almost groaned. Instead, he teased the tip of his tongue between her middle and ring finger. "Your ear?"

"It was odd, but I felt it everywhere. It made my insides tighten."

He lightly bit her palm, her finger—and then he drew the tip of one finger into his mouth and sucked.

Her thighs tightened around him. *"Oh."*

Forcing himself to be patient, Mallet kissed each finger, licked and sucked and slowly closed his other hand over her left breast.

She jumped the tiniest bit.

"Easy." She was small, firm, silky. He cuddled her, caressed, moved his thumb over her taut nipple. "This," he said, sucking at her finger, "will feel even better when my mouth is"—he lightly plucked her nipple—"here."

Groaning, she put her head back, which also offered up her breasts for his attentions.

But not just yet, Mallet thought, wanting her on the very edge of exploding—like him.

He held both breasts, teased both nipples while kissing her throat again. It wasn't easy, not when he wanted to devour her, but he took care not to mark her. He could just imagine her embarrassment if she had to explain a hickey.

As he teased at both nipples, her breath caught, her short nails curled into his shoulders. She breathed, "Michael, *please.*"

He loved her reactions, so honest and hot. "You want my mouth on you?" He carefully caught both nipples, squeezed just enough to send sensation through her. "Here?"

"Yes."

New heat sizzled inside him. "All right." He captured her wrists and held them behind her, arching her back more. "No, don't fight me, babe." When her thighs remained tense, he added, "Don't think of it as restraint or control. It's just the two of us, and we're partners, remember? You want this. Yeah, that's it, perfect. Just relax and let me taste you."

Building the anticipation, he kissed her shoulder, her collarbone, the upper swells of her breasts, around her nipple, and when she held her breath—he sucked her deep.

She cried out and almost came off his lap. Mallet didn't release her; he tightened his hold to feast on her. Her frantic movements scooted her closer to his lap until she came into stark contact with his erection.

She didn't mind, and in fact pressed against him, seeking, hungry.

Locking his free arm around her waist to keep her where he wanted her, he moved to the other breast. He licked first, gave a wet suck, and then caught her in his teeth.

She groaned again, groaned more when he tugged while stroking with the rough, wet tip of his tongue.

"Oh God, Michael," she whispered, her voice raw and breathless.

"Just trust me now, babe." He didn't wait for an answer. She was too far gone to carry on a conversation. He slid his hand down her back to her bottom, pausing to appreciate that rounded part of her anatomy.

He couldn't help but growl, "You have a very fine ass, woman." Keeping her situated, he moved them farther back on the rock until they were out of the water and he could see her, all of her, in the scant moonlight.

To quiet her soft moans and muffle his groans, he kissed her mouth—and slipped his other hand back around front, down over her belly, and between her widely spread legs.

She lurched back, but he kept kissing her even as his fingers moved over her. So wet. So sleek. Hot. And . . . so fucking tight.

Damn, but she was smaller than he'd imagined. He tried to work one finger into her, but he met incredible resistance.

The fantasy of taking a virgin wasn't nearly as complicated as the reality.

With his hand now cupped lovingly, protectively, over her, he lifted his mouth. While trying to figure out how to proceed, he gave her a one-armed, tender hug.

This was a mega first for him, and he couldn't bear the thought of hurting her.

"Michael?" She sought his mouth for a deep kiss, and he obliged. Beneath his palm, he felt the heat of her, her wetness. Her hips shifted, moving against him, seeking relief before shyness made her still again.

He wouldn't enter her, couldn't finger her the way he wanted to. But it didn't matter. With new awareness and heightened emotion, he searched over her sensitive flesh, over swollen lips, and up to her turgid clitoris.

She was wet enough to slick the way, and with the very tips of his fingers he teased her. Given the wide spread of her thighs over his lap, she was nicely open and available, unable to shy away from him, unable to flinch away.

And he loved it.

At the first bold touch, she cried out. To keep her quiet and their rendezvous private, Mallet took her mouth again and continued in his slow, concentrated rhythm.

Kayli, he found, was easy to follow, easier to please.

In no time at all, he felt the small spasms building in her, the way her muscles tightened, her fingertips digging into his shoulders and the heat that emanated off her in waves.

Lifting his head to see her as she came, he encouraged softly, "That's it." Her pleasure became his, and he felt caught up in it with her. She couldn't stay still. Her hips rolled with the pace he set, riding against him, her thighs hugging him, her scent filling his head with every deep breath he dragged in.

She squeezed her eyes shut. As she strained toward release, her head went back and she gulped air.

Through a burning haze, Mallet looked at her nipples, at the frantic pounding of her heartbeat.

Her teeth came together, her face constricted in an honest, raw show of pleasure—and then she lurched against him, groaning long and low, her thighs tensed and her belly hollowed tight.

The sounds she made nearly pushed Mallet into his oblivion.

Awed by her and her natural, carnal response, he steadied her, keeping up the rhythm until she moaned, caught his wrist with a plea.

She went boneless, so soft and female that he easily repositioned her across his thighs so he could cradle her in his arms. With a soft sound, she curled closer, and smiled like a female well satisfied.

He felt like a conquering warrior.

He felt like the savior her colony wanted him to be.

He felt more like a man than he ever had in his entire life.

So overwhelmed with emotion, Mallet found speaking

wasn't easy. He kissed Kayli's crown, nuzzled her ear, and inhaled her intensified scent. "Better?" he asked in a broken voice.

"Mmmm. Much." She smoothed a hand over his chest and shoulder. "That was . . . amazing."

Could it be her first climax? Was she so inhibited by her colony's strictures that she'd never even pleasured herself? "So this was all new to you?"

Her smile teased into a grin. "Definitely not something covered in the instructions."

Mallet couldn't stop kissing her, her hair, her ear, her cheek, and the tip of her nose. "Instructions?"

"What you would call sex education." She put a soft kiss on his pectoral muscle and her golden eyes, warm and accepting, gazed up at him. "Thank you for sharing that with me."

"My pleasure."

"How can that be?" she asked, her brows pinching a little in confusion. "You're still hard."

Was that supposed to be news to him? He shook his head. "Don't worry about it. I'm okay. It'll go away . . ." He almost choked. "Eventually."

Her eyes glittered up at him. "Maybe I could—"

At that inconvenient moment, Hauk intruded. "Kayli, your sister approaches."

Well, an onslaught of family ought to help get rid of his boner.

Kayli went rigid. "Idola is looking for me?" She scrambled out of Mallet's arms so fast that she tangled her legs with his and fell back into the water with a loud splash.

Mallet reached down and hauled her out. "Calm down, Kayli."

But she twisted away from him. "If Idola knows what we've done—"

"So I was right? Now you're ashamed?"

"No! But—"

"Actually," Hauk interrupted, "it is Mesha, and she's, ah, looking for Mallet, not Kayli."

Kayli stopped splashing. *"What?"* She turned big, suspicious eyes on him. "Why?"

"Don't look at me like that. I have no idea what the girl wants." He ran a hand over his head. "How much time do we have, Hauk?"

"Close to two minutes before she'll be able to hear you. Voices carry on the water, you know. Perhaps six minutes before she is close enough to spot you in the lake."

"Shit." He caught Kayli's arm and together they thrashed through the water until they were on the shore. That she already regretted their time together bothered him more than he wanted to admit, but he was a gentleman—most of the time—so he wanted to salvage her pride for her if he could.

"I can't believe this."

"Me, either. Now quick, take all of your stuff and hustle your pert little ass over behind those trees to get dressed." The trees would shield her from the illumination of the moon and Mesha's detection.

Even in moments like this, Kayli wasn't a good one to take orders. She ignored the clothes he tried to shove into her arms. "Why is my sister looking for you?"

Mallet was in no mood for an interrogation, especially when he was innocent of any wrongdoing. "Well now, I reckon I'll find that out as soon as you make yourself scarce."

"One minute," Hauk warned them. "And then she'll hear everything you say."

Cupping her face, Mallet gave Kayli a resounding smooch that he hoped would distract her from her ire, and then, in a lowered voice, said, "Hide, damn it. Please."

"Maybe we should greet her together?"

He shook his head, rejecting that idea. "It's clear I've been swimming. Naked. No one will think anything of me doing the forbidden, but I'll be damned if I want to hear anyone accuse you of anything ever again, even your twit of a sister."

"My sister is not—"

Mallet kissed her hard again, turned her, and gave her a stinging swat on her naked butt. *"Go."*

Over her shoulder, her hand on her backside, Kayli scowled. "All right. But I'll be listening to every word." Still mumbling, she marched away.

Seconds later, Mesha called out, "Sir? Are you there?"

Groaning, Mallet snatched up his pants and tried to step into them. Being wet made it tough, but he had them up and almost fastened when Mesha appeared with an illuminated stick of light guiding her way.

When she spied him standing there, shirtless, still fastening the pants, she froze. Her enrapt gaze was far too curious as she looked over his wet chest and clinging pants.

"Mesha, right?" Bluffing his way through the awkward moment, Mallet ran a hand over his face and then headed toward her. He strove for patience and prayed Mesha wouldn't say or do anything to bring Kayli out of hiding. Stopping before her, he cocked a brow and said, "So. What's up?"

CHAPTER 15

E VEN as his partially disrobed presence nearly sent her into a swoon, Mesha remained determined to complete her mission. It was more difficult than she'd imagined because of his dominating physique.

He was so muscular.

And hairy.

And . . . *male*.

She'd never seen a man like him, and she doubted she ever would again.

She gave a delicate cough to clear her throat and tried not to keep staring at his chest.

She failed.

The men she'd seen, never so unclothed, had smooth chests without all the muscles or dark hair. This man was so different. So bold and dark.

He was . . . breathtaking.

While he waited with seeming patience, she cleared her throat again. "Yes, I'm Mesha, Kayli's sister."

"The youngest one, right?" He picked up a shirt, shook it out, and struggled to get it on over his wet skin.

"I am eighteen."

His head cleared the material and he tugged it down over his abdomen. "You're damn near a baby."

Lord help her, that shirt clung to every swell of muscle, only highlighting his strength rather than concealing it.

Nodding at her light, he said, "Care to douse that a little? You're blinding me."

"Oh." She dragged her hand from top to bottom down the light stick, and it dimmed. "My apologies."

"No harm." After sitting on a rock, he began putting on his socks. "What are you doing out here, Mesha? Isn't it dangerous for a woman your age to be alone in the dark, in the woods?"

At least he'd referred to her as a woman this time, and not a baby. "How so?" Even his feet were big and . . . strangely beautiful. Somehow *powerful*.

He gave her a negligent glance. "You aren't worried about getting attacked?"

The questions confused her. "By whom?"

His laugh was abrupt and lacking in humor. "Attackers? Hell, girl, I don't know. Your colony might be safe as a day-care most of the time, but it has had some issues lately, right?"

"Oh." He referred to the recent infiltration of outsiders—the very reason he'd been brought in. "They always warn us before arriving."

She dared to inch closer to him, watching him don his clothes, and it suddenly dawned on her. He had been swimming. In the lake.

Naked!

Unmindful of the impropriety of such a thing, he dressed with an efficient, masculine grace. "So there are no other villains lurking about, huh?"

"No, of course not."

"What about me?" Now fully dressed but still damp, especially his hair, he rose from the rock to tower over her. "You don't know me well enough to assume I'm all that safe and proper."

She was unable to halt the small, unladylike snort. "Definitely not proper, sir, given it appears you've been swimming in the lake."

"Buck-ass," he agreed, shocking her. "Which proves my point, doesn't it?"

She didn't back up when he moved closer to her. In fact, she forced herself to lift her chin. "Kayli trusts you, and that is all the reassurance I need. She would not put her faith in an untrustworthy person."

"That's your whole logic on it, huh?"

It wasn't enough? "Yes."

He laughed, this time with a little more amusement. "I guess I can't argue with that, since I agree your sister is a smart cookie with very good instincts."

Not quite understanding, Mesha frowned and fidgeted with the light. "Kayli is very intelligent, and she's brave and strong. She's always been an excellent judge of character."

"All that and more," Michael agreed. Then he turned his head to scrutinize her. "You admire those qualities in your sister?"

"Oh yes, very much." In many ways, Kayli was her idol, the person she most looked up to. "If I . . . if I had been different, I would have joined the defense."

"Different how?"

She made a face of disgust. Touting her lesser qualities hadn't been part of the strategy when she'd set out on this mission. "I'm weak. And I can't help but cry when things upset me."

"So?" His giant shoulder lifted in a shrug of indifference. "Most females do."

Though she didn't deny it, that attitude set her pride on edge. He was sexist, which probably accounted for her mother's displeasure with him. "I've never seen Kayli cry."

His hands landed on his hips, and he frowned, as if Kayli's stoicism bothered him. In a musing tone, he said, "She's a leader."

Mesha nodded her agreement to that. "And Kayli doesn't

get panicked when things go wrong. She has a very cool head and does what she has to do to gain control of the situation."

His frown darkened more. "She's trained."

"Yes, sir, but I know those are also intrinsic qualities in her character."

"You think? I'm not sure I agree." Before Mesha could ask him what he meant, he crossed his arms over his massive chest. "So, Mesha, what's up?"

His sudden focus on her left her tongue-tied. "Up?"

"Why did you sneak out here to find me?"

"Oh." Nervousness fluttered through her, but she couldn't deny that she had snuck. "I had some . . . special inquiries that, if you'll forgive the imposition and intrusion, I think you could explain for me."

"Queries huh?"

"Ah . . . yes, sir."

"Forget that sir stuff, okay? Call me Mallet."

"But . . . oh, I could not. It wouldn't be—"

"Proper?" He laughed at her.

Just the thought of such familiarity left Mesha breathless. And then what he'd said sank in. "But I thought your name was Michael?"

His charming grin sent her stomach into flip-flops. "Yeah, it is. But friends call me Mallet."

Now a little breathless, she pointed out, "My sister calls you Michael."

The grin turned intimate. "She's more than a friend, now, isn't she?"

"Oh." Her poor sister didn't stand a chance against someone with Michael's charisma. No wonder Kayli allowed him to be so different. "Yes, of course. You will join in union."

"Exactly. So . . ." He quirked a brow at her. "Those queries, Mesha?"

Quickly, before she lost her nerve, Mesha dragged her hand down the light stick again, completely dousing it, though the moon still provided some illumination.

Mallet stirred uneasily. "Uh . . ."

"I'm sorry, sir, but it will be easier if I don't have to face you."

"Yeah, well . . ." His agitation reached her even across the area that separated them. "You know, I'm thinking that maybe this is a discussion you should have with Kayli instead of me."

"Kayli would not have the answers I need." She hedged, hesitated, and then blurted, "Is it wrong for me to be so attracted to a man?"

He muttered, "Oh shit."

Mesha rushed on before he could derail her purpose. "I want to have a union with him, and I think we will someday."

"Who are we talking about?"

"I doubt you know him, sir. The thing is, we're not yet in union, and still . . . he's . . . Oh God. He's *kissed* me." With that intimate disclosure, Mesha put her hands over her face. Embarrassed heat flooded to the surface of her skin.

"He's kissed you?"

Through her fingers, she admitted the unthinkable. "Twice."

There was a long pause, then a gruff laugh. "Yeah? So what?"

Her knees almost gave out. He didn't point at her and call her shameful. He didn't reel back in shock.

She dropped her hands and looked at him, at the slight, amused smile on his handsome face. He honestly didn't seem to think anything of her shame.

Filled with hope, Mesha whispered, "It's not wrong?"

"A kiss?" He snorted much louder and ruder than she had. "Why the hell would a kiss be so wrong?"

"I really don't know." That was just it. She couldn't understand the smothering strictures dictated by the colony.

"This guy smooching you up—he's not already in a union, is he?"

"No, of course not." Such a suggestion was outrageous. "I would never do such a thing."

"Is he a lot older than you?"

"He's two years older."

"Hmmm." Michael rubbed his chin in thought. "Exactly how old are folks before they get unionized here?"

"Unionized?" The things he said, the slang he used, was so unfamiliar that it often confounded her. "If you are asking what is the median age of those who join in union, it's early twenties, but some join in union during their latest teens."

He sized her up in the darkness. "So you're a little young, but not all that much, right?"

"Yes."

"Then what's the big deal?"

Shaking her head, Mesha blurted, "I saw you kiss Kayli, several times in fact, and she did not object. Everyone whispered about it, though."

In a rush of anger, he took one giant step and loomed over her. "Who? Who talked about Kayli?"

Mesha stumbled back and would have fallen if he hadn't shot out his hands to grab her upper arms. His reaction was so fast, she didn't have time to even think of dodging him.

In a firm hold that didn't hurt, but allowed no wiggle room, he kept her close. He didn't raise his voice—but that only made the lethal tone more alarming. "Did someone say something bad about her?"

"No!" Good God, she wanted to faint. She'd never witnessed such a defensive, protective reaction from a man. Michael's hands were huge, wrapping entirely around her arms. And this close, she felt the heat pulsing off his big rock-solid body.

Even after he released her, she couldn't move. The top of her head barely reached his shoulder. And she could *smell* him, a warm, not-unpleasant scent that sent strange swirls of giddy awareness through her belly.

"Who was it, Mesha?"

Stammering, she explained, "Mostly my friends, girls my age. We're all just . . . confused."

"A gaggle of your girlfriends were gossiping? That's it?"

"Yes." She nodded. "I promise."

He rolled his eyes. "Got it. Look, you should really talk

to Kayli about this. I don't know squat about the restrictions around here, except that I think they're overdone."

"I think so, too!"

Michael tugged on his ear. "But you know, it could be this twenty-something kid is taking advantage of you. I can tell you that boys that age have only one thing on their minds."

Scandalized, her eyes widened and her voice dropped to a whisper. "What is on their minds?"

He laughed. "Let's just say, it's usually not settling down with a nice girl."

Mesha edged closer. Finally, she'd hear the truth. "Then what?"

He took in her expression, his mouth quirked, and then he burst into a big, robust laugh. "Sorry, kiddo." Reaching out one hand, he touched the end of her nose. "The answer to that one is definitely reserved for Kayli."

Disappointment dragged her down. He treated her like a child, which was okay except that she knew he wouldn't tell her anything important.

She dug the toe of her shoe into the grass. "I tried talking to Idola about it, but she doesn't understand." She peeked up to ensure she still had Michael's attention. "I think she enjoys teasing all the boys."

"I bet," he said under his breath, and then added, "She'll probably outgrow that as soon as she meets the right guy for her."

Mesha wasn't convinced. "I don't think so. As the oldest, Idola is favored by our mother and gets to attend all the meetings at the Cosmos Confederation. While she's there, every male fawns over her. She enjoys the attention."

Michael gave her a confused look. "I thought Kayli was the oldest."

"Warriors can't inherit." Mesha lifted her arms. "For that reason, they don't really count. Idola, though, she's very important to my mother, to our colony, and she knows it. Sometimes . . ." Mesha hesitated, unsure if her admission would be taken as a whiney complaint. "Sometimes I feel like I don't have my place. I'm not a valiant warrior like Kayli, and I'm not the one to inherit, as Idola will do one day."

Her worry proved unwarranted since Michael barely paid any mind to her complaints. "That's just not right. One child should never be favored over another."

He seemed infuriated—why, she couldn't guess. Kayli was happy in her choices.

Didn't he know that?

Mesha drew a breath. "Sir, my point is that Idola doesn't understand because she isn't concerned about finding the right man for her. She has numerous choices, not just from here, but from . . . everywhere in the galaxy."

He paced away. "Yeah, she said something along those lines."

"And Kayli, until recently—until *you*—was resigned to being a warrior."

"She'll still be a warrior," Michael said, and it sounded like a vow. "Defending others is in her blood, a part of the person she is. Once we do the union, she'll just have me tagging along for the ride."

Kayli was so independent that Mesha couldn't imagine such a thing. She said only, "I know you'll make Kayli happy." She thought he already did, despite the way Kayli sometimes debated with him.

"Hey." As if just remembering why she'd come to him in the first place, Mallet put a finger under her chin and tipped up her face. "Listen, it's human to want to kiss and hug and all that shit. Don't let anyone tell you otherwise, okay?"

"Shit?"

He shook his head. "Forget that. Sorry. I should have said stuff. Kissing and touching and *stuff*."

Mesha realized he'd grown impatient, that she'd overstayed her welcome. "I'm sorry." She took one step away. "I should be going."

"Probably." But he asked, "Where to?"

"My mother's home."

More annoyance bristled in his tone. "Isn't it your home, too?"

"For now, yes of course. Until I get my own." *Until I make a union.* She sighed. Would it *ever* happen?

"Mesha? One thing before you go."

She paused. "Yes, sir?"

"Mallet," he insisted.

It felt more than odd, but she repeated, "Yes, Mallet?"

"Who's the guy?"

Putting her hands together, she smiled and dreamed of the day they'd finally be together. "Dormius."

As the young one departed, disappearing through the trees, Valder smiled. By sneaking in silently, he'd learned much tonight. Most important, he now knew that Idola was the one to take—the one that would break Raemay's stubborn spirit.

Satisfaction had him grinning, and kept him smiling as he gave up his stealth and started his orbiter with a roar that split the quiet night and reverberated off the water of the peaceful lake.

Beneath the illumination of the fat moon, he saw the dark man stiffen in realization and rage.

Good.

He wanted him to know he'd been there, watching, listening, able to attack but showing patience. He wanted them all to know he didn't fear them or the bulkier outsider they'd brought in.

How ridiculous.

No single man could impact his plans, regardless of his size.

Valder was interested in where they'd gotten the outsider, but so far the last woman they'd abducted, Lydina, wasn't sharing details. She was a strangely quiet woman, too contained and too impassive.

Soon, Valder told himself, soon he'd know all he needed to know. He didn't have to browbeat a shy woman into divulging secrets.

Overcoming any effort they made was simple. They were all so complacent in their long history of peace, so unschooled in real warfare, that they trusted when they shouldn't and had no sound plan for how to deal with the likes of him and his twenty-five years of sustained resentment.

Their skirmishes were like wrestling with children. It was fun, and his men were challenged to dominate without actually hurting any of the little women.

With a battle cry meant to send fear into the outsider's bones, Valder shot away. He was long gone before anyone could even think of trying to follow him.

HEARING the roar of the same orbiter that had come to take the AFA sacrifice sent stark fear hammering through Mallet.

His first thought was of Kayli.

He jerked around toward where she'd concealed herself, but couldn't see her at all.

His heart dropped, his knees went weak, then everything was replaced by blinding fury. *"Kayli."*

"He's gone now," Hauk said quickly before Mallet could launch into a run. "He was only here to spy."

His heart continued to punch. "And Kayli?"

"She's fine, still hiding away." Somehow the computer managed to make his voice soothing.

A deep breath helped to unclench his guts, but Mallet wasn't about to relax. Not yet.

God almighty, nothing had ever scared him more. When he thought of someone taking her from him . . .

He sucked in another deep breath and tried to still the furious gallop of his heart.

Flattening a hand against a large tree for support and needing more reassurance, Mallet asked, "You're positive she's fine?"

"Yes. He was listening to you."

"Yeah, I know that." Rage tightened his fists and bunched his muscles. *"Now."*

Had the bastard seen Kayli undressed? No, he couldn't think that way or he'd explode.

As if Hauk had read his mind, he said, "He did not show up until after Kayli had hidden. But Mallet, he was here for a while, all during your chat with Mesha."

Mallet pushed off the tree and stood there, fuming. "Damn it, Hauk. If you knew, then why the *fuck* didn't you tell me before now?"

Unaffected by Mallet's temper, Hauk said, "I deduced it safest not to."

"You want to explain that—and fast?"

"If I had told you, you would have gone charging after him."

Mallet lifted a fist into the air, wishing he could grab Hauk and shake him. "Damn right I would have! And I'd have caught him, too."

"But," Hauk pointed out, all reasonable and calm, "Kayli is the head of defense, so she would not have remained safely stashed away as you engaged in battle."

"Oh." Thunderstruck by that sound reasoning, Mallet shuddered. Good God, after that awful scare, the last thing he wanted to think about was Kayli engaging in a physical confrontation with some guy twisted enough to demand women as payment for not destroying their colony.

Scowling, he ran a hand across the back of his neck. "Damn." He hated to admit it, but knew he had to. "Yeah, okay, you're right."

"Of course I am."

Though it choked him, Mallet commended Hauk. "Good thinking. Thank you for keeping her out of it."

Still concealed by shadows, Kayli's strident voice lashed out. "No, it is not good thinking at all."

Oh shit. Mallet moved forward and the second he saw her, he realized she was beyond furious. Hurt, anger, betrayal . . . each emotion flashed over her features.

"Kayli—" he started, but nothing brilliant came to mind. What could he say in his defense? She'd overheard too much.

Her eyes glittered in the darkness. From tears?

He prayed not.

"You say you trust me." As she spoke, her lips barely moved. "You say we're in a partnership, and that you understand the importance of my position."

"I do."

Arms folded, expression pinched, she waited for him to say more.

He did trust her, damn it.

But she was still just a *woman*.

He sighed. "It will never be easy for me to put you at risk."

Sensing the static in the air, Hauk whistled.

Kayli's small body went tight with resentment. Stepping toward him, her voice low, wounded, she said, "It's all a game to you, isn't it?"

"No." He'd never been more serious about anything in his life.

"I gave up control for you," she accused. "I *trusted* you."

"Yeah, uh, if we're talking about sexual stuff—"

She slashed her hand through the air, cutting him off. "But you can't do the same, can you?"

Damn, when she went all female on him, she was as difficult to deal with as any other woman. His own temper prickled. "I told you I trust you and I do." Caring for her had nothing to do with trust.

"Oh no. Not this time, Michael." She shook her stubborn head. "You tell me what you think I want to hear just to appease me. And it usually works, doesn't it?"

His frustration amplified. "I've been honest with you if you'd just stop and realize it."

His words had no apparent impact on her. "You don't trust my ability at all, do you? Why don't you just admit it?"

Mallet hated being cornered, almost as much as he hated having words put in his mouth. Facing her anger with his own, he glared down at her. "I can't help it if my instinct is to protect you."

As if she'd hoped for him to say something different, the light faded out of her eyes. Her shoulders loosened, her expression went flat. Seconds ticked by while she visibly fought emotion.

Finally her chin lifted, and her words sounded with sadness, maybe even apology. "Then I can't make a union with you."

Mallet locked his jaw. "That's bullshit and you know it."

"I'm sorry, Michael." She didn't blink, didn't soften. "I really am."

Pointing a finger at her, he said, "You brought me here, woman. I didn't ask for any of this. You studied me, so you damn well knew the type of person I was before you propositioned me."

She nodded. "Yes, of course you're right. It has all been . . . a mistake. *My* mistake." She started around him. "It's over."

His heart skipped two beats; the wind left him as if someone had just sucker-punched him in the solar plexus.

Did she not realize all the concessions he'd made to her and her back-ass colony? Couldn't she tell that their relationship was damn special?

In a little less than a roar, he commanded, "Kayli, come back here!"

She never slowed in her determination to leave him.

Mallet saw red. She thought it was over?

Not by a long shot.

Stomping after her, he said, "You're head of defense, Kayli, so shouldn't we at least talk about the asshole who spied on us?"

But even that didn't breach her current frame of mind.

Without a backward glance, she said, "I'll take care of it."

Before he could reach her, she got on her aircycle. Her shoulders straightened, and her voice, chilled and even, reached him over the silent night. "Understand something, Michael. I don't regret what we did."

He had a moment of hope.

Until she said, "But it won't happen again. It can't." And then she was gone.

CHAPTER 16

FOR long minutes, Mallet stood there, trying to figure out what the hell had just happened. Not that long ago, she'd been soft and sated in his arms.

Now she'd just walked out on him, telling him that something he'd thought was special wasn't special at all.

How the hell could she call it quits so easily?

He blamed Kayli for the confusion, of course. She was fickle, twisting him around her little finger, then kicking him in the nuts.

Or so it felt.

She'd brought him here to defend her and her colony, but then had a hissy when he tried to do just that. She only wanted half measure, but he wasn't a man used to half-assing anything. If he did it, he did his best.

Frustration sent him pacing; worry kept his heart thumping. "Hauk?"

"Yes, Mallet?"

The sympathy in the computer's voice made him grind his teeth. "Are you with her, too?" He didn't want Kayli alone right now. She was stubborn and capable—but he'd allowed her go off alone while she was thoroughly distracted.

Would she even notice if someone crept up on her?

"Yes," Hauk said. "I'm with her. Always."

"Good." Mallet wanted to ask, but he didn't even like the idea of a computer knowing how she'd gotten to him.

Somehow, while he'd thought he was in control, accepting absurd changes and believing the unbelievable, Kayli had crawled under his skin.

He might have caused a stir in her colony, but she'd sure as hell caused a bigger stir in him. *Damn it.*

"She's okay, Mallet."

Under his breath, he muttered, "Damned intuitive machine."

Hauk ignored his continued ill humor. "She is, however, furious." He hesitated. "And badly hurt. By both of us."

Mallet wanted to howl, he wanted to punch something. "Fuck."

Commiserating, Hauk said, "Yes, fuck, Mallet."

"Oh, shut up if you can't say it right." The monotone use of such a word just made it sound comical, and there was nothing funny about his current predicament.

"What will you do?"

Good question—not that there was any real choice. "Apologize. Work on her." His hands fisted. "And find the jerk who was here, spying on us." When he did, he'd make the bastard pay, big-time.

Something occurred to him, something that would at least get Kayli talking with him. He hoped. "Hauk, I need to have a town meeting, but I need to discuss it with Kayli first."

"Now?"

"No." God no. He had the distinct feeling that once Kayli had time to get her emotions in check, she'd resent him for causing her to come that close to tears. He recalled what Mesha said, that she never cried.

No, she wouldn't appreciate that he'd upset her so much, or that he'd witnessed her struggle.

"She needs time to settle down." What an understatement. "Let's say tomorrow morning."

"Kayli might dwell on this and be even angrier in the morning. She has a habit of going over things until she gets the conclusion she wants."

"I'll take that chance." Most times, Mallet figured he knew women, knew how to get around their little idiosyncrasies.

In most cases, some warm loving worked wonders.

Though Kayli wasn't like most women, hopefully the same logic would apply. "Keep everything just between us. Don't tell her I'm going to see her in the morning. Got it?"

"Er . . ."

"Your word, Hauk."

"Computers do not have a conscience, which negates the importance of giving my word."

Mallet threw up his hands in annoyance. "Give it anyway, will ya?"

"Very well." The computer sighed. "Because I know it's not your intent to further hurt Kayli, you have my word that I will not tell her of your intentions."

"Great." Having come up with a sound plan, Mallet was starting to feel a little better about things. He'd already reconciled himself to a whole new life away from past friends and acquaintances. He was in the future—with Kayli.

Together, they'd have good sex, a lot of laughs, and great companionship. He wasn't about to let her pride change things now.

"I'll need you to let me know before she leaves her room in the morning."

Again, Hauk balked at his decision. "Er . . ."

"It's okay, Hauk. I won't forget that your loyalty is to her."

"Yes."

"And I'm glad." It assuaged some of his worry to know that Kayli had Hauk protecting her, especially since she wouldn't let Mallet take that position. Yet. "Trust me that this is in her best interest."

"If you are lying, I will do reprehensible things to you."

Mallet laughed. "I'm glad she has you, Hauk, I really am." He looked around, and realized the moon had settled behind clouds; it was now pitch-black, and he didn't have a ride. "I don't suppose you can show me the way home?"

In the next instant, Mallet found himself in his room on the spaceship. "Damn it, Hauk, warn a man before you do that."

Hauk had nothing to say to that.

"Well, since we're here already and I'm nowhere near ready to sleep, how about you get me one of those media viewers Kayli had at the hospital and some tapes on her fighting techniques." He rubbed his hands together. "By morning, I want to be familiar with all her best moves."

IT had been a sleepless night for Kayli, fraught with worry about the future and memory of what Michael had done to her.

Now, as she finished dressing, lack of sleep, frustration, and overwhelming curiosity got the better of her.

She wanted to curse Michael for bringing this on her, for making her doubt herself and her abilities, for wanting him in her life despite his dismissal of those things most important to her.

For making her ache all night long, wondering over the touches and sensations he'd already evoked, and those that might have followed had he not forced her to cut him out of her life.

Closing her eyes, she again felt the gentle touch of his rough fingertips, the power of his warm palms, and the rasp of his damp tongue over places she'd seldom ever thought about, much less touched.

Breathing a little harder, she put her fingers to her ear—but it wasn't the same. Today, without Michael's stimuli, it was just her ear.

Just her breast.

Just her . . . body.

It was Michael who had made her lips so sensitive to his, he who had made her ache and then later, filled her with the most delicious wash of feeling that exploded with immeasurable pleasure.

How he'd done it, and if it could be achieved with anyone else; that's what she needed to know.

Not that she was anxious to be with any other man. In her current frame of mind, still ridiculously hurt over what felt like a betrayal, she couldn't imagine the intimate involvement. No, with Michael banned from her life, she would naturally accept her old lifestyle back—alone as a warrior. Besides, the thought of anyone else touching her was repugnant.

Today, being calmer, she hoped to talk to Michael, to convince him to stay in the colony, while remaining separate from her.

To distract herself from her preoccupation with his possible reaction, she ordered Hauk to fill her room with some of her favorite music. It was loud, raw, with a heavy beat that helped to give her a new focus as she opened her media viewer.

Biting her lip, she called forth the images she thought might best satisfy her inquisitiveness. Settling back in a chair, she curled up her legs, crossed her arms over her knees, and rested her chin there.

Huddled like that, she watched generic depictions of unknown men and women in a variety of sexual acts.

The images, while somewhat clinical, were fairly forbidden, and she'd die if anyone knew of her interest. But now, with her own personal knowledge of the thrill of carnality, the threat of being caught wasn't enough to keep her from watching.

She was in a daze, her lips parted in intrigue and her heart beating a little too fast, when Michael said from behind her, "If I'd known you were into porn, Kayli, I sure as hell could have supplied some better stuff than this crap."

She screamed.

Her attempts to bolt were hampered by the chair's crazy shifting efforts to accommodate her.

With a roll of his eyes, Michael caught her arms and lifted her free.

Humiliation rolled over her in suffocating waves. Her breath strangled; she felt light-headed with shame.

The second her feet touched the floor, she shoved him back and gasped, "How *dare* you?" That wasn't enough to stifle her mortification, and she charged forward to thump him hard in the chest, repeating, *"How dare you?"*

Under normal circumstances—meaning any circumstance other than this—she was a calm, collected, deliberate woman who handled situations accordingly.

That Michael grinned at her, slow and easy and, oh yes, *amused*, only made her temper detonate.

She pushed up her sleeves as she backed up to put fighting space between them. "You have no business—no right—transporting yourself into my private quarters unannounced."

His blue eyes glittered in challenge. "I know." He made the mistake of glancing down at her body, and Kayli kicked out.

The strike landed hard on his shoulder, knocking him sideways. But he didn't lose his balance, didn't fall, and did not stop grinning.

"Oh ho! It's like that, huh?" He took a stance. "Just take it easy, Kayli. Everyone likes a little porn every now and th—"

Her next kick landed on his ribs, and he gave a satisfying "oof" of surprise.

"Not bad," he rasped, still watching her, still unconcerned with her mood. He straightened in what she knew was a deceptively casual stance.

His arrogance infuriated her.

"It's your fault," she told him, to keep his attention divided. "What you did to me last night left me wondering about what else there might be to do."

The look in his eyes grew heated. "Is that so?"

As she circled him, she gave a slow nod.

He kept her locked in his gaze. "You didn't have to resort to bad sex tapes to get answers, you know."

Left shoulder lifting, she shrugged. "Hauk has divided loyalties now, so I couldn't continue to ask him." She curled her lip. "And as . . . *nice* as that was last night, I'm not discussing sex with you ever again."

His eyes narrowed. "Wanna bet?"

Michael's unwavering confidence pushed her, and she switched up, kicking with her other foot. While it threw him off a little, he blocked it with his forearm so that it didn't do any real harm.

As he straightened again, his smile grew. "So we're going to do this, huh?"

She didn't answer. She wouldn't give him any forewarning of her intent.

"Clear the furniture, Kayli. Then we'll see what you've got."

Keeping her eyes on Michael, she ordered, "Do it, Hauk," and the furniture all tucked away, leaving the room mostly empty.

He flexed his neck, preparing himself as they circled. "We have a problem, you know."

"Several," she agreed. "The intruder didn't restrict himself to the appointed time. He slipped in unannounced, and undetected."

His brows lifted with approval. "Smart girl."

"Like it takes a genius." She punched, he ducked, and she ended up behind him. Before she could take advantage, he whipped around, caught her arm, and dropped her to the floor.

She rolled away so he couldn't get on her.

Then she smirked. "I always heard that the big ones were slow."

He lazily redirected his stance, and waited.

Kayli couldn't tell if her taunts got to him or not. He did a great job of hiding his emotions—as any good warrior would. "I've already called a meeting to warn everyone of the danger. We'll take added precautions, of course."

"Such as?"

Noting that he stood more on his right leg than his left, she considered her next blow. "I'll program Hauk to alert us to anyone new entering the town."

"He can do that?"

"Yes." She eased forward. "But first he'll need to be refreshed on everyone who is a legitimate part of our colony, so he doesn't send out any false alarms. We have plenty of members who come and go, you realize."

"How long will it take Hauk to get programmed on everyone?"

She shrugged again. "At least several hours, maybe up to a day or more. It depends on how quickly everyone responds to the directive. He'll have to scan all the locals and take into account new residents as well as those that have moved on. It's something that I now realize we should have been doing on a regular basis instead of waiting for a breach. I'll prepare a new order for that today. In the meantime, I've ordered a rotation of defense personnel to watch the perimeter—"

So fast that she knew she'd have to eat her words about his size slowing him down, Michael shot in on her. He grabbed her in a double-leg hold and she went down hard on her behind.

Her anger was such that she wanted to hurt him, and she did. While he wrangled for a better hold to control her, she landed several elbows and fists to his shoulders and neck, and got in one good knee to his ribs.

He took each blow without making a sound, and she almost immediately regretted the flash of anger.

That is, until he flattened her out, stretching her beneath him.

Breathing hard, still teeming with resentment, Kayli dared him with narrowed eyes and clenched teeth.

He surprised her by saying, "I watched more footage last

night of you fighting. You're good, but your moves are predictable and easy to anticipate."

Regrets were forgotten; she head-butted him, making him curse while she indulged a big, taunting smile.

Obnoxious brute. "Apparently they're not *that* easy to anticipate."

With his hands locked around her wrists, he levered up on his forearms. That kept his head away from additional attacks, but it also pressed his hips in tight against her.

Oh God. She knew this was how he'd enter her, if they had sex. And she could almost feel the press of him pushing into her body, how he'd fill her. Her nipples tightened and her heart tripped.

"I'm trying to talk with you, Kayli."

"I don't want to talk with you." She struggled to ignore his big, hard body touching her in all the most relevant places. It proved impossible. "I don't want to be protected by you. I don't want a union with you."

"Well that's too damned bad, now, isn't it." He came down, nose to nose with her, almost smothering her with his incredible weight. "You brought me here, lady, and I'm not leaving, so deal with it. And so help me, if you club me again, I'll turn you over my knee and paddle your sweet little ass. Just see if I don't."

Such an outrageous threat made her gasp, but as soon as she recovered enough to speak, she struggled against him. "If you *ever*—"

"Yeah, I know." His mood nearly matched her own now. "You'll get pissed and cut me off. From everything. How original for a woman." His scorn was a live, palpable thing sizzling between them. "And here I thought you were different."

She leaned up to scream in his face, "I am different, damn you!"

Eyeing her, he tsked. "I've been a bad influence on your language."

Oh God. She wanted to kill him. She wanted to have sex

with him, too. But right now, killing him took precedence. "Get. Off. Me."

"Not just yet." He settled more comfortably again, and instead of squeezing her wrists, his thumbs caressed. She still couldn't get free.

And her body wasn't in agreement with her mind anyway.

"Now," he asked, "can we agree to talk like two reasonable adults?"

Giving up, Kayli went limp on the floor, lifeless in his hold. She rested her head back with a sigh and stared at the ceiling. "I keep explaining to you, Michael, we have nothing further to discuss."

"I'm still here, babe. You took me from everything familiar to me, and now, over one lousy dispute, you want to kick me to the curb, leaving me floundering about all alone?"

How could he sound so reasonable? That wasn't the situation at all, and yet . . . it sort of was.

"There's no reason for you to flounder and you know it. Numerous women have already made it clear that they'd love to be aligned with you."

"Even your sister, huh?"

Oh, that hurt. "Leave Idola out of this."

"Why? She's a terrible flirt, at least according to Mesha. She did make a few moves, but mostly out of habit I think, not any real interest in me."

Kayli doubted that. How could any woman not be interested in him?

He leaned closer, put his nose near her neck, and began softly nuzzling.

She heard him inhale, slow and deep.

"Michael," she squeaked, almost desperate to interrupt him. His warm mouth touched, light as a butterfly, against her sensitive skin, and his breath teased over her, raising goose bumps. "I would have you still help the colony. We need you if you're willing. But our association—"

"Our union." His voice was gentle, persuasive.

"No." She hated to say it. "That's over."

"Why? Because I screwed up? Hate to break it to you, doll, but it's going to happen again and again. I'm human, and I have flaws."

"No, really?"

"Brat." He smiled, making the insult sound like an endearment. "Being overprotective, especially toward you, is something that's bound to repeat. All I can promise is that I'll try to give you room to do your own thing, but only if you'll allow me to give you better instruction and be a part of any threat you face."

"We've been over this." And then, because it had eaten away at her all night long, Kayli turned her head to look at him. "I have a question for you, Michael. Will you give me an honest answer?"

Wariness had him pulling back a few inches. "Let's hear the question before I commit."

Did she really want to know? Yes, she had to know. If he cared for her, if he loved her a little, then maybe they could work through their differences as he suggested.

But . . . she didn't think that was the case. Bracing for his reply, she drew a fortifying breath. "Aside from the fact that I'm the one who brought you here, and therefore most familiar with you, why do you want me?"

He frowned at her. "Why wouldn't I want you?"

Evasions were the tactics of people who felt cornered. "I'm sorry, Michael, but I need to know." She tried to sit up, but he used gentle leverage to keep her still.

"Settle down." He did adjust some, nudging her legs open so that she held him in a position far too intimate for comfort. "I like you right where you are. It's safer for me."

Like he actually worried about her as an opponent? She didn't think so. More likely, he didn't want to risk putting a scratch on her, and he thought that was best accomplished by keeping her pinned down.

And of course, his worry about her being injured was the crux of the problem. "I know what type of women you gravitated to in your own time."

"I'm all ears."

No, he was all charm and temptation, and she had to fight herself as much as him to stay on course. His preferences in women were well known to her. Remembering those preferences were part of what had kept her awake last night. "You enjoy beautiful, overtly sexual women who don't have a combative bone in their very soft, very feminine bodies."

"Sometimes." Michael shrugged without denial. "What's your point?"

Why did he have to be so deliberately obtuse? "That's not me. That could never be me." Which meant he could never really care for her.

"Oh, I dunno." He bent again and kissed her chin. "Even with all your sleek muscle tone, which I find sexy as hell, by the way, you're still very soft in all the right places." He kissed the very top of her left breast. "Here." He pushed his hips inward. "And on that killer ass of yours."

"Stop that." She could not let him weaken her with physical need. She was stronger than that.

She had to be.

He did stop, but with him so near she felt his sexual interest, could see the striations in his intense blue eyes as they studied her.

"Just making my point, because, lady, whether it's overt or not, you're plenty sexual." He nuzzled into her neck again and sent chills of sensation down her spine. "Last night, the sounds you made, the way you looked and the way you tightened . . ." He growled low. "Damn, baby, it was something to see."

"Michael!"

His gaze burned as he smiled at her. "You were so incredible, I thought I was going to embarrass myself."

She shook her head at him. "The things you say . . ." His outrageous disclosures kept her face hot with embarrassment, but deep inside, she was glad that she'd pleased him.

"You smell incredible, too." Cautiously, he eased closer again to tease the sensitive skin of her throat with his lips and tongue. "I think I'm already addicted to your scent."

Her heart started pumping too hard. Desperate to get her questions answered, she whispered, "I do *not* want you to seduce me, Michael."

"Oh, I think you do." He lowered his voice as he looked at her tightened nipples. "But I would never force you."

"I know that."

"The fact that I *could* seduce you," he continued with confidence, "even now with you still peeved at me, just goes to show how innately sexual you are. Being inexperienced doesn't change that."

Kayli let her eyes narrow. "I'm more than peeved, and you know it."

"Understood." Unfazed, he tucked his hips in the smallest bit, letting her feel his growing erection. "So why don't you tell me what I need to do to make it up to you?"

Love me. Closing her eyes, Kayli held that awesome thought at bay. She drew in a calming breath and when she opened her eyes again, she felt marginally more controlled—or at least, as in control as she could be while lying beneath Michael. "For a start, you could answer my questions."

CHAPTER 17

KAYLI saw Michael give a grievous roll of his eyes. "It's going to be that way, huh?" He softened his complaint with a smile before he leaned down and kissed her. He kept kissing her, over and over, the touch of his mouth always brief but possessive. "All right, babe. We can play things your way."

"I'm not playing." But obviously he was.

Given her mood, he forced more gravity into his tone. "I admire you."

Not trusting that, she asked, "Why?"

"If you have to ask, you must be suffering some severely low self-esteem. Do you really not know how wonderful you are?"

No one had ever called her that before. "I'm just me."

"Mesha adores you. She told me so herself. I think she's suffering a little hero worship, even."

"Truly?" Mesha was very sweet, and she always listened when Kayli gave her advice.

"And why not? On top of being sexy as sin, you're also smart and brave and protective. In fact, you have the same basic sense of protectiveness that I have." His expression turned grave. "And while I'm thinking about it, that brings up a question of my own. You're in the protection business, and I know, regardless of your doubts, that you're damn good at it."

Despite herself, the praise warmed her. "Thank you, Michael."

"So what if another warrior got into trouble, but she was the independent sort and didn't want your help. What would you do, Kayli? Would you let her be hurt?"

He tried to turn the scenario around, to catch her as a hypocrite, but she wouldn't let him. "I hope that I would respect her wishes. At the very least I'd wait to see if she could handle it herself or not."

"It's a tricky thing, to know exactly when to interfere and when to stand back. Add emotion into the mix, and it only gets tougher."

"Emotion?" she asked with a little hope.

"We'll be in a union, remember? That means we'll have a responsibility to each other. The thought of standing by and seeing you hurt is nearly impossible for me."

"Maybe I'd surprise you and *not* be hurt."

"Maybe." He grinned. "But that's just it. I haven't seen you fight except in practice, and playing around with me."

"Playing?" Now that just plain insulted her. True, she hadn't wanted to do him any serious harm, so she hadn't given it her all. Still . . .

"Oh, come on, darlin'." The grin turned to a teasing, dubious smirk as he shook his head at her. "Please tell me you weren't seriously trying to take me out during that little half-baked skirmish?"

Take him out? No. Remove his smug arrogance? Definitely.

But admitting it now would gain her nothing. It would only make her look as temperamental and moody as most non-warrior females. "I know you want to make a point, Michael, so get to it."

"In almost every situation, your instincts would be the

same as mine: to protect. But," he said when she started to speak, "I am trying. You just have to give me time to adjust to the whole role reversal thing here."

That brought Kayli full circle, making her sigh in frustration. "Tell me why, Michael. Why should I give you time? Why do you *want* more time? So you admire me. So what? I'm sure there are other women here you could admire just as much."

"It's possible, but I don't want them." Appearing perplexed, he let out a long breath. "I can't pinpoint what it is about you, Kayli. It's a combination of things, chemistry at its best. It's how you look, how you act and talk, the way you smell and taste, the unique way you make me feel."

He sounded as confused as she, but it was a start. After all, they hadn't really known each other long. For her, it didn't matter; she'd lost her heart the first time he kissed her.

But for him, a man of his experience, wanting someone was pretty routine, not a momentous occasion. "How do I make you feel?"

Frustration showed in his expression, and in the set of his broad shoulders. "Hell, I don't know. Different for sure."

"Different from other women?"

"Well yeah, since I've never met any other woman like you. But I enjoy you." His voice deepened. "I'll enjoy you even more once we're free to be as sexual as I'm dying to be."

Perhaps what she needed to do was give him more time. And then she could not only show him how capable she was, but also give him an opportunity to get used to the different roles women now played.

The problem, of course, was that being in love with him left her wallowing in unfamiliar emotions.

So irresponsible.

So shortsighted.

But it was too late now, at least for her.

She had to do the right thing, for herself and those who

depended on her. If that meant going along with his demands to get his assistance with the intruders, then that was what she would do.

Ready to wade through tricky negotiations, she said, "Let me go, Michael."

With a grumble, he released her wrists and started to sit up.

"Where are you going?" Kayli caught him with a tight hold around his thick neck. His skin was warm, sleek, and the muscle beneath thrilled her.

Cautious, he turned back to her, one of his brows lifted. "Are you forgiving me, or preparing to deck me again?"

Somber, uncertain, she said, "We'll see." She stared into his eyes. "But Michael, if we're to get along at all, you really must do your best to trust in my ability and experience."

"You have my word that I'll give it my best shot." Just as solemn, he said, "And you'll need to do your best to cut me some slack and know that even when I do screw up, it's not an insult to your ability, and it sure as hell doesn't mean I don't trust you."

Feeling more confident now that she'd made her decision, Kayli teased, "It's just because you can't help yourself?"

His grin did funny things to her stomach. "Yeah. You have that effect on me."

She swallowed, nodded. "Michael, I would ask for a concession as we both try to adjust to the differences in our time periods."

He didn't like the idea of a concession at all. "All right. Let's hear it."

She may as well get it out in the open. "I would rather not join in union."

He stiffened, his arms going straight so that he loomed over her. "Now wait a damn minute—"

"But," she said, wanting to finish before he misunderstood, "I want to be intimate with you. I want to share time with you."

Instead of being grateful, umbrage added an edge to his

tone. "So you want to fool around, you just don't want to be stuck with me, is that it?"

In truth, she didn't want him to be stuck with her when he realized he didn't love her and never would. Unwilling to bare her soul that much, she firmed her resolve. "Something like that."

His brief expression of hurt surprised her. But it faded away until he looked more offended, and then angry.

His right eye twitched, his jaw went tight as he stared at her. And after what felt like an eternity, the light of challenge entered his gaze. "Fine. While we're at it, I have some stipulations of my own."

Her heart nearly stopped. "What sort of stipulations?"

"We need to call that town meeting."

"Already done. We meet at noon."

"Perfect. Then we have some time."

Kayli waited, her breath held.

"Before the meeting, I want to show you some better moves. We'll start with the basic stuff, and then after today, we'll spend an hour before each practice with some old-fashioned one-on-one time to finesse what skills you already have." He looked at her mouth. "Just you and me, Kayli. Understood?"

Kayli all but snarled. Maybe she'd cut loose and show *him* a thing or two. "No problem."

"You won't hold back when we're sparring. I need to know exactly what you can do, how fast you can do it." His warm breath brushed over her lips, and he emphasized, "How *hard* you can do it."

Her lips parted.

Michael looked at her mouth, but he didn't move. "And then after practice, instead of running off and hiding from me—"

"I did *not*—"

"I want to see your house."

That wasn't what she expected at all, and it made her mind go blank. He wanted to see her house? But why?

She didn't live there, and he knew it. For her, the house was more about owning property. She wanted something of her own for when she retired—a very long time from now. Eyes narrowing, she asked, "Is there a reason you want to see it?"

"It's a part of you. Let's just say I'm curious and leave it at that."

She had no choice but to accept his explanation. "I can arrange that."

"I want *you* to show it to me, not anyone else. I also want *you* to teach me how to operate the different vehicles you have."

Because she lacked patience, she wasn't the best teacher. But she only shrugged. "Okay."

A smile teased at the corner of his mouth. "I do love an agreeable woman."

Love. Her throat constricted and she went mute.

Michael didn't seem to notice. "But for now, I want to talk to you about . . . other things."

Now what was he up to?

His fingers tunneled into her hair, massaged her scalp, then just held her. "You gave me one hell of a shock this morning."

Did he mean with her attack? He'd deserved it. "You came into my room unannounced."

"And busted you watching that skin flick—"

Her hand smashed over his mouth, cutting off the rest of what he might have wanted to say. Assuming that *skin flick* referred to the sexual images she'd been studying, she told him, "Do *not* bring that up."

He nibbled on her finger, then curled his tongue around it.

Her stomach went all fluttery. She wanted to stop him . . . but then again, she didn't.

It seemed every time Michael touched her, kissed her, he showed her something new, made her feel something different and exciting.

Kissing his way from her wrist, up her arm, over to

her chest, throat, and chin, he left tingling skin in his
wake.

By the time he reached her mouth, she was starving for
him in a way she hadn't known existed. Right before he took
her mouth, he whispered, "Not to hit a sore spot, but it was a
major turn-on to see you watching that."

"Michael," she warned, without much heat.

"Damn, woman, but I do love how you say my name."

He sure felt comfortable flinging that "L" word around a
lot. His good mood and her own overwhelming emotions
battered her resolve.

"There's nothing wrong with watching." He brushed his
mouth along her jaw before settling back to smile at her.
"Next time, if you want, I'll watch with you."

The thought made her dazed with embarrassment. "No,
never."

His hand opened at the side of her face. "In that case, I
guess there's no reason for me to wait to say what's on my
mind."

Bracing herself, Kayli asked, "And that is?"

He caressed with his thumb. "Anything you saw, we can
do. If it interested you, count me in."

Oh wow. She got an immediate image of Michael as the
male star of those movies, naked, sexually aggressive,
aroused to the point of fulfillment.

She wondered if he'd throw back his head, grit his teeth,
and groan long and low as the male in the movie had.

Burgeoning need made her voice thin and a little too
high. "I wasn't . . . sure about some of the things they did.
That is, I didn't know if they were . . ."

The smile widened. "You can ask me anything you want,
and I promise that I'll always give you a straight answer.
And just so you know, I also do a really good show-and-tell.
You might want to keep that in mind in moments of . . .
curiosity."

Kayli imagined that he did, and a dozen questions came
to mind. "When would you want to—"

He sucked in a breath. "No time like the present." And

then he kissed her, and Kayli didn't want him to stop. Ever.

LEAVING half of his twenty-man team behind, Valder and the rest crept into the heart of the colony, using the tall buildings as cover. He didn't see Raemay, but then, he hadn't expected to.

He'd wanted to. Oh yes, he definitely wanted to see the witch. But his Raemay wasn't stupid.

Never that.

Instead he saw many women and a few men milling about. Girls played in the street, outnumbering the boys three to one. He didn't see a single warrior, or a male of any competition.

He didn't see anyone worth taking or challenging.

"Remember," he said to the men behind him, "we are not here to steal away more women."

A grumble of grudging consent was the only reply. Though he knew no man under his leadership would ever go against his will, many were still without mates, and therefore anxious to remedy the situation.

But Lydina, the last woman he'd appropriated, wasn't adjusting well. She didn't seem unhappy, per say, but she continued to deny all the men and her expression remained unemotional, as if carved in stone.

It worried Valder more than he wanted to admit. He was a hard leader, ruthless when need be, but he wasn't a man to force a woman to suffer.

Before her, none had.

Most of the women, unable to find a mate in their own colony, were overjoyed to find more than a few for their choosing.

But not Lydina.

When he heard the feminine giggling, Valder sought the source and located a pleasingly plump, dark-haired waif. She was smiling, talking intimately to a scrawny fellow who showed signs of honey-dipped joy over her nearness. Before they parted ways, he took her hand and kissed it briefly. After he'd gone, the woman sighed wistfully, put her hands to her heart in melodrama fit only for females, and closed her eyes.

The very young woman was rounded in an adorable way that Valder knew his men would appreciate, so he made his tone stern as he cautioned them.

"Her," Valder said. "I'll grab her, and we'll question her. Nothing more."

As the girl began strolling again, she paid little attention to her surroundings or any possible danger. Smiling, Valder was about to step out in front of her when the young man suddenly turned and called out to her, saying, "Mesha!"

She ran to him as if she hadn't seen him in ages. The young man peeked around, didn't know he was watched, and kissed her, quick and light.

Hand-in-hand, they veered off in a different direction.

Disgusted, Valder watched them walking away until another woman came into range. This one was older, not quite as attractive but still appealing, especially to a group of men suffering from a shortage of females.

Before he lost another opportunity, Valder came out from behind the building.

"Hello, darlin'."

She stopped abruptly and stared at him with widening blue eyes. Pink tinged her skin as she took in his size and unfamiliar clothes. Strangely, she didn't appear afraid so much as intrigued.

"Hello." She looked around, confused by his sudden presence. "Are you new here?"

"Very new."

Head tipping to the side, mouth twitching with a nervous smile, she inched closer—and within reach. "Are you a friend of Michael's?"

Assuming she drew a correlation from their heights, he asked, "Big fellow, loud and pushy?"

"Yes, that's him." She started to relax. She even eyed him

head to toe with appreciation. "I didn't realize that he'd brought any friends with him."

Valder smiled over her assumption. "We know each other on a basic level. You see, darlin', we're adversaries—whether he knows it yet or not."

"Adversaries? But then that must mean . . ." Without finishing that thought, she tried to dash away. Valder caught her before she even got turned around. Clamping a hand on her mouth, he dragged her back behind the building. Her wild thrashing did her no good, and Valder tried to calm her by shushing into her ear and saying nonsense words of comfort.

"Easy now, woman. I won't hurt you. I only want to ask you some questions."

The second he uncovered her mouth, she screeched. Quickly, Valder clamped a hand over her mouth to silence her again. He held her back tightly to his chest, and bent low to speak into her ear.

Her long, curly hair tangled as she continued to struggle with him.

His men watched on, some of them frowning in concern, some unwillingly drawn to survey her lush body. His second in command, Toller Bryn, had an altogether different look that Valder recognized too well.

Toller wanted her.

"Woman," Valder warned, anxious to have this bit of business over with, "that won't do. I only need you to stand here a few moments, to quietly answer my questions, and then I'll let you go. But if you can't collect yourself, I'll have to take you back to my colony with me—where no one will hear your screams."

Toller didn't like the threat, but he held himself silent.

"Which would you prefer?"

She pondered the question for far too long, drew an uneven breath, and stopped fighting him.

"Better." Valder regretted the need for brute force. She might have ample padding, but she was still a woman, delicate as only a woman could be. "Shall I take that for agreement?"

She nodded.

Cautiously, Valder lifted his hand.

She stepped away from him, turned to slowly face him. In a defiant pose that he admired, she asked, "What do you want?"

"I already told you. A few answers, nothing more."

She cast a cautious glance around at his men, and got caught on Toller's intent stare. She blinked, forced her gaze back to Valder, and said, "I'll try."

"Good choice." He crossed his arms over his chest. "Let's start with your name."

"I am Nayana."

Nodding, Valder asked, "And the other girl? The one who was just before you?" He shrugged toward where he could still barely see her with her beau. Why it mattered to him, he couldn't say, but he felt compelled to know her identity.

"That one is Mesha Raine, daughter of the Arbiter."

Valder's heart slammed into his ribs. He felt his men stirring around him, saw the confusion on the woman's face. "She is Raemay's daughter?"

"One of them, yes." Her gaze was far too astute. "You know our Arbiter?"

"I did. Years ago." He needed a moment to collect himself, but that was a luxury that'd have to wait. He should have known; he'd seen the resemblance in the petite build, the smoldering eyes, the dark, silky hair. "She resembles her mother."

"As does Idola."

"Ah, Idola. The reason for my visit." New inspiration came to him, and Valder held out his arms. "I need to see Idola, but it's a surprise, so I don't want anyone to know."

Nayana's brows pinched down with suspicion. "See her for what?"

"As I told you, I haven't seen Raemay for many years. I'd like to set up a . . . reunion." And what a reunion it would be. He could barely wait to witness Raemay's reaction. He would bring her to her knees—which was where she'd left him after she'd run away. He shook his head, knowing he needed to advance one step at a time. "I want to surprise her. As the heir, Idola can assist me."

"I see." Nayana didn't look entirely convinced, but she wasn't alarmed, either. She kept glancing at Toller, distracted by his presence and the way he focused on her. "When did you know our Arbiter?"

"It's been more than twenty years, before she married and had children." He fashioned a look of concern. "I understand that her husband passed away."

"Yes." She said nothing more for several moments, then she looked around at all of them. "I am a loyal member of my colony, as well as a close friend of Raemay's. I will not betray her."

Valder's brows went up. "No one asked you—"

"Neither am I stupid." She said it in a chastising way. "You are the infiltrators, the ones we are at odds with." She turned to Toller. "You are the men who are stealing women, are you not?"

Toller gave a slow, lazy smile. "The women we've taken have no complaints."

"Truly? We had all wondered since we never heard back from them."

Because Toller stepped forward, Valder allowed him to explain. He had a feeling they'd be taking another woman after all.

"We have yet to allow them correspondence, but it is their only restriction. Most have taken union with men from my colony. They have set up homes, and they are happy."

"Then why not let them—"

Toller put a finger to her mouth, silencing her. "You ask too many questions, Nayana. There are things that do not concern you." He traced her mouth. "Make up your mind right now."

She swallowed. Against Toller's finger, she asked, "About what?"

"We will not take you by force—but I would be pleased if you came with me all the same."

Valder sighed. "We haven't found out what we need to know."

"But we will," Toller told him. "Isn't that right, Nayana?"

Her chin lifted, and her eyes challenged them all. "Perhaps I will go with you, and if I agree that the women are happy, then . . . I may choose to assist you."

Toller turned to Valder. "She rides with me."

"Of course."

As they all started to exit, Valder again looked toward Mesha, but she was no longer in sight.

Raemay's daughter.

If Raemay hadn't betrayed him, she could have been *his* daughter, too. He'd missed out on so much, on family and home and love . . .

That damned lump formed in his throat. Damn near twenty-five years was far too long to pine after a woman. When he finished with Raemay, she'd be exorcised from his soul, once and for all.

CHAPTER 18

D ETERMINED to win her over the old-fashioned way, with hot sex, Mallet turned up the charm and the seduction. "Tell me what you want to know, Kayli. Tell me what you saw?"

She chewed her bottom lip, making him a little crazed. Her fingers caressed his nape, and every so often, she squirmed, moving her body against his, amping up his desire.

"Do men really . . . well . . . kiss women *everywhere*?"

Oh hell yes. *Easy*, Mallet, he cautioned himself. She sounded very tempted, but also tentative, so he couldn't jump her the way he wanted.

Moving slowly, he went to the side of her and brought his hands to her breasts. "Here, definitely."

Bending one knee, she shifted and licked her bottom lip. "I know. You already kissed me there. It was . . . I felt it everywhere."

"Between your legs?"

She nodded.

Hold on, Mallet. Go slow. He fingered a middle seam in

her tunic, but couldn't quite figure out the opening. "How does this fasten?"

Kayli put shaking fingertips in the neck, tugged, and it parted down the middle like silent Velcro.

Hotly anticipating his pleasure at seeing her again, Mallet opened it the rest of the way, leaving her upper body exposed.

She didn't wear a bra, and the top all but fell away. "Futuristic chicks wear some awesome clothes." He loved looking at her, at her delicate breasts with the rosy nipples, her narrow midriff, her hip bones and concave belly.

She held herself rigid, breath suspended in expectation of what he'd do.

When he only looked at her, enjoying the sight too much to rush himself, she asked, "Are you going to kiss me there?"

"Damn straight." He covered each bare breast with a palm, loving the contrast of his big dark hands on her delicate pale body. "Soon."

She gave a small groan of protest.

Her nipples were already taut, and as Mallet cuddled her, her breathing quickened. "Patience, honey. Before we go there, I want your mouth."

"Okay." Anxious to get things rolling, she leaned up to meet him halfway. This time she knew exactly what to do. At the first touch of his tongue, her lips parted, and she welcomed a deep, scorching kiss that quickly ran out of control.

He'd made out plenty of times, but never with anyone like Kayli. Everything he did with her was different and fresh and better.

Hotter.

More personal.

He left her mouth to kiss her throat, and then worked his way down to her right breast. Teasing her, he got close to her nipple without actually touching her there.

At the same time, he toyed with her left breast, rolling his thumb over the ripe peak, stroking around it. Just as he closed fingers and thumb on that nipple, he sucked the other nipple into his mouth.

Kayli lurched up with a sound of primal pleasure; her hands caught his biceps, her fingertips dug deep into the muscles.

"The way I'm kissing you here, Kayli . . ." He drew her in again, worked her with his tongue, taunted with his teeth. "That's how I'll kiss you between your legs."

Just saying it fired his blood. With agonizing slowness, Mallet drifted one hand down over her trembling belly, between her parted thighs, until he cupped her. "Right here."

She gave a ragged moan of understanding, but for Mallet, it wasn't enough. It wouldn't be enough until he tasted her pleasure, until he heard her coming.

"Let's get the rest of these clothes off of you." He sat up and helped her get her arms out of the tunic, and then stripped the stretchy, trim-fitting pants down and off her long, slim legs.

He thought she'd be modest, but instead, she rushed him, ridding herself of the clothes as fast as she could. As soon as she was bare, she reached for his shirt.

Mallet stilled her hands. "Hold up, baby. One of us has to stay dressed or I'll forget myself."

"But I want—"

"Yeah, me, too." He held her knees and pressed her thighs wide apart.

Automatically she started to close her legs to conceal herself, but Mallet held her open, and she slumped back in shock. "Michael?"

"God, woman, you are beautiful." He stared at her sex, all soft and pink and now, because she was excited, glistening wet. His heart pounded as he put his fingers on her, stroking a little, feeling her, enjoying the easy glide and the heat.

Mallet lifted his gaze to hers. "Right here, Kayli." Spreading her moisture, he moved his thumb over her clitoris, and heard her sharp inhalation. He smiled. "Right here is where I'll kiss you. I'll suck you into my mouth, tease you with my tongue, and you'll love it so much, you'll come for me."

Her chest rose in frantic tandem with her breaths. She stared at him, face flushed, lips parted. "Okay."

Damn, but her agreement nearly did him in.

With a groan, Mallet bent and bit her soft belly, left a hickey on her hip bone, put more love bites on her inner thighs, behind her right knee.

She shifted and moaned and lifted her hips to encourage him.

Moving down between her legs, Mallet parted her. She sucked in a breath and went perfectly still, waiting, waiting . . . He gave her one long, leisurely lick that sent shudders through her body. While she was still reacting to that, he closed his mouth around her.

Sucking gently at her turgid clitoris, he felt her swell, inhaled her tangy scent. He wanted to fuck her so badly, he wasn't sure he'd be able to stop himself this time.

But for now, for this moment, this intimacy was enough. Her pleasure, her open acceptance of him and the carnality they shared, made him determined to help her feel everything that she could.

Her hips rocked up to meet the rhythm of his tongue. Mallet reached up for her breasts and plied her nipples with just the right touches, alternating the pressure to keep her tight with expectation.

Her moan was long and ragged. Her feet settled on his shoulders and her thighs opened more. Her head tipped back, eyes squeezed shut and jaw clenched. As the pressure built in her, her body bowed, strong in her reach for release.

To keep her still, Mallet flattened one hand to her belly, clamped his other hand on her thigh, and seconds later she climaxed. Her long, shuddering cry sounded raw and real, and it was more exciting than anything he'd ever heard.

Her pleasure demolished his good intentions.

Rising up over her in a rush, Mallet took her mouth hard, startling her, demanding from her.

He pressed a hand between her legs, fingered her slick, swollen lips and, unable to stop, he pushed past her natural resistance.

As she lost the badge of her virginity, she cried out again, this time in a twinge of pain.

"Oh God," Mallet said against her mouth, feeling her tighten around his finger, feeling the incredible smallness of her, knowing how good she'd feel around his cock. "Did I hurt you?"

"Yes, a little."

"You're all mine, Kayli." Knowing it to be true, he struggled with raging need. She was his, his alone. No other man had touched her.

No other man ever would.

He swallowed down emotion so strong, it overwhelmed him. This wasn't sex. He didn't know what the fuck this was—but he liked it. "I'm sorry."

"It's okay." Her hips twitched again, this time seeking. Sounding awed, she whispered, "You're . . . inside me."

"Not the way I want to be. Not the way I will be after we're in a union." What the hell was he saying? He couldn't wait that long. He'd never outlast her. "Kayli—"

"Okay."

Her naked breasts were against his chest, her heartbeat thundering, her sex squeezing around his finger . . . It was understandable that his brain didn't want to function properly. "What?"

"Okay, I'll join you in union." Her arms came around his neck and she pressed her face against his throat. "I don't think I can wait, though. Can we do it tonight?"

He didn't want to misunderstand. "It?"

"The ceremony." She opened her mouth on his skin, licked him, and then returned one of his love bites before whispering, "And have sex."

Mallet reared up to catch her gaze. His hand was still between her legs, and she was so damn wet.

So ready for him.

He opened his mouth—and Hauk said, "I really do hate to intrude, but there's an incident that requires your attention."

Mallet groaned. Although he wasn't at all sure if a computer could actually *see* them or not, he disentangled himself from Kayli's sweet body. Talk about *bad* fucking timing . . .

Kayli covered her face, sucked in a couple of deep breaths, and then dropped her arms to her sides. With her head back and her eyes closed in dismay, she asked Hauk, "Whose attention? Michael's or mine?"

"Not for me to say. But Kayli, after you ordered a reconnaissance of the colony's perimeter, the men now in training found out. They're highly insulted that only women were ordered to take part in the current security. They, along with many women from defense, are gathered in the training field, looking for one or both of you to settle the matter."

Mallet wanted to tell Hauk to go away, but knowing how important Kayli's responsibilities were to her, he dredged up a pained smile and cupped the side of her face.

"Do you need a minute?"

She opened her eyes and stared at him with raw emotions he didn't want to identify. "No. But what about you?"

"I'll survive." He sat up beside her. "Barely."

After she scrambled to cover herself, he asked, "So what do you want to do?"

"About?" She got her top on easily enough, but he'd turned her pants inside out when he stripped them away.

"The men. I think they're ready to help out, but it's your decision. You've been handling things long enough to know what's best."

She paused in the middle of dressing herself, and blinked at him. After a moment, she smiled and, making an obvious concession, asked, "I would enjoy your opinion before I decide."

Mallet knew an olive branch when he saw one. He grinned, too. "Fair enough." He hauled her to her feet. Without looking away from her golden eyes, he said, "Get lost, Hauk. You can tell the rioting horde that we'll be there shortly."

"Understood." Hauk didn't say another word.

"He's gone?"

"Yes." Her smile went crooked. "I doubt they're actually rioting."

"Who cares?" Mallet cupped her face in his hands and put his forehead to hers. "Promise me one thing, honey, okay?"

"What is it?"

"We'll have that union tonight, no matter what."

Her small hand briefly moved over the bulge behind his fly. "Tonight. I would insist even if you did not." Then she took his hand and started them on their way, and Mallet wondered if he'd live through the rest of the day.

THRILLED that Michael had deferred to her, Kayli listened without prejudice to his advice. It made sense to her, and they came to an agreement before they'd reached the training fields.

As she stepped off the aircycle, she asked him, "Do you want to tell them, or should I?"

"Go ahead. I'll just go with you to back you up."

Back her up. Yes, that's what she'd always wanted, and now Michael seemed determined to give it to her. Of course, the real test would be when they faced the actual threat, but she'd deal with that when she had to.

Hopefully there'd be plenty of time before that eventuality where she could better showcase her skills for him.

Until then, she just wanted to enjoy him. Being with him again in such an intimate way . . . well, it just heightened everything she felt. Physically, he was a beautiful man, rock solid with muscles and very handsome of face.

He was so big through the chest and shoulders that she couldn't get her arms all the way around him. Even the smallest movement he made sent muscles rippling and bulging.

And yet, when he touched her, he was so sweet, so incredibly gentle.

How could she possibly stay angry at him?

Michael took her hand as they walked toward the dais where she'd address the disgruntled men and righteous women. Along the way, Kayli spotted her mother. She stood off to the side with Idola, both looking harassed by the circumstances.

It was very uncommon for them to have two gatherings of large, angry crowds in such a short time.

When they reached the platform, Michael let go of her and put his hand at the small of her back. Everyone went silent, watching them.

"Michael and I have discussed the situation, and together, we've made a decision." No one spoke. No one even moved. "Because the women are best trained and most familiar with the duty of protecting the colony, at least half of those patrolling the perimeter will always be established defense members. However, the men are quickly learning what they need to know, so we will alternate the front line with long-time defense members and newly recruited men. That'll give us better coverage of the area."

There was some grumbling from the women, both from warriors and non-warriors. Of the non-warriors, a few got extra attention from their men as they spoke in their ears, offering comfort and reassurance.

The defense team got ribbed, until a couple of the women tossed the guys, shutting them up.

Kayli hid her grin. "Save the energy for when we start practice. Now, Michael has some things to add to our new strategy."

She nodded to Michael, indicating it was his turn.

The corner of his sexy mouth tipped up, and he nodded back before addressing the crowd. "So that those on patrol will remain alert, we'll change shifts every four hours. Kayli will make up the schedule, and you'll all stick to it. Do not be late when it's your turn to relieve someone, and don't balk when it's your turn to step down. In between shift changes, we'll continue our training."

One of the men stepped forward. "What will we work on next?"

Clasping his hands behind his back, Michael said, "Now that you're all in better fighting shape, I want to work on some defensive moves. The men we'll go up against are a lot bigger than you. But that won't matter if you know what to do. Because it's a certainty that you'll get knocked down, we'll start practicing how to get back to your feet fast."

Kayli watched as Michael took over—again—but this

time it didn't bother her. The ability to lead was one of the qualities that had drawn her to him, and since he was being fair about it, she saw no reason to hold her grudge.

She faded back; when he didn't notice, she left the platform and joined her mother. She could still hear Michael explaining.

"Once I think you have that down," he said, "we'll work on submissions that don't require brawn as much as speed and technique. Even if you're knocked to the ground, there are ways to bring your opponent down, too, so that you'll be in the dominant position."

Raemay shook her head. "They hang on his every word."

"He's a good speaker," Kayli agreed. "And he knows what he's talking about."

Idola stared toward Michael, but spoke to Kayli. "When will you join him in union?" Her lashes fluttered, as if she had mixed feelings on the matter. "Or have you changed your mind about that?"

"Actually," Kayli said, taking advantage of the opening, "we decided to do the ceremony tonight."

Raemay stirred. "Tonight?"

"Does that not please you?"

"It should," Idola said. "You and your man have caused quite a bit of gossip, and many of the women are now anxious to follow your lead."

Lifting a brow, Kayli asked, "What does that mean?"

Raemay waved a hand. "It's nothing, really. It's just that some of the colony members have expressed a hope that your behavior will become acceptable."

"My behavior?"

"Oh, don't be coy, Kayli." Idola smiled, and there wasn't any real animosity in the amusement. "You and Michael have been most . . . demonstrative in your affection. It surprises many, me included, because we never saw that side of you. Somehow it makes you much more human."

Kayli frowned.

"Before Michael, we viewed you as almost superhuman

in your dedication. But now . . . well, if you don't join in
union soon, we could see many couples forgoing the tradition of a formal ceremony."

"Nonsense." Raemay grew flustered. "Your sister would
never be so improper."

"Thank you, Mother," Kayli said, and she almost choked
on the gratitude. If they hadn't been interrupted, she'd be
back in her rooms right now, being *very* improper with Michael.

Idola winked. "Not that I am entirely against such a
change. It would be most freeing."

"Tonight then," Raemay said in a rush. "Shall I make the
arrangements?"

"Yes, please. I would like to stay here and work with Michael and the others."

"I'll help Mother," Idola offered. "And I bet Mesha will
want to be involved, too. Do not worry, sister, we'll organize
everything." She shooed Kayli away. "Go, take care of your
duties."

Because she couldn't think of any reason not to, Kayli
did just that.

Michael had already joined the men on the ground, starting their practice hours earlier than originally planned.
Kayli doubted if anyone had had a proper meal yet, but no
one complained.

The women vied to outdo the men, and the men wanted
to prove themselves worthy of Michael's trust. The end result was that everyone worked extra hard.

Michael exhibited a move, allowing one of the trainees to
throw him to the ground. He rebounded to his feet so fast, it
was almost as if he never went down. Kayli watched with
interest, but she wasn't a woman to stand by idly when she
could be physically involved.

She stepped forward. "Try it with me."

And Michael, with a twinkle in his eyes, held out a hand.
"Whatever you say, sweet."

CHAPTER 19

MALLET drew Kayli in close—maybe even a little closer than necessary. "You've been watching?"

"Yes."

"I'm going to toss you, and I want you to—"

She surprised him by tossing him first. He hit the ground hard on his back, shot back to his feet, and grabbed her to swing her in a wide circle while he laughed out loud.

To their audience, he said, "And that, folks, is how it's done!"

Kayli laughed, too, which made smiles appear on many faces.

Enjoying their new camaraderie, Mallet put her back on her feet. "Sneaky wench. Is it my turn to drop you now?"

"All right."

He knew better than to temper his strength too much, but there was no way in hell he'd hurt her. He wouldn't put his all into practice with any woman. He wanted them to learn, and they would, but not by getting bruised.

He put Kayli down, and she got back up faster than he'd

expected, but not yet as fast as she'd need to be. After instructing her, he set up teams, men with women to help
balance things, and set them all to practicing.

It was pretty hilarious, really, given that the trained
women were so much better than the men. But the men, taking his example, laughed at their own shortcomings, and
teased the women about their strengths. And they learned.
All of them.

He now understood why his friends enjoyed coaching so
much. Both Dean and Simon had left the ring to train other
fighters, and they seemed as content doing that as engaging
in the actual competitions.

It was a rewarding thing, to see others learn from his instruction.

They broke for a rest, with the agreement that those not
on patrol would return in the late afternoon for more lessons. The respite would give everyone a chance for a light
meal.

Before Kayli could come to him, Mallet sought out Raemay. "I need assistance."

She was in conversation with a group of young girls, but
at his interruption, she excused herself. "How may I help
you, sir?"

"Michael. If we're going to be family, you can't call me
sir."

"As you wish."

"I'm sorry to interrupt, but . . ." He ran a hand over his
head, aware of Kayli watching him from some distance
away. How long did he have before she came after him?
"Kayli and I will join in union tonight."

"So she told me. I was just instructing some of our young
ones on the occasion. They will help with making announce-
ments and gathering flowers."

"The thing is . . . I don't have a ring for Kayli."

"A ring?"

"Yeah. You know, a ring to give her. I assume you have
places to buy them here, but I'm pretty sure my credit cards
have expired."

She smiled. "It is a lovely thought, Michael, but the tradition of giving the woman a symbolic ring ended a long time ago. If a woman wants jewelry she can purchase it for herself."

It figured that in even this, he'd be out of the loop. "So call me old-fashioned, but I want to give Kayli something. If not a ring, then what do you suggest?"

Raemay thought for a moment, then nodded. "I do understand. Sometimes a gift is simply a gesture of caring." She studied him. "And you care for her?"

"Yeah, I do."

Her smile warmed. "At first, I worried, maybe more than I should have. But I think you will be good for my daughter."

"Count on it."

Pulling a ring from her right hand, Raemay said, "This was a very special gift given to me a long time ago. I had thought to one day pass it on to Kayli, but now . . . I think there will never be a better time."

Mallet stared at the ring. It was a delicate piece of work with a thin, braided silver band and an intricate heart topped with a natural pearl. "It's beautiful, Raemay, but I didn't mean—"

She folded his hands around it. "Please, I insist. The ring has much meaning for me, and for Kayli."

Mallet didn't like the way she said that. "For Kayli? How so?"

But Raemay shook her head. "It is not important." Her smile now was tremulous and determined. "Just know that wearing it may bring Kayli added protection when she encounters conflicts outside our colony."

Again, Mallet examined the ring. But it was more the look in Raemay's face that convinced him. He tucked the ring deep into his pocket and, taking her by surprise, pulled Raemay into a big bear hug that lifted her off her small feet. "Thank you."

When he set her down again, she was bright pink and laughing. "Go on with you." Patting her hair, she said, "Here comes Kayli. Will you give her the ring now?"

"In private, if that's okay."

"It suits perfectly." And with that, Raemay waved to Kayli and turned to go the opposite way.

When she reached him, Mallet held out a hand. "You hungry, babe?"

"A little." Kayli used a forearm to dab sweat from her brow as she watched her mother's retreat. "What did you discuss with my mother?"

"Just making peace with her, that's all."

Appearing unconvinced, Kayli said, "I'm relieved. As our Arbiter, it is important that you get along with her."

"I was more concerned with her role as your mother, but whatever." He drew her around to face him. "You ever been on a picnic?"

Confused, she shook her head.

"It's where you pack some food and eat outside, usually under a nice shade tree. I thought if you were game, we could grab something simple and head off by ourselves. Along the way, you could tell me how to operate the aircycle."

"How much time do we have?"

"Enough. I promise to be a fast learner."

A little dubious, she shrugged. "Okay."

Obviously his plan had worked even better than he'd expected. He'd given her just a few small tastes of sexual pleasure, and she'd turned into an agreeable, adoring woman.

She pleased him so much that Mallet had to kiss her. "I can't wait till tonight."

"The ceremony?"

"After that." He tucked her in close and hugged her. "But speaking of the ceremony . . . I have no idea how this all works. I don't need to dress up, do I?"

"Somewhat. I'll have Hauk supply you with appropriate clothing."

"Nothing pansy-ass, okay?"

She laughed. "Denim is not appropriate, nor is the clothing you wear for practices. But I will endeavor to suit your demeanor."

"Yeah, whatever that means."

"It means, nothing pansy-ass."

Mallet laughed, and it seemed he didn't stop laughing for hours. The instruction she gave him on the aircycle was almost comical. She was an incredible trainer, but when it came to teaching anything else . . . her patience ran thin. She expected him to get all the nuances on the first go-around.

He had an affinity for all things mechanical so he didn't disappoint her. And still she was a harsh taskmaster, grumbling about every little thing until he abruptly stopped the aircycle, wrestled her to the ground, and tickled her till she cried for mercy.

While he had her down, he showed her a few moves far progressed from the routine training they'd been doing with the others.

No matter how complicated the move, Kayli caught on quick.

What she lacked in muscle she made up for with speed, technique, and agility. Mallet tried a hold on her, and through a little fumbling, allowed her to get him in a rear naked choke. She squeezed—but he was laughing too hard to take the move seriously.

That is, until she got her knees in his back, and really cranked. He tapped her arm, letting her know she had the upper hand, and she turned him loose.

She was on her feet before he drew in a long, much-needed breath.

Every bit as cocky as a seasoned MMA fighter, she stood with her hands on her hips and a victorious smile on her mouth. She wasn't breathing hard. She hadn't strained herself overly.

More proud than he should have been, Mallet stood and grinned down at her. "Not too shabby, Kayli. If I'd been a real threat, you could have forced me to pass out."

"Yeah right." She gave him a playful slug in his shoulder. "Except that you *let* me get you in the choke in the first place."

"Trust me, most men will let you get them in that hold. They won't know enough to avoid it. But you've got the knowledge, and you know how to use it to your advantage. As long as you can stay calm in a crisis situation—and Mesha swears that you do—then I think you'll do great."

She glowed, that was the only word for it. Mallet knew then how much his doubt had hurt her. He felt like an ass, and vowed to do his best never to underestimate her again.

HOURS later Mallet found himself standing before a large crowd, dressed all in white. He felt like the freakin' bride, or maybe a sacrificial virgin. The clothes were comfortable enough, with loose drawstring pants, a billowing tunic-style shirt, and sandals.

When Kayli, flanked by her sisters, strode onto the scene in a long dark dress, he felt especially out of place being all in white.

She looked like she was headed to a funeral. Well, except that her eyes glowed and her lush mouth held a timid smile that promised him unspeakable pleasure.

The long sleeveless gown made her look even taller, slimmer. She wore no makeup, but a faint blush colored her cheeks. As she walked, Mallet saw that she wore dainty slip-on black sandals.

Spellbound, he watched her. Hard to believe that soon she'd be his.

Raemay appeared at his side. "She looks lovely, doesn't she?"

Mallet had to admit that the contrast of her pale blond hair and golden eyes against the sleek black gown was stunning. "Yeah." He couldn't look away from her.

Her sisters were decked out in fancy-wear too, but they wore pastel colors.

"It may be the only time either of us will see her in a gown."

Mallet grinned. "She looks great whatever she wears."
Or doesn't wear.

"I'd like to talk with you."

"Again?" Seeing that Kayli was engaged with the others, he offered Raemay his arm. "Let's find a quiet spot then, but not too far. I don't want Kayli to think I'm bailing on her."

Slipping her arm through his, Raemay shared a genuine smile. "She would not. From the time you've been with us, you've made it embarrassingly clear that you care for her."

Now if only Kayli would realize it. "So what's up now?"

"Today, when you wanted a symbol for Kayli . . . You've surprised me, that's all. Before knowing you, I expected a man of brute force, who would live that lifestyle. But you're unexpected in many ways. You joke around—far too often as a rule—and I've heard only praise about you from those in training. So I . . ." She stopped them near a pillar, just out of range from where the union would be blessed. "I felt I owed you an apology."

"Why, Raemay," he joked, pretending to stagger with a hand on his heart. "You'll put me in a faint with that lavish praise."

She shook her head at him. "Oh stop. You're a terrible tease."

Mallet wanted to sit down, or lean on something. But he just knew he'd get dirty and that might ruin Kayli's big day. "You were worried about your daughter. I get that."

She stared toward Kayli. "Things aren't always what they seem."

"With you?"

"No, I meant with . . . people. With . . . men." Flustered, she took a few steps away. "I have found it's best to go forward with caution."

Feeling his way, Mallet asked, "You're talking about in romance?"

"In life," she snapped, then immediately showed regret for her tone. "I'm sorry, it's just that you have turned my assumptions upside down."

Gently, Mallet told her, "Assumptions are like that—not very solid." Niggling suspicion crawled in, stirring his protective instincts. "Raemay, did some jerk hurt you? Physically, I mean?"

She went so still that Mallet felt his anger surging toward that unknown man, that unknown situation.

Unable to take the stricken look on her face, he promised, "It won't happen again. Not while I'm around. If the asshole shows up, just point me in his direction. Understand?"

She blinked hard and fast, twittered on a disbelieving laugh, and quickly covered her mouth. "Thank you." She got herself together and smoothed her hair. "As I said, you are . . . unexpected. But enough about all this. This is your and Kayli's day, and I didn't mean to intrude with my silly concerns."

Mallet put a hand to her shoulder. "Hey, for better or worse, you're my family now, right? Your concerns aren't silly."

Her expression almost crumbled. "Thank you. Again."

Kayli stepped in close at his side. "Mother?"

"I'm fine." She twittered again, sounding almost like a schoolgirl. Then she held out her arms. "Oh my. I never thought to see this day. You look beautiful, dear."

Kayli embraced her. "Thank you."

Mesha and Idola joined them. They, too, were full of smiles over the forthcoming ceremony.

Mesha grinned up at Mallet and asked with mock sternness, "Did you twist her arm, sir?"

"Several times," Mallet admitted. He flicked Mesha on the end of her nose. "Getting your sister to the altar was not an easy feat."

"Altar?" Idola asked.

Being surrounded by Kayli's family wasn't an altogether unpleasant situation. With Kayli in a dress instead of loose-fitting fighting wear, they made a show of pure femininity.

But as always, Kayli stood out with her different colored hair and eyes, so different from the rest of the colony.

"Altars are where we held weddings, our version of unions, back in my time frame."

Idola was very serious. "Here, we have the ceremony in front of the reception hall so that all of the colony can join in." She gestured, and Mallet looked around.

Without him noticing, streets had become crowded with people, and with the high ratio of women to men, there were a lot of flowers everywhere. It seemed every woman wore them in her hair and carried them in her arms.

"They must have razed the landscape to gather together so many blooms."

"They all adore Kayli," Mesha said, as if that explained it.

"The flowers are thrown after the ceremony as a sign of acceptance." Idola squinted through the bright sunshine, one hand on her head to keep her hair in place against the cooling breeze. "Though I always assumed I'd be the first to join in union, I'm pleased to see so much support. Not just for Kayli, who has always been a very important part of our colony, but for you, too."

To Mallet, it seemed that Idola also wanted to make amends. "I'm sure you'll have a union whenever you want it, Idola."

"Of course," she said without thought. "But I am particular and will wait until I find the right man."

Dryly, Mallet said, "Good thinking."

"Oh, I did not mean that Kayli is rushing the matter. Not at all." She faced Mallet, far more serious than the situation warranted. "Kayli has inspired me to patience. I want to wait until I find a man who will adore me as you adore her."

"Idola!" Kayli protested.

"But I do," Mallet told her with a kiss to her hot cheek.

"He does," Mesha agreed, and she laughed at her sister's embarrassment. "I believe I have found my man. He's not like Michael, but he is wonderful."

Flabbergasted by that revelation, Raemay started to speak to her youngest daughter, then appeared to think better of it. "I'm not surprised by the colony's support," Raemay stated. "It seems that people like a modicum of change on occasion."

Mallet slipped his arm around his very quiet woman. "What do you think, Kayli? Do you like change?"

"Some, perhaps." She turned her face up to him. "You've brought many good changes. I have hope that, with your help and so many additions to the defense, we'll soon be able to get back all of our members."

Mallet sighed. Even now, on such an important personal day, her mind was on her duty. At least in part.

Once he had her alone, he had no doubt that her thoughts would turn carnal.

Raemay began steering them toward the front of the wide stairway. While everyone found their position and their audience continued to whisper, he asked Kayli, "Is it customary for the guy to wear white and the woman to wear black?"

Showing uncustomary timidity, she smoothed her hands over his chest and stared at his chin. "The white signifies that you come to this union with your soul free of doubts or regrets."

"True enough." He held her upper arms and fought the urge to jump the gun and kiss her.

"Black for the bride represents that she's leaving her old life behind, giving herself to a new life in union, forever shared with another." Her fingers fretted on the seam of his shirt, and she met his gaze with worry. "Once the ceremony is complete, we can never change our minds. We can never leave the union."

Emotion burned inside Mallet. "Do you think you'd want to?"

"No." Her lashes fluttered. "But you—"

Damn it, he lost his head and scooped her in for a ravenous, dead-serious kiss. "No."

Limp in his arms, Kayli stared at him. Then she swallowed. "I think you just messed up the ceremony."

He looked around and saw everyone staring. Then Dormius grinned, and beside him, Mesha laughed. One by one, the Council Mavens joined in. Even Raemay fought a grin.

"Shit. I'm sorry."

She put her forehead to his chest and snickered.

Raemay held up her hands for silence. When everyone

quieted, she addressed the assembly. "We're going a little out of order, but with our guest, that is not uncommon."

Folks chuckled again.

She faced the Council Mavens. "I trust you all approve this union?"

One by one, they stepped forward and offered their consent.

Raemay looked out at the colony members. "What say you?"

The cheers were deafening.

Kayli tugged at his neck, and when Mallet looked down at her, she shouted about the noise, "*Now* we should kiss. Just as a formality."

He was so edgy with new and unfamiliar sentiment that it took a lot of control to kiss her as was proper, instead of how he wanted. Cuddling her close in his embrace, Mallet bent her back just a little, and planted one on her.

They were pelted with flowers of a dozen varieties, all of them fragrant and colorful, until they stood surrounded by the blooms.

Mallet kept her close as he fished the ring out of his pocket. "I know it's not customary for your colony, or in this time frame, but none of this felt right for me without a ring to give you, so . . ." He lifted her hand and slipped it on her ring finger.

"Michael." She blinked fast with a rush of emotion. "Thank you."

"It was your mother's, but she insisted I take it instead of getting you a new one."

Curling her fingers around the ring, Kayli nodded. "I have always admired it. That you would want it for me matters more than the item itself."

Idola tapped Mallet's shoulder. "Sir? You must present yourself to the colony now, hands held, before you depart. They're waiting."

Kayli pulled away, squeezed his hand, and together, they joined Raemay.

The old girl had tears in her eyes, and that, too, made Mallet full with good feelings. Raemay did love her daughter. Maybe not the way he thought a mother should. Or maybe she had her reasons for her odd reserve around her oldest daughter.

But she cared. A lot. And that was what mattered. He saw a mother's love in the way she watched Kayli, in her pride, and in the way she smiled.

Voice low and full of reverence, Raemay pronounced, "It is final, now and always. You will go forth with our many blessings."

The trembling of Kayli's hand gave away her nervousness. Mallet, on the other hand, trembled for an entirely different reason. He'd finally have her.

And he damn well couldn't wait.

Leaning down to her ear, he asked, "It's okay if Hauk just transports us out of here?"

"A credible idea." Kayli said, "Good-bye Mother." She waved to everyone, then said, "Hauk, whenever you're ready . . ."

Before she finished, they were in a room, not on the vessel, but definitely Kayli's.

As surprised as him, she looked around and said, "Oh, Michael, this is my home."

"Yeah?"

"This is . . . my private quarters."

He held her waist. "Your bedroom. I know." He was so anxious that he wanted to drag her to the floor and take her with all the pent-up need he'd accumulated since meeting her.

"Yes." She stepped back from him, drew a breath, and with little more than a tug, she stripped away the dress.

Mallet's eyes widened. He hadn't seen that one coming.

Kayli cleared her throat. She stood before him in barely there black sandals, flower petals clinging to her fair hair, and nothing else.

The "nothing else" struck him, and while soaking in the sight of her, he asked, "Does the union usually include a honeymoon type trip? I didn't even think of that." Never mind that he had no idea where he'd take her, since he knew only her colony.

As if she'd anticipated that question, she fidgeted and said, "No. That's an antiquated custom. And as Claviger, I can't afford the time away. I need to be nearby in case of emergencies, but particularly now, with the current situation."

"Later then, after we have things resolved and I've learned about some of your more recreational areas."

"That's not necessary. You have already given me so much."

That snapped Mallet's attention up to her face. "No way, babe. When it comes to giving, the scales are definitely tipped in your favor. But I promise to do my best to even up the score."

Stepping out of the sandals, her hands folded behind her, she gazed up at him and whispered, "You could start by making love to me. That is, if you're ready?"

Ready? Truth be told, he'd been ready since the moment he first saw her while still in that hospital bed, physically devastated, his body almost crippled, his mind in a funk.

From the moment he'd met her, she'd improved him; his mind, his spirit, his body. Now he'd finally have her, and he didn't give a damn if the moon dropped out of the sky, he wouldn't let anyone interrupt them.

CHAPTER 20

KAYLI felt horribly exposed, on display, and so anxious that she trembled. She wanted to please Michael, but she knew it wouldn't be easy. He'd had plenty of experience, and from what she'd uncovered in media research, the more experience, the better.

She had none. Before Michael, the few kisses she'd shared were all but inconsequential.

Because he just stood there, staring at her body, his hands fisted, his nostrils flared, his cheekbones slashed with dark color, her nervousness amplified.

She cleared her throat and said, "Take off your clothes, too." Maybe if he was naked, she wouldn't so keenly feel the lack of covering.

Without taking his searing gaze from her belly, he reached over his shoulder, caught the back of the shirt in a fist, and then stripped it off over his head. He dropped it to the floor.

His chest rose and fell on deep inhalations. He took a step toward her.

"The pants, too," Kayli said in a rush, knowing that if he

touched her, she might lose the opportunity to see him as he'd seen her. And she wanted to, badly. Her curiosity over his body was a burning thing inside her. She'd dreamt of it, of him, and now the dreams would be a reality.

So that he wouldn't think he'd tied himself to a virago, she licked her lips and added, "Please."

His jaw tightened, but he kicked off his sandals, untied the waistband of the loose, white slacks, pushed them down, and stepped free.

He straightened without a single hint of modesty.

And why not? He had the most magnificent body she'd ever seen. Forgetting her nervousness for the moment, Kayli approached him. Her palms tingled with the need to touch him. Everywhere.

"I never imagined a man like you."

His neck stiffened, but he held himself still. "No?"

Flattening her hands over his shoulders, she stroked downward, over the crisp hair on his chest, over solid muscle and incomparable strength. "Before searching you out through time, I expected all males of your power to be cumbersome, maybe awkward. When my research brought me to your sport, and then to you, I was thoroughly mesmerized."

Slowly, she dragged her hands along his body to the smoother skin of his hips, farther to his long, powerful thighs. Deliberately, she didn't yet touch his sex. It . . . intimidated her.

How they'd fit, she didn't know.

But she wanted to find out.

Her gaze met his. "Still I'm enthralled. More so now that I've gotten to know you."

Narrowed eyes burning with intensity, Michael stared down at her. His arms hung at his sides, his big hands curled into fists. At her approach, he'd braced his feet apart as if in preparation of an attack.

A sensual onslaught.

"The contradictions of you are enchanting. You possess so much physical strength, yet your personality is playful, charming. You tower over others, and still you treat every-one as an equal."

His erection moved, insisting on attention, and Kayli, feeling so daring, wrapped both hands around him.

He made a sound like a groan of pleasure and pain, and when she looked at him, his eyes were closed, his throat working.

She felt powerful, too, through her effect on him.

Moving a little closer so that she breathed in his scent and felt the touch of his heat on her bare skin everywhere, she stroked him.

He grew a little longer, a little harder still.

"This part of you is so alive." A drop of fluid appeared on the head, and without considering it too much, she dragged her thumb over it, spreading it.

In a flash, Michael's hands clasped her wrists. His voice guttural, he said, "You have to stop or I'm going to come."

Heat bloomed inside her. The idea of him losing control that way captivated her. She wasn't sure what it meant in terms of the two of them, but she wanted to find out.

Unconsciously, her fingers tightened around him.

"Kayli . . ." he warned.

She did not want to stop, so she tried to distract him with more of his contrasts. "You easily overwhelm women with your size and your strength, but instead of seeing that as an advantage to take what you want, you see it as an obligation to protect."

He misunderstood and took her words as a complaint. "It's not an obligation, it's an instinct."

"Not all men with your qualities would see it so." She felt him pulsing in her hands, and was prompted to explore his length, to touch that intriguing liquid again, to cuddle the softer flesh beneath. "The men attacking us obviously feel no obliga-tion to protect. They take by brute force."

"I can't think when you're doing that, babe."

"Good. I don't want you to think."

"But there are a few things you need to know." So saying,

he put his hands over hers, one around his shaft, the other beneath, holding him in her palm.

Instruction would be most welcome. Now that she had him to herself, she wanted too many things to know where to start.

"Here," he said, squeezing her hand around his shaft, "I like a firm hold. Stroking is good, but not when I'm this primed already. Later, maybe after I've had you a dozen times, you can try that, okay?"

A dozen times? The words did funny things to her insides, and she nodded dumbly.

"But here—" He winced and loosened her grip. "Easy goes it on the family jewels, okay? That's a place where guys are most vulnerable. One shot there will cripple a man for a few minutes at least, longer depending on how hard you hit him. If you're ever in danger, that'd be the place to attack."

She looked down at his "family jewels" and cuddled more gently.

"Yeah, that's better."

"Hitting a man there will really affect him?"

"It'll bring him low, I swear. But hey . . ." He tipped up her chin and frowned at her. "Don't ever slug *me* there, okay? No matter how pissed you might be."

Fighting a smile, Kayli nodded. "I understand. I would never want to seriously harm you."

"Never say never. We've already agreed that I can be infuriating, remember?"

"Yes." His intoxicating scent, as well as the visual of his chest, drew her. She put her mouth to his left pectoral and lightly bit. "You smell so good."

His hands settled on her waist, tacitly giving her permission to do as she pleased.

She kissed his chest, the smooth skin of his shoulders, his throat, and jaw. Just when she wanted his mouth most, he took over, cupping one hand behind her head and kissing her hard, deep, and wet.

His other hand went to her bottom and palpated the softer flesh there, lifting her to her tiptoes.

"Woman?" he rumbled against her mouth. "Turn me loose so we can get this show on the road."

"Oh." Kayli realized she held his sex in an iron grip, and immediately released him.

In the next instant, he had them both on the floor and his hands were all over her. He plumped up both her breasts and sucked at each nipple in turn. She'd almost disbelieved her perception of the sensation evoked—but now it was proved again. His mouth made her feel things in places he hadn't yet touched, but soon would.

He came back up, kissing her throat while sliding a hand down between her thighs. His fingers searched over her, making her moan, and just as he worked one finger into her, thrilling her, setting her on fire, he said, "Got a question."

She couldn't think, didn't understand.

"Kayli, love?" Now that he had that finger pressed deep, he held still and waited.

Love? She opened her eyes to find him watching her closely. She couldn't get any words out, and so lifted a brow in query.

"What do you futuristic chicks do about birth control?"

Her brain went blank. She knew that in his time period, the earth had been overpopulated, and many people prevented birth through various methods.

But such wasn't true anymore. It was assumed that once you joined in union, you would accept children as a blessing. There were methods of stopping conception, but . . . she didn't want them.

Michael put several small, teasing kisses along her shoulder. "Cat got your tongue?" He pressed his finger in a little more, making her catch her breath. "I don't mean to stop the action, but I need to know how to progress here."

It was most difficult to measure her words at such a time, with him over her, touching her so intimately, looking so incredible, but she knew she must.

Tentative, measuring her words, she asked, "Do you not want children?"

"I want you. If kids come along, and you're happy about it, then hey, I'm happy, too."

That sounded far too noncommittal to Kayli. "I would not want to trap you into an undesirable situation."

His mouth slowly lifted into a grin. "The situation we're in is pretty damned desirable." Capturing her gaze, he eased his finger out, and then worked two back in.

Her body strained against him. It was a very tight fit, and she felt herself stretching—and a whole lot more.

Michael lowered his voice. "In my day, it was the gentlemanly thing to protect the woman from an unwanted birth. Only a selfish prick would have sex without a rubber. But things are so different here, I need to know the norm."

Her thoughts swam, sent adrift by the pulsing pleasure. "It is . . . it is customary to progress as nature intended."

"Meaning no rubber." As if that excited him unbearably, he ravaged her mouth again.

Kayli locked her arms around his neck, opened her legs more.

"I don't want to hurt you," he rasped.

"You won't." Only if he stopped now would he injure her. She needed to feel him, all of him. "Please, Michael."

He moved over her, opening her legs more with the press of his knee. "Tell me to stop if I hurt you."

"Okay." She would not.

He held her face and stared into her eyes. "Try to relax for me."

"Okay." She *could* not.

He reached down between them, opened her, adjusted himself, and then . . . he was pressing inside her and he was far bigger than two fingers.

The groan came unbidden, as much urgency as apprehension.

"Easy," he whispered, fondling a breast and kissing her mouth. "Easy."

It burned, the stretching of her intimate flesh, but even

so, she felt the moisture build, the heat and sensitivity. Excitement turned her breathing to pants, mingled with moans.

"Put your legs around me, babe." He helped, lifting her thigh up along his waist, which sent him a little deeper.

They both groaned.

Through his teeth, he said, "I've never fucked without a condom. Never."

The coarse language only added to the carnality of the moment. The look on his face added to the intimacy.

That she would give him something special meant a lot to her. He was her man now, and always. She wanted this to be the best for him that it could be. He'd given so much to her, to her colony.

She could give this to him.

Putting a palm to his face, she smiled past the overwhelming intensity. "I want all of you," she whispered. "Now."

He ducked his head down; his shoulders bunched, and with a raw sound of anticipated pleasure, he drove into her.

Kayli lost her breath and stiffened, but the intrusion pained her for only a moment before other sensations rose up, wild and hot. *"Michael."*

His body trembled as he fought himself. He withdrew with painstaking care, pushed back in just as leisurely.

Kayli locked her legs around him and put back her head.

He took advantage of that, kissing her throat, pawing both her breasts as he sank in again, withdrew, came back slow and deep.

Each thrust heightened what she felt, sharpened it until it became a different agony. Her heels pressed into the small of his back, trying to encourage him to haste.

But he wouldn't be swayed, moving at that slow, methodical pace, taking his time as he toyed with her nipples, sucked at the sensitive skin of her throat.

A wave of feeling crested, but receded before she got where she needed to be.

"Please."

"Soon," he promised on a ragged breath.

Again and again he thrust into her, and each time the pleasure built, and went away. Each time it grew stronger, more necessary until she thought she'd scream for the need of it.

And when it washed over her, consuming her, she did scream out, squeezing him tight with her legs, putting her teeth to his shoulder to try to contain it all.

Finally letting himself go, Michael hammered into her. Kayli was barely aware of him sharing that awesome moment with her, it was so voracious. But as her climax faded, she heard his harsh groans, felt the wild pounding of his heart and the wilder pounding of his body.

She saw her teeth marks in his shoulder, and licked them by way of apology.

"Oh God," he said, straining over her until, spent, he slumped down to give her all his weight.

And she loved it.

She loved him, but was unsure about telling him so. Instead, she ran her fingers through his damp hair, over his hot shoulders, along the indentation of his spine.

He was a beautiful man. He was hers.

Now that she knew what that meant, she'd never let him go.

MALLET was still trying to get his brain or legs to function—either would have been a major accomplishment—when Kayli whispered, "Thank you."

She had to be kidding, but just in case, he struggled up to his elbows, and saw the seriousness of her expression. How could she twist his heart so easily?

And it was his heart. Not his gonads, not his sense of duty, not an obligation, and not mere protectiveness.

He'd fallen for the little warrior, and he wasn't at all sure how he felt about that. "My pleasure, and I mean that."

She touched his mouth, tracing his lips. "You said I should ask you things."

Well yeah, that revived him, assuming she meant sexual things. "Anything. Anytime." Better him than any other person, male, female, or computer.

"Would you really be able to do that a dozen times tonight?"

" 'That'?" Mallet laughed. "It's called making love—"

"Not sex?"

"It's more than sex." Even with her inexperience, how could she not know that? "And while I hate to disappoint you, probably not."

"I am not disappointed." Next she traced an eyebrow. "I wasn't sure if I'd be able to. I've never felt so . . . relaxed."

He grinned. "Should we test you to see?" Even now, with his boner fading, it was incredible to feel her and only her, all slippery wet, still squeezing him in small aftershocks, still accepting him.

"Perhaps in a bit, if you think we'll both recover enough." When he laughed, she poked his shoulder. "You know more about this than I do."

"We'll get you schooled in no time."

Her look turned teasing, sensually ripe. "I hope so."

Damn, she pleased him. He gave her a tickling, laughing smooch, and because that felt so good, he came back for another. He'd thought he was dead for a while, but the kiss turned deep, not so much with lust, but with that special something that was more profound.

Lifting up to his elbows, he looked at her.

Her golden eyes were soft and slumberous, her silky, fair hair wild around her head. "Damn, woman," he growled low and with feeling, "you are so fucking beautiful."

Smiling a little, she turned her head to study him more, and her mood turned sober. "Thank you, but you are far more beautiful than I could ever be." Her fingers teased along his upper chest while she ate him up with her eyes. "Especially after you've just had pleasure. Your eyes are so blue, they could enchant me. They *have* enchanted me."

Uncomfortable with the praise, Mallet laughed. "Yeah, uh, most men don't want to be called beautiful."

"But you are."

"How about cruelly handsome? I like the sound of that."

Slowly, she shook her head. "That would never do because there is nothing cruel about you. Remarkable, yes. Outstanding, most definitely. But never cruel."

He twisted his mouth. "What the hell, woman. I give you sex and you go all mushy on me?"

"I'm being honest, not mushy. Never did I think to find myself in this situation. In this position." She bent her knees along his hips, deepening their intimate embrace. "But you are more special than I anticipated, and now I'm doing a lot of things I never considered."

Things she didn't want to do? Things he'd coerced her into? "I don't want to disrupt your life." What a lie. He wanted to turn her entire world around. But he also wanted her happy, damn it.

She frowned in incomprehension. "Yet you've done nothing but." Then she kissed him. "And while it's taking me time to adjust, it's not all unpleasant."

No, it wasn't all unpleasant—because she liked the sex. Mallet wanted to curse himself. Somehow, with the role-reversal of her time, she'd managed to turn him into a fretting woman who feared being used sexually.

It burned his ass big-time.

"Look, I'm not a paragon, not a hero—"

"Yes, you are."

He groaned. "But I'm not a villain, either."

"I know this." She studied him. "Why does the truth upset you so much?"

"Because you're making assumptions. We haven't known each other long enough for you to . . . hell, I don't know. Hold me in such esteem?" He felt like an idiot, but he didn't want to accuse her of hero worship. Somehow he didn't think that'd go over real big with a woman as independent as her.

"It feels like I've known you forever." She pulled him

down for another kiss, and each touch of her lush mouth nudged him further away from tiredness and closer to full-blown lust again. "Each day, in a dozen different ways, your character is revealed to me."

"Yeah, and as I recall, my character has put you in a snit more than a few times."

She went all serious on him again. "I've thought about that, and concluded that it was my own insecurities that caused resentment. I like being in control of all things, but under my control, my colony has been endangered. I have to accept that I need your help, and that your help might include your leadership over mine."

Mallet brought his face closer to hers. *"No."*

"Yes." She smoothed a hand over his rumpled hair, then held his face. Her thumbs stroked his jaw. "Being in a union requires that both people give a little. It requires adjustment. I will do my best to adjust in the ways that you need me to."

Mallet didn't like the sound of that at all. Guilt that he'd pretty much forced her into the union added a nasty edge to his irritation.

He was happy. Hell, he was in love with her.

But she gave no indication of feeling the same. From what she'd said, she only suffered him for the sake of her colony.

And for the sex.

Just looking at her now, how she stretched so sinuously, she *loved* the sex, and truth be told, that made him feel about a hundred feet tall.

But he wanted more. He wanted her to love him, too, damn it, not just what he gave her in the sack.

"What if I disappoint you, Kayli? I'm a fighter with skill, but still just a man. What if I can't make a difference? What if the intruders attack and it doesn't go well?"

She pushed him to his back and sat up to look at him. All of him. With her gaze on his lap, she whispered, "You're doing all that you can do, more than I ever hoped for. You've already made an amazing difference, in so many ways. If we fight and lose, it won't be your fault. It will be mine."

She ended that statement by wrapping her hand around his cock.

"Kayli . . ." He wanted to say more, wanted to explain that she took on too much responsibility for a woman so young, a woman going up against men. But she squeezed him, and all he could manage was a groan.

"Oh look, Michael," she said with enthusiasm. "I think you are ready again." Golden gaze warm and anxious, she sank down to his chest, whispering huskily, "That's good, because I am ready, too."

CHAPTER 21

AFTER Mallet stepped into pants and Kayli pulled on a loose shirt, they headed to the dining room for sustenance. Even with the clean lines of the utilitarian furnishings he saw, her house still looked far more cozy and comfortable than her spaceship.

Unlike that cold metal vessel, her home had color.

Not bright crayon color, but subtle, warm colors of the earth. The windows were without shades or curtains, but darkened for privacy into a matte deep tan hue.

The floors in the hallways lit up as they walked. Like a cross within the home, the hallways all led to a single focal point: an enormous tree growing out of the center of Kayli's living room. The tree had a smooth trunk and waxy leaves, and grew all the way to the top of a high ceiling.

Mallet stopped and stared in amazement. "You have a tree in here."

As if such a thing wasn't at all unusual, Kayli shrugged. "I don't get to see much nature when I'm on the vessel. I miss it." She trailed her hand along a low, twisting branch.

"It won't grow any taller than its confines, and it gives off a woodsy scent that I enjoy."

Mallet sniffed, and grinned. "Smells a little like my favorite cologne." Thinking of men and their grooming habits led his thoughts along a different path. "It's unusually quiet here. You don't have any AMAs milling around?"

"No. I'm not home often enough to need assistance."

Home. Yeah, that's what made this different from her spaceship. Even without a lot of personal clutter or knick-knacks, the place felt like home, like a specific design that reflected Kayli's personality. "What about for cleaning up?"

"That is unnecessary. The house maintains itself."

Of course it did. Shaking his head, Mallet looked around at the soft, modular furniture, a flowing water feature in the wall that also fed into a narrow groove to nourish the tree, delicate wind chimes hanging from multiple floor stands, and some pretty funky lighting effects.

The walls in this room were made of thick glass that could either be clear or frosted for privacy. With a touch, Kayli frosted them.

Before they headed for food, Kayli took Mallet on a quick tour. At the end of each of the hallways were separate areas, including the bedrooms and bath, a media and tele-commuting center, a professional workout and training area, and the dining and cooking areas.

As he walked, each of Mallet's footsteps glowed on the strange floor. Depending on the area, the muted hues changed shades. The hallways had the brightest illumination, the bedroom the dimmest.

He learned more just by watching Kayli as she moved modifiable walls to adjust the sizes of each room. The walls slid in and out of place as easily as a closet door would.

In her dining room, the floor was slate-like tile that she said came from the mountains beyond, traded from a different colony. Like most of Kayli's house, it was sparsely appointed, holding only pod-like chairs and an oval, frosted-glass table that adjusted at a touch.

Instead of hanging pictures as adornment, large blocks of artistic color themes bisected the creamy beige walls.

"Cool artwork."

"Thank you." She glanced at him with an impish expression usually foreign to her character. "Do you remember the mood rings of your time?"

"I've seen them."

"Watch." With a touch of her finger, the colors in the nearest collage changed.

"No way. Mood *art*?"

"The panels are built into the wall. Sometimes they pick up my feelings just through my nearness."

"Huh." Tonight her mood was soft and mellow, swirls of butter yellow, pale melon, and softest blue. Uncertain what that might indicate, Mallet nodded at the color collage nearest her. "Does that mean you're happy?"

"It means I'm content."

Not quite what he wanted to hear, but he supposed that would have to be good enough for now.

"I'd like more light in here." Just that easily, the ceiling opened up to allow in the last rays of the fading sun. "Are you very hungry?"

Mallet turned a circle, taking it all in, making note of her preferences. "I'm not starving, if that's what you mean. Whatever is easiest is fine." Hell, this was sort of her honeymoon, though there was too much going on in the colony for her to take any real time off.

"It's all easy. I was thinking about some ripe fruit, and perhaps some cheese and crackers?"

Standing there in nothing more than a shirt, her long shapely legs bare, her hair tousled, she looked more than adorable. Mallet didn't care what they ate. He just wanted to make sure that she did because after they finished, he'd probably keep her up most of the night. "If that sounds good to you, it works for me."

She turned away to speak into a microchip in the wall.

The meal came up out of the center of Kayli's dining table along with a chilled, green-tinted drink. Kayli gestured for him to sit, and after he did, he pulled her onto his lap.

Knowing her bottom was bare teased him, but for the moment, he felt sated enough to just enjoy the closeness of cuddling her.

She reached for a glass and handed him one before settling back against his chest.

Mallet sniffed the liquid. "Are you trying to get me drunk?"

"No." She put her nose to his throat and breathed in. "Such is forbidden."

"Should have figured." He tried the drink, liked it, and drank about half before starting on the food. He alternately took bites for himself and fed her.

If he had his way, he'd always take care of her, but he had a feeling this was a one-shot deal, an aberration brought on by the discovery of her sensual nature. She wouldn't see this as a routine, more as a celebration of their union.

"This is decadent," she said, agreeing with his thoughts. "But tonight, I don't care. I'm enjoying it too much."

"Me, too." While he had her in an agreeable mood, Mallet asked, "Do you think we could live here, now that we're in a union?"

As if the question surprised her, she hesitated, and then sat up on his lap. "Did you want to live here?"

He wanted a real life with her, with her in the role of wife instead of soldier. It wasn't likely to happen, and he felt like a bastard for trying to change her, but he needed to know she'd be safe.

Being in a home, as a couple, was a start. "I like it here. It's cozier than your spaceship."

"My vessel is not meant to be cozy."

No, it was meant to facilitate her role as Claviger. "Can you handle your duties from here as easily as you do the spaceship?"

"Yes. If I needed to be aboard, Hauk could transport me in a second."

"Transport *us*," he corrected. She wasn't going anywhere,

definitely not into danger, without him. Now that they were in a union, he had certain rights—and he'd damn well exercise them.

Kayli chewed it over before looking around the dining room as if just seeing it. "We could live here, if that's what you want."

"I do." He kissed her for being so agreeable. "Know what else I'd like?"

"Sex?"

She did have a one-track mind. Mallet laughed. "Always, but for right now, let's finish eating and then take a late flight on your aircycle. What do you think?"

Kayli let out a sigh. "I could show you the clouds and, when the sun goes down, the stars. I haven't ridden high at night in a very long time. It will be better if we take the Sky Slider, though. It has an autopilot feature so that we can . . . entertain ourselves instead of steer."

The future looked bright, with Kayli in his life. Mallet hugged her, and said, "Let's do it."

VALDER stewed in silence. From a distance, he saw his good friend Toller walking with his new woman, Nayana. In such a short time, they had fallen very much in love. Toller was nearly as big as Valder, and had been twice as wild, most especially with women. But he'd taken one look at Nayana and his expression had warned away the other men in their hunting party.

He had claimed her the same night they brought her home, and the next day they had cemented their relationship for all time.

Valder envied them. Instead of love, his heart overflowed with resentment and discontent.

While he lingered in the shade of a building to watch his friend on his stroll, children ran up to him with squeals of excitement.

Valder scuffled with them for a few moments, laughing at their antics, pretending to let them tackle him to the ground.

They crawled all over him, trying to tickle him, smothering him with their enthusiasm. The boys grabbed his limbs, practicing their fighting moves, while the girls harassed the boys for their exuberance.

There were twice the number of boys than girls, but in his colony they were all rowdy and filled with life, regardless of their gender. The young ones grew up happy and free, the males protecting the females, and the females nurturing the males.

Valder enjoyed them all. A lot. But he had no young ones of his own, no offspring to carry on his name, his heritage.

He should have taken a woman as his own, procreating with her to give his colony a dozen beautiful little children. But somehow, after Raemay, the thought of commitment didn't settle right.

Most of the children ran to the strange one, Lydina, when they saw her approaching. She almost always had something to show them—a butterfly, a flower, sweet treats, or magic tricks. In her expressionless way, she entertained them.

Valder considered returning her to her own colony. If doing so wouldn't make him look weak to his opponents, he would have already. That Lydina remained distant and uninterested in engaging the men or befriending the women led him to believe she would never be happy here.

It was intolerable for him to add sadness to any woman's life. Well, except for Raemay Raine. He wanted her to feel the same sadness, to be as bereft as he was.

Toller and Nayana walked up to him, Toller frowning in anger, Nayana in confusion.

Straightening from his relaxed posture, Valder asked, "What is it?"

"She has something to explain," Toller said, pressing Nayana forward with a hand at the small of her back.

She dug in her heels and spun around to face him. "And why should I when you won't tell me why it matters?" Nayana shot right back.

She was a spunky one, Valder thought, perfect for Toller's dominating personality. It amused Valder that the only people Toller had ever deferred to him was himself, and Nayana.

Because his friend turned red in the face, Valder asked, "Is there something I should know?"

When Nayana didn't answer, Toller snarled, then said, "The new one, Lydina, is an AFA."

Ice ran down Valder's spine. His eyes narrowed and his body tensed. "What say you?"

Toller nudged Nayana again. She hesitated, but when Valder turned his burning attention on her, she pinched her mouth. "I do not know why it matters so much, but yes, I did ask about that one"—she pointed to Lydina—"because she is an AFA, and she looks just like one we have back at our colony."

"This is now your colony," Toller pointed out.

"Yes, of course." It was her turn to roll her eyes. "But I meant the colony from which you took me."

"She is an *android*?" Valder asked, disbelieving such could be true.

Nayana pulled back in real surprise. "You truly did not know?"

Feeling like a total fool, Valder said nothing. He didn't want to frighten Toller's woman with his reaction to such a deception.

Toller said to her, "You are sure of this?"

"Yes. The one who looks just like her belongs to Kayli, Raemay's oldest daughter."

Valder took that disclosure with an equal measure of shock. "Oldest daughter? But I understood that to be Idola."

"Idola is second oldest. Mesha is the youngest."

Raemay had three daughters? In one big step, Valder closed the space separating him from Nayana. "Idola is not oldest, and yet she will inherit? How can that be?"

Toller pulled Nayana to his side, offering protection that was not needed, but served to comfort her in the face of Valder's rage.

She cleared her throat. "I am not sure why you need to know this—"

Toller squeezed her, and spoke with quiet assurance. "No games, woman. This is not a matter to drag out."

She scowled at both men. "Only because I know you will not harm any of the women of my colony . . ." She hesitated, and asked, "Correct?"

Rigid enough to snap, Valder nodded.

Toller, irritated by such a remark, snorted. "You should not even need to ask." Then, in a lower voice, he said, "Have I not treated you quite well?"

She gave a sly smile. "Yes you have."

In no mood for their bliss, Valder growled, regaining her attention.

"As the second eldest daughter, Idola is the name carrier because Kayli is a soldier and therefore cannot inherit."

Raemay's daughter, a soldier. Valder held his fists so tight, his knuckles ached. He might have encountered her during their scrimmages and not even known it. If the women didn't wear those useless helmets, he might have recognized features similar to Raemay's.

Unaware of his thoughts, Nayana continued. "That is, Kayli could not have inherited before. But much has changed since the outsider came."

"How so?" Raemay had duped him, was probably even now laughing at his gullibility in believing an AFA to be a flesh-and-blood woman.

If he were as ruthless as he wanted to be, he would not have suffered guilt over Lydina's assumed unhappiness. God, how it galled, knowing that he'd worried for the emotional damage done to a fabricated being incapable of real emotion.

If he were a coward who raped women, he would have known immediately that she was an android.

He'd wanted Raemay to believe such vile things about him. And why not? She had not believed the truth of his nature, had not cared that he was loyal and honorable and that he loved her . . . *"Answer me, woman."*

His barked order made Nayana jump. Toller narrowed his eyes over the slight, but after a whisper into Nayana's ear, she nodded and relaxed again.

"Before the outsider, no soldier could ever form a union. The career path was believed too risky to involve family."

"By your Arbiter's order?"

"Yes. But he changed that by joining Kayli in union. Now . . ." Nayana shrugged. "It may be possible that Kayli will inherit after all. She is already Claviger, even though she has been claimed by Michael."

"Michael?"

"The big one," Toller clarified. "The stranger."

So it was probably his plan to dupe Valder. The man had come in and accomplished much, accomplished what none other had managed since Raemay left him: to make a fool of Valder Wildoon.

As the silence stretched on, a plan formed in Valder's mind. He could strike a single blow, and cause much devastation.

By taking Kayli Raine.

She was Raemay's rightful heir, her oldest child. Raemay would be destroyed to lose her.

Kayli was in union with the outsider, a placeholder for him within the colony. Without her, he'd be nothing to them.

And as Claviger, her colony needed her more than they needed Raemay, the Arbiter. All of the people relied on her for leadership against attacks.

Once Valder had her, the outsider, Raemay, the entire colony would be lost.

Valder showed his teeth in a look no one mistook for a smile. "In the morn, we ride."

Toller nodded. "Then tonight, we plan."

Valder watched as Toller took Nayana's arm and led her away. Neither man paid any attention to her shrill protests.

KAYLI woke before the sun, felt the weight of Michael's arm around her, his warm breath on her shoulder. She smiled with a bone-deep contentment she'd never known—and was afraid to trust.

Being this way with him scared her, when so little ever had.

But with him, she was a different person. She no longer knew herself. What she felt for Michael kept her from prioritizing her duty as she should. Now, her thoughts divided between responsibility and a predominance of happiness.

Over the past ten days, since the eve of their union, they'd fallen into a wonderful routine. They rose early, showered and dined together, talked endlessly about everything, and then saw to the business of the colony.

Each day included strenuous training. Michael didn't let up on any of them, including her. But she loved it. She loved testing her strength and endurance, her speed and reflexes. Learning new things about her body, her capabilities, was thrilling.

When it rained each afternoon, Michael found a place to cuddle with her, and sometimes more. Often he had Hauk transport them to her vessel, sometimes to her house. He showed her the ecstasy of long, leisurely lovemaking as well as the urgency of a frenzied mating that he termed a "quickie."

She loved it all.

She loved him.

In the evening, they swam in the lake. And they discussed things important to her, things important to him. He shared with her his old dreams, and dreams that were new. She wanted to share, too, but all of her dreams now included him, and she worried that she might smother him with her feelings.

Each night when they returned home, he made love to her.

Home.

It had so much more meaning now. Not just in the physical sense of a comfortable dwelling where she resided with her man, but in the sense of well-being, the sense of belonging.

Little by little, Michael had accumulated belongings of

his own, so that her house was now his house, too. He had several changes of clothes sharing space with hers in the closet. An old-fashioned razor that he insisted on using hung on their bathroom wall. On her shelves she found manuals and menus he'd created for the trainees. He even had his own pick of music and media.

And strangely enough, he liked flowers. He often left a bouquet for her in the dining areas or in their sleeping room. Sometimes he placed a single bloom on her pillow; she'd awaken to the sweet scent and find him watching her.

She'd thought being Claviger defined her.

Nothing defined her more than the things she felt for Michael. She'd loved before, of course. Her family, her friends. Her work.

But this was so different, so all-consuming. It changed everything about her.

"Hey you."

At the sound of his deep, sleepy voice, she turned to him with a smile that came from her soul. "Good morn."

He stretched, showing her a breathtaking display of thick muscle and sinew. After he resettled into the pillows, he dropped a hand to her thigh, caught her gaze on his body, and asked, "What are you thinking?"

Seeing no reason to lie, Kayli admitted, "That I enjoy my man."

His brow went up. With his hair so rumpled and beard shadow on his face, he looked roguish and unbelievably sexy. "Your man, huh?"

"Are you not?" She lounged atop him and played with his chest hair. Everything about him was so masculine, so appealing.

Her morning mood was such that she had to test him. Just a little. "You do belong to me now. You realize that, don't you?"

Smiling, he cupped her backside with both hands. "Damn, but I do love a possessive woman."

Every time Michael used that *L* word, her heart ached and her stomach clenched. Never had he said, "I love *you*," only that he loved things about her body or her personality.

Was it the same? She didn't dare think so.

Unsure if she should laugh or not, Kayli waited and her silence stole his grin, turning him somber.

"Hey. What's wrong?"

Making one small admission would be preferable to laying out her heart. "I suffer some guilt."

Concern softened his touch. "Why?"

"I shouldn't be so blissful."

"Blissful, huh?" Judging by his expression, he liked the sound of that. "And why shouldn't you be?"

Resting her elbows on his chest, she propped up her chin. "Members of my colony are still held captive, Michael. I should be concentrating on a plan to free them, to bring them home. I should be—"

"Bullshit." Michael sat up so fast she didn't have time to scramble away. He lifted her, plopped her to the side of him, and scowled at her. "No one has done more than you to try to figure out this mess. We've prepared so that when he attacks again, we'll be ready. But you know as well as I do that for now, that's all any of us *can* do."

If only that were true. He had done much, but she'd been very ineffectual. "You're preparing everyone, and you thought of sending the AFA. That has at least bought us time. But it has been weeks now." She pushed the sheet away and stood. "It eats away at me, wondering when he will come again, who he will take next."

"Look, babe, I love how dedicated you are, but—"

"Enough." How could he keep saying such things? Emotions frazzled, Kayli glared at him. "You use that word too often."

His brows shot up in confusion. "What word?"

"Love."

The way she practically spat it at him instantly turned his mood. Expression darkening, Michael came to his feet to tower over her. Kayli had a strange foreboding of things to come, things out of her control, and she almost backed up in denial of the inevitable.

"You," he said, leaning down into her space, "never say it at all."

A complaint? She shook her head in confusion. A dozen different times, the words had burned her throat with her need to share them with him. Only because she didn't want him to feel trapped by her emotions had she kept silent. She had brought Michael here for a reason, for a specific purpose.

It was probable that he had chosen to make a union with her because, in a totally unfamiliar area, she was the one closest to him. That he enjoyed sex with her made his adjustment easier, and she found no complaint with that part of their deal.

It *had* been a deal. Hadn't it? Tone tentative, she asked, "Did you *want* me to?"

Seeming distant and guarded, Michael folded his arms over his chest. "Depends on if you mean it or not."

Her mouth fell open. So . . . did he mean it when he said it to her in those abstract ways? Her heart raced with yearning, and with that aberrant fear. Oh God, if she admitted she loved him, would her world forever change?

Hadn't it already?

Shaking his head, Michael said, "Forget it. I didn't mean to put you on the spot." He left for the bathroom, leaving her with her own chaotic thoughts.

Love. It had been more unattainable than union, so abstract in her mind that she wasn't sure how to deal with it, what to do for it.

Her stomach hurt and she wrapped her arms around herself.

For as long as she could remember, she'd given herself to her duty as Claviger. But now, with the enticement of so much more . . . did she even want to continue in that path?

Without realizing it, her hand flattened to her belly. Even now, she could be carrying his child. Tears welled in her eyes. Would she dare risk something so precious just out of a sense of duty?

No, she would not.

The second she made the decision, she felt stronger, more powerful than she ever had.

Smiling past the tears that continued to track down her face, she stood.

She was about to call out to him when he came back into the room, freshly cleaned and dressed. He took one look at her and froze.

"What is it? What's wrong?" A strange, alert expression shone in his blue eyes.

Smiling, her heart full to bursting, she said, "Michael—"

And then Hauk's voice interjected. "I am beyond remorseful to interrupt you lovebirds yet again, especially at such a tender moment, but there is a problem that requires your immediate attention."

After a long, measuring look at Kayli, Michael said, "What is it, Hauk?"

"It has just been discovered that Nayana is missing."

Kayli gasped, but Michael asked, "Who's Nayana? You mean another woman's been kidnapped?"

No, Kayli thought. It was impossible. The intruders had snuck in after she'd put such careful checks in place? "When was she taken?"

"According to Lydina, she was taken right before your union."

Lydina, the AFA that they'd sent in place of a human woman? Kayli's heart dropped to her knees. "You've been in contact with Lydina?"

"She has been returned to us," Hauk explained.

"Returned? By who?" Michael demanded.

"Valder Wildoon—the man you gave her to."

CHAPTER 22

"TALK fast, Hauk."

"He left Lydina at the border and she walked in," Hauk explained to Mallet. "As soon as she reached our boundary, I detected her. She said that Valder is just beyond the lake, awaiting you. He wants to meet man-to-man."

Mallet grinned with anticipation. "Perfect." He started out of the room.

"Damn, damn, damn!" Kayli shouted. "Michael, don't you dare leave here without me!"

He glanced over his shoulder to see her scrambling after him, her body bare and her hair tangled. He was still pissed that she continued to keep him at a distance. "You're naked, dollface. Not a good way to confront an enemy."

"Stop!" She swiped a shirt from the floor, but nothing else. "I mean it, damn you. We are a team. You said so yourself."

Her deteriorated language was a bad habit she'd picked up from him. Raemay wouldn't like that a bit, but her mother's reaction wasn't a priority right now.

Doing what she'd brought him here to do was.

Seeing Kayli charge naked after him, seeing her small breasts bounce, was an interesting thing—but Mallet refused to be sidetracked.

He wanted to be so much more than her fucking teammate. He wanted to be . . . everything to her.

At times, like right now, he thought he wanted the impossible.

"Exactly," he agreed, having no intention of putting her face-to-face with any bastard who kidnapped women against their will. "We're a team. You go round up the troops and I'll head to the lake."

"No!" She tripped, snagged him by the back of his shirt, and almost took them both down.

"Kayli," he said, trying to sound reasonable as he helped her to catch her balance. "We don't have time to argue about it. He wants to meet man-to-man. With me."

"You won't go alone."

Damn. "Look, Hauk can oversee things, right, Hauk? If it's a trap, he can transport the lot of you over to join me."

"I can do that," Hauk said, but he sounded very reluctant.

"There, you see?" Mallet didn't want her to worry too much. "Now go sound the alarm—do whatever it is you do—and get everyone ready."

Both her hands fisted in his shirt. "You will wait for me."

Mallet pried her hands loose. Time to make a stand. "Wrong. You brought me here for this, remember? Not for anything else." Not for love. Not for a life together. "Let me make your effort worthwhile."

Her eyes filled with panic. Strange for her, considering she was supposed to be cool and collected at times of crises.

"Many things have changed since then."

"Like?" Would she admit she cared for him? He waited.

But she shook her head. "Michael, stop and think. You have not fought him. I realize that you are very good at what you do, but you don't know how good he might be. It would be better if—"

"Now you have doubts about my ability? Thanks." He'd seen the man, and felt not the least challenged by him. But when Kayli only looked more stricken, Mallet softened. "Look, I'll detain him, that's all."

"But . . ."

"This is our best chance for you to shake off that guilt, babe." And then, just maybe, she'd be ready to forge a real life with him as husband and wife, in every sense of the word.

She shook her head. "No, Michael, please. We need to form a plan."

"And then he might take off again and we'll have lost the opportunity. Have a little faith in me, will you?"

"You are worth more than a little guilt to me."

Well, that was something, at least. It wasn't love, but what the hell. Maybe once he rid her of her nemesis, she'd learn to love him. "You can't talk me out of it, Kayli. Not everything is in your control."

"I figured that out for myself already."

His smile took him by surprise. "Sorry, love, but this is one of those times where you're just going to have to accept my nature." He set her away from him, looked at her naked legs, her unprotected head. "Hauk?"

"Yes?"

"Can you get her properly dressed before she joins the defense team?"

A beat of silence sounded like a ticking time bomb. Hauk cleared his throat. "She has special gear for engagement with enemies."

"Perfect. Be sure to stick the helmet on her head, too."

Hauk said, "Yes, of course. But if I could offer a suggestion—"

"I'm the boss, Hauk. You'd do well to remember that." Mallet knew that if he hesitated at all, if he showed any weakness, Kayli would follow hot on his heels. And in fact . . . "Hauk, wait. After you get her attired, take her to the reception hall so she can round up the defense team. I don't want to see her anywhere near the lake until she has everyone with her as backup. You got that?"

Hauk sighed. "Yes. Got it."

Kayli didn't argue. She dropped her hands and stepped back from Mallet. She looked so utterly devastated by his decision to exclude her that it felt like he'd taken a shot to the liver.

She stared at him, eyes big and wounded, and then in the next instant, she was gone.

Mallet fought the unavoidable remorse. He had no idea if he'd done the right thing or not. He only knew that he couldn't risk her.

"She is not angered," Hauk told him. "She is despondent. But she is now in full gear at the reception hall where the troops are already assembling."

Mallet supposed that'd have to be good enough. Even he couldn't get away with removing her from the defense team entirely.

"Get me to the lake." If he could destroy the bastard before Kayli got there, it'd be a moot point.

"Do you require special gear?"

"No. I fight barefoot, usually in shorts, but the pants are fine. Just get me there. Now."

Mallet didn't have time to regret his decision before he found himself at the lake.

Unfortunately, he was alone.

Valder Wildoon was nowhere to be seen.

Mallet strode along the shore, searched the edge of the woods that marked the colony's boundaries, but he saw nothing, heard no more than the occasional insect, the lapping of the water on the shore, and the breeze rustling through the treetops. What the hell? "Hauk?"

"Yes, Mallet."

"Where the hell is he?"

Another long sigh. "It appears that his instruction to Lydina was a setup."

Oh, shit. No, no, no. "Explain that."

"Please recall that I did try to suggest to you the probabilities."

Mallet's blood ran cold. "Explain it now, you fucking chunk of metal, and fast!"

"Twenty men were hiding outside my radar, with more in readiness should they be needed. They entered the center of town."

An eerie calm settled over Mallet. "Near the reception hall." Where Hauk had taken Kayli.

"They only wanted you out of the way so they could storm the colony from another direction. I sounded the alarm, of course, and even now, the intruders engage with the defense team."

Pinpricks of light flashed into Mallet's vision. He'd never known fear like this and he didn't like it worth a damn. All his training had taught him to remain calm and methodical, but chaos reigned in his thoughts. He was far too emotional.

"They specifically want Kayli."

"Put me there." An invisible fist squeezed his throat, making the words raspy. *"Now."*

Hauk, damn him, remained composed. "Shall I drop you anywhere in the middle of the conflict, or would you prefer to be near where Kayli fights?"

Ah fuck! His brain scrambled, but he forced himself to draw an icy breath of control. "Yes, damn you! Next to her."

In a flash, Mallet found himself in the middle of a conflict, bodies smashing into bodies, fists and elbows flying. He ducked a strike and automatically retaliated with a kick that landed against his opponent's temple.

The guy crashed down like a fallen tree.

While fending off other attacks, he searched for Kayli and found her engaged with a big blond man who smiled as he taunted her. She wore a uniform and helmet, but Mallet recognized the shape of her body, her stance, the tilt of her head.

He had only a second to watch her before the man tried to trip her and found out what Mallet already knew—that she had incredible skill.

Her elbow smashed into the man's jaw, snapping his head back. Then her knee came up into his gut, once, twice, again to land on his chin . . . and down he went.

Fluid and fast, she turned and launched herself after another man.

Pride burned inside Mallet.

Hot damn, she was good. Better than good. His little woman knew how to kick some serious ass.

The intruders were outnumbered. It was clear they hadn't expected to find men fighting with the defense team, and while the women warriors showed more skill, the new male recruits contributed strength and power.

In part to ensure her protection, but also to fight alongside her, to encourage her, Mallet tore through the intruders to reach Kayli's side.

Left in his path were broken and disabled men.

Just before he got to her, Mallet recognized the blond dude as the same one who'd ridden the loud cycle the night Lydina was taken.

Valder Wildoon.

Grabbing Kayli from behind, Valder lifted her completely off her feet. She bloodied his nose with an elbow, brought her heel back, almost hitting his groin.

He grunted, and squeezed her so tight that she couldn't breathe.

Tuning out everyone and everything else, Mallet stopped in front of them.

Valder greeted him with a smile. "Michael Manchester. We finally meet."

Mallet didn't blink, didn't move. He was so focused on Valder, he saw his every thought, and he knew that this attack was very personal, and very deliberate.

The man should not have used Kayli in his twisted plans. Sounding almost bored, Mallet said, "Big mistake, Valder. Now you're a dead man."

Valder gave an earsplitting whistle, and all around them, silence fell. His men, many of them bloodied and limping, retreated to stand behind him.

The defense team took a stance with Mallet.

Feigning amusement, Valder asked, "Will you risk her to get to me?" Slowly, he wrapped an arm around her throat, caging her into his steely hold. "Or will you stay out of matters that don't concern you?"

"Nothing concerns me more than her." Mallet needed to see her, needed to know her expression. "Besides, you're the one bleeding."

Valder wiped a forearm across his face. "She is fast."

"More so than you realize."

Kayli used her elbow again, striking Valder in the ribs and knocking his breath from him a rush.

He cursed, faltered, and quickly readjusted to keep her in front of him.

But not once did he hurt her.

"Take off her helmet," Mallet ordered. If he could see Kayli's eyes, he would know her state of mind.

Valder quirked a brow, laughed, and said to Kayli, "Do it, little bird. Let him see your fear."

Mallet watched Kayli slowly reach up and release her helmet strap.

It was then that Valder saw the ring on her finger. It was almost imperceptible, but Mallet noted his surprise on such a deep level.

He recalled what Raemay had said—that Kayli would be safe while wearing the ring.

Happy for an opportunity to distract the man, Mallet said, "You're here for Raemay, aren't you?"

Valder didn't reply. As Kayli lifted off the helmet, Valder waited with his breath suspended.

And Mallet saw what he had so hoped to see.

No fear.

Kayli's golden eyes conveyed a message to him.

This time, he had no choice but to trust her, but it didn't matter. He saw the intent there in her expression; he knew her well enough to know what she'd do, to anticipate when.

He smiled, encouraging her.

The helmet hit the ground, and in moves so fast and economical they seemed a blur, Kayli locked her fists for added impact as she brought her elbow back once more, this time in a crippling liver blow. Air left Valder in a whoosh, loosening his hold just enough for her to turn and drive a knee hard into his groin.

Just that easily Kayli was loose—and Mallet stepped in with fury boiling through his bloodstream.

FOLLOWING the protocol applied to the Arbiter, Raemay waited in her chambers for news. She had finished her morning meal and had just begun brushing her hair when the alarm sounded, and her nerves were still jangled from the awful sound.

She worried for the women of the colony. She worried for Kayli, now distracted with her union.

She even worried for Michael, knowing he would put himself in harm's way to protect all others.

Pressing a hand to her mouth, she said aloud to the empty room, "I can't just wait here."

"No," Hauk said, "you can not. It is time for you to confront your demons."

It had been so long since Hauk belonged to her, since he had come to her that way. Not since Kayli became Claviger so long ago and Hauk stopped answering to her had she heard the abrupt intrusion of his voice. Hearing it now had her jerking in shock.

"Hauk!" A fist pressed to her thundering heart, Raemay asked, "What are you doing here? Is Kayli all right? What's wrong?"

"Kayli is happy now."

Some of the awful panic receded. "Yes, yes she is. Are you saying that because of her happiness, she is not involved in this conflict?"

"You care for Mallet."

"Michael?" What was Hauk getting to? "Yes, I like him very much. He's a good man, and he is good for Kayli. Not at all what I always . . ."

"Feared?"

"What is going on, Hauk? Do you know something about Michael that I do not?"

"I know that he is about to tear apart Valder Wildoon, unless you stop being a coward."

Her legs gave out and she slumped to the edge of her bed. Vision fading, then exploding bright again, she whispered, "Valder is here?"

"He tried to take Kayli."

"No."

"To get even with you. To make you pay for hurting him so badly."

Raemay covered her ears with her hands. Never had she wanted to hurt Valder. But she'd had no choice, had never had choices . . .

"Time for us to go, Raemay. There can be no more hiding from the past."

Tears welled in her eyes. "Yes." Her daughter had always been noble. Michael was noble.

Time for her to be noble as well.

KAYLI watched as Michael grabbed Valder and hauled him upright. His men started to surge forward, but Valder shouted, "No!" and they all stepped back again.

"Man-to-man, huh?" Michael taunted. "And you just let a girl lay you low."

"Because of that ring," Valder said, and there was something in his face, something stricken that incapacitated him. "Look at her hair, her eyes—"

Michael hit him in the jaw and his head snapped back hard. Valder fell onto his backside but shot back to his feet in an instant, spitting blood, shoving his hair out of his face. He didn't watch Michael as he should have.

He stared at Kayli. Beseeching. Apologizing.

She saw his eyes then, eyes so much like her own. Golden eyes—unlike anyone else's in their colony.

Michael must have seen it, too, for he looked at Valder, then at Kayli.

She heard Michael say, "No way," very succinctly. Then

right after that, he muttered, "Fuck it," and he kicked Valder in the head.

The man went flying, landing hard on his side.

Again, he got back to his feet, but not quite as quickly this time. He held off his men with one raised hand. Blood trickled from his nose, a purpling bruise rose on the side of his face, and he wasn't quite steady on his feet.

Again, he paid no mind to Michael.

"How old are you, child?" he asked Kayli. "Exactly how old?"

She couldn't answer. For some reason, seeing him so battered hurt her heart. "The women you've taken," she whispered. "How do they fare?"

His swollen mouth tipped in a crooked smile. "All are happy in union. Some are with child. They choose to stay. I have not held them against their will."

"You swear it?" Kayli asked, unable to trust something that was so opposite of what she'd believed for so long.

Nayana spoke up from the crowd. "It is the truth, Kayli. The man suffered, not understanding why he couldn't make Lydina happy. Not until I told him she was an AFA did he know." She stepped forward so all could see her, and her face was pink with a blush. "I, too, have taken union. They are good men, just short on women as we are short on men."

Michael threw up his hands. "You're taking all the fun out of this, Valder. I need you to fight back so I can kick your ass."

Valder shook his head without taking his attention from Kayli. "I will not. Not now." He took one step toward her, but Michael stepped into his path.

"I don't think so."

"Look at her!" Valder shouted with volatile emotion. "Look at her hair." And softer, "Look at her eyes."

Michael glanced at her, put his hands on his hips and dropped his head to mutter, "Fuck, fuck, fuck."

Kayli drew a shaky, uneven breath.

"How old are you?" Valder asked again.

And Raemay said, "She was born eight months after I left you."

Valder's head shot up and he searched for her, found her picking her way around the field. Rage replaced the shock. His mouth twisted in a snarl. "You did more damage than I ever realized." He thumped a fist to his chest and bellowed, *"You stole my daughter from me."*

Michael looked as undecided as Kayli on what to do. Then, giving up on more violence, he came to her and put an arm around her.

Simple support.

But she needed it so much, just as she'd so badly needed him to know that she had the situation under control with Valder. And he had. He'd trusted her, he'd smiled at her, he'd let her handle things.

Until she realized that Valder was . . .

Her *father.*

She wanted to crawl in on herself. No wonder her mother had always treated her differently. No wonder she couldn't inherit.

She was a bastard.

"I'm sorry." Tears tracking her cheeks, Raemay came to Kayli. "I am so very, very sorry, Kayli."

Even now, with the proof there for the entire colony to see, Kayli couldn't believe it. "He's . . . he is my father?"

Raemay reached out to her. "Darling, please understand. I could not tell you—"

With a roar of fury, Valder took an aggressive step forward—which prompted Michael to do the same. With his body, Michael protected Kayli and her mother.

Valder drew up short in impotent fury. Red-eyed and crackling with rage, he pointed a finger at Raemay. "I loved you! I would have cared for you and our daughter."

"Your way!" Raemay screamed back at him. "Can't you see, Valder? Your colony does not value women."

Valder looked truly shocked by that accusation. "That's not true!"

Raemay's lip trembled, then curled. "Women are second-class citizens, never quite equal to men. Even now, you take what you want. You took our women, stole them with threats against my colony."

His jaw locked. "To get even with you. You think my men need to resort to abduction? Every woman taken was charmed into union within days of joining my colony. They are happier than they've ever been here. None are anxious to return. What do you think of that, Raemay? What do you think of your leadership that sends women joyfully to other colonies?"

"Harsh," Michael said to him, his arm tight around Kayli's shoulders. "If you're trying to win her back, you're batting a big fat zero."

Valder stared at Michael, then shook his head. "You make no sense."

"Bullshit. You're here acting out of wounded pride and lingering love. Why not be a man and admit it?"

Valder looked struck by that observation. He turned to Raemay with a frown.

She shook her head. "Please, Valder, you have to understand. If I had stayed with you, I would have lost everything. I would have been forced to give up my inherited title and position in the colony."

"You would have had me."

Raemay covered her face and turned away. Her shoulders shook.

Rolling his eyes, Michael said, "You gotta see it from her perspective, dude."

Valder looked ready to attack him. "This does not concern you."

"Wrong again." Michael tightened his arm around her. "I love Kayli, and Raemay's her mom. So their business is my business. Deal with it."

Kayli went weak in the knees.

In the middle of pure bedlam, Michael made that incredible confession. She grabbed his shirt and jerked him around to face her. "You *what*?"

CHAPTER 23

INSTEAD of answering her, Michael gave her a resounding smooch on her mouth—and then he stuck her behind him as if she needed protection from the chaos.

He addressed the crowd, saying, "Show's over, folks. This is personal stuff, so stop gawking. Head back to your homes. All of you." He looked at Valder. "Your people, too, Valder. Get rid of them."

Valder nodded, but he looked around with no clear idea where to send his men.

Dormius, with Mesha at his side, moved forward into the fray. "Sir, I could take them all, including our . . . er, guests, to the reception hall. Does that serve?"

Michael slapped him on the back. "Good plan, Dormius. Have Mesha order up drinks or something. Keep them all busy, okay?"

"Yes, sir."

Not about to cower behind Michael, Kayli stepped around him and caught Dormius's arm. After all, she was still the head of the defense, and should have been the one giving the orders. "Have my second in command watch over everyone.

Tell her there will be no disputes on this day. All will behave, or face consequences."

"Yes," Valder agreed. "My men will not cause conflict."

"Understood." Dormius tried to lead Mesha away, but she
resisted.

Blinking first at her mother, then at Kayli, she made an
"oh boy" face and then touched Michael's arm. "Good luck,
sir."

"Thanks, doll."

Once everyone had filed a respectable distance away,
Michael stepped away from Kayli. He folded his arms over
his chest and addressed Valder with obvious pity. "Face it,
man. You do have a primitive way of doing things—stealing
women and all."

Valder slashed a hand through the air. "It was the only
thing I could think to do after I found her again."

"Raemay, you mean?"

"Yes."

"So you were looking for her?"

"Looking? I searched for her for years." His anger on the
rise again, he made a point of not looking at Raemay. "We
were in love, or so I thought. But she left me without a single
word, and I did not know if she lived or if she had died. For
such a long time, I suffered suffocating grief."

Raemay wrapped her arms around herself.

"Time faded the pain," Valder confessed. "But no other
woman appealed to me." His laugh was rough, suggestive.
"No one can claim I have been a saint, but I've never formed
a union."

Kayli found it very telling that he had never committed
himself to a woman.

"Raemay?" Michael prompted. "You got anything to add
to that?"

Her face tear-streaked and her eyes red, Raemay lifted
her shoulders helplessly. "I can only apologize for things
that were out of my control."

"Out of your control?" Valder's piercing stare said he
didn't care about her circumstances. His gaze burned with

resentment and lingering rage. "You kept my child from me. That is unforgivable."

Kayli's heart clenched with so many painful repercussions. Valder—*her father*—was truly devastated that he'd missed time with her.

She felt devastated, too, knowing her life to be a lie. Her mother had done much damage to so many.

Seeking comfort, she took Michael's hand and said a prayer of gratitude that she had him with her. As soon as possible, she would let him know that she returned his love in all ways.

MALLET felt the chill in Kayli's hand, the way she shook, and wanted only to protect her. But he knew the easiest way to get beyond a hurt was to face it, expose it, and then deal with it.

She'd fought with valor and courage, only to find out that the man she'd faced was a father she'd never known. Kayli hadn't needed his help, but once Valder realized she was his daughter, he stopped resisting her rather than chance hurting her.

Mallet had to respect that.

There were so many wounded feelings at play. As the one least emotionally involved, Mallet hoped to help them all sort it out.

"Did the guy you were in a union with know that Kayli wasn't his?"

Raemay nodded. "Oh yes, he knew." A faint, dark memory flickered in her gaze, there and gone. "I owed him that much. You see . . . he saved me."

"From *me*?" Valder sneered with renewed fury.

"No." More tears glistened in her eyes. "From my father."

When Kayli stiffened beside Mallet, he put his arm around her and tucked her in close to his side.

Valder's face went blank with horror.

Putting a hand to her stomach, Raemay nervously glanced

at them all, and then moved closer to Valder. "Danta Raine was my father's closest confidant. He . . . he did not love me, but when my father rejected all other suitors, Danta wondered why. You see, my father . . . he was Arbiter before me, hero to many."

Expecting the worst, Mallet glanced at Kayli, and saw the same dread in her eyes.

"Those of the colony loved my father for his fair leadership. But at home he was a harsh dictator." As if shamed by the truth, Raemay turned her gaze away from everyone. "Because the bruises on my back and legs were always hidden, not many knew of Father's true nature, of his hot temper."

"He *beat* you?" Valder asked.

She nodded. "But then Danta witnessed the tail end of one of the beatings, and within the week, he told my father of his intent to join me in union. He was the one man my father could not reject without raising suspicions within the colony."

Valder stared at her, tormented, Mallet knew, by the fact that she'd been hurt, and more so that he couldn't demand retribution on her behalf.

Her father was long gone, well out of his reach.

"Valder still loves her," Mallet whispered to Kayli.

"I think you are right," she whispered back, and she put her head on his chest, surprising Mallet.

Eyes clouded with regret, Valder said, "God, Raemay, I did not know."

As if she didn't hear him, Raemay continued. "Danta was kind. He protected me and my father never touched me again after that. But . . ." She glanced again at Kayli, her eyes filled with apology. "Because he felt no passion for me, because he'd accepted me through pity, he often sought his pleasure with other women."

"Bastard," Valder raged.

Mallet had to agree.

"He kept me in material comfort, and on occasion, when he thought of having a son, he came to me in the dark. But otherwise, we lived as dear friends."

Valder charged two steps closer to her. "You should have left him."

"Perhaps." She shrugged her shoulders in defeat. "But he had sacrificed much for me, and though it broke my heart to know I was in a loveless union, it battered my pride more so that he showed little discretion. Many knew he was unfaithful, that I could not . . . keep him happy."

"You felt indebted to him," Mallet said, stating the obvious.

"Yes." She gave another flickering glance toward Kayli. "And had I left him, my father would have taken it as a personal slight. Such was not done, not by the daughter of an Arbiter." She twisted her hands together, and her voice trembled. "As my father aged, his health failed him, and that only made his temper more volatile."

Valder thumped a fist to his chest. "I would have protected you. I would have taken you in union."

Raemay bit her lip and struggled with her emotions. "You were wonderful, Valder. You were there when I needed you most and I will always love you for that."

For such a sturdy man, Valder almost staggered at the mention of love.

"But," Raemay continued, "you are a dictator in your own right. No woman in your colony can serve in a position of power. For you, women are there to be protected and pampered, unable to make their own decisions, limited in the destinies they can fulfill." Tears spilled over. "For you, they are still second-class citizens."

Seeing Valder ready to explode, Mallet stepped between them. "If what she says is true, then she has a point, Valder. Get with the times, man. Women are equals."

He didn't agree. "They are smaller, more delicate. They are not physically or emotionally equipped to endure the hardships of—"

"I'd stop right there if I were you," Mallet warned. He didn't bother looking at Kayli or Raemay; he already knew how those independent women would feel about Valder's sexist attitude.

"It is our way to protect, to treasure our women!" he avowed. And then he demanded, "What would you have me do? Put women at risk as Raemay has done?"

So much now made sense to Mallet—Raemay's determination that women could be the aggressor, *should* be capable of defending themselves. And the strict moral code she'd instituted . . . it had come straight from her own shattered nobility. "If I were you, I'd try a little compromise."

"Compromise?" To a leader like Valder, the idea appeared foreign.

"Come on, man." If at all possible, Mallet hoped to save Valder from himself. "You do know what it means, don't you? You give a little, Raemay gives a little."

Valder eyed Mallet head to toe—and made note when Kayli came forward to stand at his side, silently agreeing with him, backing him up. "You would do this?"

"What the hell do you think I've been doing?" He put his arm around Kayli and landed a quick kiss to her temple. "You think I liked seeing Kayli in battle with you? Fuck no. It took everything I had to keep from taking over, which would have included killing you."

"I did not hurt her."

Mallet grinned. "No, as I recall, she worked you over pretty damned good—and that was before you realized she was your daughter, so don't tell me you 'let' her do it."

Valder's mouth tipped into a crooked smile. "She took me off guard more than once." He touched his swollen nose, now discolored with bruises and dried blood. "She is faster and stronger than expected."

"Pride, Valder?" Maybe there was hope for him after all. "For a female warrior?"

"Pride for my *daughter*," Valder charged, not yet willing to admit to anything more. Then his eyes closed with renewed pain. "God in heaven, when I think of what might have happened to her . . ."

"It was *your* men I saw bloodied and limping, not the defense team—which until very recently was all female," Mallet pointed out. "Don't get me wrong, the new male recruits are coming along, but they're not up to snuff yet. Without the women, the defense team wouldn't be nearly so effective."

"But how do you bear it?" Valder asked Mallet with feeling. "If you care for her—"

"Care for her? Hell man, I'd lose the use of my legs again to keep her baby toe safe. But her independence and the defense of her colony are important to her, and that makes them important to me." He gave Valder a long look. "And let me tell you, it's a hell of a lot easier than going two decades without her."

Valder slowly nodded. "Point taken."

Kayli pushed back from Mallet to stare at him. "So you really do love me?"

He rolled his eyes. "Why do you look so surprised, baby? I've told you so a dozen times."

"No," she accused, frowning at him as her hands fisted in his shirt. "You have only said that you love things about me."

"*Everything* about you," he corrected. Catching her by the waist, he lifted her up so he could plant a thorough kiss on her mouth. Regardless of what happened between Raemay and Valder, he wanted them to know that Kayli was his and he wouldn't be giving her up. "I even love your take-charge personality. The only problem is that it clashes with my take-charge personality. I guess we need to work on that, huh?"

She hung limp in his arms, her expression still dazed, bewildered. And happy. Slowly, she smiled. "Truly, you love me?"

Mallet laughed. "Woman, you're the one who has a problem with that word, not me. What the hell did you think? That I support your life as Claviger because I enjoy seeing you charge off into conflicts?"

"I know that you do not."

Mallet laughed at the dry way she said that. "It kills me a little to even think about it. But for you, it's worth it." He kissed her again, lingering just long enough to tease, but not so long that he embarrassed her. Too much. "For you, I'd do anything—and that includes protecting you when I think it's necessary, even when it pisses you off."

Astounded, Raemay lifted a hand toward Mallet. "Yes," she whispered. "Yes, you understand."

"Understands what?" Valder asked.

But it was Mallet who answered. "The overwhelming need to protect those I cherish most, regardless of the consequences."

Raemay nodded. "As Arbiter, I could ensure that my daughters had every opportunity. I could help other women in so many ways." She stared regretfully at Valder. "But none of that would have been possible if you knew Kayli was your daughter."

"Because I would have claimed her," Valder said. He tangled a hand in his hair, caught between anger over what he'd lost and a struggle to understand Raemay's reasoning. "I assume that's why she could not inherit."

Keeping her head down, her shoulders heavy with guilt, Raemay said, "Even after Danta died, I had to ensure Kayli was not heir. As such, she would have gone to the Cosmos Confederation."

"She has very unique coloring. My coloring."

Raemay acknowledged that with a small smile at her daughter. "From the time she was a young girl, she looked so much like you, Valder. Others would have noticed the resemblance. It would have only been a matter of time before word reached you. It scared me so much, not knowing what you would do."

With no hesitation at all, Valder said, "I would have come for both of you."

"But it was not just Kayli and me. I had two other daughters by then, and a duty to my colony. Many people would have been shocked and shamed by my less than respectable behavior with you."

"No." Kayli smiled at her mother. "I believe you are more critical of yourself than others would be if they knew the whole truth."

Her generosity and understanding pleased Mallet, and it
nearly crumbled the last of Raemay's defenses. She covered
her face with her hands, but only for a second. Then she
squared her shoulders and faced the repercussions to her actions. "I made many mistakes and I know it, but I've tried to
correct them."

Agonized, Valder went to her. "What happened that
brought you to me that first night?"

Showing less tension now, her voice soft, Raemay wiped
away the last of her tears. "For many days, I had noticed you.
You were so attentive, always flirting with me, flattering me."

Valder took her hands. "I fell for you the very first time
I saw you."

In Kayli's ear, Mallet whispered, "I know the feeling."

She smiled at him.

"Earlier that day one of my meetings was canceled. I returned to my quarters and found Danta with one of his lov-
ers. I reacted out of anger, hurt. I knew it was wrong, knew
I had no future with you. But I needed to feel . . . wanted. I
needed to know that I was still a woman."

Valder swallowed hard. "You spent two months with
me."

"Because you were so tempting, and being with you was
the happiest I'd ever been. I thought of breaking union. I
thought of a life with you. Danta did not come after me, and
I assumed he would not mind. My father was so very sick, I
knew he could not hurt me again. But then . . . I got news
that Father had passed and I was heir and . . . grand plans
formed."

He dropped her hands. "Plans to leave me."

"Plans to protect the women of my colony. Plans to protect all women from the hurt I'd suffered, both physical and
emotional. Danta had his own obligations to the colony, and
other than the occasional attempt at siring a son, he left me
to do as I pleased. I had dishonored myself enough, so if
Danta had not been killed in that terrible accident, I would
be with him still."

"How did he die?" Valder asked.

"A freak explosion in space incinerated his vessel. He and all of his crew were lost. It was not long after Mesha was born. Though he treated the girls well, I knew that he was unhappy that I'd had yet another daughter instead of a son."

Valder braced himself. "You grieved for him?"

"Yes. He had become more a supportive friend than a life mate. Mostly," she confessed with sadness, "I grieved for what I would never have."

Valder stood mere inches in front of her. "When I chanced upon your whereabouts, when I discovered that you had married, that you had children of your own . . . You can not know what that knowledge did to me."

"I'd say that it made you stupid," Mallet interjected. "Only a fool would get even with a woman by using other women."

Kayli nodded. "It was not a good plan."

Valder didn't take offense. "True." He shared a self-deprecating smile. "Though I had wanted you to think otherwise, my actions were not all motivated by revenge." He put his hands on his hips and paced a little. "My colony is in need of females."

"You don't say." Mallet quirked a brow at Raemay. "That's kind of serendipitous, isn't it, considering your colony is short on guys?"

Cautious now, Raemay said, "I suppose that it is."

Valder again took her hands in his. "I would like to see if . . ." His voice broke, and he cleared his throat. "I believe we can . . . fix this. Compromise, yes? That's what your visitor suggests. If we sit down and talk, is it possible that we can find a middle ground?"

Raemay drew in a deep breath, her expression a mix of hope and worry. "It would not be easy. As Arbiter, I have many duties. My colony relies on me. I don't know that I can give up everything I have worked so hard for."

"I would." Kayli put her arms around Mallet's neck and stared up into his eyes. "For my man, I would give up everything, because I love him, too."

Inside, Mallet's stomach dropped, but outside, he pretended to falter on his feet. "Woman! You said the word."

"Love," she said again, enunciating clearly, half laughing. "I love you very much, Michael Manchester, and if my father had not chosen this morning to attack us, I would have told you so."

Damn, but she could take his knees out so easily. "Say it again."

"I love you. I want you to be happy. If you need me to give up my position as Claviger—"

To cut off that offer, Mallet kissed her hard and didn't want to stop. But he had her mother and father both watching him, so he lifted his head and smiled at her. "No, Kayli. All I need is for you to love me. We'll work out everything else."

Valder came forward to slap Mallet on the shoulder. "Formal introductions have gone awry, but I hope it's not too late to say that I am pleased my daughter has found you."

"And it wasn't easy," Mallet told him, "considering she had to travel back through time."

Confused, Valder frowned over that, until Raemay said, "I am most pleased, too. At first, his attraction to her nearly panicked me. I knew that if he pursued her, she would become more noticeable to others."

"To me," Valder said.

"Yes. I have some deeply ingrained reservations about large, powerful men. But when I saw how happy Michael made my daughter, I started to doubt many of my decisions. He's bigger than you, Valder, and every bit as dominant, but he takes great care with Kayli's feelings."

Valder went to one knee in front of her. "I would care for your feelings, too."

Kayli squeezed Mallet again. "I think we are proof, Mother, that love can temper longtime beliefs. I never thought something could be more important to me than my position as Claviger. But compared to what I feel for Michael, it is nothing."

Mallet grinned. Damn, but he'd never get used to hearing her say that. "You see, Valder? Compromise pays off."

Raemay touched Valder's jaw. "I don't know how you could ever forgive me."

Valder smiled. "I searched the galaxy for you, woman. Do you think I created that colony next door by accident? Do you think I stumbled across you by chance? It was destiny. We are meant to be together."

Mallet glanced at Kayli, saw that she was smiling now, too. "Yeah, I think Kayli and I will mosey on and let the two of you hash things out."

"Wait." Valder, still clinging to a silent Raemay's hands, turned to his daughter. "I owe you much."

"No."

"You are my daughter. And I'm so very proud of you. More proud than I can say. My chest wants to burst when I look at you."

Kayli laughed with tears in her eyes. "Thank you, but you have other things on your mind right now. You and I can . . . catch up later."

"You promise?"

"Yes." She tipped her head. "I'm most curious about you. If you and your men would like to stay over, we can accommodate you easily. Just let me know."

Raemay said, "I could make the arrangements."

And Valder, pleased at Raemay's interest in keeping him around, grinned at them.

When he started to say more, Mallet shook his head. "Later, Valder. One hurdle at a time." He winked. "Right now, I want a moment alone with my lady."

THE moment alone took over two hours to get. On their way to privacy, they got waylaid by the colony members who needed reassurance that all was well. Mallet stood back and let Kayli do her thing, putting all at ease.

She really was terrific in the role of leader.

Then Toller, Valder's good friend and apparently only

one of a few who knew of the torch he carried, wanted to know how he fared with Raemay. Mallet wasn't one to gossip, so he said only, "If you trust him, that should be enough, right?"

Kayli added as an aside, "My mother is much touched by his sincerity."

Toller grinned at that and went off with Nayana.

Before they could leave, they saw Idola making eyes at a man who didn't preen for her, didn't fall at her feet. But he made his interest clear.

"I can't believe it," Kayli said. "Idola looks much smitten."

"Must be something in the air today, huh?" Mallet squeezed her close and said, "Now, for a little privacy . . ."

"Wait!" Mesha ran up to let them know that she hoped to form her own union very soon because it was all so romantic how theirs had worked out.

Beside her, Dormius held her hand and stared at her with adoration.

Mallet looked at Kayli, but she appeared as much at a loss as he was. "I think that's one for Raemay to figure out." He tugged Mesha in for a quick hug. "Just don't do anything right now, okay?"

Dormius, the little rascal, blushed, but Mesha chuckled. "Do not worry, sir. Now go. We've held you up long enough."

Mallet looked up at the sky and said, "Hauk?"

"Where to, Mallet?"

"Anyplace where we won't be interrupted."

In a blink, he found himself alone with Kayli near the lake. The sun was high overhead. Wildflowers dipped and swayed in the breeze. Water lapped the shoreline while the surface twinkled like a million diamonds.

Kayli sat on a boulder and watched him. "I love you."

Mallet smiled as he removed his shirt. "One more time."

She pulled off her boots. "I love you. More than anything."

When he was naked, Mallet went to her and helped her finish undressing. "Will you tell me that every day?"

"Yes."

"At least twice a day?"

She laughed. "Yes."

Not to press his luck, but . . . "Any reason it took you so long?"

"Many reasons, but they all seem most insignificant now."

Pensive, Mallet took her hand and they waded waist deep into the water. He pushed back her pale hair, held her face, and kissed her incredible mouth.

It was a peaceful moment that filled him with too many emotions. "Kayli, love, I'd like it if you shared the reasons with me anyway."

"Okay." Dipping her hands under the water, she found him. "I feared that I would not keep you happy."

"I love you." He closed his eyes. "Of course you make me happy—especially when you do things like that."

Smiling, she said, "I feared that you were drawn to me because I was most familiar to you. I had taken you from everything you knew and dropped you into a situation that few would have been able to accept."

"You're here." He covered her breasts with his hands. "That's all that matters to me. The rest is just backdrop."

"I feared that I would lose my identity and that I didn't know how to do anything other than be a warrior."

His brow went up. "Oh, trust me, babe, you know how to do other things."

Laughing aloud, she said, "You are a very sexual man. That pleases me."

Before he got totally off topic, Mallet said, "I want you to go on being Claviger for as long as you enjoy the job. You're damned good at it."

"I will do that for you, if you will do something for me."

"Anything."

"Do not change." She put her arms around his neck and wrapped her legs around his waist. "Keep being protective of me and everyone else. Keep influencing my people—now your people—with your outrageous attitudes. Continue helping us to train and improve. Tease my mother, care for my sisters, and make love to me every day so that we can procreate and make a family."

Emotion got a stranglehold on him. "It'll be my pleasure." He started to kiss her with all the love he felt.

And Hauk said, "You have twenty minutes kiddies, and then your mother wishes to make an announcement."

Mallet laughed. "Can I give Hauk back?"

"No." She tightened her legs around him. "But you can show me again the details of the quickie. And afterward, we will face everyone together."

"Always."

EPILOGUE

DREW Black couldn't believe it when he found Dean and Simon sitting with their heads together on a bench in the locker room. In an hour or so, the preliminary fights would start and they both needed to be out front, schmoozing the crowd and racking up the publicity.

Instead, they were playing show-and-tell with photographs.

Walking beside him, Harley asked, "What do you have there?" He joined them at the bench, took one look at the photos, and grinned. "I'll be damned. He looks great, huh?"

Scowling with curiosity, Drew walked over to them. "Why aren't you guys out front? The crowds are screaming for you."

"They'll wait," Dean said, and then he handed a photo to Drew. "Check that out."

The photo showed Mallet with the slim, gutsy blonde he'd met at the hospital. They were waist deep in a big lake, the woman's upper body shielded behind Mallet as she wrapped her arms around his neck and peeked over his shoulder. Her hair was slicked back, her eyes were bright with laughter.

Damn. When Mallet had disappeared, they'd all wondered where he went, and why he'd left with only a note as farewell. The little broad had gotten to him in a very big way.

"Here are a few more." Simon handed him several photos. They showed Mallet and the woman lounging in some odd chairs, riding some weird looking cycles, and one was even of them sparring. Each picture was a scene of pleasure. "Seems his legs are fine now."

"Must've been one hell of a progressive hospital," Dean added, "to be able to get him completely healed."

"She's cute," Harley said. "And he sure looks sunk on her."

"Yeah, he does." Drew flattened his mouth. "Guess I fucking well better give up on the idea of him coming back."

"He said he's not." Dean handed over a note, and explained, "He's married now, happy where he's at, and he just wanted us all to know he's okay, given the funk he was in when he left."

Simon lifted his brows. "It's nothing short of a miracle, I say."

"I'm damn glad she found him, or he found her," Dean said. "However it worked out, it worked out for the best. I can see that."

Harley finished reading the note himself and nodded. "You have to admit, he sounds like his old self again."

"Strange envelope, though." Simon held it up for all to see. "It was delivered special courier to the gym, without a return address, by some jumpy fellow who was there one minute and gone the next."

Drew took the envelope and looked it over. It was all too fucking strange, if you asked him.

"But it's definitely Mallet's handwriting on the note," Dean pointed out. "And he does sound pretty damned content."

Drew read the note, had to agree with the others, and then smacked it down on the bench. "Now where the fuck am I going to find someone to replace him?"

"It's been months," Simon pointed out. "You were still counting on him to commentate?"

"The fans think of him as a hero." Rubbing his head, Drew said, "So yeah, I was holding the position."

Harley slapped him on the shoulder. "You'll figure it out, Drew. You always do."

"And when he does," Simon said, sotto voce, "he'll find a way to make a fortune off it."

Drew ignored that. "Mind if I hang on to these for a while?"

Shrugging, Simon said, "I can get them from you later. No big deal."

Dean, Harley, and Simon headed out of the room, talking to themselves, all obviously happy for their friend.

Drew again looked at the photo of Mallet and the woman in the lake, and he shook his head. "Damn it, you lucky SOB, you do look deliriously happy." Grinning, he tucked the photos and note back into the envelope, concealed them inside his suit coat pocket, straightened his designer tie and, said to no one, "Where the hell am I going to find another fighter like you?"

FAR, far away, in a different time and place, Mallet smiled as he turned off the viewer.

"They have no more need to worry about you." Kayli hugged up to Mallet's side.

"Satisfied?" Hauk asked.

Mallet kissed Kayli. "You heard Drew. I'm more than satisfied. I'm *deliriously* happy."

Don't miss the next
SBC Fighter Romance featuring Drew Black

Following is a special excerpt from this
upcoming novel from
Lori Foster

Coming soon!

GILLIAN Noode stood against the back wall of the popular bar, Roger's Rodeo, where many fighters hung out. She was close enough to observe him, but not close enough to get noticed. Yet. At least, not by him. Plenty of other men had already given her the once-over, showing appreciation for her trim black skirt, her low-scooped white blouse and strappy sandals. A few had even tried to strike up a conversation. She'd politely declined.

She'd come here for a reason, and Drew Black was it.

Dressed in well-worn jeans and a comfortable black T-shirt bearing the logo of the SBC fight club, the president of the sport sat at the polished bar. Currently, he was holding close conversation with two long-haired young women whose bloated busts defied believability. No woman *that* slender had breasts *that* large.

But Drew showed no signs of disbelief. Like a king of his own making, he ogled with commitment to the boob ruse.

From the many interviews and television spots she'd watched, as well as her current scrutiny, Gillian surmised he had a fighter-type physique, not quite as shredded as the actual fighters, but sculpted with muscle, strong and capable. Obviously his ego demanded he stay in shape since he was often surrounded by younger men in their prime, elite fighters with rock-hard bodies and astounding ability.

Drew Black intrigued her beyond the job at hand.

As an entrepreneur he showed great intelligence; no one could have accomplished what he had without smarts. He'd taken a mostly dead sport, banned in many states, and turned it into an astounding success.

And motivation? The man had it in spades. He couldn't possibly sleep more than six hours a night given his enthusiastic workload and insane social calendar.

Good looks, great body, intelligence, enthusiasm and money . . . Drew Black would be quite the catch if he wasn't such a sexist foulmouthed jerk with the tact of a goat.

Her external analysis complete, Gillian moved closer, just a short ways down the bar. She could now hear Drew's deep voice—not that she expected much enlightenment from his conversation.

But Drew surprised her.

"Will you call me?" Bimbo One asked him with a pout.

"No." His laugh was low and mellow, but lacking malice.

Look-alike Bimbo Two said, "How about me?" She toyed with his ear in a way that made Gillian twitch. "I can promise you a good time."

"I bet you can." Drew took her wrist and moved her teasing hand away. "But I'll pass."

Gillian raised a brow. She'd expected him to suggest a threesome, and instead he'd rejected them both.

Interesting.

The bimbos combined their whining complaints and attempts at persuasion until Drew sent them away. "Girls, what the fuck? C'mon, I have shit to do and it doesn't include having my ears ring. Go find something—or someone—else to do, okay?"

"We waited a long time to get to talk to you." Bimbo One sulked in a juvenile fashion.

Drew leaned around the woman to eye his male companion. "A little help here?"

The man, who Gillian recognized as a fighter, held up big, capable hands. "Sorry. I have a girl waiting at home."

"We aren't at your home, Brett."

He smirked. "Yeah, well, Sarge doesn't like to share me."

Drew pulled back. "Sarge? What the fuck kind of name is that for a female?"

"The kind that suits her." Unruffled by the implied insult, Brett finished his drink. To Gillian, it looked like juice. She gave Brett points.

"Look," Drew said to the closest bimbo, "you're too fucking young and frankly, too pushy."

"We have to be pushy to get near you. You're just so popular—"

"How about I give you a couple of tickets to the next SBC fight instead? Good seats. How's that?"

The girls bounced with enthusiasm. Gillian couldn't take it. She asked the bartender for a martini. By the time she'd been served and taken a few fortifying sips, Drew was alone at the bar with Brett.

"You're brutal, Drew."

"Did you see those girls? Not only were they phony from head to toes, the damn giggles were wearing on my nerves." He worked his shoulders, as if releasing tension. "Jesus, I do have some standards you know."

"Yeah? Like what?"

"You want the whole list, huh? Well, it doesn't apply here, but she has to be less than forty. Older broads are too independent."

Brett laughed. "The two of them together weren't forty. So what else?"

"She has to be childless, because let's face it: The whole kid thing is a pain in the ass. No way am I fucking anybody's mother. And before you say it, yeah, I know, those two are still children themselves."

Brett saluted him with juice.

"On top of being good-looking and sexy, she has to have some intelligence—at least enough that I can carry on a conversation with her. And no squealing. God, I detest broads who squeal."

Brett commiserated. "They were squealers."

"Can you imagine how they'd be in bed?" Drew laughed. "I'd need fucking earplugs."

That mouth of his. Gillian shook her head. It was a sexy mouth, but the things he said, the crude language he used, was not befitting the force behind the fastest growing sport in history. That mouth had gotten him into trouble, whether he realized it yet or not.

It was her job to clean up his act, and to make him a more presentable figurehead for the SBC franchise.

Daunting, but maybe not impossible.

The trick would be to beat him at his own game, to always keep the upper hand, and to grow a skin so thick that her feminist core wouldn't be damaged in the process.

She'd also have to remember that he was a jackass, albeit a sexy one, so it would behoove her to keep her emotional distance.

Sadly, he was the first man she'd found exciting in a very long time.

He was the *last* man she could ever get involved with.

Picking up her glass, Gillian moved down the bar, took the vacated seat beside him and crossed her legs. While watching him, she removed the olive from her drink and ate it.

Both men stared at her, not so much because of her looks, which she knew to be average, or her figure, which was a little more voluptuous than currently popular. But because she'd invaded their space—and was now staring back.

Drew turned on his stool to fully face her. Without a word, he looked her over, lingering on her legs, her cleavage, and her mouth. When his gaze met hers, he said low, "Hello there."

Oh, men were *so* easy. Gillian held out a hand. "Hello."

A very warm, firm hand, twice the size of hers, enveloped her fingers—and held on. "I'm Drew Black."

"Of course you are." Smiling, she retrieved her hand from his. "Gillian Noode."

"Nude?"

Of course he wouldn't let that one slide. With a chastising look, she spelled, "N.O.O.D.E."

His mouth quirked. "Hell of a name."

"Yes, and I've heard every joke there is from every schoolboy out there." She reached beyond Drew to the fighter. She'd heard Drew use his first name, but she liked proper introductions. "And you are?"

He took her hand gently. "Brett Bullman, ma'am."

Unlike Drew, who shaved his head, Brett had shaggy brown hair a little too long, a little too unruly, and gorgeous green eyes.

He also had a name familiar to her. "I've read about you. You're touted as a self-taught phenomenon taking the fight scene by storm."

He shrugged with indifference, and shared a friendly smile that had surely melted many female hearts. "So they say. But I haven't been really challenged yet." He gave a nod at Drew. "We're working on that."

"And I'm interrupting. My apologies." She stood to leave. She could wait for their business to conclude. "Congratulations on your recent success."

"Thank you, ma'am. But please, don't leave on my account. We're all talked out. I was just finishing my drink."

Drew agreed. "I'm all yours, so why not park your pretty ass back on the stool? We can get acquainted."

Gillian's teeth locked, but her smile didn't falter. To Brett she said, "Call me Gillian, please."

He nodded. "All right, Gillian."

"When do you fight again?"

"It's still being set up. After that last win, I got recruited by a team, so I'll train with them for a while before I fight again."

"No more going it alone?"

"I started out that way because I didn't know how to get in a good team." He shrugged. "I'm always open to learning from more experienced guys."

Drew lounged back, elbows on the bar, and copped an attitude over being ignored. "After some promotion, I'll give him a main fight on a pay-per-view."

"I find it fascinating how this all works." Gillian turned back to Drew, but did *not* reseat herself. "So. I suppose we really should talk."

"You heard Brett. I'm all talked out." His brown eyes challenged her. "But hey, you got anything else in mind, count me in."

Gillian might not have an extensive social background, but neither was she obtuse. Drew was sexually interested. "I'm sure nothing more than talk would interest you."

A brow went up. "The hell it wouldn't."

This time her smile was snide. "But I don't meet your many requirements."

His gaze went over her again, slower this time, lingering in places in a way meant to discomfort her. "Honey, I think you fit the requirements just fine."

Rather than be offended, Gillian felt . . . warmed. That annoyed her. So he had a type of raw sex appeal. It was so raw as to be dangerous.

She put an arm on the bar and propped her chin on a fist. "But Drew, I'm forty-one," she lied. "That puts me beyond your age stipulation."

His mouth twitched into a grin and he took up the game with practiced ease. "You sneaky broad. You were eavesdropping on us."

"Yes, and on top of being ancient, I have five . . . no, let's make that six children."

"You're a terrible fibber." He turned his head to study her waist in the snug skirt. "I'd put you at no more thirty-three. And any idiot can see those are not the hips of a childbearing woman."

Brett coughed, then made a point of looking at the ceiling.

Gillian leaned in closer to Drew. "Perhaps you're right. But why do you think I'd lie?"

"Modesty?"

Gillian pursed her mouth. "Or maybe I stretched the truth to deliberately place myself on your list to avoid your personal interest."

Drew got closer, too, looking at her mouth. "So you assumed I'd be personally interested?"

"You did suggest certain things you'd like to do."

"Yeah. They involve getting naked and sweaty. You interested?"

"Ah . . . no, I'm afraid not." For her own peace of mind, she moved away from him again. "You were probably too hasty in sending away the groupies who, I'm sure, would have been more accommodating."

"They didn't interest me." He made a face. "Too artificial for my tastes."

"The laughs?" she guessed.

"The boobs." He gaze veered to her cleavage and stuck there. "I like things a little more natural."

Gillian fought a blush. "I don't see much difference between breast implants and the bright red lipstick I'm wearing. Both are meant to make a woman more attractive."

"Yeah, but one is surgery, and the other"—he closed the space between them again—"can be licked off."

Shocked both at his audacity and her innate response to it, Gillian straightened away. The man had no shame, no boundaries. She was out of her league, so she'd have to play it a little safer.

"Now don't run off," Drew said. "Things were just getting interesting."

Gillian shook her head. "You might be willing to bend your rules, but I'm not. And mixing business with pleasure is considered my number one no-no."

Caution replaced some of his amusement. "If we have business together, I don't know about it."

"I'm here to inform you." It was evil of her, but Gillian felt positively gleeful to set him straight. She put her shoulders back and smiled. "I've been hired as your new publicist, slash handler, slash miracle worker. And I daresay that with a lot of hard work on your part, I'll transform you into a man fit for polite society."

Drew came to his feet. His face tightened and his brows came down. "What the fuck are you talking about? I never hired a publicist."

"Slash handler, slash miracle worker," Gillian clarified.

Brett came off his stool. "I think that's my cue to excuse myself."

In a sotto voce whisper, Gillian said, "You may be right. It'll be safer from across the room."

Brett looked her over. "You don't look worried."

Gillian shrugged one shoulder. "I get paid the big bucks to take all the risks." She swung her gaze back to lock on Drew's. "And the owners of the SBC are very big payers."

And now a special excerpt from the next book
in the chilling new series by **L. L. Foster**

Servant: The Kindred

Coming soon!

G OD, *please, not now.*
For long minutes, what began to feel like an eternity, Gabrielle Cody fought the inevitable. Naked on Luther's king-sized bed, she stretched taut as sweat beaded on her skin and her teeth locked.

The agony grew.

And she fought it.

As her heart buffeted too hard in her chest, she repeatedly fisted her hands, clenching and unclenching them as she grasped the smooth, clean sheets beneath her. Exiguous moonlight snaked through a part in his heavy bedroom drapes, sending a silvery dart to cross the floor and crawl, with painstaking slowness, up the wall.

Clean. Organized. Masculine. Everything about his home, a *real* home, felt nice, smelled nice.

So inappropriate to the likes of her.

That Gaby could hear Luther in the bathroom finishing up a hot shower was the only salvation, the only measure to fight the staggering call. It dragged at her, commanding acceptance, gnarling her muscles, relentless in its claim on her.

She squeezed her eyes shut and thought of Luther, re-membered his pleasure as she'd capitulated to his demands.

Demands to join him, to try for a normal life—to give them, as a couple, a chance.

He was a fool. *She* was a fool for accepting even the slight-est possibility of a normal life, a real relationship.

Before excusing himself for the shower he'd smiled at her, thrilled to have her in his home, anticipation bright in his eyes. Luther thought he'd gotten his way. He thought he had Gaby where he wanted her.

Be careful what you wish for.

Another shaft of pain pierced her. It was always this way—the bid to fulfill her duty was a wrenching agony she couldn't fight. Whenever she'd tried, the pain had grown insurmount-able.

As it did now.

Sweat trickled down her temple to soak into Luther's pil-low. Already she soiled his fine home. If she stayed, she'd turn his entire existence black with depravity.

Her breath caught as the shower turned off. Luther would not expect to find her in his bed. No, he thought she was downstairs, waiting, where she should have been, where he'd left her. He wanted to go slow, to give her time.

But God knew, time wasn't always something she had.

Tonight, right now, her time had run out before she'd even begun.

Damn her plight. Damn her *duty*.

For so long now, Detective Luther Cross had tried to worm his way into her dysfunctional, psychotic life—and she'd resisted.

With good reason.

No matter his claims of "knowing" her, of "accepting" her and her strange eccentricities. He might think he had an inkling of what she did and why. But he didn't, not really. He couldn't.

Why had she come here?

Tears, salty and hot, trickled along her temples, mingling with the sweat. Her body strained as she tried to find just a few minutes more, just enough time to have Luther. Once. A memory she could keep forever . . .

But the relentless pull and drag on her senses, the encompassing pain that twisted and curdled inside her told her to stop being fanciful.

Should she leave without telling him? Make a clean break of it and let him wonder, let him worry?

Let him give up. On her.

On them.

Or should she try trusting him?

No, no, never that. She couldn't.

The pain lashed her, impatient for obedience, and Gaby knew she couldn't resist it any longer. As she sat up, she cried out—and the bathroom door opened.

Luther stepped out, buck naked, tall and strong and oddly beautiful for a man. That stunning golden aura swirled around him, bright with optimism, with promise of all that was good.

All that was the opposite of her.

Seeing her, he drew up short, stared for a moment. His hot gaze moved over her body, but not with lust as much as concern. "Gaby?"

"I was waiting . . ." She gasped, nearly doubled with the physical torment of the calling. "For you. I was willing, Luther. I was anxious. But . . ." She staggered to her feet, unseeing, choked with the need for haste. "But now I have to go."

He remained strangely still, watching her. "Where?"

How could he remain so composed, so . . . detached, in the face of what she was, what she had to do? "I don't know yet."

She fumbled for her shirt and dragged it on.

Words hurt. Leaving felt like death.

But she was a paladin, and being interested in a man, even a man as good as Luther, didn't change that.

Luther didn't ask any more questions, he just dried with the speed of a man on a mission. "I'm coming with you."

"Don't be fucking stupid." She stepped into jeans, almost

fell, and had to stop, had to gnash her teeth and squeeze her eyes shut in an attempt to contain the overpowering draw. But she knew the only relief would be to give in. And she would—once she was away from Luther. "I work alone."

"Not tonight." Already dressed in a black T-shirt, jeans, and sneakers, he reached for her. His hand touched her face, smoothed back her damp hair, and some of the awful, distorting agony dissipated. Almost sad, definitely accepting, he whispered, "Not tonight."

He'd always affected her this way, bringing clarity in the midst of the blind calling, easing her misery, calming her heart.

With the short reprieve, Gaby slapped his hand aside and pushed her feet into casual shoes. "I'll say it once, Luther. Stay out of my way."

And then she gave herself over to her duty.

Once accepted, it lashed through her, shocking her body, rolling her eyes back, straining her spine. In the peripheral of her senses, she felt Luther there, not touching her, not deterring her, but keeping pace as she moved forward, out of his bedroom, out of his house—and into the hell that was her life.

New York Times bestselling author

LORI FOSTER...

"Writes smart, sexy, engaging characters."
—**Christine Feehan**

"Doesn't hesitate to turn up the heat."
—*Booklist*

"Delivers everything you're
looking for in a romance."
—**Jayne Ann Krentz**

So don't miss...

Causing Havoc

Simon Says

Hard to Handle

Available now from penguin.com

M277AS0408

HER DESTINY CAN'T BE DENIED.

SERVANT:
THE ACCEPTANCE

THE SECOND BOOK IN THE SUPERNATURAL
URBAN THRILLER SERIES

BY LORI FOSTER WRITING AS
L. L. Foster

Gabrielle Cody has accepted her destiny—for she is fated to destroy all evil. But she wasn't prepared to see Detective Luther Cross ever again. He's the beacon of reality in her life, the one thing that makes her feel human, like a real woman.

But Gaby must resist involvement with Luther now, for she is protecting streetwalkers. Her life of retribution is far too dangerous, and this time, it's not just their hearts that won't come out unscathed.

penguin.com

M361T1008

MORE PRAISE FOR
LORI FOSTER

"The pages sizzle."
>—Christine Feehan, *New York Times* bestselling author

"Fun, sexy, warmhearted . . . just what people want in a romance."
>—Jayne Ann Krentz, *New York Times* bestselling author

"Foster outwrites most of her peers." —*Library Journal*

"Lori Foster delivers the goods." —*Publishers Weekly*

"Known for her funny, sexy writing." —*Booklist*

Titles by Lori Foster

THE WINSTON BROTHERS
WILD
CAUSING HAVOC
SIMON SAYS
HARD TO HANDLE
MY MAN, MICHAEL

Anthologies

HOT CHOCOLATE
(with Suzanne Forster, Elda Minger, and Fayrene Preston)

SINFUL
(with Maggie Shayne, Suzanne Forster, and Kimberley Randell)

WILDLY WINSTON

THE POWER OF LOVE
(with Erin McCarthy, Rosemary Laurey, Kay Stockham, Toni Blake,
Lucy Monroe, and Dianne Castell)

CHARMED
(with Jayne Castle, Julie Beard, and Eileen Wilks)

DOUBLE THE PLEASURE
(with Deirdre Martin, Jacquie D'Alessandro, and Penny McCall)

Writing as L. L. Foster

SERVANT: THE AWAKENING
SERVANT: THE ACCEPTANCE

Simon Says

"Delightful . . . an enjoyable, fast-paced read. Foster turns up the heat with Simon and Dakota's relationship, which makes the story even more satisfying . . . A double thumbs-up!"
—*Roundtable Reviews*

"Exhilarating . . . readers will enjoy going the distance with this fine pairing of two champions." —*Midwest Book Review*

"Quintessential Lori Foster . . . This would make a good beach book—although it's spicy enough that you may want to read it in air-conditioned comfort rather than sitting in the sun!"
—*The Romance Reader*

"Has delightfully familiar faces as well as intriguing new ones."
—*Romantic Times*

Causing Havoc

"Foster is at her best *Causing Havoc* with this delightful combination family drama, romance, and a bit of a mystery that all blends together into a wonderful contemporary."
—*Midwest Book Review*

"She writes about real people that are easy to connect with yet flawed enough they seem true to life and lovable. The plot is intricate, interesting, and entertaining, making this yet another page-turner that you can't put down. The sexual chemistry between couples in *Causing Havoc* palpates and explodes off the pages of this sizzling book . . . There is no doubt in my mind that you will love this book . . . You can't go wrong with a Lori Foster book."
—*Two Lips Reviews*

"Foster supplies good sex and great humor along the way in a thoroughly enjoyable romance reminiscent of Susan Elizabeth Phillips's novels."
—*Booklist*

"Convincing, heartfelt family drama." —*Publishers Weekly*

PRAISE FOR THE NOVELS OF

LORI FOSTER

Hard to Handle

"Intense, edgy, and hot, Lori Foster delivers everything you're looking for in a romance."
—Jayne Ann Krentz, *New York Times* bestselling author

"Tension, temptation, hot action, and hotter romance—Lori Foster has it all! *Hard to Handle* is a knockout!"
—Elizabeth Lowell, *New York Times* bestselling author

"Another success for Lori Foster. The humorous bantering and friendship among the characters makes for an enjoyable escape into the world of hunky SBC fighters and the women they love . . . a sweet read."
—*Fresh Fiction*

"A well-written tale with lots of details . . . Emotional, warm, stressful, and humorous moments keep the story interesting. Reading the previous books will add some background, but this book stands well on its own. *Hard to Handle* is one book not to miss."
—*Romance Reviews Today*

"An enjoyable book with great characters and plot that flows well."
—*Love Romances and More*

"With many familiar faces and a delightful secondary romance, Foster's latest is a wonderful, heartwarming story with plenty of action, a suspenseful mystery, and a glimpse into the sport of fighting. This very pleasing third addition to Foster's series is one that even readers who don't like sports can enjoy."
—*Romantic Times*

"An entertaining contemporary tale."
—*Midwest Book Review*

continued . . .